"Who are you?" the man asked, sounding so inspired that Breanne returned to his side and touched his cheek.

"Shhh. Rest now. You have a long journey ahead of you." Then she bent forward and kissed his forehead, giving in to an urge to feel how soft his skin was. Part of her knew she shouldn't be so intimate, tender. It took advantage of his vulnerability and compromised trust. A healer walked the fine line of trust with any charge.

But, she didn't regret it when her lips pressed his skin, warm, moist with sweat. His hand covered hers on his cheek and then touched her cheek. His fingers trembled. Breanne inched back and lowered her gaze to his. What she saw there startled her. Never before had she seen such intensity, such heat in another's eyes.

Breanne leaned her cheek into his palm and searched his eyes. His hot gaze trapped her, spellbound and unable to retreat or progress. She needed to do neither, as he did for her.

His hand slid back and into her hair. She covered his hand with hers, her touch intrigued by the change from stubble to smooth texture. He pulled her gently. His lips caressed hers, a whisper of touch, and his eyes closed. Breanne's closed as well and the feel of his lips on hers magnified. A dizzying hunger for more took root in Breanne and she pressed her lips onto his, opening her mouth. The hunger grew, spreading through her limbs, down her belly, between her thighs.

A shockwave tingled there when his tongue met hers, soft and warm. He tasted sweet. His lips on hers were so firm but pliant. She gripped his hand and leaned in for more. His tongue swept into her mouth, jolting her with pleasure.

She reveled in this new experience and grew bold. All thought beyond the feel of it, of him, escaped her. She matched his sweep with her own, suckling his lower lip, letting her teeth drag against it, savoring the plump feel.

The tingle warmed, changed, into an ache unlike any she'd ever known. It made her heart beat harder, her breathing feel desperate. She needed something more, craved a satisfaction she could not name but sensed it there in his lips pressing hers, his tongue twining and tormenting her mouth.

His hand stroked her jaw and explored lower, brushing her throat, tickling her collarbone and all the while taking Breanne's hand with it. She couldn't let go and as it drew farther and farther down, a strange, wonderful beating of anticipation built in her.

~ ~ ~

"This fantasy was captivating…alluring and suspenseful. It kept me on edge of my seat. Having so many turns, the ending was a stupendous surprise. Personally, it is a very gratifying read. I would be delighted to see a few spin offs from this novel as well."

~Bitten By Books, 4 ½ Coffins

Irish

Moon

Amber Scott

Chapter One

Tir Conaill, Ireland 1315

"Quiet, Finn. I canno' hear with all your purring." Breanne pressed her ear back against the gap between the heavy door and the stone wall. She swore the cat was doing it apurpose, goading her into leaving. He did not quiet, so she barely heard the voices discussing her future.

Finn licked his chest, ignoring her, but at least he remained in his wood floor seat this morn. Nearly every other one for the last fortnight they'd come to her mother's chamber door to listen. And each became a waste when Finn grew restless and left, forcing her after him empty- handed. Her mother's only rule of tolerance for the large cat taking residence with them was that he never be left on his own, a sure opportunity for mischief and destruction.

Today he stayed, and Breanne's ever patient eavesdropping sounded as though it might bear fruit. For once, her instincts might prove accurate.

"I see no reason to press her," her mother, Ula, said.

"She is well past a marrying age. Good men have asked for her hand. I am running out of excuses to give them."

Breanne O'Donnell strained to hear her mother come

to her defense. Soon, Niall would be Ula's husband and have fatherly authority over Breanne. For now, he spoke merely as guardian and chieftain.

Ula replied softly but clearly. "She is interested in her studies and has only half completed her apprenticeship with Heremon. Allow her two more years to completion. Then, I promise, we'll see her settled."

"Two more years? She's seen nineteen already," Niall said, his voice rising. "You encourage the lass too much. Following the old ways puts her at risk."

Breanne winced, but pressed her ear closer, careful not to breathe so loudly. It was worse than she'd feared.

"But, she may not be able to tell a husband of her training and I can't deny her Ovate status, not when she's so close. Even Heremon has come to agree it is her calling."

"She is a healer. It is well known that Heremon is tutoring her in herbs and tonics. Why shouldn't a husband be aware of the same? Dinna' forget, there is her inheritance to be seen to." Niall's voice rose to a bellow.

Breanne pulled her head away a moment. She chewed her lip, knotted a strand of strawberry blonde hair around her finger. Her stomach clenched at the memory of her childhood home, left so many years ago.

"The keep is hers to do with as she will. Why not discuss the property with her instead? Mayhap she will rent it or even take residence in it, taking a guard along to protect it."

"A husband will protect her."

She would protect herself. Were she born a few hundred years before, she'd be allowed a hermit's life if she wished. She'd be allowed to fight as a warrior, though she'd never choose to. The damned English Pale seemed to be influencing even their own northern tuath nowadays. Before long it might spread across the Giant's

Causeway to encroach the Highland clans.

"Ula, she's been asked for again. If I excuse her unmarried state much longer, people will think me soft or worse of her."

Breanne wanted to walk in and demand answers. Who had asked? Quinlan? Another? When had she been asked for?

"I don't want to force her. She is no princess. Her marriage will not end a war or cause one. She should choose. And let them talk."

Breanne silently thanked Ula. Her mother was the only one she had to stand up for her, and she was doing it well. Being stubborn went against her mother's demure and nurturing nature, so her firm words bespoke the issue's importance to her, as well.

There was a moment of silence. All she could hear was her heart thumping hard enough that her throat quivered. "Shane Ferguson is a good man, comes from a good family. A husband will give her a family, Ula." His voice became softer. "And allow us one, as well."

Finn's tail swatted her skirt, shushing across the floor, leaving her unsure she'd heard the last of it right. She couldn't have. Her mother was no longer young and though she bore Breanne at sixteen years, nineteen were certainly too many years for a womb to wait.

And allow us *fun*, as well? *Some*, as well? She searched her brain for a suitable word to make sense of what she couldn't have heard correctly.

Alarm shot through her at the light tap of footsteps coming up the wooden stairway. She could not remain there. Besides, Heremon surely awaited her in the grove. If she arrived late again, she'd be punished with another deplorable jar dusting.

Five long years of study and she was finally nearing the topics that had sparked her ask to become an Ovate within the nigh extinct order. The Druid master didn't like waiting and though her mother hadn't finalized the decision, Breanne could not risk lingering.

She stood summarily, scooping Finn up with her, and shot down the hallway to the stairs. Few men lingered in the main hall, most busy outside practicing in arms, but of all of them, Quinlan was the last she likened to see. Reaching the bottom stair, Breanne scowled and lifted her chin, continuing her fast pace, hoping to look unapproachable.

She failed. Quinlan's face lit up upon seeing her and he stepped in pace beside her. She glanced sideways and forced a small smile on her face. His smile grew and lit up his face. "I've been looking for you, Breanne. I thought you might enjoy an afternoon ride."

"I canno'," she said faster than she intended. He was so handsome he was nearly pretty with his copper brown hair and bright blue eyes. "I have preparations for the wedding to attend to," she lied. Not only were her lessons to be kept private, she feared he would offer to escort her. She had absolutely no romantic interest in him. Not anymore.

"These are for you," Quinlan said, suddenly in front of her and shoving a handful of lavender and heather to her nose, forcing her to stop.

Breanne's mouth fell open to speak, but she found she could barely breathe. They were lovely, the very kind of bouquet she'd picked as a girl to bestow upon herself, pretending they were from him. Suddenly her childhood dreams of becoming Quinlan's wife took on a sickening feeling.

"Thank you," she said. She smiled weakly and inhaled their scent. She didn't want to hurt him. She searched his eyes, didn't want to see them filled with pain at her rejection.

He smiled, showing even white teeth, and her stomach grew more sickly. He was handsomer than St. Kevin himself.

How could one simple kiss change so much? She hated the question and the truth of it even more. One kiss that she'd dreamed of she would now remove from existence, uncast, were she able. The memory of it only worsened her urgency to leave him.

Thankfully, they were in plain sight of others in the hall, assuring he couldn't kiss her again. It was bad enough that most were snickering and cooing over the obvious sign of courtship.

Quinlan stared at her a long awkward moment until she gestured past him. His face flooded with color. He stepped out of her way, coughing into his fist. She glanced uncomfortably away, no words coming to her, and gave up the effort. What could she possibly tell him to ease such palpable tension between them?

She ignored the pang in her chest at his crestfallen face, held Finn a bit tighter and left through the kitchen. Outside in the crisp spring air, Breanne slipped through the postern in the fortress yard, confident none saw her exit the small gate.

The lightness her escape of the bailey walls typically offered her didn't come. The unusually sunny spring day was perfect for a ride. Or for a walk. Alone. If she hurried, she could reach the grove in time.

She wore a green cape attached at the shoulders of her lighter green gown to help blend and disguise her rushing form. She'd made the steep walk in worse weather, with less time to spare, and feeling less harried than she felt now. A funny nagging feeling in her belly seemed to grow with each step.

"A husband. The last thing I need now is a husband. Who could I possibly marry, let alone why?" she asked

Finn through panting breath.

"Quinlan appears to be ready for the call of that duty," Finn answered, the lisp of his feline mouth coating an extra layer of sarcasm. Once away from the keep, Finn made up for his forced quiet by having opinions and sharing them at every opportunity.

"You are a vile beast," Breanne said and dropped the enchanted cat inherited with her third year of lessons.

He landed expertly and trotted after her. "He's perfectly enamored with you. Anyone can see that." Finn's tone brimmed with gloating sarcasm.

"Oh? Even besotted, enchanted cats?" Breanne kicked a rock his way, knowing it would miss. She hated how right Finn was.

"France did well by him, I think," Finn said. "He's gotten some pluck since he returned."

She'd hardly name the silly doe-eyed look as pluck. But, it seemed the only one Quinlan bestowed on her since his autumn return from six years abroad. Finn kept in stride with her, pouncing from rock to grassy dirt with springy ease.

"And what would you know about it?"

She knelt at a bush and retrieved the chalice hidden there. Setting the bundle of flowers down, she bent over the stream and captured water into it. Its encrusted rubies and sapphires warmed and brightened in the sunlight.

"You're not my first mistress," Finn said, teetering on a rock to dip his mouth to the water. "Do recall that I did exist long before you came into my life."

Breanne resisted the strong urge to push him in.

"Pluck. I would have used a more explicit word, myself." They'd each grown up during the six years and apparently his feelings for her were now adult in nature. "Brute comes to mind."

Not a fortnight ago, he'd cornered her outside her

chamber and kissed her soundly, pressing into her. His attraction was more than obvious, stabbing her hip. Although a curt slap had ended his assault, it had done little to dissuade him since.

"Mayhap he'll ask for you."

"Bite your tongue. I would rather marry you."

"How terribly flattering. But, not possible since you cannot see fit to lift the curse, and after last night's miserable failure, I don't see it happening anytime soon."

Breanne ignored the jab and his sour tone. She told herself again that she had so much more to learn, that it was still early to be expecting the kind of magick he needed to come readily. As Heremon always told her, magick takes more than talent. It takes persistence and study and practice, practice, practice.

"Hush now, you old lecher, we need to focus," she said.

If a cat could roll its eyes, Finn nearly did, but quieted nonetheless. Craggy hillside met lush valley, carpeted with heather and grass. The gurgle of water grew louder. The grove lay ahead. Breanne paused at the base and breathed in a gulp of air to clear her head. If she joined Heremon preoccupied with Quinlan or the conversation between her mother and Niall, he might send her right back where she came from.

Likely, Finn was saving the rest of his teasing for the jaunt home, as usual.

Breanne exhaled, filling her heart with love and asked the goddess and ancestors for a blessing. She thanked the land and trees and asked for their welcome.

Spring leaves shivered under the cool answering breeze and the two entered the grove in silence. The trees and bushes blocked out the cool air and warm light, giving way to a dim comfort. The place never lost its spell on her. Any doubts that ever grew about her choosing this path in life shrank away here.

She approached the largest oak and knelt before it, spilling the water out of the chalice onto its roots with a silent prayer. Finn licked himself, lapping loudly. Breanne finished her offering and glared at her companion.

"For a victim of curse," she said. "You are certainly more and more insolent. Is it so much trouble to be reverent toward that which will aid your release?"

Finn yawned.

Breanne shook her head and continued to Heremon's altar. The old Druid stood with his eyes closed and his face tilted skyward, one hand on the large stone slab. Seven white candles' flames lit the small clearing. Heremon's dull athame lay at rest, on a folded red wool square, with the white handle pointing south, blade north.

Breanne sat before him and waited for acknowledgement. Finn trotted after a flitting object that she hoped wasn't a fairy. Of all the magick this grove held, a fairy would be the best to see true. All things secret, Heremon promised, would reveal themselves in time. With less than two years remaining in her tutelage, she couldn't see why all the things she worked for still failed to happen.

"We have much work to do," Heremon said and joined her on the mossy forest floor. "I have received the prophecy and we must prepare. A stranger will join us, become one of us."

His pale eyes bounced as he spoke. Was he still in a trance? Her cleared head flooded with unease.

Breanne watched and waited for him to continue. Her stomach tightened up with the same sick feeling from before when she had listened in shadows to Niall O'Donnell's words. *A husband will protect her.*

She would protect herself.

"He is yours to keep," Heremon said. "See the emeralds, know the key."

Breanne's mind halted. Her heart skipped. She knew better than to read the literal into any vision's meaning, but several ideas formed in her head unbidden. Surely, his words could not be linked to Niall's.

Heremon had assured her that once she began seeing, she would better understand the nature of second sight and that it in fact made the future less clear than before. But, how could foreknowledge not help in life? She hoped to soon know the truth for herself.

"Tell no one." Heremon's hands shot out, clenched her knees. She moved back, startled. His eyes danced, looking through her. "Protect him."

Another presage, or did the first continue? Protect what? It would be pointless to ask as he would not recall his words. He never did. By the look of his eyes, it wouldn't be long. The cloudiness in them receded, the shaking slowed. Within a moment, Heremon's irises returned to dark green and focused on her face, adjusting to the light.

"Breanne." He blinked at her with surprise. "When did you arrive?" He let go of her knees as though they'd not been touched at all.

"But a moment ago. You greeted me, Heremon. Do you not remember?"

He looked past her and tilted his head as though listening to the wind.

"The storm last night," he said.

"Yes, it has passed already. The sun shines clear with not a single cloud."

He looked back at her, his forehead wrinkled with trouble. "I've promised you a lesson, haven't I?"

Not again. She nodded patiently. His graying red beard was a tangled unkempt mess and helped distract from the fraying, torn blue cloak he preferred. Distraction seemed his nature of late and still he had managed to become the wisest, oldest Druid priest in all of Ireland, well, leastwise the north of it.

"We are scheduled to review my Grimoire, my most recent attempt to free Finn, and you were to give me five new herbals." She left out her least favorite, gathering, hoping he'd forget, and refused to feel bad for taking advantage of his daze.

"Yes, yes. We haven't much time, though." His voice faded with each word. "We will meet again tonight at the spring. The moon is waxing to fullness. The end of it nears."

Breanne scowled, not only because he seemed about to cut their lesson short, but because his words weren't making much sense.

"The end of the moon? Not near at all, Heremon. For if the lunar cycle has a fortnight to wane...."

"What's this? Are you still here, then? Off with you. We mustn't tarry." He shooed her with his hands, standing briskly.

Breanne's frown deepened. Heremon was truly out of sorts. With last night's failed experiment and a week since the last lesson, which she was hardly able to sneak away for with of all her mother's nuptial arrangements, she couldn't help feeling keenly disappointed.

She stood, ready to argue for at least an hour of his time. She needed it. With all the husband discussion and wedding plans and changing friendships in her life, the one thing that kept her levelheaded was her Ovate training.

Breanne took a deep breath and squared her shoulders. Heremon blew out his candles and tossed each into his deerskin bag, dropping one in his haste.

"Heremon, I can see you have important things to

attend to and I can't relay how truly appreciative I am of all your time and wisdom, but I beg of you, please allow me my lesson," she said, trying to sound at once imploring and firm.

He didn't reply as he scooped up the fallen candle, shoved it inside and cinched the drawstring.

"At least tell me of the herbals," she said, her hands wringing, voice trembling. Breanne bit her lip. She was not going to tear up.

Tears would seem weak, desperate even, and though she was weak with desperation, such displays would not build Heremon's confidence in her. The tolerance of a woman learning anything, let alone studying the old ways, lessened with every passing year and she considered it her duty to never appear unsuitable because of an inability to control her emotions.

Heremon walked past her, his gaze on the mossy ground, head tilted. His mouth moved silently.

"I will write down the herbals and study them for our meeting tonight," she said to his back, following after him.

He didn't answer her, didn't even glance up and acknowledge her. Breanne stopped and let him go. A single tear slid down her cheek and she clenched her hands into little fists.

"That was fast," Finn said.

Breanne swung around and pinned him with her eyes.

"What?" he said, a licked paw hanging mid-air.

"He left." She threw her hands up. "Simply rescheduled our lesson, gathered his ceremonials, and walked away as though I wasn't standing right here in front of him. In all my days and nights, I have never seen a person act so strange. Not a soul." She threw her hands again, letting them fall hard and heavy against her gown.

"The man is old, Breanne. His mind likely went soft and I assure you he was never quite right," Finn sounded unconcerned.

She might've stamped the grassy dirt, but to what good?

"I feel something terrible may have happened," Breanne said. "Or will. If you'd seen him, you'd not be sitting there as though you haven't a care in all the world. You'd be after him and frightened." Breanne's voice rose with each word, but the cat wouldn't stop looking so damned unaffected or take her seriously.

Finn blinked. "You feel?"

"Heremon had a prediction and is now wandering about, talking to himself, as though he didn't see me or hear me."

"When will you meet again?"

"He said tonight, but I am not sure he knew what he was saying. I will not be surprised if I come tonight, assuming I am able to sneak away with all the clansmen underfoot, only to find the forest empty."

"The grove is never empty," Finn said, his gaze fixed in the air rather than on her, tail swishing arrogantly.

Breanne blew a stray hair from her brow. "You know that I mean--Heremon not present. I canno' believe he knew what he was saying, not with the way he said it. Had you not wandered, you'd have seen with your own eyes."

"And I didn't. Can we return to the keep now? I'm hungry."

Breanne turned around and eyed the barely discernable path Heremon left by.

"No," she said.

She jutted her chin upward and trounced after the old sage, telling herself that something was very wrong and he needed her. And if she happened to secure a quick tutorial on the five herbals, secrets that would potentially--finally--unlock her own potential, all the better.

The idea quickened her pulse. Her long formed hope to practice true magick had recently taken on a desperate feel. Instead of sheer excitement over dreams of the magickal and wondrous accomplishments, the threat of an uncertain future loomed like a hungry wolf in a dark corner where light used to shine.

Heremon's path wove in and around pine and the occasional blessed oak tree, deeper into the forest, toward the coast. Her worry grew as her irritation with Finn dissipated. She wished she'd grabbed the cat. She could have snatched him up and under her arm without a scratch in seconds. If she had, she'd now be happily arguing with him instead of fighting to keep prickling fear at bay.

She'd not taken this path before. She knew where Heremon lived, in theory, knew the lay of the land she'd been born to and explored through to adult years. So there really was no reason to be frightened. And she had her sheathed boline dagger strapped to her thigh as well as the confidence to use it lethally if necessary.

Thinking of the blade and imagining lifting her skirt, retrieving it, and slashing through whomever or whatever happened upon her in the dense foliage, worsened the quiver in her veins. She stopped her careful tracks and palmed the sharp weapon, paying no mind to her fingers' slight tremble. The action helped a bit, as did a long deeply indrawn breath and prayer to Morrigan.

Continuing after the trail of winding footprints and sunken moss spots that mapped Heremon's path, Breanne's fingers traced the carved pattern on the dagger's handle. The side she felt held a pointy-tailed, horny dragon. A lion adorned the other side, but she needed the dragon, which represented the Otherworld, magick, to her. Mayhap its ever-elusive magick, a protection better than any man, would aid her.

The copse of pines and birch gave way and glimpses of ocean took the place of sky in the gaps between them. Breanne slowed her pace and realized how hard she was breathing. She paused at the edge of trees and caught her breath, scanning the open area for a dwelling. When she found none she stepped further, feeling exposed but alone, and followed the remaining marks Heremon left behind.

"Are you lost?" a whisper said.

Breanne swung about, weapon ready, shards of panic snapping through her. To the left, the right, her eyes shot. Nothing. Nothing more than the trees and grass and sounds of spring humming met her searching gaze.

A deep chuckle carried upward from her ankle and immediately Breanne's fear changed to anger. "Finn! You scared me, you evil thing."

A deeper, purring chuckle with no apology. "I couldn't resist after watching you sneaking along with that ridiculous excuse for protection held like your life depended on it. Truly, Bree, if you'd seen yourself...." His chuckle broke into coughing guffaws.

Breanne could kick him, she really could, if not for the fact that he was stuck as a creature more helpless than she. And if she weren't so nice a person as she was. Even so, the idea was worth fantasizing, however briefly and unrealistically as she could. Breanne dropped to the ground and wiped her sweaty brow, the boline forgotten.

"I swear I dream of the day that I will no longer be the source of your twisted amusem—."

"Shh. Did you hear that?" Finn said, suddenly recovered and his ears pricked low.

Breanne frowned, listening. The distant rush and crush of waves below the cliff, the chirp of birds and crickets, leaves rustling behind, no more. Her eyes narrowed on Finn. Paying no mind to her skepticism, he crept forward, nearing the cliff.

Breanne watched and crouched lower herself, unwilling to move and risk the noise of her gown and limbs alerting someone or overbearing whatever the cat's ears had picked up.

Finn inched closer to the perilously sharp, rocky edge. Breanne breathed shallowly and strained her senses to detect something, anything within the sunny, spring day around her.

He looked back at her then pranced sideways, arching his back. The hair along his spine stood up as he hissed at the cliff's edge.

Breanne crawled as close to him as she could, without allowing the deathtrap waters to reach her line of sight, on her belly.

"What?" she whispered. "What do you see?" She couldn't bring herself to look over the sharp edge.

He hissed again and she slammed her head to the ground, heart pumping, and ready to retreat back to the woods fast. She closed her eyes. Something touched her hair. She screamed out the last stitch of air in her lungs and blindly raced back to the woods.

Finn's chortle of laughter brought her to a stony halt. She should have known. Not bothering to turn back around, she stormed through the brush and returned the way she had come. If she didn't move fast, she might end up living out that kicking fantasy despite the threat of tumbling over the edge and plummeting into the bleak waters after him.

Although, he would be tumbling first.

Chapter Two

The flames scalded. He could feel them lick over his face, crawl over his skin, sear his very soul. He tried to scream, but no sound came out. They were burning him alive. Through the blue-orange flames Ashlon made out their laughing faces. They were dancing.

A flash of cold wet him, dowsing the flames down. Their faces changed. They saw him. They saw that he still lived and one vicious man came forward. It was Jacques. Jacques was alive.

Ashlon rejoiced, certain his old friend simply had not known what he'd done, who Ashlon was. But Jacques's smile was twisted, contorted with ugly intention. Ashlon shook his head, trying to speak, but his jaw and lips and tongue failed him. All he could do was plead with Jacques with his eyes to stop this madness.

"Quiet now," Jacques said and wiped his face with his cold hand. Jacques's face went blurry as his voice drew nearer. "Don't struggle. Relax. You're safe here."

His friend's face vanished and in its place, Ashlon looked into the kindest green eyes. Even so, the eyes belonged to a stranger. He should reach for his sword. He couldn't move, so weak he feared trying to. But those crinkling eyes reassured him along with the brittle voice.

"Rest now."

Ashlon let the nightmare leave him and his eyelids drooped shut. The continued cool pressing and wiping soothed him like a baby in its mother's arms. He succumbed to feverish fatigue.

* * * *

"I must say, I thought you'd come straight away, dancing and bubbling with joy this morning, Bree. Did you not see Quinlan just this morning?" Rose McRoarty pedaled the spindle as she spoke.

"Aye, we spoke in the hall, but not regarding anything worth bubbling or dancing, Rose," Breanne said and kept her gaze on her embroidery.

None of the women around her yet noticed she'd made not a single worthwhile stitch, so preoccupied was she with this morning's events. Leave it to Rose to unwittingly add to her worries. She'd completely forgotten about Quinlan's waiting for her, or their awkward exchange, so rapt in thought, planning methods to escape into the night in seven or so hours.

Rose's delicate red brows arched, probably both in surprise and suspicion. As Breanne's best friend and single confidante, she knew of the decade long infatuation Breanne had had with Quinlan who was also Rose's brother. Ten years she'd loved him. In all those ten years since the two had come to live within the keep, orphaned, Rose had patiently listened to her best friend vie and long for her older brother and never interfering on either party's behalf. No easy feat.

Today, she no doubt knew of Quinlan's attempt to begin officially courting her, might've even suggested what kind of flowers he should gather. And so she had reason to raise those beautiful brows that Breanne now peripherally saw, and silently cursed. Breanne found herself stuck.

"Oh," Rose said after a moment of consideration.

Breanne could only hope that she'd yet to see and question Quinlan concerning the success or disaster of his morning's best intentions. Mayhap, she'd be smiled on and he'd not tell Rose at all, give up easily and allow their long friendship (minus her long-standing obsession, of course) to resume as though nothing had gone amiss.

"Did you not see him this morn?" Rose asked.

Dratted persistent thing that she was, Rose would ask for more from one, eventually both, of them, until the whole sordid truth surfaced. Well, not easily, Breanne decided and looked up from her piteous knots to hold her best friend's gaze as steadily as she possibly could. A steady gaze seemed the best way to convince Rose of the lie about to spit to life.

"Only for a moment," she said. "Long enough for a quick good morn greeting. He appeared to be in quite a hurry and so I left him and attended to, er, Finn. He desperately needed a bath." A bath? A BATH? Felines bathe themselves, remember? But she nodded and returned to her embroidery. If she unknotted the last stitches and began again, the small wren might look less like wet horse droppings.

When she looked away, she didn't miss the pure disbelief flit to life and death in Rose's cerulean eyes. Breanne didn't know when the lies had started. Weeks, months mayhap? They weren't really her fault and in fact protected Rose in the end.

No one could know about her training with Heremon aside from Ula and Niall. The first few years of her study she didn't have to lie, simply told part truths. She was learning to be a healer. But, when she'd begun acting as a healer and concern from her uncle, the abbot, had risen, secrecy had been decided upon. Strict secrecy.

While most things Druid were incorporated into religion, what she studied was not. By some standards, it could be misconstrued and considered witchcraft, heresy, and devil worship. Breanne made the choice between stopping altogether and absolute concealment to the point of denial easily.

And regarding lies of Quinlan, well, what else could she do? At least that's what she told herself when pangs of hurt shot through her heart.

The truth about Quinlan seemed more harmful than any lie could be. And how could she begin to explain such a dramatic change of heart to the one woman on the whole of Ireland who loved Quinlan? She wished fervently she could, too, in the way she did the very second before his lips locked onto hers.

But, she didn't.

She didn't know what she felt any longer. Breanne didn't want to call it revulsion, despite it being the closest descriptor to the sick stomach turn his lips and tongue and bulge churned up in her.

"Did he stink so terribly?" Rose asked with a touch of sarcasm.

"Who?" Breanne frowned. "Oh, Finn, you mean. Of course." Damnation. She was appalling at this. "Yes. He rolled in carcass, I believe. All night, he smelled so foul that I swore I would wash him clean first and foremost that very morning--this very morning." Thankfully, Finn had yet to return to the keep and her side, so he couldn't be offended which he'd doubtless seek vengeance for.

Rose laughed deeply, making Breanne feel both relieved to see her friend did not see through her fabrication and guilty by the lies. "I'll wager that was not simple. Such a big feisty thing, he is." Her cheeks and eyes were bright with cheer.

"Aye. He is and never more than this morning. I took him by the scruff and lowered him straight in. He kicked and yowled," she detailed, enjoying the chortles of laughter as well as the attention it drew. Rose could light a dark room with her joy.

"And not a scratch on you. I'll say you've missed your calling, Bree."

Breanne looked back to her cloth and needle, still smiling. The words rang through her with a painful truth she didn't want anyone seeing. Had she missed her calling? Heremon's strange behavior circled back into her thoughts, again consuming them.

Her mother's gentle hand on her shoulder startled her. "It's good to see you smiling," Ula said, not to her but to Rose.

Breanne furrowed her brow. As she began to ask why Rose wouldn't be smiling, her mother's expression stopped her. It held a seriousness that unsettled her. She half knew what words were coming.

"Niall and I would like a word before you bathe for the evening meal, Breanne." Ula stroked and cupped Breanne's cheek warmly, then walked away as demurely and quietly as she had come.

Breanne wasn't sure she could withstand any other emotional struggle today, but neither saw a way clear of it. A husband. She dissected the feel and parts of the word, turning it over in her mind.

"What's this then?" Rose asked, speaking low so none of the others would hear them in their corner of the Grianan.

"I do believe I've been decided for, Rose," she said, the words feeling strangled.

Rose gave her a sympathetic look and cluck of her tongue as Breanne walked past her. She followed the way her mother had come, through the main hall and into a small room filled with books, inks, rolled tapestries and Niall O'Donnell's broad frame.

It wasn't the walk she'd taken this morning, sneaking up the stairs to her mother's door. This walk, all could see and most did. The curious stares and hand-covered mumblings made putting one foot in front of another, trying to appear casual but proud, difficult. She swore the clusters of men and their speculative mutters were worse than any of the women. They seemed to relish a good tongue-waggle much more than any of the numerous females Breanne grew up listening to.

Before entering the room, Breanne stopped and swung full around, her hands on her hips, and glared at every man she could meet eyes with. Most had the decency to look away. One smiled toothsomely right at her. Shane MacSweeney. What had Niall said when Shane asked for her hand? She might be about to find out.

Niall's earlier mention of him to her mother recalled in her memory. She narrowed her eyes on him, raised her chin a notch. *We'll be seeing about that, MacSweeney.*

She knocked on the heavy door causing it to open. Bravely, she stepped in. Her stomach roiled with nerves and her pulse slammed.

"My lord has asked to speak with me," she said, with a deep feminine bow. Though she disliked the idea of her mother marrying the man her father had died protecting, she couldn't resent him.

"Breanne, yes, please come in," Niall said in his booming voice.

He looked distressed, his brow heavily creased, mouth tight-lipped. Breanne did as asked and came forward. He rose from his seat and came around the table. Ula remained seated. Her mother's distress showed singularly in fidgeting fingers toying with the hem of her blue and silver gown.

Niall circled the room, closed the door, and continued. "Please, be seated."

Breanne took the deep chair opposite her mother. She bit the inside of her lip when it trembled. She fought to maintain outward calm, as well. Niall did not. He paced the floor in large circles, his big hands clasping behind him, moving to the front, to his chin and returning to his back.

She wanted to scream out. She wanted to order him to speak so they all could breathe again. But, she didn't.

"Breanne, how are your studies coming along?" he asked, a relief in his tone belied the procrastination.

"Very well. Aside from today, that is."

He stopped, met her eyes, and frowned. "Oh?"

"Heremon was distracted and saw fit to reschedule for a more opportune time."

"Distracted." Niall looked away. "When?"

Breanne gulped. She couldn't very well tell him midnight tonight. While he was quite aware of her tutelage, her safety being risked would not be tolerated. Since the death of Breanne's father, Ula's husband, Niall O'Donnell took his role as their guardian and protector on earnestly.

"Tomorrow morn."

"Has Heremon related to you your progress? When will you complete it?"

Even his voice grew direct. Breanne breathed deep and didn't fidget. "Nearly a year, depending on frequency of meeting and lesson quantity."

"Too long," Niall said to himself and shook his head. "Too long," he said to her. "I'll not meander about. Breanne, you've been asked for. It is time you marry."

There they were, the words overheard in her head and from the shadows, real and alive before her. Breanne exhaled inaudibly and sat up a bit straighter.

"I agree."

Niall stopped, scowled at her. "You agree."

"I agree," she said again and felt the strength in the declaration. No longer did she feel helpless. Now, it was her decision. "I would like some time to choose, of course, but not an unreasonable amount."

Niall's scowl darkened. Ula's hands twittered to her chest.

"Are you not curious who asked?" Niall demanded, his eyes narrowing.

She realized she should be and used the first excuse that came to mind. "Quinlan Blake made his intentions clear enough this very morning. I assume he spoke with you." His intentions were likely wagging tongues already after the display of flowers. Which meant Rose must know, Breanne suddenly thought.

"Quinlan Blake?" Niall looked appeased and the tension in his face lessened. "Nay, not him."

"I have another suitor?" Breanne said to her mother, her hand to her chest.

Ula nodded and smiled sweetly enough that Breanne's chest pricked a bit. She wanted Breanne to marry?

First Rose and now her mother. She was going straight to hell to burn a thousand deaths for the deceits coming out of her more readily and convincingly each hour.

"Gannon O'Shannon, your uncle's most promising scribe," Ula said and leaned forward to touch Breanne's knee. "A learned man, a student. You will have so much in common."

Breanne certainly didn't have to feign her surprise. Her shock might be the first honest thing about her day. Gannon? Sweet, shy, Gannon? Breanne and Gannon O'Shannon? Laughter tickled her. She coughed to rid her throat of the entirely inappropriate, not to mention rude, response. Gannon was a dear sweet young fellow after all. But, in all her days and nights, she hadn't guessed he held affection for her.

"When will you decide?" Niall asked, making her feel dissected, exposed.

"Decide on Gannon?" How could she? Her mind still spun from the notion. Kiss Gannon? Feel Gannon press his bulge into her? No. Gannon wouldn't be lewd and overbearing like Quinlan. He'd be gentle.

"How long before you planned to choose?" Niall asked with an exasperated sigh. He bent forward and crossed his arms, in wait for her answer.

Breanne's eyes shot from him to Ula and back to him. Her mind slammed to a stop. He was asking her to name a deadline. The sense of control she'd momentarily lost grasp of returned. She licked her lips and laughed. It sounded affected but she didn't care.

"No later than All Hallows Eve. I will have been officiated and that offers me enough time to consider among these men," she said and nodded sharply at the end.

Niall met her gaze steadily. A grin grew on his face and for a wonderful moment, Breanne thought she'd cleanly averted disaster.

"Beltane," Niall said. "Not a day later. You may choose in the tradition which has kept you from your choice."

"Beltane? But, my lord, that's nigh two months hence. You canno' possibly expect me to…."

"If you do not. I will."

"You will." Breanne shot to her feet. Her voice rose. "You will? I am not chattel to be given away at your discretion or whim."

"No," Niall said. "You are not. But you are my responsibility and you are not going to live the life of a hermit, which for some reason I cannot fathom, you appear to be attracted to."

"Niall, please," Ula said and stood, as well. She

stepped between them. "Breanne. This is for the best. And you said yourself that you agree. Please don't make me rue the liberties we've allowed you out of a mother's love."

"My apologies, my lord." Guilt kicked her heart. "Do forgive my insolence. You have both indeed indulged my aspirations. Forgive me." She bowed her head.

Niall swept a hand through the air. Ula sat.

"We will discuss this further tomorrow," Niall said, sounding tired. "The dinner hour approaches. You may leave us, Breanne."

Her face was hot with color, but she was grateful despite the embarrassment of losing her temper. She had no right to speak to him so disrespectfully and not simply because he was the local king. Niall O'Donnell had been naught but good to her and her mother since their arrival eleven years ago.

Breanne left and part of her was glad that she couldn't stay and eavesdrop. She didn't want to hear what they said about her outburst, didn't have to.

The hot bath waiting for her in her bedchamber washed away hot tears and the day's troubles. Finn wasn't even there to vent on, still hadn't returned to the keep. He was probably roaming the forest for fairy mounds again.

Plaiting her hair into an intricate braid, she wove gold baubles in sporadically. Two, potentially three, very different men were about to become a daily nuisance and she didn't have any way out of any of it. She did want to marry. It wasn't that. One of them certainly would be suitable if she could settle herself with their inevitable manly passions.

And though six weeks time sounded brief, she knew of courtships that completed in days. Why, hadn't Rose set sight on her husband, Ryan, exactly one week before they handfasted and now had four babies to prove their love, if not lust, for one another?

And her husband need not necessarily be selected from the three. If she actually began looking, she might find another suitable man among the clansmen and frequent inter-tribal travelers.

Were she more daring, the Beltane feast and fire could become her hunting ground. What a lovely thought. To walk up, pick a man, and just be done with it. To not bother with the mess of any of it, the wooing, the choosing, the hurt feelings and quarrels, until the last minute. Breanne smiled at herself in the mirror and covered a giggle. The idea was ridiculous.

Ready for dinner, she stood and braced herself. She honed in on the single thought that would lift her spirits and help ease facing four long tables filled with knowing faces. In six short hours, she'd be deep in the woods, and might glimpse some magick.

* * * *

Hunger woke Ashlon. He opened his eyes and adjusted to the dimly lit area he was in. Carefully, he sat up, making the table he lay on creak loudly. He looked around, trying to remember where he was and how he got there. But nothing came. The last distinct memory he had was of falling asleep in a cave with his arms around Jacque's treasure.

Abruptly, Ashlon looked about the small room. He rolled from the table, careless of the small wool covering dropping to the floor. He located his mantle, his sword, and his shoes. But, nowhere did he see the chest.

A man's voice sounded outside the stone walled room. Ashlon stopped. He listened to… singing? It drew closer. Ashlon promptly palmed his sword and took battle stance.

Brittle notes of song carried nearer, a language foreign and beautiful to Ashlon's ears. The door knocked about and the song changed to cursing and finally the man kicked the wood open and froze in place.

"What are you about now, lad?"

Ashlon lifted the sword a degree, the friendliness of the stranger adding to his defensiveness. "Who are you? What have you done with my possessions?" he demanded in English.

"There now, lad. You'll ruin my ministrations." The man directed his gaze to Ashlon's midsection.

He followed the gaze and saw the clumps of leaf and mossy root about to fall from his middle. He put one hand over the poultices and held his sword steady with the other. The heathen guised man had fast explaining to do or he'd feel the thick end of Ashlon's blade. Pointing his sword at the man, he motioned him in. It was then that he realized the stranger carried a steaming bowl. His gut ached with the hunger.

"I demand to know who you are and where I am. I require the return of my belongings immediately."

The man entered the small room slowly, set the bowl down, all the while nodding gently. "Calm yourself, lad. You're in my home. Tir Conaill, Ireland home of the clan O'Donnell and all who are welcomed here along their travels."

Ashlon's arm lowered a fragment. He was losing his strength by the second. "Who are you?" He needed to lie down.

"My Christian name is Shamus Heremon Dermot O'Brian, descendant of The O'Brian, descended of Niall of the Nine Hostages." The man smiled, showing aged folds in his cheeks. "You may call me Heremon, as do all others."

Ashlon's arm wobbled inside. His sword felt like a

hundred pounds trying to drag it down. He had the man's name, but it told him nothing concrete. He needed more. "How did I come to be here with you, Lord Heremon? Where have you put the chest I traveled with?" he asked, biting for a minute more of strength.

"Why, I saved you, lad. And I know of no chest."

In a loud clang, Ashlon's sword fell from his grip to the stone floor. He used the free hand to support his body before it collapsed on the spot. A wet pile of leafy mush landed next to his blade.

"Enough of that now," Heremon said. Raising his voice made it sound more tinny than brittle, but kind nonetheless. "Lie on your back. There. Go easy on yourself there. It's no feather sack you're putting onto."

Ashlon eased as carefully as he could onto the wood table. His body shook from exhaustion and his vision swam. How could such little effort drain him so rapidly? "My belongings," he muttered between gasps for air. "A square wooden, well worn... oak, I need to...." It was too much.

Heremon lifted his head and placed a rolled bundle beneath it. Before Ashlon could try the words again, a mouthful of bitter tasting broth filled up his mouth from a small wooden bowl. Heremon's movements were sure for a man his apparent age. The broth didn't spill or slosh as he brought it repeatedly to Ashlon's lips.

Despite the bitter taste, Ashlon drank hungrily. A small suspicion that the soup held poison gave way to deep gratitude. The man had saved him from the cave, the storm. If only he could recall a moment past the cave. Logic explained that he must have succumbed to fever as he slept. But, something in that conclusion unsettled him. If the man had saved him from the cave, how in the world did he come upon him in it?

"Your belly wants more, but will put it right out if

we don't rest a spell," Heremon said.

Ashlon closed his eyes. He felt groggy. Numbed. He opened his mouth to speak but only a snore escaped.

Heremon smiled at the rumpling sound and patted the young knight's arm. Near dead yet swift as a lion to stand brave and order answers. The vigor of youth and ambition hadn't yet given way to wisdom for Ashlon Sinclair, but soon enough it would. Soon enough.

Heremon set about straightening the small space before blowing out the single candle and leaving his charge. The difficult part was over. In a week's time, Ashlon would be standing and able to fight again, so long as he allowed his body to heal.

In the outer room, Heremon put ink to paper and began the hours of assiduous preparation for Breanne's arrival. The girl, a woman now, he had to remind himself, was on the precipice of her destiny. She despaired, he knew. But he also knew that soon she would be living her dreams, her long years of work bearing fruit.

Heremon sighed and rubbed his eyes. He dipped the quill tip into the inkwell. He blotted and wrote the words that designed what seemed a lifetime past. In a sense, they were exactly that: a lifetime.

He had thought it would be harder than it was, to proceed with the necessary arrangements as he now did. But, perhaps the years of preparing for this end caused some desensitization. He was appreciative for it. He had never considered himself a courageous soul and the numbness prevented him from running in fear from obligation.

He lifted the parchment and gently blew on it. Once the ink dried to satisfaction, Heremon rolled it, tied it and returned to Ashlon's meager temporary quarters where he hid it among the items Breanne would take. Ashlon slept soundly thanks to the herbs and his body's desperate need to strengthen itself. He would need it.

Mouse quiet, Heremon closed the door and locked it. He trusted Breanne to be resourceful enough to find the key, and the man, in that order, just as the ancestors had shown him. Nostalgia crept into his heart. He would miss her. The knowledge that they would meet again when the veil between his new world and hers became thin didn't console him. But, he couldn't change the course of destiny and fighting its will only made the course of things more difficult to survive in the end.

The knock came, loud and abrupt, right on time. Heremon opened the door without delay. He saw this final act of answering straight away, his last act of courage. The man on the other side was the only surprise amid the events that had been foretold nearly forty years before.

Wordlessly, Heremon gestured the man to enter and met the eyes of his fate unwaveringly.

Chapter Three

Two bards arrived that day and joined the chieftain at his table as welcome. The night promised to be full of new songs and poems, a preview of the performance they came to give at Niall and Ula's wedding feast.

The large hall was overwrought with guests and residents dining, laughing and sharing. Excitement and welcome permeated the room Breanne forced herself to enter gracefully into. Not many noticed her entrance, a good sign. She released her held breath after walking a few rods when she got no snicker or stare. The room full of pointing, laughing family and friends she'd envisioned gave way to an average, perhaps somewhat special evening.

Rose's waving hand caught her attention. Breanne smiled. She gladly joined her best friend at the long table. Ula and Niall weren't likely waiting on her to join them after this afternoon's exchange.

"You're just in time, Bree," Rose said. "Ryan has returned and will join us, as well as Quinlan." She wiggled her eyebrows up and down.

Already seated, Breanne forced herself to smile. She chose unpleasantness here over mortified there, readily. Besides, what could Quinlan do with so many surrounding them? It wasn't as though he could kiss her right there, paw away for all to see. And he'd already given her the flowers. Oh damn and double damn it.

She'd left the flowers by the stream, hadn't she?

The bump on her shoulder made her look up. Quinlan grinned down at her sheepishly and gestured to the seat next to her. Before she could protest, he took it.

"Good evening, ladies. You both look beautiful this fine eve," he said cordially, his gaze steady on her face.

They thanked him and he nodded and took the opportunity to absorb every visible inch of her with his eyes, leaving her feeling bare and doubtless of his interest. When his gaze flew back to hers she glared fiercely back. He blinked. Interest fell away to blushing red cheeks and Breanne cursed herself under her breath.

She didn't want to hurt his feelings. Truly, she didn't. She simply wanted him to stop. It had been a reflexive reaction. Damned guilt plagued her and Breanne found herself making more than necessary friendly attempts to engage Quinlan into conversation.

"Are you settling back in very well, Quinlan?" she asked and speared a sweet meat with her knife from the piled trencher.

"Oh, I would say he's happy to be home," Ryan said behind them. "Why, he's been skipping around like a little girl, that one."

Rose squealed in delight, jumped from her seat and into her husband's arms. She nearly knocked Breanne into Quinlan's lap in the process and they both went rigid with embarrassment. Righting herself, as did he, Breanne waited for another opportunity to make conversation.

She decided that if she kept on neutral subjects-- warm but very unromantic and definitely not flirtatious by any stretch-- that he would perceive the underlying message. Could they please be friends and not become desperate with lovesickness?

"Have you decided whether you'll hire onto Niall's guard or not?" she asked Quinlan while Ryan and Rose's reunion settled.

Quinlan looked at her strangely and immediately Breanne realized her mistake, an additional blunder. Her father had been Niall's first warrior, the most elite of his hired warriors, assigned to fight for and protect the king. He had died doing it. And as honorable a death as it might be, Breanne had a hundred times already told Quinlan that his living would have been better.

Since childhood, she'd tried to dissuade Quinlan of the idea and he, in turn, would press it on her. But, that was before her feelings for him changed. Now, it seemed, since he would not become her husband, any career should be a good choice so long as he was happy.

Quinlan stood.

Breanne opened her mouth to try to take back the callous sound her words took on in her mind and, so obviously, in his, as well. But, what could she say? So sorry Quinlan, I hadn't thought that one out? I'm distracted with an ultimatum and concern for my strangely behaving friend and mentor?

He walked away before a reasonable apology came to her.

"What was all that, then?" Rose asked. Ryan kept his arm around his wife, unhearing.

"I've said the wrong thing." She put her forehead into her hands. "Oh, Rose, I'm mucking things up good today. Promise me you'll forget every last thing I say today?"

Rose rubbed her back sympathetically. "Always, Bree. Why, I'll even forgive the pile of lies you laid at my feet this afternoon."

Breanne gasped and looked up.

"Don't look so surprised. I have ears and eyes." Rose's eyes twinkled and smiled reassuringly. "You don't have to tell me the truth of things unless you want.

But, I've known you too long to not smell a rotten fib when you spew one."

Breanne shrank down in her seat. She felt caught. Rose chuckled. She couldn't help laughing, as well.

"Am I truly so terrible at them?" Not for the first time, she wished she could be so gay and forgiving as Rose.

"Aye. The whole Grianan, every woman in the room, begins to look about at each other for whoever filled it with stink when you've left a lie behind," she laughed out.

"That's my Rose. She can make a warrior blush." Ryan shook his head and let his arm fall to eat.

"Stop now, Rose," Breanne said. "You'll have me crying if you don't." A tear slid out anyway.

"And then I inevitably get the blame." Rose had tears, too. "But you're my dearest friend and if that's not worth suffering a few prim glares, what is?"

Breanne's heart warmed. She hugged her friend close to thank her. Leave it to Rose to remind her that life can't be taken so seriously.

"And you no longer have the blameworthiness of being with child right now," Breanne said, "I had better stop before they bar you from the Grianan." Her stomach and cheeks ached from the ongoing jest.

"Ah, let them." Rose waved her hand and leaned back against Ryan. "Give me a reason to stay in bed."

Ryan responded with appropriately lewd hip gyrations and soon the two were in their own secret jest that by the look of things and all the kisses, Breanne needn't be in on.

She glanced about for Quinlan, caught Shane's eyes on her and felt eager to escape to her bedchamber— without him or any other following. She hoped the visiting bards would be enough of a distraction to allow her to slip away unnoticed. She needed to prepare to steal away, no easy feat with the likelihood of revelry lasting into the night.

As the food cleared and the music began, Breanne slipped into the kitchen. Dishes sat in wait, the room otherwise empty. She needed a cloak and her book from her room and Heremon had said midnight, but also she recognized that easily, she could slink out now and not be missed.

With one glance and three short steps, Breanne sneaked out the door, the best path of avoidance. She liked this better than any entertainment, especially when the cool night air gusted on her face. The smell of heather was strong from the recent rains and Breanne sucked air into her lungs. She felt released.

She stood there only long enough to ascertain no one followed or wandered nearby, then slinked through the shadows, past the walls of the dun, and through the postern. Jitters of excitement danced through her. Her only regret was that Heremon wouldn't get to examine her notebook, her developing Grimoire.

She could hear him now, "No, no. This chant is all wrong". Surely he would understand she had to take the opportunity when presented?

"Too late now," she said aloud. The moon would be full in less than two weeks and looked like a glowing smile surrounded by freckles of stars.

"Too late for what?"

Breanne screamed and turned to the direction of the too familiar voice. Pins and needles of fright rushed her shoulders and scalp. With her hand over her thumping heart, she glowered at Finn's scruffy, pleased countenance.

"Why do you so love to come upon me like that, cat?" she said. Thankfully, he'd waited until she'd cleared reach of the keep to frighten the clothes right off of her. She should be used to it, should expect these little acts by now.

Finn joined her walk without so much as a chuckle of satisfaction. His step was heavy, purposeful.

"Where have you been?" Breanne asked, his quiet making her wary.

"Hunting fairies, preying on pixies." His usual sarcasm held a note of disturbing sobriety to it. "You know they are quite tasty, the little people."

"Heremon won't arrive at the Grove for some time. If you'd like, we can try again when we get there," she said, guilt over her failing him gnawing her.

He didn't reply and she didn't repeat herself. Obviously, Finn felt bent to brood and who was she to stop him? If she'd waited half the number of years as he, she'd be more than pouting, too. Once they got there, he'd probably let her try again. But she didn't have her book. No matter. Perchance starting from scratch would turn out more successful. The idea assuaged Breanne's guilt and focused her mind.

Night's sounds sang in the breeze. Crickets chirped, frogs croaked, water burbled louder as they neared the wooded area. They headed to the usual meeting place after Breanne completed her ritual blessing and offering.

"I can't see a reason to bother with it." Finn lay on the grass and thumped his tail as he watched her bend, poke, pick through the foliage.

"We have time." She chose to ignore the snide remark, but smiled at hearing signs of his usual self.

"Are you no longer worried for Heremon? With all the fuss and froth this afternoon, I thought you'd be rushing to find him first chance presented," Finn said, his tone venomous.

Heat climbed Breanne's neck. She clenched her fists.

She would not let him bait her tonight, not after the day she'd had. He couldn't be expected to empathize with her plight, but might appreciate that she did his. She pursed her lips tightly, refusing to spit harsh words back at him.

"I believe I overreacted earlier," she said. "Given time to consider the events of the day, I've decided to trust that Heremon is well enough, wise enough to care for himself." Taking the high moral ground and turning her cheek felt good. Why give him what he so clearly wanted?

"Interesting. Do tell me then, Breanne, what will you do if he fails to show, unaware that his devotee is patiently awaiting a lesson he doesn't recall scheduling?"

His voice was less sour, closer to the dry wit she'd grown accustomed to. But the words needled her worse. Damn. He was too good at this vicious game. Breanne steadied her breathing so that her mind and emotions would follow suit.

Moonlight broke free from a cloud, brightening the cluster of trees they walked through. She had no candle to light, no book to be reviewed and possibly no lesson to be heard, but she refused to give in to climbing regret. Finn wasn't right, he was simply most happy when making her unhappy.

"I will check in on him," she said succinctly and began searching the small clearing for ingredients to make a potion for Finn. Perhaps that would make him happy. In the underbrush a swath of white caught her eye. Recognizing it, Breanne bent and retrieved a candle that her master must have missed.

"Of course you will, brave girl that you are," Finn sneered.

Carefully, she set the candle upon the stone altar and closed her eyes in concentration. She raveled up her thoughts into a little bundle, compressed the bundle into a ball and chanted the words in her mind. Breanne had successfully created fire only twice before, and neither occasion were close in proximity, but she might as well try.

The small orb slowly spun until it grew and colored to a deep blue. Breanne opened her eyes, looked at the wick and blew. She could feel the glowing orb's energy deep in her chest and breathed inwardly to catch it and push it out of her. When the burning sensation left her body, nothing happened. She sighed in resignation.

Suddenly, a tiny flicker of light sparked the candle's tip. A small happy shriek escaped her open mouth as she saw the flame take hold and dance.

"Finn. Finn, I can hardly trust my eyes. Have I done it?" She searched for him.

"Astonishing. You make fire. Forgive me if I don't dance a jig, will you?" Finn blinked slowly, his ears pitched back.

Her smile widened. Finn was back to his old self and as annoying as that persona was, it also comforted her. She'd had enough of change today to last some time. Turning back, Breanne watched the flame she'd charged from her own mind and felt lifted.

I can do this. I am meant for this.

The joyous thoughts buzzed her veins with promise and certainty. She rested her chin on her bent knees, feeling like she could wait all night for Heremon. And if he did not arrive, she would take heed of Finn's words and check in on the old Druid priest.

Beeswax melted faster than tallow. Or was it the other way around? Breanne couldn't remember, but quashed the urge to ask Finn for verification and decided that of either substance, this one had burned well long enough to warrant seeking Heremon out. The beeswax was nearly all puddle, the flame dwarfed with so little wick left to consume. Heremon hadn't shown.

Breanne blew the candle out. The darkness spread out around them. It was colder and the moon looked to be on its descent. She should return to the keep. If her mother had looked in on her, there would be more than hell to pay. Breanne stood and brushed at her gown. She nudged Finn with her toe to wake him.

"We must go. You were right. Heremon hasn't come."

The cat yawned and stretched but didn't rise. "I'll wait here."

She realized that he thought she was going to find Heremon. She'd intended to, but the cold and the dark, along with a nagging rawness in her chest, changed her mind. Finn lay his head back down and peeked up at her through one eye. He didn't have to speak a word for her to hear the gloating. She could see it in the slit of his eyes, the swish of his tail, that he thought her a self-centered coward.

Mayhap he was right. Was she here only to get in her long awaited lesson? Was her concern for Heremon truly because of his strange behavior or in fact a result of her discontent at missing out on five new herbals and praise for her Grimoire? Was he acting strange at all or had she conjured it all as a convenience?

"I don't know where his home is," she ground out, knowing full well that she had just taken his bait. "I need you with me."

Swish. Blink.

"Please." She'd look in a window, mayhap knock, say hello, farewell and be warm in her bed within the hour. And if he chose to stay, then she'd be there all the sooner.

After staring at her at length, eyes squinted, Finn leapt to his feet, stretched and pounced in a westerly direction toward the sea.

Breanne clamped her jaw and trudged after him, letting her cape drag and catch as it pleased along the way.

The trees grew sparse as they neared the edge of the forest. The piney scent of it mingled with the salty sea air pushing up the Slieve League cliffs. When the crisp blue of ocean came into view, Breanne stopped. She didn't have to peer over the dizzying three-furlong drop to sense its danger. She could hear it in the quality of the waves hissing against the rocky walls.

"How much further?" she asked Finn, her voice quaking.

He ignored her and inched to the edge. Breanne's breath caught, her belly clenched watching him. Terrible by day, the stony precipice felt horrific and cavernous by night. She could almost see his small, fat body plummeting to the bottom to his death and it made her ears ache and skin crawl.

Right as she readied to call him back, he stopped. Breanne looked up and down the coast for a dwelling of any size or shape, but saw none. The cliffs made her feel naked and she turned around for escape into the cover of trees. Then she saw it.

The home was modest and exactly what she'd expect of a man such as Heremon. She went to the stone house and resigned to knock. With no light inside, it was her only option. Breanne rapped her knuckles on the splintering wood door. It sounded hollow. She glanced to verify Finn hadn't plunged, then knocked again, harder. The skin on her knuckles protested the combination of cold and hard colliding.

"He's not answering," she called to Finn.

He eyed her over his shoulder for a moment and finally joined her. A wind picked up and whipped at loose tendrils from her braid. "Could we have missed him?" she asked. "Mayhap he came as we went?"

Either way, she'd come and could now go. All she needed was certainty that Finn knew she'd tried.

"Is it locked?" Finn asked, his tone strange, almost caring.

Of course, he had known Heremon much longer than she. Longer than she'd fathom a guess at. Though Heremon never gave her such detail, she gathered that Finn's curse began some time ago, long enough ago for him to have been through five other priestess hopefuls only to have them fail him.

Breanne tried the door. The dark wood slab fell open. Silence. Finn looked at her in agitation and Breanne stepped inside. Warmth enclosed her body and she understood how chilled she had become. Her skin prickled gloriously and she stepped further in. She could hear Finn follow and suspected that he might actually be uneasy.

They left the door ajar and Breanne lit a candle off the remaining, almost ashen embers. Four additional candles made the room fill with enough light to see two things clearly. Heremon was not present, which they confirmed after searching the adjoining rooms, and something was wrong. Breanne didn't know if wrong was the right word to define the gut feeling she had. Amiss might be more suitable, or different, but nothing appeared to be out of the ordinary, no fallen chairs, no signs of departure.

Neither spoke the words, but Breanne knew Finn sensed it, as well. He took as much care as she in keeping all movement quiet and delicate. After a fast search, she went through each room again, trying to pinpoint evidence to support her increasing worry. She came to a stop. Cool air brushed in at the open door on her. She frowned at Finn. He hadn't joined her on the second turn, sat shaking his head for the twentieth time.

"Where do you expect he's gone to?" she whispered.

"Mayhap nowhere. Have you not thought to try the fourth door?" His voice bounced off the walls.

"What door?" She turned, scanned and found it. She couldn't believe she'd missed it. Leave it to Finn to sit and watch her muck along, missing the obvious.

The door was well hidden by shadows and a long narrow table piled high with books. Seeing that the door was not so obvious made her feel somewhat better. Breanne cleared the table, slid it away and tried the knob. It turned easily and she peeked into the darkness. She needed a candle.

"What was that?" Finn's voice was a whisper. His ears tucked back and he crouched, looking into the night.

Breanne froze in place, hand an inch from a candle. The hair on her neck tickled with fear as she watched the cat slink low and creep to the door. Surely, it was Heremon returning, she told herself.

Finn stole into the darkness, forcing Breanne to choke back the tremble rising in her throat and follow. Her eyes penetrated the shadowy obscurity, rushing to adjust to the lack of light. Movement in the grass caught her eye and she followed the small form that could only be Finn's.

By the time he neared the edge, she could fully see. She wanted to call his name but remained quiet, trying to calm the thudding blood in her head. The breeze shushed the tall grass around them, a hiss barely audible above the low roar of waves so far below them. The sounds concealed her clumsy movements as she crouched to the ground midway between the cliffs and cottage.

Time slipped like fingers drumming a surface. Breanne's pulse steadied along with her breathing as she eyed Finn. She wondered how far down the coast they'd been this afternoon. Could she have simply walked a spell and found Heremon right there in the bright of day had she not given in to her temper?

He was toying with her again. After so many moments of Finn hunched, hind legs readying over and again, what else could it be? Breanne sat upright and exhaled in annoyance. Not that he would hear her, or care. She moved to rise. Then she heard it. Faint and low, but definite. She heard a grunt. Finn stood taller and peered down over the lip of rock.

"Heremon," Finn said, his voice full of anguish so sincere it brought Breanne forward.

She went flat to the ground and belly crawled to him. They were so high up, her head and vision swam a little just at the thought of what lay below.

"Oh no," she gasped, feeling the same anguish she'd heard. "Heremon. Can you hear me? Heremon?" The Druid's figure didn't move. "Heremon," Breanne called again, using her hands to cup the sound and help push it down and out toward the man. The rocky, moss covered spot he lay on looked impossible to reach. How in the son of the lord's name did the old man get there?

"Can you get to him?"

Finn paced, testing the rocky edge, but couldn't seem to find a suitable angle. Then in a streak of fur the cat bounded down and landed a breath away from Heremon's limp arm. Breanne put her hands over her eyes, then down to her mouth. The moaning sound came again.

She glanced toward it, the left, saw nothing and returned her attention to Finn and her teacher. "Is he breathing? Oh, what have I done? I knew. I knew and I stood there rather than trust myself as he's always telling me and now he's hurt." She scooted closer. "Is he breathing?" she called louder.

Finn flashed her a look of panicked anger and sniffed Heremon. The slope he lay on became more clear as Finn tried to negotiate it and help without moving him. Hot tears dripped down her face, the gusts off of the ocean hitting them cold.

Please be alive.

But the longer Finn sniffed and peered, the larger her certainty became. He was not. She knew it and it numbed her, panic and fear leadening her mind.

Finn leapt back up and hung his head. "He's gone." The misery in his voice surprised her. She'd never seen the beast show any emotion outside of annoyed, amused or bored. Later, thinking back she would feel a small shame for her surprise and for her sudden complete lack of her own utter sadness.

Somewhere someone had moaned. Matter of factly, her mind told her this. She stood and walked in the direction she'd glanced moments ago. The wind brought the sound. The wind also had pushed it down to bring their focus to Heremon, but the low sound of pain they'd heard was not his. The numbness seemed to aid her in these conclusions, helping her walk without fear and listen.

Behind her, Finn yowled, as close to a human wail as she'd ever heard from a hurt animal. But, she stepped on, unmoved in any emotional direction. Three immediate needs showed clear and foremost in her mind. She first must locate the source of the second sound. Next, after assessing its source, she must take appropriate action. Third, she must get Heremon off of that sloping ledge before he fell from it and washed out to sea.

The second meant considerations and decisions unlike the other two. Once she found the person making the sound, should she dispatch that person? Was he or she lying wounded from battling Heremon? Or could they have witnessed her teacher's tragic demise and need even more priority and help than Heremon?

Breanne lifted her skirt for her boline. But it wasn't there. It lay in the grass somewhere south of this place, tossed and forgotten when she'd stormed back to the dun.

Another step brought answers. There in the brush, Breanne saw the gleam of skin, a man's leg. She rushed to the form and found him, eyes closed and body askew. No more than breeches covered him from the elements and her startled eyes.

Chapter Four

He moaned again. She observed no marks on him save a few scrapes, no wounds to speak of. She knelt at his side and felt his head. A fever.

Breanne looked back to Finn. He lay on the ground, curled over himself and yowling into the wind. She could see he would be no help and hunted the area for fallen branches. She retrieved four, tore her cape from the shoulder fastenings and worked the branches and material together. She didn't have time for perfection. Heremon needed her and this man would die if his fever couldn't be reduced fast.

Somewhere in her mind, a voice ordered her to leave for help, insisting he was too big for one woman to haul anywhere, let alone to Heremon's home that might not be safe. Breanne ignored it. If she left him, he would die.

She rolled him from the bed of heather onto the tied branches and dragged him, headfirst to the small stone cottage. The man lay limp, unperturbed by her clumsy hauling of his person. Her muscles screamed in pain from his dead weight's pull on them.

She managed to get him in and the door closed. She laid him flat, near the fireplace and piled two small wood pieces on top of a peat moss clump. The fire lit, she scurried through the house, ransacking cupboards and drawers for Heremon's herbs. He was a Druid priest for Christ's sake, where were his herbs, potions? Her mind tangled with hurry and panic and she forced herself to stop and think.

He moaned again and she returned to his side. Only after she paused next to him did she notice how out of breath she'd become rushing as she had been.

She placed her hand to his brow. Damned but he was dangerously hot. Breanne wiped beads of sweat from his brow. Then she remembered: the door. Grabbing two candles, Breanne rushed to the forgotten room and flooded with relief when the light revealed shelves brimming with jars and bowls and papers and books.

Breanne set both candles on the long table in the center and searched through the glass bottles. The labels were hard to read but she found what she was looking for at last. Finn's mewling carried softly from outside. Her heart, no longer so numb, ached for him. She couldn't fathom the agony he must feel to loose Heremon. Her own sorrow would come soon enough, she knew, and set to grinding the herbs while she had the wherewithal to do so.

Mixed with warmed water, she lifted the man's head and brought the bowl to his lips.

"Drink," she said as sternly as she'd ever heard herself speak.

He sputtered in protest, wasting part of the mixture. Breanne used her knee to prop his head, curled an arm around his neck and forced his mouth open. She poured another mouthful in and covered his mouth tightly. He coughed and choked a bit, but ingested most of the hot liquid.

She repeated the process until the remaining liquid was gone along with her strength. The man spoke slurring words she didn't understand. But he didn't open his eyes, he settled down.

While she wiped a wet rag over his face and neck,

her mind worked on a strategy to retrieve Heremon. She would leave Finn with the man, hide them in the room. Mayhap the door could be locked. If not, she would have to hope re-disguising it would suffice. Then she'd get back to the O'Donnell keep, wake Quinlan, no, Niall. She would be in serious trouble, but that was that. It couldn't be changed and certainly was not so important that it took precedence to getting some men and some rope and bringing Heremon up from that tiny little ledge.

How could he have gotten there? Had he gone mad and fallen? Had he been pushed? But, the fall was not so far that he wouldn't survive. Breanne couldn't see Heremon to have died of natural causes, standing at the edge of rock, only to then fall on his own and land so mysteriously.

Breanne viewed the nearly naked man on the floor. His skin was flushed with color. He had the answers she needed. And if Niall couldn't get them from the man, she would find a way. She might not succeed with a potion, but knew a poison that disrupted the bowels so much, a man would beg for death.

Breanne felt his forehead. It still burned, but not so hot as before. She nodded to no one and ran a hand through her loosened hair. The braided strands pulled painfully against the movement. Sighing, she began to unravel the thing and twist her waist length hair into a knot instead. She realized that Finn had gone silent. His silence was worse.

The first waves of sorrow were accompanied by fear. And soon guilt joined in. She should have come earlier. She should have followed him sooner. She should have told someone. A tear slid down her cheek and the first sob coughed through her. Breanne covered her mouth almost as though to keep the pain inside or lessen the outward force of it. But her hand only served to muffle the sounds of crying.

Heremon wasn't an easy person to know. His affection was difficult to win and praise came in meager supply. But, she had grown to respect and even love the man. He was her teacher and had believed in her. She knew that, not because he told her but because he showed her. He had taken the time and withstood risk and ridicule by taking her on as his primary student.

"Bards come and go and believe themselves the blessing of life itself. But an Ovate is rare to discover, a hard win, and worth a thousand of them," Heremon had said to her more than once.

Breanne smiled weakly as tears and her eyebrows gathered tighter. With her knees to her chest, she tipped back and forth, and didn't notice the door had opened. They were no longer alone.

"Kill him." Finn's eyes glittered with malice. He stopped at the man's waist.

"I canno', Finn. He may know what happened to Heremon. He may be here with Heremon for a reason."

Finn slowly shook his head. "Nay. He clearly killed a man you clearly do not fathom the worth of. He doesn't deserve to breathe the air I take into my lungs."

Breanne's heart ached again for Finn. Had Heremon's death sealed his curse, never to be lifted now? Seven times failing proved that she couldn't lift it on her own. Or would Heremon's death change the prophecy that an Ovate would end Finn's enchanted sentence?

"I understand your anger, but this man may not be at fault. We canno' assume blame with only his presence here to evidence it."

Finn's stare locked onto hers and she saw his pain, raw and fresh. But killing the man did not bode well.

"Slit him open and leave him to choke on his own

foul blood. We must get help before Heremon falls from that ledge. We cannot afford your uncertainty."

"This man is in no shape to kill anyone and can't have been for some time. If you take pause for a moment and view the man as he is, you will see I speak truly." She waited while he grudgingly turned to view the gleaming body he meant to slaughter. "A fever such as this is not brought on in minutes. He may not make it past whatever ails him and no man is strong enough to kill in this condition."

"And pushing an old man off a cliff takes immense strength, does it? If not for luck having Heremon's body finding that ledge, it would be lost to the sea."

She wouldn't acknowledge his tone by responding in like. She must remain calm, speak calmly. "Even walking to that edge himself would be impossible." She wasn't certain she spoke the truth, but she felt deep in her bones that this man must live. She must persuade him to wait. More than persuade, he must be convinced because Breanne couldn't leave the man alone, yet had to get help before Heremon fell and was lost to the sea.

Finn eyed the man and Breanne watched for the venom in his expression to give way to compassion, understanding, or at least acquiescence. "He isn't going anywhere. I will bring Niall and others for Heremon. Niall will see the man answers for what he may have done or find the person who should. Heremon was his most trusted advisor, was his Brehon advisor for years."

Finn lowered his head slightly and closed his eyes. Breanne's hope rose then fell again when the cat shook his head. "You will not give this man over to Niall."

Taken aback, Breanne scowled. "Of course I will. I must. He may know something."

Finn glared at her in his typical condescension. "Don't you think Heremon would have brought the man to the keep if it were his intention? Has it not crossed your mind that the man is here for a reason?"

Breanne didn't know how to gauge this about face other than as another outlet for his sorrow and anger. "No. I found him outside, fallen. I didn't conclude that Heremon had him here at all, let alone by secret." A strange and disquieting sensation took hold of her as implications and fears scrambled her thoughts.

"At this rate, Breanne, I will live a thousand years in this cursed place." He shook his head slower. "The table? Did you not notice the pile of men's clothing, a sword, next to the table in the herb closet?"

Breanne shook her head equally slowly. She hadn't. She'd been so keen on finding the herbs that she'd barely noticed the table itself. She rose and went to the room and was struck by the obviousness of the pile, particularly the large, heavy-looking sword. Its hilt was encrusted with three large emeralds and a trail of sapphires inlaid in gold filigree. Beautiful.

"I still see no reason not to tell Niall. He needs care. He should be moved to the keep."

"Do you recall what Heremon spoke of in his presage?" Finn said the name reverently. A new note of misery rang in his words.

Breanne furrowed her brow and struggled to remember the words from what felt like days ago, longer. She wanted to leave. She'd made a plan and Finn was changing it all. Niall would know what to do. Niall would care for this man, retrieve and handle Heremon's body. She couldn't do it, none of it. She wouldn't.

"I don't see how that pertains to any of this or how Heremon may help us now. I'm going for help. Stay or leave, just don't kill the man." She strode for the door.

"You'll kill him yourself if you give him to Niall."

She ignored his words. He was barbing her again

and she would not give in. Breanne counted her breaths and paced them with her steps. It gave her direction and kept her mind clear to think.

She'd rouse Niall, bring him and whoever else he saw fit back to this place. The pines lead to a small cluster of birch and then to a line of oaks. The path was clear if you focused. Focus. Remember, so you may make it back.

"How would I kill him? I am trying to help him. He's the one that was ready to gorge him on the spot." She talked to herself to keep the anger at bay, and the guilt.

Niall would command the situation far better than she or Finn. Yes, he would be equally distressed by Heremon's death. But, he was a levelheaded man. He certainly wouldn't kill the man directly. He would make certain death was deserved.

What could Finn have meant? She knew better than to conclude he'd thrown the first lie at her that came to mind. He was far too calculating a beast to do so.

Think, Breanne. How could your leaving kill the man? Would Finn complete what she thought she'd stopped? No. She'd seen the change in him. Heard it.

She pushed away low branches as she walked. A branch slapped at her cheek, leaving a stinging stripe. She rubbed at the pain, her mind on the path and Finn's words still. Her skin felt warm where the branch whipped her.

Suddenly, the realization sprang to mind. Mayhap Finn meant literally her departure would kill the stranger. Mayhap, he needed her there. But, how could Niall be brought? She didn't wait for her mind to answer. She turned and went back, moving fast and deftly back to Heremon's home. The fever. The man would succumb if she didn't wait for it to break.

She broke through the doorway and rushed to the stranger's side. "Has he worsened?" She felt his head. It was cooler, much cooler. Then he didn't need her here. She straightened.

Finn stood and joined her from his position at the man's feet. "He's English."

"What? How do you know…?"

"He spoke. Mumbled. The worst French I've ever heard in a distinctly English accent. And he's nobility. The Irish may be the most hospitable people, but even hospitality has limitations when a former Brehon advisor to his clan's chieftain, a Druid priest of high respect, has met a mysterious demise with an English noble in residence."

She wanted to say he was reaching, that the conclusion would be based on loose evidence and that Niall had better judgment. Surely an Englishman would mumble his native tongue. But, Heremon's words chose that moment to spring back into her muddled brain. The emeralds…he is yours…tell no one. Protect him.

Breanne looked at the stranger's face. No. It couldn't be. Not her. Not him.

She looked at Finn, searched his eyes suspiciously. Had he been there to hear the words and already concluded the obvious that she always seemed to miss at first glance? So be it.

Breanne stood and surveyed the room. She needed to hide him and get back to the keep. His head was cool and he should sleep for a day with as much valerian root as she'd ground into the mixture. "They will want to search the place. Where can I take him?"

Finn smiled his cat's grin. Gloating beast. "If you believe you can better disguise the closet, we may put him there. Or," Finn rolled onto his back as though to scratch it.

"Or what?" Breanne fisted her hands into her skirt.

"There is a cave nearby."

"How close?" She knew her limitations in successfully dragging a man this size.

"Close. It is sacred. He will be safe there." Finn's tone was casual.

"And your thirst for blood? Where is it now?" Breanne pinned him with her eyes. If she would have to trust him with more than simply watching the man whilst she left, she wanted assurance.

"Rest your fears, Breanne. If I still wanted his head, I'd have had it while you were off wandering the woods." He managed to sound bored.

Though his point rang honest, Breanne trusted the instincts that sprang up alongside the prophetic words. She would take him to the place Finn suggested, ensure he was safe there herself, but Finn would come back with her. She'd drag him by the tail if need be.

It took her a full and arduous fifteen minutes to get the man from the cottage to the cave, despite how close it turned out to be. And though just a few cubits inside the forest boundaries, the small cave was concealed well by foliage. If a person didn't already know it was there, they'd be hard pressed to detect it.

Breanne laid the man on deerskin and wrapped him in every woolen blanket Heremon owned. Hopefully, the items wouldn't be missed when Niall's men inevitably searched the dwelling. With one last press of her hand to the man's cheek, she silently promised him he was safe and to return posthaste, then left.

Finn joined her on the path freely, and relieved her of the ugly imagery her mind had formed of carrying him back by the neck scruff kicking and yowling and scratching. They made good time and once within the keep walls, Breanne knew he would be forced into silence. Now was her last and best opportunity to speak what she must.

"You will tell no one, Finn. Heremon said tell no one. Out of respect for Heremon, I will ask you to obey my wish, his portending."

Finn nodded soberly and Breanne entered the kitchen door, where she'd snuck from only hours before. She left Finn in her bedchamber with a bowl of wine and a plate of leftover venison to go wake her soon-to-be stepfather. Sadness ached inside of her as she tried to prime herself for Niall O'Donnell's disappointment.

He answered soon after her first knock and looked disheveled but alert. "What is it?" Urgency rang in his words.

"It's Heremon, my lord. He has fallen. Please dress quickly. We must retrieve him." She couldn't meet his eyes and her hushed words felt inadequate.

"Fallen. Fallen where?"

"He no longer lives, my lord." The tears stung before they fell. She tried to stop them and couldn't. "The cliffs. He's fallen from the Slieve League. Near his home. We must retrieve him." She wiped the tears and met his gaze.

Niall closed the door hard. Dumbfounded, Breanne reached her fist up to knock again when the door flew open. Niall exited, fully dressed and motioned her to follow. "You saw him fall?" With surprising efficiency, he had four men ready and waiting within moments of her first knock.

She shook her head. "I found him. I thought I heard something and found him on a small outcrop some twenty feet below the edge." She stuck to his queries, grateful to save explanations of why she'd been there for later.

"Where in proximity of his home did you see him, Breanne?" He tightened his sword belt and tucked his mantle as he spoke.

She understood that they weren't taking her with them and explained in as much detail as she could where he lay. She bit back the sobs that threatened her composure. He needed her calm, not blubbering with emotion.

The five armed men left into the night air with the remaining household undisturbed. The quiet was unsettling. Breanne sat on the bottom stair where Niall had left her with a dogged nod.

She hugged her knees close and rested her chin on them. Finally free to do so, she exhaled and let the sorrow come. Her world felt inside out, backward. This pain in her chest that radiated from her heart wasn't foreign. It was familiar despite the years of healing and burying she'd done. She had known this loss before and every fiber of her recognized it.

Life is change, she reminded herself but it didn't help dry her tears. She liked her life. It had become steady and simple again after her father's death and all the change it produced.

She and Ula had left their home and joined the O'Donnell chieftain in his. Being an only child, Sean O'Donnell left no brothers to care for his family. Niall took them in both as Sean's cousin and as the man he'd served and died for.

For ten years, that home sat empty aside from the caretaker Niall assigned to it. With her mother marrying, the home became solely her inheritance. An only child herself she had no brother to share it with nor a sister to split the estate into suitable portions for each to take with her own marriage. Only her, only her marriage.

She wondered what it would be like to return to it after so many years. Would it hurt? Would it feel like a different place entirely after so long? Soon she would know, unless she chose a man with property of his own and they chose to rent or sell the manor.

"Breanne, why are you crying?" The softly whispered words startled her, though she knew immediately who asked them.

"Danny. Did I wake you?"

"Nah. I can hardly sleep is all. Are ye all right?" He came down the stairs to sit next to her. His rumpled hair and bedclothes made her smile.

"Aye, lad. I'll be perfect now that you're here to keep me company." Breanne wiped her face dry and gave the boy a warm smile. He rested his head on her shoulder and she hugged him into the crook of her arm. "Look at how big you're getting on me. It feels like yesterday you were in my lap and now I only get hugs in secret when no one else can see."

"I'm almost a grown man, Breanne. I can't have the other men seeing you and my mum coddling me. They'll poke at me 'til I bleed with it."

"A man already, Danny? Here I was hoping you'd wait at least another four or five years before I lost you to brawling and warring and rutting. Can you not wait a bit longer?" Breanne meant her words, though she said them in a playful tone. Ten years old was too young to be thinking of growing up. She wanted to see him remain a sweet boy, blushes and all, the little brother she never had.

"Mayhap a little longer, I suppose," Danny told her after a consternate rub on his hairless chin. "But only when the men are not around. I can't have you giving me kisses in front of them."

"I promise," Breanne said and bent to give him one on each dimpled cheek. "But, I'll miss it dearly."

"Breanne?"

"Yes?"

"Why are you crying?" Danny's face flushed with tender concern.

"A bit of a rough day is all. Now that you're here with me, it all seems trifling."

"Is it because you have to marry?" Danny fingered the edge of his bedrobe, avoided her gaze.

His directness both refreshed and discomfited her. Children could be so perfectly honest. "In part, yes. I had hoped I'd fall in love before I chose a husband. It looks like I may have to go the other way about it."

"Like the tale last night? The pretty one about the fairy princess and the mortal she took to the Otherworld?" Danny gestured grandly as he spoke, his voice filling the empty passageway with the music of childish wonder.

Breanne nodded eagerly. "She took him then? Did she clobber him over the head and drag him back with her?" Danny chortled with laughter. "Think you and I shall go about it in the same manner, Danny? I'll need a big club." Breanne tapped her lips, pretending to think of where she could find such a thing. Danny giggled, covering his mouth to hide a snort.

"Ah, Breanne, was he not the best bard you ever heard in all you life? His words made magick right there before us all. I swear I saw the princess walk right through the room," Danny said, looking for her agreement.

Breanne nodded. It sounded like she'd missed quite a show and she'd be lying if she said she didn't wish she'd been there instead. A little pang of jealousy shot through her at Danny's praise for the bard. Their words were magickal, held more real power than the boy guessed. She wished she could say the same about her own.

"Well, Danny, I best be off to bed. I think you ought

to as well before your father finds us and fines me three embroidered tunics for keeping you up late. We have a big day ahead tomorrow, well, I do leastwise, what with finding myself a club and all." She didn't let herself remember what tomorrow really brought, or of everything that had ended today.

Danny giggled harder, but nodded. He threw his arms around her, breaking her heart with happiness and love. Breanne rocked his small frame to and fro in hers.

"I love you, Dan," she said and kissed his head.

"I love you, too," he said with such feeling that Breanne knew she'd better leave fast or end up crying again on his shoulder.

Chapter Five

In the light of dawn, Breanne woke with a single panicked thought: what if he wakes and has no food or explanation? Will he leave? She yanked the covers from her, the cool morning air feeling good on her hot skin, and dressed hurriedly. She had to get back to that cave and the man now, before Niall placed an inevitable hold on her leaving the grounds without escort. With a murderer lurking about and no studies for her to be leaving to, she'd lose her freedom fast.

Finn lay unperturbed at the edge of her bed, sleeping soundly. Breanne nudged him. He rolled over but didn't open his eyes and she knew by the limpness of his body that he wouldn't soon be rising. She didn't doubt he'd finished half the bottle of wine last night, perhaps more.

No matter. Far better that he stayed. The less he dealt with the stranger, the less he could interfere and have her second guessing her actions. Her belly quivered at the thought of meeting the man alone, by daylight, with him awake. She blamed hunger and left without preamble for the kitchens.

The scent of bacon roused her stomach as she entered the busy room. Several freshly baked loafs of grainy bread cooled on the open window's ledge. The servants, some fuidir and others free and part of the feine, spoke and moved with liveliness, paying her no mind as she filled her satchel with a loaf and choice meats. News of Heremon's death must not have reached many ears, Breanne concluded and was glad she'd woken when she did.

She headed for the same door as last night but stopped short when Erin Burke's plump frame blocked her way. "And where do ye think you're off to this morning, Miss O'Donnell?"

Breanne rushed to the first lie her brain could formulate. "To the Friary. Gannon O'Shannon. My uncle has invited…."

A loud crash behind of something distinctly ceramic stole Erin's attention and Breanne took the chance to slip past her and sprint down the slope of yard before the old cook could follow and call after her.

Just past the gate, Breanne stopped to catch her breath and peek-check for Erin barreling after her. Could Niall have already warned the staff that she was not to be out alone any longer? Seeing the coast clear, Breanne continued in a fast walk down her usual trail with the hood of her evergreen cloak concealing her blonde strands.

Eating along the way, she skipped her usual blessings and prayers until she reached her destination. There she knelt outside of the cave, asked Morrigan for her protection and sprinkled a few crumbs of bread on the mossy ground. She entered the cave slowly, her belly fluttering with turns of fear and excitement.

When she saw him, she stilled. Sunlight filtered through from both the entrance and a small hole in the stone ceiling. Breanne looked at the hole in wonder and followed its path down to rest her gaze on his face. Her breath caught for a moment. Tiny sparkling dust particles danced in the stream of light bathing the man's smooth, whiskered skin.

His strong jaw lay tilted up and his features were

cast in lovely relief in the morning light. His features appeared so chiseled they could be that of a sculpture. Thick black eyebrows arched over his heavy, long lashed eyes. Soft black curls framed his face. His lips were full and soft looking.

Breanne reached her hand out to touch his cheek and only then realized that she'd walked over and knelt next to him. It startled her from the distraction seeing him had cast on her. Her cheeks filled with heat and she thanked the lord and goddess that no one had witnessed her foolish behavior.

English. Yes, he looked English. Were he well, the two or three days growth of beard that shadowed his jaw would be cleanly shaven. Her eyes traveled over the rest of him, evaluating other signs of his heritage. He was tall yet still broad shouldered and lean. His chest was bare of any hair and Breanne wondered what his skin would feel like on her palm.

Her belly flip-flopped and shivered. Again, she blushed and mentally shook herself. Such thoughts were new to her. Even her girlish crush on Quinlan hadn't evoked such lasciviousness.

She did have to touch him though, to ensure he remained free of fever. Why not on his chest, a small impish voice asked? Tentatively, Breanne reached her hand forward to hover above the outlined of pectoral muscle, where his heart would be. Would she feel its beat, she wondered, mesmerized by the tingle of emotion swirling through her?

Slowly, she placed her hand on him. His skin was warm, not hot but the surge that went through her body was. The sensation jolted her and she jerked her hand away. No fever. That is all she needed to verify. She should leave him the food and go. But she didn't. She replaced her hand, keeping a watchful eye on his face for signs of awareness.

He didn't stir. She pressed her palm slightly and felt his heart thump steady and strong. It assured the healer in her but stirred another part. Breanne gradually slid her hand down his skin, fascinated by the smooth texture and warmth. More wondrous was the heat his body seemed to send into hers. Not heat as the sun gives, or fire, for this did not feel at all uncomfortable. It didn't warn not to get too close. This heat did not burn, and yet did somehow.

The man's skin goose-bumped under her touch and Breanne jerked back her hand. She tore his eyes from his sleeping face and focused her attention on placing the satchel and wineskin in an obvious and close place. Too late, she thought to include a note warning him not to leave the cave. It was enough food to last more than a day and she didn't know when she'd be able to return.

Worry made her movements hasty and her brow furrow. She couldn't tarry much longer or Niall would have a search party after her and of all her luck it would include Shane MacSweeney. She rued her lack of forethought but couldn't see a way around it. He'd wake no later than tonight, surely. She would simply find a way to return, explain, and get some explanations, as well.

The idea made her feel immensely better. "Until tonight then," she whispered. Her hushed voice echoed in the small stone room and the feeling she had of quiet awe when she entered, returned.

On her walk back, Breanne tried to find the hole that created the tunnel of light, but gave up as the pressure of time closed in on her. Within ten minutes, she slipped back through the gate and remembering her lie, headed in the direction of the friary. Just in case.

"Breanne O'Donnell," a man's voice said. "You've got yourself some explaining to do."

Breanne's heart skipped a beat when she recognized the voice to be her uncle's. She stopped and faced the man with her most charming smile to placate the annoyance she heard in his words. "Uncle Patrick. Good morning to you. Why, I was on my way to see you just now and here you are."

"I doubt such a story," he said gruffly, his eyebrows sharply raised. "What route were you takin' that could send you so far off to eat a good hour to get to be standing at the very place you started from?"

Breanne struggled to maintain her smile and add a look of innocence as her mind ran to find an acceptable fib. "An hour. Why did you expect I'd be seeing you an hour ago?" She choked out a weak laugh but maintained steady eye contact.

"My soon to be brother-in-law informed me not five minutes ago of your plans. I'll tell you I got him worried when I told him I hadn't seen you. Best we plan a visit another day, Breanne. I believe you'd better check with Niall just now." His brow lifted higher in disapproval before he left her standing in the yard.

Breanne nodded curtly, shut her mouth and went back inside. She wouldn't have believed a person's brows could reach that level had she not seen it for herself numerable times. The look still impressed her not just by its contortion but by the undeniable effect it had on her. She'd been reduced to a seven-year-old miscreant caught in naughtiness, not the best way to approach what would likely be an inquisition about more than her morning's activities.

* * * *

Noisy activity outside the cave woke Ashlon. The angry chirping of birds first entered his dreams then penetrated them and he sat up groggily. He tried rubbing the sleep from his eyes but it clung to him like a spider's web, dulling his awareness.

Rock surrounded him and for a moment he thought he'd dreamed the heathen man and missing chest. He jerked his body around to view the small space and still saw no familiarity, but recognized that he was in a cave. No water, no skiff, a different cave than the one he'd taken shelter in when he'd oared his skiff into the cove, his last memory before the fever took hold.

To his left lay a satchel and wine skin. He reached for both and his arms shook from the effort. Daylight poured in from above and before him. He opened the satchel and found food. He ate slowly, refusing to give in to the desire to gorge himself. He surmised that his recollection of the kind-eyed man was real and that for some reason, he'd brought him here. Beyond that he couldn't hope to understand the actions of an Irishman but was thankful for the food and independence.

He was safe, although weak, and had found Tir Conaill despite the storm, lack of a map, and cover of night. He counted himself more than lucky. If luck continued to be on his side, he'd find the chest where he took shelter, bring it to its destination and be left to start anew.

He stuffed in another mouthful of bread and chewed. It was the most delicious food he could recall having. The chirping that woke him continued outside the small shrub shrouded entrance and he guessed a mating season's lover's quarrel. He was too weak yet to look and verify his conclusion but it amused him nonetheless.

He felt surprisingly optimistic for having woken in a strange place, obviously in poor health. No, that wasn't right. He didn't feel poorly so much as weakened, hungry, and foggy. Otherwise, life seemed to be gloriously going his way. And why shouldn't it after so many years of hardship, lies and caution, he asked himself and tore off another piece of peppered venison?

Finally, the end was in sight. The end of a long journey he wished at times another man had been given. But, Jacques had been clear that he was the only one who could accomplish the undertaking, even indicating that he was meant to. Sitting in the cave, covered in furs and wool, Ashlon still didn't see why another knight had not been given this fate. For the first time in a long time, he was glad it was him.

Strange thing to feel happy about such circumstance, but he did. At that moment he couldn't fathom a single other place he'd rather be. His future was nearing, he could feel it and the knowledge brought with it a sense of wonderment.

Comfortably full and satisfied that the food would stay down, Ashlon evaluated his surroundings and plotted. The cave was no taller than he at its highest point and much shorter at its mouth. Rich earth scented the air. The light above filtered through a gap in the stone where the earth fell away. Or perhaps the hole was manmade, a primitive dwelling. The idea fascinated him and he looked for other signs of inhabitation. The floor was mostly earth, even and a table-like stone sat at the far end.

He'd seen a similar stone slab before, during one of many initiation rites of the brotherhood. The stone symbolized the power of the brotherhood's bond, unity. In his own rite of passage into the Templar, he'd placed his hand on stone and sworn his oath of duty, honor. He had believed the words to his core.

He still did, though they mattered not now. The brotherhood's name was so besmirched, so shamed that even its brethren, the weaker of it, had disavowed themselves. It came down to cost, Ashlon reasoned. He had no price to pay for continuing to believe, even now, on his own.

Ashlon removed the covers. His skin prickled in the chill and he moved slowly to the mouth of the cave. The movement offered two things: he tested his strength after having eaten and he judged his outer surroundings. What he saw, sent him back in, retreating to the depths to hide in shadow. The rustling of footsteps in brush got closer. Ashlon snaked the strap of the satchel with his foot to drag it back from the stream of sunlight.

Just outside, a twig snapped. Ashlon's hand involuntarily went to the place where his sword should be. He felt foolish upon finding it empty. He saw only one defense. In a quick movement he grabbed the pile of blankets and swept them over his crouched figure. Enveloped in darkness, the sound of his labored breathing flooded his ears. He strained to hear above it for a sign of danger approaching.

"MacSweeney," he heard faint and muffled. "Over here."

"What have ye found?" The man's voice was so close and low that Ashlon envisioned him bent, ready to enter the cave.

* * * *

"Leaving the explanation aside of why you were out, on your own, without a single other person knowing of it, at such an hour, answer me this: did you go inside?" Niall stopped his slow methodical pace to stand in front of her, bent at the hips with his arms crossed.

Breanne forced her gaze up to meet his eyes while mentally rifling through what she could and could not tell him. "Yes." She decided to be brief and obtuse in order to barter more time to figure out the details of her forming falsehoods.

"Before or after?"

"Before or after what?" she hedged. The hard wood

seat creaked under her when she shifted as though to announce her nervousness.

Niall's eyes squinted, assessing her. "Before or after you found Heremon on the ledge some twenty feet below. Before or after you happened to see a man, lying prone and surmised him already dead and gone to the Otherworld."

A throat cleared behind him and Niall said, "to meet his maker," in correction.

"Before. I knocked, peered in the window. It was cold." Breanne filtered out details about Finn, about the groan she heard. "I tried the knob."

"And?" Niall's face reddened.

"It wasn't locked, my lord."

He resumed his pacing of the room. The three men behind him wore stoic expressions and almost appeared to be guarding the door. Against intruders, of course.

"What did you find there?" he said in rhythm with his pace.

"I found it dark, empty." Did they already know of the stranger Heremon had took in?

"Did you notice anything amiss?" Niall asked.

"Amiss?" She wasn't stalling. She wanted clarification.

"Embers still burned in his fire when we arrived. Furniture had been moved."

Breanne's heart picked up speed. Had they located the closet? "I lit the fire, my lord. I thought it best to wait for him, that he must be out and would return."

"And the furniture?"

"I can't say I would notice any different. It was my first time inside the man's home, you see." She felt better speaking as much truth as possible.

Niall nodded contemplatively upon hearing the last. "How did you find him?" His voice was soft.

Breanne's chest panged. "I thought I heard something outside. I looked about, began to worry. When I peered over the cliff's edge, it was more to assure myself than anything." Her stomach turned over remembering the stark edge and Finn braving it. But, omitting Finn's presence was imperative, for both their sake.

"And you found him there." Niall's shoulders drooped, his head lowered.

Breanne had a hundred questions she hungered to ask of him. But she bit her tongue, seeing they would have to wait until the suddenness of Heremon's death faded. One, however, she couldn't suppress. "How did he die, my lord?"

When he didn't answer or perceptibly react Breanne thought she spoke too quietly. She hated to repeat the grim inquiry.

"Interesting that you ask, Breanne." He straightened and confronted her. "I was hoping you might be the person to tell us that very terrible thing."

Breanne's breath whooshed out of her like a felled animals. His stare met hers resolutely. "My lord?" Her voice squeaked.

"Before I attend to announcements, or burials proceedings, I need to be certain that no foul play arrived at Heremon's door. I have men searching the area, as we speak, for any signs of conflict or malicious intent. Their information combined with your intimate knowledge will offer the insight I need to rest the concern."

Relief came slow but steady, plumping Breanne's limbs back to life as she realized his meaning. He needed her to examine Heremon. For a bewildering moment, she'd concluded that he suspected her of far more than hiding a man in a cave or protecting an enchanted cat. For being mistaken, Breanne silently thanked the Virgin

Mary in all her blessed wisdom.

"When shall I see him, my lord?" Breanne said, bowing her head respectfully.

"Straight away," Niall answered and motioned for her to rise and follow.

Breanne prepared for the worst. Heremon's body would not be the first she'd examined but was the first she knew. If Niall had no guess of cause of death then perchance he had died of natural, albeit tragic, causes. She recognized the idea as a desperate hope, knew deep down in her flesh and bones that it was not the case. But, it helped her face the chore, prodded her reluctant feet forward when the door opened in front of her. Access granted.

She nodded formerly to Niall and the three men. Only Niall remained with her. The silence between them hung ominously like a storm cloud on the horizon. There would be no rainbow at this dismal storm's end.

Heremon's blue lips were parted. His eyes were wide-open, surprised looking, disturbingly similar to the expression she last saw on his face. Crazed. His body was still wooden stiff and the faintest trace of death assaulted Breanne's nostrils. She began with his hands as taught. The iciness of his skin when she touched it broke through her wariness and instantly Breanne no longer thought of the body before her as Heremon.

The whites of his eyes were slightly yellowed. Liver. His palms were pale, unmarked. No wounds, scratches. If he'd been attacked, he hadn't resisted. If he fell, he had not gripped rock on his way down. She probed his neck, rolled him to feel his spine. No breaks. She examined his feet. Calloused, scraped.

Breanne tried to recall ever having seen shoes on the man but for all her days and nights couldn't conjure a single image. Sitting, kneeling, walking, all of her memories contained the long blue cloak and no more.

"When did you last see him well, Breanne?" Niall asked.

She guessed he needed to keep his mind busy. She understood the inclination. "In the grove, early afternoon." How much detail should she offer? Guilt pressed down on her as she remembered Heremon's strange behavior and her lack of action upon seeing it.

She forced the mouth open and put her nose above it. She inhaled. The stink of death masked it somewhat, but she identified the barely discernable scent of poison. She took another whiff, ignoring the growing putridity and searched her mind for what the third scent's identity. Its sweetness was familiar, like a comfort smell. Roses? Roses.

"My lord, in truth, I had not seen Heremon well since the week prior, our last tutelage together." She did turn around when she spoke, not yet ready to brazen further inquiry or the guilt beneath her answers.

"Explain yourself," he said in a gruff tone.

Breanne faced Niall, certain of her conclusions regarding both Heremon's cause of death and what she should reveal.

"When I met with Heremon, he rescheduled our lesson within moments of my arrival. He appeared more disheveled than normal and out of sorts." She took a steadying breath, aware of her shaky voice. "I should have followed him then, rather than returning at night. My lord," she said and met his eyes. "He died of poisoning."

Niall's stern expression crumbled into one of sad confusion. He shook his head over and over, opened his mouth and closed it wordlessly. Breanne's heart ached for him, for her murdered teacher, for herself.

His death was real now, material. Incontrovertible.

She couldn't think of an appropriate consolation and so, sat next to her chieftain, stepfather, in silence.

* * * *

The man passed, his attention on whatever his companions had found. Ashlon used the opportunity to bury the satchel and skin, adjust the coverings, and hug the cold cave floor as close as his body would allow. He picked up bits of conversation so long as he remained motionless and breathed shallowly.

"He wasna stabbed, daft mule," one said, a smacking thud followed.

"The king said anything odd, anything at all… marks unusual," another answered derisively. "What have you found, you stinking old boar?"

Thumps and tumbles. Then a clear, young voice resonated. "Enough! You waste valuable time here… report… my responsibility. If I left such an item in either of your hands…."

The voices left earshot and Ashlon tore his head free of the smothering wool and fur. He sat up and breathed in the cool air in deep gulps to calm his pounding pulse. They were gone. He'd wait some time to be certain of it, but couldn't deny relief coursed through him. Five steps into this stone hole and he'd be found.

Friend or foe, he couldn't know, but had learned long ago to trust his instincts and when that man had threatened his discovery, instinct said hide. They now said be calm. In a short while, he would be free to leave this place. In the meantime, the men where gone.

Ashlon rested his head and closed his eyes. Twenty or thirty minutes should do it, he estimated, but within ten fell soundly back to sleep. The world outside blurred and dreams stole his senses.

* * * *

"I ask for your word, Breanne, that no one, not a

single other living soul in the whole of the tuath, hear those words."

Breanne nodded quickly, though confusion made her frown. She heard the gravity in his tone, but she still wanted to question such a decision. Heremon had been murdered. Had she not made that clear? Would Niall not wish to find the killer of his most esteemed and sage advisor?

She opened her mouth to speak but he cut her intention to the quick. "Not another soul, Breanne. Do you understand?" His eyes glittered as he gritted each word out.

She snapped her lips together, stepped back and nodded again. "Yes, my lord. No one save you and I shall know unless you wish it so."

He seemed satisfied. "It will be announced as a tragedy, which I believe we can agree, it is."

She nodded and suppressed the swirl of ifs and howevers in her brain. His decision must be trusted, respected, she remembered.

"I will make the announcement. He will be buried tomorrow morn. The abbot, your uncle has made the arrangement. If any inquire to you, you will answer directly that you were not, in fact, the person who discovered Heremon. You were called at an early hour for your services which proved not to be needed." Niall paced. His voice restored to the even and authoritative level she was used to. "He died from the fall. A broken neck."

He wanted her to lie? She should be used to lying by now, be comfortable with it, schooled at it. But she was not. "As you wish, my lord." She meant what she said, for the most part.

They left the corpse to be readied for burial. "That will be all, Breanne," Niall said to dismiss her.

Ten steps and one very deep breath later, the words she thought she'd escaped called to her. "And do not leave the grounds again, Breanne. Not without escort."

She exhaled loudly but didn't turn around to acknowledge him. His footsteps and those of the men already rounded the corner and hit the stairs as Breanne closed her bedroom door, the last in the long corridor.

Finn slept soundly, unmoved from where she had left him. Breanne flopped down next to him and stared up. How would she get to the man? Not going back to the cave was not an option. He would wake, need more food, more ministerings. She glanced the cat's way. His eyes were open and looked straight through her.

"Ale," he said, his voice thick. "I require a bowl of ale straight away, Breanne."

"Not now, Finn, I have plans to make that take precedence over yours." She would need a distraction of some sort. If only an accomplice were available, aside from Finn, whom she still didn't trust.

"Breanne, you may not yet realize that with Heremon's death, my own life is now over. I am stuck in this miserable hairy form for the remainder of my days. Since I count you at fault for my sealed fate, the least you might do is help me return to a drunk oblivion."

Breanne pursed her full lips into a sour pucker of censure. Finn appeared unaffected, rolling onto his back and stretching his limbs. Even if he could be trusted, he was useless. She wouldn't let him get to her this time, though. Breanne left without a backward glance.

Chapter Six

When Ashlon woke for the third time since washing ashore, he felt beaten. His muscles ached so badly, he thought the pain came from his very bones. It was dark, nearly black inside the hole he lay in and whatever euphoria he'd earlier experienced, what could have been hours or days past, was gone.

Ashlon sat upright, pushing himself past the all-encompassing pain. He couldn't stay here, wherever here was. He knew that. Any man could have happened upon him since he last woke and easily slit his throat as he slept.

"Christ's blood," he cursed through clenched teeth as another round of throbbing coursed through his body. He needed to move though, to a better sanctuary. He needed his sword and to figure out where he was exactly.

The gaps of blackness in his memory bothered him almost as much as how difficult moving was. He wasn't used to being powerless. He had long been on his own, answering to no person save Jacques de Molay. The Grand Master took him on to train personally and from the start had granted him a kind of immunity that both isolated and elevated him among his peerage. Though he had never entertained the headiness power gave some men, he did enjoy its autonomy.

He moved to his knees and a sheen of sweat surfaced on his brow and lip. Both the exertion and cooling it gave felt a relief. He paused a breath then moved to all fours.

He crawled toward the blue night framed by cave wall. If he could just make it to the mouth to view his surroundings, he would feel better, in control again.

He remembered the sack of food he was leaving behind but turning back for it might waste the energy he needed to get to the entrance. He grunted. As he moved the pain throbbed less and less. His muscles strained and pushed as he willed his body forward.

A deep sorrowful howl echoed in the night, reaching his ears. Wolves. And he lay in a cave. Ashlon reached the mouth and sat with a panting gasp. He propped his back against one side and threw a leg across the threshold as if the small exit would ring victory and convince his body to end its game of straining.

Another howl answered the first, too loud for Ashlon's temporary comfort to last. Using the outer wall for balance, he struggled to his feet. He regretted forgetting the sack but not as much as falling asleep. Foolish, he thought, to trust a bedraggled heathen. He should have left the place when he woke rather than trust he meant no harm.

Where had the man gone to in all this time? One thing Ashlon did feel certain of, at the minimum hours were wasted in sleep if not days. Not just the obvious change of day to nightfall told him so, or his desperate hunger and weakness. He also could feel it, a strange panicking dread that he'd missed some vital window of opportunity.

On his feet, Ashlon scanned his surroundings. To his left, the woods gave way to lush mossy grass and beyond lay the horizon. The sky was clear and the air was dewy but comfortable. To the right and front, the trees grew thicker and wound in clusters, creating patches of clearings. Grass and shrubbery of varying breeds filled gaps.

The air smelled inviting. He'd wager the hour passed midnight recently and looking around, Ashlon fought back the urge to climb back into the hole, eat and wait for morning light. Wolves, he reminded himself, and galloglass. He'd heard enough about the fierce and fearless Scots soldiers to make certain he was armed when he met one. And he'd come too close to one's notice already. By luck, the man had been distracted and not come upon him and batter his skull with a mace.

Jacques would not have sent you here, were it not safe, a voice inside him argued. "And what better place to hide it than in the wild," he said out loud for no one to hear.

He took a gulp of air and a wobbly step. Instantly, he became more aware of his near nakedness. "Bloody heathen," he said. "Drugged me and robbed me is what he did, then left me for dead." Dead but fed, that voice argued again. He nearly told it to shut up, but remembered he'd be telling himself to and laughed.

"You're losing your mind, Ash. Stay focused. You need to find the man, get your clothes and sword and be on your way. If you don't find what you've lost, there will be far uglier things to concern you." As he muttered each word, he stepped, until the small stone house peeked into his view. With a circling glance around him, Ashlon pursued it.

He only had to stop once, a fact that struck him with pride. As well, the pain had dulled considerably along his short tenuous trek to the door he readied to knock on. He kept his expectations low and prepared a reasonable story for his shocking state to whoever answered.

He knocked hard several times, allowing time for the resident to rise and decide to answer their door at such an ungodly hour. A robbery, he decided would be the most plausible excuse for his lack of dress and unkempt appearance. And it would be—might be—true. Perfect.

When several moments, certainly enough for a person to hear him and waken, passed, Ashlon felt the owner had slunk low behind the door, and listened there, debating if he should risk opening his home. "My sincerest apologies for the rude interruption of your slumber, sir or madam. I am Ashlon Sinclair, of the Remington Sinclairs, and have met the misfortune of marauders. They've left me without a stitch of clothing and in need of your charitable assistance," he said in his most soothing and approachable tone.

He was a gentleman, a knight schooled in chivalry. He was no threat, yet the door did not open. At last he supposed the home empty and tried the crude knob. It gave and opened. Warm air enveloped him when he stepped inside. "Hello there," he called, hoping now that someone would be there.

His vision warbled and he turned to the door. Before he could reach it, he vomited. The heaves racked him but produced no results save a pithy amount of bile. Ashlon gasped, lowered to a crouch and sat next to the liquid. He was in bad shape. He hated admitting it but he needed help. Better than that, he needed that help to come find him because he couldn't be sure he'd make it back to the cave. He'd pushed too far and his body committed mutiny.

* * * *

Breanne's heart beat hard and fast. Someone was following her. She didn't see them or hear them but she couldn't shake the feeling and walked as fast, as quietly fast as humanly possible. It wasn't Finn. She wished it were Finn with another one of his sick pranks. Finn was passed out drunk when she'd left him to steal into the night.

She prayed Niall hadn't assigned a man to watch

her. He constantly scolded her headstrong nature behind closed doors to her mother. Day upon day of eavesdropping outside their chamber door gave her that insight as well as the one about marrying.

Breanne stopped and tucked between two close oak trees. She closed her eyes and spoke a prayer for concealment and protection. Sorely, she missed her boline. She'd nearly brought her athame as a temporary replacement but the casting blade was too small to fit her thigh sheath and at the last minute she decided it wouldn't damage well enough to bother.

Now, she regretted the change of mind. Listening for signs of footsteps, Breanne held her breath for several counts in turns. It calmed her racing pulse and cleared noise. The oak's woody scent calmed her, too. Soon she breathed regularly. Surely, she'd lost anyone who tried to track her?

With a chant of gratitude, Breanne sprinkled breadcrumbs and stepped out of the shadows. The moon's light hit her path well and Breanne saw the coastline in the distance. She hurried along, this time with anticipation. Would he be awake, she wondered? Her belly trembled at the thought.

She approached the cave slowly after lingering outside long enough to light a candle. She entered the cave and found it empty. Absolutely empty. Turning and gasping, she looked about, kicked the covers. Only the food sack lay beneath them. Both annoyed and worried, Breanne rushed from the cave and skimmed the area.

Nothing. She saw him nowhere and not a single sign of him. Not even a strand of grass pressed into the earth. Breanne threw her hands in the air and sprinted toward Heremon's. The men. What if the men had discovered the stranger, or worse?

Before fear took hold of her, she saw Heremon's

door stood open and rushed to it. The candle's light almost extinguished, flickered and returned to life once inside the house. She saw him before the room glowed, recognized his silhouette. Immediately she went to her knees in front of him. His closed eyes slammed open wide and pinned her with an accusatory look.

She reached to touch his brow and his hand snaked around her wrist. She winced. "I will not harm you," she said in English, shaking her head.

His eyes narrowed but he dropped her arm, his falling to the floor. Accusation in his gaze gave way to entreaty. She smiled to reassure him and held a finger up.

"Don't move," she said.

As though he could, Ashlon thought. His vision blurred in and out as he watched her. As she moved, the room grew lighter and just as he was about to ease the panic rotting his gut by calling to her, she returned. She put a bowl to his mouth and he recognized the bitter taste and scent. He drank it.

The broth traced a path of warmth down his gullet into his raw stomach. He prayed to keep it down and thanked God for sending him an angel of mercy in his darkest hour yet. Ashlon closed his eyes and repeated words of thanks until he noticed that the drink was working.

When he opened his eyes he found her sitting before him, apprehension showed on her delicate features. Bow shaped lips pressed together. Wide but dainty eyebrows furrowed together making a crease in between them.

"Are you feeling the effects then?" she asked him.

Ashlon could only nod. He opened his mouth to speak but she shoved a chunk of bread into it before he formed the words. His mouth salivated painfully upon tasting the soft morsel and he slowly chewed it and swallowed. Her eyes appeared a dark brown but he suspected they were much lighter than the dimness appreciated. The color of honey. Honey, sweet and golden.

A strange buzzing feeling formed in him. A reaction to her beauty or a result of the broth, he didn't care. The sensation was miles away from the retched misery she'd saved him from. She continued to feed him and he continued to stare.

Her hair was a coppery tinged blonde and the strands that escaped her braid curled into little ringlets. The tip of her braid rested and swathed her hip. His gaze traced the outline of her hip delineated by shadow and light. Ashlon reached out a hand to touch it with his index finger but his hand fell away weakly before hitting target.

Breanne looked down wondering what he'd been attempting, what fascinated him so. Finding no more than the drape of clothing, she dismissed it as the pleasant haze of her concoction.

"More," she said firmly. Obediently, he opened his mouth for her. Breanne stifled a laugh at how readily he obeyed. The lazy smile on his face made her belly flip over. When his eyes locked with hers, it flipped again.

"I don't know what you were thinking, leaving the cave as you did. You may not realize, but your life is in danger and you canno' be moving about as all that," she said, placing another piece of meat between his lips. The color returned to them and she wished it had not. She couldn't seem to take her eyes off of his lips.

"Apologies," he said, a mumble. A crumb of food spit forth when he spoke.

Breanne stifled a laugh. He was better than drunk and wouldn't be wandering again for a few good hours now. She touched his forehead to ascertain his ill health. Feeling cool skin under her palm, Breanne nodded pertly and set about making a fire.

"Who are you?" the man asked, sounding so inspired that she returned to his side and touched his cheek.

"Shhh. Rest now. You have a long journey ahead of you." Then she bent forward and kissed his forehead, giving in to an urge to feel how soft his skin was. Part of her knew she shouldn't be so intimate, tender. It took advantage of his vulnerability and compromised trust. A healer walked the fine line of trust with any charge.

But, she didn't regret it when her lips pressed his skin, warm, moist with sweat. His hand covered hers on his cheek and then touched her cheek. His fingers trembled. Breanne inched back and lowered her gaze to his. What she saw there startled her. Never before had she seen such intensity, such heat in another's eyes.

Breanne leaned her cheek into his palm and searched his eyes. His hot gaze trapped her, spellbound and unable to retreat or progress. She needed to do neither, as he did for her.

His hand slid back and into her hair. She covered his hand with hers, her touch intrigued by the change from stubble to smooth texture. He pulled her gently. His lips caressed hers, a whisper of touch, and his eyes closed. Breanne's closed as well and the feel of his lips on hers magnified. A dizzying hunger for more took root in Breanne and she pressed her lips onto his, opening her mouth. The hunger grew, spreading through her limbs, down her belly, between her thighs.

A shockwave tingled there when his tongue met hers, soft and warm. He tasted sweet. His lips on hers were so firm but pliant. She gripped his hand and leaned in for more. His tongue swept into her mouth, jolting her with pleasure.

She reveled in this new experience and grew bold. All thought beyond the feel of it, of him, escaped her. She matched his sweep with her own, suckling his lower lip, letting her teeth drag against it, savoring the plump feel.

The tingle warmed, changed, into an ache unlike any she'd ever known. It made her heart beat harder, her breathing feel desperate. She needed something more, craved a satisfaction she could not name but sensed it there in his lips pressing hers, his tongue twining and tormenting her mouth.

His hand stroked her jaw and explored lower, brushing her throat, tickling her collarbone and all the while taking Breanne's hand with it. She couldn't let go and as it drew farther and farther down, a strange, wonderful beating of anticipation built in her.

Ashlon groaned from deep in his belly as an all-consuming want drowned what little rationale the concoction left him with. Somewhere he knew no good could come of it but he couldn't seem to stop. His body awoke, his attraction hardening with powerful swiftness. He fought the urge to allow his hands exploration of her breasts, close as they may be, sensing she might not be aware of how well her kisses and soft panting undid him. Yet he did not stop either. She felt so good, so lush and vibrant until, like a slap to the face with icy water, she broke away.

He opened his eyes and saw shock and fear and confusion take turns expressing in her eyes. Her parted lips glistened, were red, from their kiss. Damn his body but it wanted more. He wanted to return his mouth to her, to taste her more deeply, to touch the flesh.... He felt a catch in his chest as she withdrew another inch.

He reached for her, an entreaty. But she jerked back. Ashlon dropped his head back and rolled his eyes heavenward. What had he done? He was no scoundrel, but the kiss proved such a vigorous endeavor it left him no strength to move after her. She retreated and stood.

"Apologies," he mumbled again and bore his eyes into hers. "Won't happen 'gain." Ashlon closed his eyes and his last remarkable thought was that he'd just offended an angel. Then he succumbed to sleep.

Breanne exhaled loudly. He slept. She couldn't keep drugging him so, or he'd never be awake long enough to give her answers let alone be on his way from here.

She ran a hand over her brow and sat in the nearest rickety chair. He'd kissed her. Or had she kissed him? Both, she decided. And what a kiss it was. Sweet St. Bridget that experience placed her only other kiss in stark relief. The difference amazed her. This man's lips were like a charm, spinning into her body, caressing depths she didn't know existed.

Compared to it, Quinlan's kiss became sloppy, rigid, and forced. How could a stranger's mouth, one he was barely aware of due to the herbs' effects, feel so natural and yet surreal all at once? So startling and magickal?

She didn't have an answer and didn't soon want one. Any man having such an effect over her was dangerous. With a touch he'd make her witless and vulnerable to his very whim. She didn't trust it, or him.

The remainder of the week was all she'd give him. If he wasn't well and off within this very week, she'd be forced to give him over to Niall. She'd have protected him well enough, as Heremon's sight had seen her to, and she refused to feel guilty. He was not her responsibility after all. Heremon was. Once he gave clarification, assuming he saw nothing and caused nothing, regained good health, what was left to protect?

Breanne opened the closet door, apparently unfound by Niall's men, and dragged the man into it. She couldn't manage getting him onto the table, so moved the long narrow piece to the far wall. His belongings sat in a pile, undisturbed since the last she spied them.

Jutting rectangular emeralds on his sword's hilt glowed in the candlelight. Breanne touched her fingertip to one. It was a finely wrought weapon. It's seams were flawless, the design equally strong and elegant. Unusual to place the emeralds in such a way, as though they stood rather than lay on the metalwork.

The man's breathing became a snore. Breanne chuckled, watching him. In sleep, his face showed an innocence that reminded her of Danny, young and impetuous. But, she couldn't recall a trace of innocence in his awaked countenance. Signs of the boy in the man, she supposed and brushed a wavy lock off his forehead.

"What have you done here?" she asked him but wasn't sure which one of them she referred to.

She left the sack of food, the skin, blankets retrieved from the cave, and closed the door. Before leaving, she wrote him a brief note and slipped it under the disguised door.

Four more days and she could return her attention to the normalcies of life. Spinning, learning, husband hunting. Breanne sighed but it didn't help alleviate the new heaviness in her heart. She looked back at the stone cottage and walked away.

Chapter Seven

"Please, Breanne, be seated," Niall said when she knocked on the open door. He closed the door and took the chair across from her, the one her mother had mutely sat in only three days ago.

"May I ask the reason for this summons, my lord?" she asked, coming straight to the heart of her worry.

"With Heremon's death and burial, my time has been consumed."

"As has all of ours, my lord," she said, trying to sound understanding, docile, but needing to move from chitchat.

He placed a hand up, stopping her from further interruption. "I intended to speak with you sooner. Regardless, we have much to discuss and I ask that you hold your tongue until I finish," he said in a scolding tone.

Breanne lowered her gaze but her chin raised a notch. She doubted she wanted to hear anything else from this man. In mere days, he'd turned her world inside out with his demands. First, forcing her to choose a husband, then protracting a solemn swear of secrecy. Now what?

"It should first be known by you that Shane MacSweeney proclaimed intention of pursuing your hand in marriage. When Ula and I spoke with you previously, I failed to mention his name and I only do so now so that you may appreciate the seriousness of which I called you here for." His large belly forced his thighs to sit wide and bulged when he leaned forward.

Breanne frowned. She didn't comprehend what the man was attempting to tell her, but she kept silent, as he wished. Prodding his temper would make her request all the more difficult to ask.

"MacSweeney met with me this morning and begged off." Niall paused and pierced her with a severe look of disapproval.

"My lord, I—"

His hand shot up again, quieting her. "Better that he did. A fine gallowglass he may be but a fine husband, I can't imagine. As to his sudden change of mind, I asked, concerned for your future, our departed friend's past, and mild curiosity, too, I propose."

Please, come to the point of this diatribe. Breanne bit her lips and counted for patience. The knots in her belly tightened.

"An' he did so mighty fast, I'll say. Not five days ago, he asked for you with stars in his eyes, eagerness in his words. And just this morn, a gruff and muttered inquiry as to yourself and then simply retracted the aforementioned intention." Niall shook his head and stroked his full beard. "So I put the question to him, to have the answers. You've not much time after all, to be choosing and of all things, he can't answer me." He swept his hand out in front of her like displaying the words before her.

Breanne tilted her head, confused and biting back interruptions. She crossed her legs and shook her foot rhythmically to the count in her head.

Niall stood, leaving a deep impression behind in the red velvet cushion. Breanne wanted to stand, as well, to pace as he did. But, she couldn't. She sat, foot-shaking, lip biting for an eternity while Niall meandered through to reach his conclusion.

"He does not speak a word to me. He offers no explanation nor apology. Had you not agreed already to choosing five weeks hence, had I informed you of his intentions, I'd have held him to them. But as I've said, I don't." He paused to estimate her with his gaze. Then with a florid gesture and bow he produced a dagger in his palm.

Breanne recognized the weapon instantly. "My dagger. Where did you find it?" She reached for it, happy to have it returned.

Niall snatched it away. "I'll be doing the asking, Miss O'Donnell." His voice held such menace. He'd never regarded her so before. Always, since the day she and Ula walked into his home as wards, he'd called her Breanne.

Breanne's brain began to scramble for answers. Shane MacSweeney brought him the dagger? Where had he found it? How? More of import, why would locating it end his desire to wed her? She swallowed hard against her throat's hard beating.

"You've left out important information surrounding your lucky discovery of Heremon. I'll have it now."

"My lord, I canno' give what I do not have. I am perplexed and feel as though I did not hear you correctly." Her voice lilted up. "I left that very blade on the ground quite a good distance south of Heremon's home. I last saw it there, hours before I found him in peril." The small part of her relieved at Shane's decision now felt betrayed, as though the man had set her up to take some fall.

Had he been following her that day? How else could he have found her blade? Niall watched her fixedly. Breanne squirmed inside but met his gaze steadily.

"I canno' presume to guess at Shane's motives in bringing you this or speculate why it's delivery would cause you suspicion." Her chin rose. "I will have it back, if you please, my lord."

Niall's eyes narrowed on her. "My men searched Heremon's by the light of day, Breanne. Among other curiosities, this knife was found, sheathed in the ground within a whispers distance of the departed's front door," he said in a furious whisper.

Breanne's mouth fell open. "Mark me, my lord, it is not possible. I left it on the ground as I said. Whomever brought violence upon Heremon, must have found my boline and left it apurpose."

"How did you come by this weapon?" He sat again and it eased some of her fear.

"Heremon," Breanne said and her voice trembled. "I have two matching knives. The one you held, I carry as protection. The other is my athame."

Niall sighed and scratched his head. "Where and how in the name of our lord did Shane know it to be yours?"

Breanne shook her head from side to side, slowly. Shane MacSweeney might gaze upon her now and then but in all her days, they'd spoken no more than a handful of occasions. "I canno' guess, my lord." She took a shaky breath. "I do not know. Mayhap the two are independent of one another?"

Niall considered this, tapped the arm of the chair with a thick finger.

"Is it possible he's heard of my being the one who found Heremon? Could he be begging off upon hearing such tittle-tattle?" Breanne knew it was a reach, but took it, desperate to keep his questions away from that night and all the details she'd omitted. Omissions she didn't trust herself to succinctly recall under this level of duress.

Niall winced, a small crinkling formed around his eyes. "I will look into it." He sounded appeased.

Breanne slouched a bit, the pressure and fear dissipated by his words and tone. For a moment, she thought he might be set on accusing her of Heremon's death. If he did so, her only help would be from a talking cat she hadn't seen since yesterday morn or a sick stranger she hadn't returned to assess. The former would likely show up bedraggled with splotches of memory loss. The latter could be roaming the countryside.

When Ula had whispered the summons to her an hour prior, Breanne had prepared herself to ask for more time to choose a husband given the recent tragedy. Now, as she watched Niall puzzle over his erroneous conclusions, eyeing her in turns but remaining uncomfortably silent, she cared less about marriage than ever before.

She would marry a mule rather than face that tone and look of betrayal again. But, he'd believed her and was all she cared for.

"I should have inspected the area myself," he said. "Third hand information muddies waters that would have been clear had I studied the area firsthand." He seemed to address himself more than her. "I propose I shall do just that at the earliest I may."

"My lord?" Breanne hoped she'd misconstrued his ramblings.

Niall looked up at her as though suddenly recalling she still sat in wait for his dismissal.

"Notwithstanding, Breanne. MacSweeney is no longer a suitor and as you did not know of his intention originally, there will be no remorse for lack of interest now, do you hear?"

Breanne nodded. Bowed and retreated, she exhaled

loudly and the exasperated sound echoed off the corridor walls. At least he'd not asked she swear by her statements. The lord surely would have struck her down for taking his name so vainly under the guise of protection. She entered her chamber and strapped the returned weapon to her thigh.

If Niall chose to investigate Heremon's personally, how much time did she have to remove the stranger, she ruminated? Two days and nights had passed since last she saw him. She had left the note along with provisions. Might he be well and gone? Breanne's belly flipped. She would likely not see him again if he left.

The afternoon clouds dimmed the sunlight. She could not wait until nightfall. If she went to him, it needed to be soon. In the years she'd known him Niall did not practice procrastination.

Breanne went to her window and measured the drop below. At least four cubits, she estimated, to the ground. Luckily, her narrow window faced the rear of the keep and the bailey there generally sat empty. If she missed the evening meal, her mother would look in on her. Unless….

She eyed her bed a moment then stuffed the plump covers with three gowns, shaping them to look like a sleeping form. Satisfied, Breanne nodded at her handiwork. Now all she needed was an accomplice. Only one name came to mind among those she could implicitly trust. He was one person Ula would not distrust, who would also not question her, nor try to dissuade her.

Ula secretly spoiled the boy like a grandchild but without any signs of public affection or approval. Danny had seemed to learn early her mother played by rules with him. Breanne never wondered at the private affection, what she saw as respect for his mother's role. Danny's mother loved him to the moon and stars and back again. Breanne kept her affection discreet at first as well, following her mother's lead but soon realized she didn't need to.

That boy was loved and coddled by so many women, the one that ended up with his heart would have extreme standards to live up to. Breanne hurried before she changed her mind about embroiling the boy in her well-meaning deceit.

She descended the stairs two at a time and spotted Danny right away. As she made her way to him though, Rose called to her from the Grianan entrance. Breanne stopped, torn between her plan and appearing suspicious to her friend. Danny's attention was rapt in play with a boy two years senior. Elias, she believed was his name. Rose beckoned.

Breanne hid her defeat as best she could and walked to Rose. The youngest of Rose's four girls sat upon her wide hip inside the doorway. When she saw Breanne, Kimber reached for her gleefully. "Beene," she said, one of the six words the toddler knew.

How could she feel overly disappointed with such a welcome? Breanne took the child to her, smooching her chubby cheek noisily.

"So?" Rose looked at her expectantly. "What did the auld Donnell have to tell you this time?" she whispered.

Breanne followed her into the room, gaining a few glances from the other women busy spinning, sewing, mending. The other children paid her little mind, though Rose had another older girl, Sheena, at her hip straight away.

"Nothing of import," she whispered back as they sat in Rose's usual corner. Breanne adjusted Kimber on her lap.

"Do you have to keep all of it to yourself, then? Every last bit. Can't you spare a wee bit for my hungry ears?"

Breanne smiled at her dramatic tone. Ryan must be out scouting, for she only got this way when he first left her. She wished she could unload some of her burden on Rose. "Shane MacSweeney is no longer interested in asking for my hand," she said low, with a shrug.

Rose inhaled sharply and Breanne stifled a guffaw at her friend's greedy curiosity. "He was at a time then? Interested in you?"

"Aye, apparently. But, he's changed heart just today." She retrieved a tunic to fold from the basket at Rose's feet.

"Whatever for?" Rose asked sounding both awed and defensive. "Does he think he's such a catch, then?"

"I care not, Rose. I'm happier for it. Two others are plenty to handle with all else happening of late," Breanne said and too late realized she'd not yet told Rose of the other two.

Rose's accusatory look proved she'd caught the juicy tidbit quicker than a fly in a web. Kimber scampered from Breanne's lap at the sight her mother's expression.

"And who might the other two fellows be?"

Breanne was trapped. She almost felt good about being cornered into spilling some of the information brimming in her brain. Her stomach tightened despite the bright thought.

"Gannon O'Shannon for one," Breanne said, then waited in hopes that one name would be enough food to tide her friend over.

"Truly? Gannon?"

"Aye," she answered, not liking the amused tone in her friend's voice. "I've yet to hear it from him, but Niall has spoken for him."

"But, Bree, he is so young and so," Rose said,

stammering a bit. "So, well, skinny. Although, they do say he carries all his muscle in his britches." She wriggled her eyebrows.

Breanne's face colored red. "Rose," she exclaimed.

"Come now. Tell me you do not wonder about some of them," Rose said. "A husband is a lover, Breanne. Don't you wonder what to expect? A big man is a treasure. That, I promise."

Breanne covered her face and shook her head. "Do not tell me, Rose. We may speak of any man but Ryan."

"Admit to it then," Rose said, half-laughing.

"Admit to what?" Breanne's hands moved to her ears, ready to plug them if Rose said another word about Ryan or his britches.

"To spying on the soldier's at bath with me when we both were still girls. To playing the games of guessing that we played. Admit that you're not the prude I suddenly see sitting before me simply because you'll finally be taking a man to your bed." Her voice threatened to rise with each word so that all the other women heard her lewd talk.

"Yes, I wonder," Breanne said in a hiss. "But not of your husband."

"Well, I should hope not. If I'm catching another woman on my husband's prick, it better not be you." The seriousness in Rose's stare betrayed her easy laugh.

"Do you worry of it, Rose?"

"I think not, Bree. Back to the subject at hand, Gannon's girth." She paused so they both could giggle. "If he can claim the prowess I've heard speak of, then I claim he'll do well by you."

"And where do you hear such speak?"

"Breanne, my dear friend, you've had your nose buried so deep these last years, you've forgotten the richest source of information is right here, surrounding you."

Breanne tipped her head in acknowledgement. What Rose pointed to was true. She had not been a part of this inner circle for some time, always off to a lesson or practice. No more. She no longer had reason to shirk contribution to the household.

"He's more than a healthy prick, I hope," Breanne said seriously.

"Let's consider," Rose said, equally sober. "He is a scribe and so is an artist and a scholar which I believe would suit you well."

"Aye, but what of my holdings? Can he protect them, or me for what is relevant? Can he hold an axe and wield death?"

"But, you've said you do not wish to have such a man. Why you've kept my brother from his intentions to train in the gallowglass with your fervor."

By some means, they'd reached the very person Breanne hoped to avoid. Mentally cursing, Breanne tried another approach. "I want both. I want a man who can protect but who does not crave bloodshed." As her father had.

"I fear they all do. Even the docile one's like Gannon thrive on lust. Lusting us or lusting war, either seem sufficient."

"Then I'll have to keep his attention on lusting me," she said and they both smiled. If only 'twere so simple as that, she knew. Ten years without a raid on Tir Conaill after so many of clashing with the O'Doherty clan to the north or Norman's seeking a new country, were wonderful.

But, the clansmen sought out what didn't arrive at their door. Less than three sennights past, a group had lifted cattle from the McRoarty's to the south.

"I'll not touch on it until you do, but I'm not sure

how much longer I can wait," Rose said after a moment of silence between them.

Breanne frowned, hesitated to ask. But did. "Touch on what?" She reached for another stocking from the basket.

"My brother."

Breanne looked down, busied her hands by searching for holes needing mending. "He kissed me," she said. She couldn't look up though Rose's silence disconcerted her.

"Aye, I know. A disaster you'd say?"

Breanne couldn't believe the rush of relief and sadness that flooded her when she nodded and lifted her head. Tears welled in her eyes. "Aye," she whispered. "Disastrous indeed." One hot salty drip ran down her cheek. Rose reached for her, wiped it dry.

"Ahh now, none of that now. There's naught to cry for. Quinlan will not shed a tear, I'll promise you that."

"Likely, you're right."

"I am right. He spoke of it yesterday as though relating the daily reports on the stables. 'Twas like a job he needed improvement on but sounded certain he could perform better next time."

Breanne gasped, horrified. Was the kiss as meaningless as all that to him? Rose must have guessed her thoughts. "He's practical, Breanne. It is not to say he lacks passions, but that he doesn't easily shirk a challenge."

She didn't respond, focused on getting her tears under control before any more fell. The confession was so cathartic that Breanne struggled to keep the rest of her burdens atop her back.

"You've loved him for so long, Bree. I thought you would be happy to hear it, to know your fairy prince may still come true." Rose put her hand on Breanne's. "Don't fret about it now. There's plenty of time to choose, and remember, the choice is yours and only yours."

The missing weight of worry offered enough liberation that remaining beleaguering felt intelligible for the first time.

"Quinlan speaks of the women abroad, women who are given as property, that have no say in their own fate." Rose leaned in. "You and I should feel privileged. They may war and lust, but we may choose for ourselves which lusty, bloodthirsty clod we take in union."

More than one glance their way made Breanne feel like more of an outsider. She should leave, relinquishing Rose's attention on her back to them. "Was it so complicated for you and Ryan?"

"Oh aye. Plenty. Love seems to enjoy complications," Rose said, looking about the room. "Now then, I'd better be joining the ladies before they pact against us and poison our ale."

With a kiss and hug she left Rose, offering a broad smile to the other ladies along with a polite farewell. Not one smile back could be counted as sincere. She promised to stay longer next time and gladly shut the door behind her. Perhaps she would return above to her chamber?

She'd barely sighed her relief when Quinlan stepped in view. Though he held no flowers, his eyes held the promise of a proposition. Recalling what Rose had said, Breanne stood her ground. And there was too little space of time or distance to bolt.

Lord the man was beautiful. Nearly pretty with his auburn hair and deep brown eyes smiling at her now, firm mouth struggling to find words.

"Would you take some air, perhaps a ride with me, Breanne?"

"A ride sounds lovely," Breanne said. And,

surprisingly it did. It might help soothe her harried mind.

His smile widened and his heels popped him happily up. "I'll bring two around, then?"

And he did. Not ten minutes later they rode down the hill. Storm clouds draped the afternoon sky in gray. A blustery wind iced their cheeks red and felt good. The somber tone of Heremon's burial two days prior left her, the strangeness of the week past, as well, seemed to sweep away with the wind, leaving Breanne sparked with vigor.

When they reached the bowl of green valley, she returned Quinlan's bright smile readily. "Thank you for this invitation. An excursion is exactly what I needed."

"It is my pleasure to share it with you, Breanne. And if I may say, you look like yourself again."

"I expect I've not quite been myself Quin. More than you might believe, I have been out of sorts, thrown by recent events." She brought her white mare up in stride with his. The taller bay nickered softly and Quin gave him his head.

"I fear I owe you an apology, Breanne." Quinlan cleared his throat.

Breanne winced. "Shall we ride much further? It feels like a downpour may be on the way inland."

He shook his head. "Allow me to finish, Bree. I 'ave no easy time saying what I must to you." His Adam's apple moved down as he swallowed.

Breanne's stomach squeezed. "Aye, Quinlan."

"If my intentions have not been clear, may they be so now. I am of a mind to win your hand in marriage. I am aware of the new discomfort between us and I take full blame for it. Please know that I count you as a friend, my closest and dearest." He swallowed again. They veered southeasterly between two hills and through the edge of woods.

"I hold our friendship very dear also," she said, his silence prodding her.

He chuckled. "Breanne. I was not finished."

She had the good grace to blush.

"I am full aware of competition for your affection and will not be daunted by a bit of competition. Considering, the incident in the corridor, I offer my apology and assurance that I will insinuate no other such intimacies unless I have first asked and gained your permission." The ocean, the cliffs, came into view.

Breanne waited, not sure he had finished though his attention seemed caught by the scene before them. The tide pushed forward in tall, foamy waves. The sky was steel colored, textured with heaps of cloud.

"Was it near here?"

Breanne knew his meaning and nodded once. She pointed and his gaze followed. Heremon's roof top showed among the trees, peeking around the curve of a low hill the man had once claimed to be a sidhe, a fairy mound, in fireside conversation after three too many ales.

Quinlan clucked his bay to a trot. Breanne followed, panic rising. She tried to quell the sudden shaking coursing through her veins by reminding herself she'd left the man well, prepared. He might be gone and if not, surely hidden well as she'd made quite clear he must be until she could return.

She had been so rapt in Quinlan's speech, she had failed to recognize how close they were to the dwelling. Breanne urged her mare after him. "We should return to the keep," she called loudly at Quinlan's back as he brought his steed short in front of the door. But, his stare was on the ocean.

Breanne pulled on the reins and leapt down after him. She glanced surreptitiously from the quiet looking cottage and back to Quinlan. Her mind worked at ways to move him to leave. A small, rebellious voice told her to go inside now when she had the chance. Slip in, it said, while he's distracted. Get to the man before he comes to you.

Breanne stood outside the door and took a single step backward. She just wanted to touch the wood, to feel the door, hold the knob. But, the irrational voice that whispered for her to find the man inside grew louder, more insistent.

Quinlan walked further away as though entranced by something below the wall of rock and moss. He will follow if I go in, she argued to the voice. *He will find the man, unless he has left the cottage as he did the cave.* If not now, it shot back, when?

Tonight. I will find a way to return tonight.

"Did you say something?" Quinlan asked, facing her.

Breanne pinched her lips and shook her head. She shrugged her shoulders. To her left, well within Quinlan's view, she swore a shadow passed over the windowpane. Behind her, she released the cold metal.

"We should head back," Quinlan said, before she could, eyeing the sky.

Before he finished, Breanne had mounted and urged her mare back the way they'd come. She bit down the impulse to glance back and make certain he followed. Drizzle began wetting both of their noses as they kicked their steeds and galloped home.

Chapter Eight

Ashlon stared at the final chunk of food in his hand menacingly. Rain thrashed the roof and walls around him and though he certainly felt grateful for shelter in the storm, he itched to be out of the small room, to finish things.

He plunked the venison into his mouth and chewed slowly. His stomach would not be satisfied with the meager fill it had just received but had little choice. The barely legible letter he woke to concisely stated the danger he'd be avoiding by staying put.

He wondered again as he chewed, who had penned the missive laid on his bundle of clothes. The angel or the heathen? He mostly hoped it was the heathen and that the angelic face he couldn't get out of his mind was no more than illusion brought on by illness.

For if she weren't real, then neither was the inexcusable kiss. The last seven years of exile had taught him more about women than any of the preceding twenty-four, eight of those spent becoming a man among the Knights. Women were undeniably the lord's creatures. They could lift you up or tear you down. Succor your soul or tempt it toward hell itself.

He'd learned the lesson the hard way when a particularly beautiful and welcoming Spanish Duchess had taken him in shortly after James de Molay and so many others were captured. Spain could have remained a safe haven. From the beginning, both her estate and the Duchess herself gave safe harbor--until he'd offended her.

Duquesa Maria Santiago, widowed and young, took Ashlon as her lover. The more time they spent in each other's arms, the more possessive and manipulative she became and pressed for marriage. He refused. She exposed him and nearly caused his own capture.

Thereafter, Ashlon took caution in all regard of the female gender. Of the many more who took him in, protected him, welcomed him in every way, he made clear that marriage would never be an option. The more deceptive ladies still tried, but by keeping his distance, Ashlon managed to avoid so insulting another.

And Ashlon couldn't see a way around the fact that he'd thoroughly kissed that angelic face and wanted to do far more. If she were in fact real as all of his sensibilities dictated, then that kiss risked more than he would allow himself to ponder. She could be married, spoken for, a maiden, all of which could be grievously insulted by his actions, fathers and husbands aside.

His actions were a clear violation and despite the inclination to lay blame on the tonic she had fed him, he should have controlled himself. As soon as the storm let up, he would leave. It was his best option now that he was well and regaining strength.

The room provided little entertainment. Rows of jars, mixing bowls, grinders, parchment. The only item of interest was a thick leather bound book found tucked in a corner and wrapped in red wool. The words inside were a language he did not understand. He assumed it to be Gaelic and though some words resembled familiar English ones, he didn't presume any accuracy in defining them.

It felt good to walk the room, however small a space

it was, and to be clothed. His sword hung at his hip, though he felt a bit silly placing it there alone as he was. The familiar weight comforted him. He paced the short length, the scant light dimming as the day closed, and paged through the thick volume.

Elaborate scrollwork graced the edge of each page and fascinated him. An intricate knotted design hid small birds, lions, dragons, all interconnected. The time and patience and love such artistry displayed impressed him. He felt tempted to keep the treasure if no one returned to the shelter. It might even be prudent to do so, could be used as a bargaining piece.

But, the old man did not know of the missing cargo, he reminded himself. He'd seen it in his eyes. Honesty. Surprise.

The room grew darker. Ashlon's gut ached with hunger. His mind longed for diversion. He tried the door. It eased open a fraction and stopped, blocked by an obstruction. A crack of dim light helped little. Carefully, taking pains not to make overmuch noise, Ashlon pushed. A thud and a scrape felt loud as gunpowder blasts in the silence.

The rain had stopped.

Sunset glowed through the window and bathed the empty room in gold outside the door. He'd gained six inches, enough to reach an arm out to hold the stack of books on the narrow table and shove.

Walking like a mouse, he felt drawn to the window. His body pulsed as he hazarded a look. Thick clouds covered the sky. They were gray and turning pink and gold as the sun sank into the dark water line. Birds chirped, the eaves dripped and the wonderful smell of clean earthiness saturated the air.

As his pulse slowed and he drank in the beauty, a faint, low thunder sounded. Hoof beats. The sound was unmistakable. Swiftly, Ashlon returned to the small room and pulled the door closed. He couldn't move the table well in his hurry and knocked several books to the floor in trying to. He hated running, hiding like a thief, a common criminal. In all the years of exile, he'd never been forced under beds, into closets or alleys. He'd found a balance between concealment and exposure.

He held his sword ready. The hooves neared and stopped. The outer door slammed open. The table scraped, clattered. Ashlon's heart slammed. The door he'd closed flew open as Ashlon raised the blade high then stilled.

The angel had returned. Golden pink light shone behind her, illuminating her hair. Small gold orbs woven through her coiffure tinkled as she came abruptly short in front of him. Wide coppery brown eyes latched on the menacing figure his sword must have presented before lighting on him.

"I've but a few minutes. If I linger longer, I'll certainly lead men here," she said and pulled his arm.

"What men?" Ashlon said and retrieved his arm.

"The men who will follow my trail, find you and either kill you directly or capture you. Quickly, collect your belongings. We must leave now."

She strode to the window, peered out and rounded back to him.

"I demand to first see the man called Heremon. He has something that I will not leave without."

Her eyes narrowed, pain flashed in them. "Your request is denied. As you are likely already aware, he is dead, possibly killed by you. Tarry longer and those men I mentioned will assume exactly that."

Ashlon chose not to argue and had no belongings to gather. He took only the book without a second thought. All he owned, he now wore. Wordlessly, he followed her and her led horse into the thicket of woods.

"Where do you lead me?" he asked.

"To the cave you left. But, I warn you not to leave it again. Leastwise not until morning." The orbs in her hair tinkled in rhythm with her hurried stride.

The man was dead, killed, she had said and he saw the truth glittering in her eyes. Yet, he'd left Ashlon in the care of this ethereal lady.

And he'd kissed her.

The cave was well hidden and Ashlon saw the chance of his finding his way back to it on his own slim to none. He would be safer here and at least able to come and go. And though she treated him so curtly, she was helping him. He could not fathom a reason why she should though.

"The man, Heremon, he sent you then?" he asked and bent to enter the cave. The book jabbed his stomach from its position under his shirt.

She didn't look at him. "I find 'sent' isn't the best word but yes, I am responsible for your care which I can see by your color and energy you will no longer need." Her eyes went over him.

She exited and reentered with a bundle balanced on her hip.

"How did he find me?"

"You have no memory of it, then?" she said.

"I rowed into the cove then awoke lying in that room," he said, feeling as though she should already know this.

"I canno' know. He died before giving me specific instruction or detail regarding your arrival to his home. Here is food, ale. The storm has passed and I do not recommend a fire. The night should be mild and these coverings should keep you warm." She plopped a bundle to the floor.

Ashlon watched her move about, straightening, directing as she spoke.

"Come morning, I will count you as well and free to go as you will." With a flutter, she met his gaze. "I've mapped the area as best as I could. If you follow north and then the line of forest, you may reach Tir Conaill on foot in reasonable time. All roads meet where you will be welcomed."

Ashlon's chest pinched. "'Tis not that I am ungrateful but, I must ask m'lady, why you have aided me so well?"

She stared at him, her eyes went to his mouth then tore away. As though looking through him, she said, "Do not speak of these past days to any man if you wish to live."

He could see the refusal, did not need words to understand that she would not explain herself. And it made him all the more intrigued.

She handed him a square piece of hide, the map she referred to inked onto it. "I must go."

She rushed past him and he followed, grasping her hand as she passed. He held her hand in his. Her gaze fell to it. He could see the fast rise and fall of her hard breathing. "What is your name? Where--how may I repay your kindnesses?" Her hand was small and soft in his.

"You may repay them with your silence, good sir." She pulled her hand from his and left, her eyes on the ground but her chin high.

* * * *

Breanne cursed the man. His questions and doubts had stolen precious minutes from her and now she was sure to be missed. More than missed. Caught. And not a single equitable explanation came to her panicked mind while she pushed her mare to the limits.

The horse ran hard and fast, Breanne sitting low and

tight in her saddle. Both breathed loud.

He'd been dressed and aglow with better health and the sight of it had knocked her breath out of her. The innocence of sleep she'd witnessed was now hard to recall, replaced by the image of a warrior standing fierce and ready.

And now she was free of the encumbrance. Those embattled green eyes would not beckon to her again. She slowed to a canter only when the keep and stables reached view. Coming in slow and at the rear proved successful. She dismounted in the inner bailey and neared the kitchen entrance.

Danny waited there whistling and twiddling his fingers, thumbs jabbed into his tunic. He was the worst looking emissary she could imagine and wanted to kiss every last freckle on his face for it.

"Any inquiries, my lord?" Breanne said with a formal bow.

"Three m'lady," Danny said. "The cat Finn asks where you've gone off to, the Lady Ula requests you filch a sweet scone for your trusted agent, and Quinlan Blake inquired thirdly."

"Finn is speaking now, is he?" she asked, only to ascertain if his reference was in fact part of the game.

Danny winked. "He circled thrice and that always means 'Where is my mistress?'"

"I see," she said and ushered him inside with her arm around his neck. She snaked her hand about a cooling scone, nearly dropping it when its heat almost scalded her, as they walked through.

The loud and crude goings on of preparation provided them with an easy cover. Up the stairs, Breanne pressed Danny for more detail.

"Your mum didn't really ask where you were, and I may have stretched the truth a bit on that scone part there." His mouth was half full with said scone. "Quinlan was the only person who did any asking. I told him like most all else 'round, you'd be bathing for the evening meal. He punched me arm and left to the stables."

"The stables. Did he follow me then, Danny?"

"If he did, it was on foot. Yours was the only horse leaving or entering, far as I spied."

"You're the best," she said and kissed his head. "Now I'd better be looking bathed soon or we'll both be suspect."

He smiled, plopped the remaining scone into his mouth and hugged her waist. Down the stairs and out of sight, he left her. Breanne stared after him. Had she ever been so carefree or always guarded, even as a child? She shook her head and enclosed herself in her chamber to ready.

As she sat before her mirror, unbraiding her hair, Finn slunk out from beneath her bed. "Is he for the worms yet?"

"If you mean the knight we found at Heremon's, no. He is well and of no consequence to either of us," she said.

"Fascinating. And when, pray tell did the stranger become a knight?" Finn's tail swished her skirt.

Breanne pursed her lips. Had she said knight? Well, of course the vision of him lifting his sword had led her to the assumption. And what could be wrong with that? Her belly quivered over the memory of seeing him, standing in shadow and the look on his face. He'd gone from intense to surprised so instantly. And the surprise that lit his features sent a thrill through her.

She felt powerful.

"I couldn't say when as I hardly know the gentleman. And is notwithstanding since he needs no further aid." Her voice sounded too pitchy by half as she spoke. Likely a consequence of her haste. She simply needed to compose herself.

"You don't need to thank me or tell me how correct I was. Both are understood." Finn licked a paw and rubbed behind an ear. "Did he witness Heremon's death?"

Breanne rolled her eyes at Finn. He'd been ready to skin the man until she'd talked sense into him. And now he spoke of the whole affair casually, unaffected. The cat's nerve and arrogance went beyond comprehension.

"He said he didn't and I believe him. He spoke as though Heremon lived, seemed put out by the tragedy."

"Were there very many mourners? Was Heremon well received?"

Was that why he'd disappeared then? To avoid the burial and feast celebrating the renowned druid priest, the scholar, philosopher, and sound judge? A shame, to be sure. Attending the rite gave Breanne a feeling of finality and she came to peace with the changes she faced. She'd decided that the loss could only detract her to the extent she allowed.

"Aye. Nearly all attended. Part of me wished he'd been sent off in the old way, into the sea, afire. But, Uncle Patrick spoke beautifully, incorporated as much of the old as he could. Clearly, he respected and knew Heremon well."

"The method matters not. Gone is gone, blessed or burned. Dead is dead."

"I suppose so," she said.

Breanne braided her hair, forgoing interweaving the gold ornamentation. Her cloak had remarkably protected her gown well enough that she needn't change, saving her additional time.

"Did you enjoy your binging and pillaging of the forest? Find any fairy mounds?"

Finn blinked unperturbed by her sarcasm. "Sidhes

lost their worth to me long before your reign over my fate, Breanne. And I doubt you hold any true interest in my activities."

Finished, Breanne faced him. "Finn, think it true or not, I have always taken my duty to you seriously. And, though I have no teacher, I have skill. I will free you."

He looked unconvinced but what else could she do or say? Empathy didn't change the facts. Finn needed to return to the Otherworld, released from a centuries old curse, or die as he was, a mangy cat bullied by hounds and humans alike.

"If you like, we may try again soon."

Finn's ears pricked up. He tipped his chin to her. "When?"

The single word held such emotion, Breanne's heart panged. "Perhaps tonight? We canno' leave the grounds but, we might try in here or—."

"Agreed. Now, don't forget my wine." He leapt to the bed, circled once and lay down. Breanne left him.

She walked through the corridor feeling composed and in control. The shocks of the last few days' events were fading. With the knight gone, Niall distracted by Heremon's death and his wedding approaching, even facing a meal aside Quinlan seemed manageable. Her life felt to be back on course.

She would focus on continuing her study independently, choose a husband and take command of her inheritance. As she walked to the main hall, she planned, and with each step, she felt more sure, more solid and capable than before.

She would not lie down and be trounced on by life's challenges. She joined Rose at the long table and piled her trencher full.

"Might I join you Lady O'Donnell?"

Breanne looked up. Gannon O'Shannon's gentle

blue eyes showed hope in them. She smiled warmly, ignored the catch in her throat and nodded. Gannon. She'd nearly forgotten about Gannon.

"Good evening to you, Master O'Shannon," Rose said. "How is the good lord treating you of late?"

"Verra well, thank you. And please, call me Gannon. I've yet to feel grown enough for another title."

Gannon sat across from them. He was charming and easy on the eyes, she supposed, watching him glance from one woman's face to another as he knifed chunks of meat. And, he was a scholar.

"I meant to pay a visit to you three days past, Gannon," Breanne said. "But I was buttonholed by my mother's husband to be."

He met her gaze openly. "A pity. I'd have enjoyed your company though I must say I mightn't have been verra good for it myself. The abbot has me right busy of late." He leaned in. "He's all afluster for the arrival of a relic."

"A relic?" Rose asked.

"Not so loud, my lady," Gannon said and winked at Breanne. "The arrival is known by no one. In truth, I only know of it accidentally and of my own conclusion."

The twinkle in his eye had Breanne ready to kick him under the table for pulling their legs. A relic, of all things, to arrive in Tir Conaill.

"I mean no jest, Breanne—your pardon—Lady O'Donnell. As logically as one and one forming two, I've concluded and found out the Abbot's secret." Gannon winked again and Breanne saw that the twinkle wasn't from amusement so much as pride. "You would draw the same conclusion I think."

"Breanne," she said. "Please, call me Breanne."

"Aye. Breanne." They exchanged a conspiratorial smile that had Rose's eyebrows lifting skyward.

Breanne widened her eyes at her friend. Not a word, she silently warned but saw that Rose's reaction was not due to Gannon and her exchange at all. Something else held her friend's attention.

Rotating in her seat, Breanne scanned the hall for the source of her friend's sudden, "Oh my. Would you look at that." Quinlan bowed to Niall some fifteen heads down at the next table. Niall stood. Together they took to the entrance as Quinlan obviously bent his ear to some issue. The two men stopped short of the entrance, under the arcade of carved arches that led to the doors.

Niall reached a meaty hand forward and the motion of a dozen more heads followed, peering. With one step, he came out of shadow and into light. The knight she left not an hour ago safe, hidden, well, knelt before Niall O'Donnell. Of all the turned heads, none were as captivated as Breanne.

And why should they be? A stranger joining the hall to dine was not uncommon. Niall was well renowned for his left arm being longer than his right, that his was among the most hospitable kinships in all of Ulster.

"He's a handsome one, that. Remind me Bree of how well I love my Ryan?"

Breanne couldn't speak. How—why was he here? And bathed and dressed and smiling like no man in his recent condition or circumstance should.

"I'll bet you a sennight of laundering he's kin," Rose said at her back.

Breanne stood, balled her fists, then realized she only gained unnecessary speculation and sat back down equally fast. Did this man have a wish to die? Was he mad?

"Are you well, Breanne?" Gannon asked.

"Aye," she said. "Adjusting my skirts is all." Breanne focused on the young face looking eagerly back at her, banishing the other one, his, from her mind.

"Are you certain? Yer face is flushed red as an apple's skin. Do you need to take some air?"

Breanne shook her head, her mouth tight, and smiled. "A bit thirsty, perhaps." She drank a long gulp of ale. Better. So long as she didn't turn around, finished her meal in short time, she should be able to conceal the riot of emotion within her.

* * * *

Ashlon spotted her long before she turned around, curiously looking about. And he didn't miss the expression of horror when he'd kneeled before the local king, Niall O'Donnell. She must think him quite arrogant to have disregarded her wishes, warnings, and arrived here.

But, he counted himself as lucky, not arrogant. From the moment he set sail as passenger on the merchant ship from Spain to Scotland, luck had followed him. Luck of the Irish, Jacques would have said, often did when Ashlon's life went right in the most wrong of circumstance, though his blood ran English tracing back as far as could be traced.

Ashlon had set foot outside the cave with a full belly and a mind to explore, map in hand. By good chance, Quinlan Blake came upon him without menace and brought him directly here, to the very man De Molay had instructed Ashlon find should anything go awry.

Awry seemed too weak a descriptor for his mislay. But, with resources such as Niall O'Donnell at his avail, Ashlon wouldn't feel defeated quite yet.

In quick order, he was bathed, his garments seen to and freshened, and brought to dine. Yes, luck was his companion of late and he hoped it would not end now.

"You are welcome at my table, Sir Sinclair under one condition. My men and I will hear of your journeys

and particularly of that which brings you to our tuath."
Niall clasped his hand with both of his, gave it a sturdy
shake that matched his nod.

"My eternal gratitude, my lord. Though I have little
adventure to tell."

"Nonsense. We all have tales and if it is true then
we'll count on the bards William and Wallace for our
imaginations' delight."

"Again, I thank you, sir. And you as well, Master
Blake."

Ashlon stole a glance her way as the two men seated
him and themselves among the two rows of scarred and
bearded men. One by one each were introduced to him.
A nod here, a good shake there, lineage and relationships
explained so well that by midway through, Ashlon
struggled to recall even the first man's identity.

She kept her head down and her back to him. Good.
No reason to raise suspicion or cause a scene. She clearly
wished to be rid of him back at the cave and he would
honor both her request for silence and divestment.
Leastwise, he would once he got her alone and showed
her what he'd found.

Chapter Nine

Breanne didn't mind being the first to arrive in the Grianan. Actually thought it might behoove her, demonstrate eagerness on her part. But when an hour passed with no other woman joining her, she began to think she'd chosen badly. But she had naught else to do. Rising with the dawn had become such a habit as a child, it stuck.

When Heremon was alive, she'd fill her mornings with study, transcribing notes and potions into her Grimoire, ornamenting the pages with drawings. Being in her room for those hours every day, she thought by the noisy activity outside, that the entire household rose early as well.

Re-braiding her hair a third time, Breanne guessed it to be nearing the seventh hour. She didn't dare leave or poke her nose out the doors to look for another female soul. If she did, she might run into *him*. Twice yesterday and four times the day before, she'd found herself in his vicinity and had to reroute not only her path but her schedule, as well.

Finn had stopped speaking to her after three more failed rituals. Being unable to go outdoors unescorted made Breanne feel like a trapped animal, too.

So, she came here, the only room Ashlon Sinclair couldn't follow her to other than her own. Sir Sinclair. She swore the man was utterly daft. From the fever mayhap. His name seemed to be on everyone's lips, so fascinating were his tales over mealtime.

She for one, cared not, was glad *not* to have suffered what was likely to be tall tales of grand chivalry. A knight. But, no gentleman, to be sure. What kind of chivalry kissed a woman like he had her?

When the door swung open, din from the hall carried and followed Rose inside. Breanne beamed.

"In St. Brigit's name, where have you been all morning Rose? I thought I might perish waiting for you and the other women."

Rose looked up, startled. "What are you doing here, Bree? Have you lost your way?" she said, recovered.

"If I'm marrying, I had better be acquainted with the ways of running my household. So, I'll be spending my time here among the fairer, my peerage, learning."

Rose's eyebrows drew together. She grinned. "Who are you hiding from, then? Niall? O'Shannon?"

"Neither. Is as I've said, naught else. I thought you would be pleased."

"Your mother will be, for certain." In a burst, the door opened again and Rose's girls stormed the room. Kimber went straight to Breanne on sight. The others greeted her and went about their fairy make believe.

Rose sat next to her with a huff. Her eyes were puffy, dark circled. "Have you not slept well, Rose?"

"I have. Slept like the dead but can't seem to get up and about. Exhausted is what I am."

"Are you feeling well?"

"Tired is all." She yawned. "Whenever Ryan is off, I feel more worn than when he's home. The help he is with the girls, I imagine."

"Shall I make you something to help?"

"Ah, no. I'll be fine, you'll see. Sheena, none of that now. We speak like ladies, don't we?" Sheena's cheeks reddened and she covered her mouth when she nodded. "Kimber, play with your sisters and let Breanne be for now."

"She's fine, really."

Rose helped the little girl down, kissed her cheek. "It's not for your sake. It's for mine. Little ears pick up big words and I have a favor to ask of you. But, first, let us move to my corner or Rhiannon will be steaming from her eyes discovering you in her chair. We can be as territorial as a buck in spring in here. Some would leave their mark if they could."

Breanne chuckled at the image despite the kernel of worry for Rose. She looked more than sleepy. Three more ladies entered the room, chattering, pausing to give Breanne raised eyebrows then settled into their areas.

"Are you very schooled in herbs, Breanne? I know I'm callus and a poor friend indeed for never asking about your study before, and I'm hoping you'll forgive me for it. It's just that I have need to know now where, before I didn't." Rose tossed an unfinished embroidery piece onto Breanne's lap. "It's not that I'm only tired, Bree."

Breanne's mouth fell open. "What is it, Rose?"

Her friend jabbed the dull end of a needle into her hand. Breanne took the hint and plucked it through the cloth. Rose held a broad smile on her face while she spoke, cueing Breanne to follow suit.

The kernel expanded.

"Rose. You're scaring me."

She snorted. "No need to be scared. I'm with child is all. Well, I think I am. I'll know for certain within a sennight or so."

Breanne inhaled but clamped her mouth shut when Rose's eyes pinned her with warning. She forced the smile back.

"Ryan, he wants a son so badly, a boy to rough and tumble, to pass his name. Men, they don't feel like men without another prick in the home to prove it."

"I canno' foretell the gender so early as that, Rose. Not until midway through, and I'm not certain you should rely on my say as I've never done it afore."

"You can tell me if it's a boy?" Rose frowned.

"Aye, well, perchance. But, that is not what you were asking me, is it? Rose, what are you asking me?" The expansion of worry spread to her chest.

Rose lowered her gaze, the smile stuck. "Kimber is but a year and a half grown. I've had them all right behind the next and I love them more than my own life, more than anything, but Breanne, I feel beaten with this one."

Breanne shook her head slowly. Not that. Rose couldn't ask her to do that.

"You've no idea what it feels like, Bree. No better than a broodmare, I am."

"Do you know what you're saying, Rose? Have you lost all your senses?"

Rose shook her head, the smile barely moved when she spoke. "Is it better it kills me, leaves my girls without a mother, Ryan without a wife?"

Breanne saw the desperation glittering in Rose's eyes and the worry inside of her became fear. "You're right, Rose. I do not know. But, I do know that I may be able to help you so that you might make it through and if you do, you'll not rue it."

Rose shook her head still. Breanne's words didn't seem to penetrate her. "I want Ryan to have his boy and I know in my heart that this babe is male. Leave it to a man to exhaust me so, make me wait so long. Just like his father." Her smile became tender. A tear slid down her cheek.

"Aye. A boy like his father. Rose," she whispered. "Take a breath. My mother has come in."

Within a breath, Ula spoke Breanne's name and rushed to their corner. "Do I trust my eyes? My very own daughter, here, among us? Why, I haven't seen you in here in the morning light since you were eleven years."

Breanne returned Ula's embrace. "It canno' be such a shock as that, now. As you said, I will soon have my own household to run. Where better to prepare for it than here with all of you?" She spoke loudly and gained a few of the smiles she'd been soliciting with the remark.

Only Rose would see through it, she hoped, and Rose was under enough burden of her own that she might not press the matter.

"A splendid idea. Now, give me that. Embroidery was never your best talent and is a pleasure you'll not have time for until your later years if your marriage is successful. And of course it will be. Here, why don't we polish your spinning skills. Rhiannon, will you be a dear and help Breanne with her spinning this morning?"

Breanne glanced back at Rose, hoping she could see the promise to finish their conversation. Sheena stole Rose's attention away before she could be certain, making her first spinning in four years time go even worse.

Sucking on her index finger, stuck for the second time, Breanne silently cursed Sir Sinclair and his mesmerizing kiss for forcing her into a punishment worth all her sins—women's work.

* * * *

"Only a man with a wish for death will go through that door," Quinlan's distinct voice said.

Ashlon turned in its direction, head cocked. "Oh, and why is that Master Blake?"

"Quinlan, Sir Sinclair, if you please, and that is the

Grianan. One must be of the fairer sex to enter though what man in his right mind would want to? A veritable nest of hens, clucking away all day long, that it is."

"Grianan?"

"Aye, it is exclusive to the ladies of the clan. Built in the sunniest corner of any man's castle, to keep them happy and out of our hair."

Ashlon suppressed a laugh. Quinlan Blake had a lot to learn about women. But, who was he to point it out? "I am in search of his Highness, King Niall O'Donnell."

"Allow me, good sir," Quinlan said, without question.

Ashlon followed, feeling the pull to stay despite the young man's warning. She could not remain in the room forever, though. Eventually, he would gain a private word with her, be able to steal a note her way. And meeting with Niall was an inevitable necessity.

The man seemed to talk in circles and Ashlon wondered from the start, sitting across from him at his table of men, if he'd injured his head during his spell of illness. No other appeared to have difficulty understanding Niall O'Donnell, but Ashlon struggled to find the man's meaning at times. So, he'd put off the conversation in hopes that speaking with the girl, Breanne O'Donnell as Quinlan informed him yesterday, would end its need.

Quinlan rapped his knuckles on the ajar door. "Sir Sinclair to see his Royal Highness."

Hearing Quinlan's sarcasm followed by Niall's guffaw, Ashlon prickled with annoyance.

"Send him in Quinlan. Send him in." Niall approached the door, waving inward.

"Ashlon, my good man, I thought I told you we're kin in these parts and none of this royal high and mighty hog's farts around them, then? I eat with my men because I am a man. They've chosen me to lead and so I do but, it makes me no better a person in theirs, mine, or the good lord's and goddess' eyes now does it there?"

Ashlon pressed his lips together and bowed. They had appointed this man as leader? What could they, or Jacques, have been thinking in giving this man a grain of influence over their lives? Did he confuse his enemies to death?

"I've come to ask for a private audience with you, my lord, of a personal theme. At your pleasure and leisure, of course."

"I will be pleasured now, Ashlon," Niall said. "Come in, sit. But no more formalities, do I have your word?"

"As you wish, my lord." Ashlon took the nearest seat and waited for Niall to join him. When he did not, Ashlon proceeded with the dreaded inquiry. "I have been welcomed so well by your clan, my lord and wish to express my sincere gratitude as well as--."

"It is our pleasure, Ashlon. You will soon be more Irish than we ourselves are Irish, so as the saying goes from the Normans, Gaels, Picts. We all love the land and it becomes a part of us like flesh on our bones. So much so that you're willing to chew off another's flesh to keep yours alive and well. So, I'd say Ashlon Sinclair that you should begin working up an appetite."

Ashlon squinted, watched the man pace and gesture as he spoke. "Your land and people have been most giving. I am sure it is the very reason Jacques de Molay sent me to you."

Niall nodded somberly, gaze held aloft by a high window. "I shall marry soon, Ashlon. I marry Lady Ula in less time than I can quite believe. It will be a grand celebration I promise you've never seen the likes of.

Have you taken a wife yet?"

"No, my lord. In service of his holiness, I had not considered the possibility." But that had not really been true for seven years. With exile and disbandment came a change in Ashlon's prospects for the future that he didn't allow consideration yet. A wife. A home. Until he ended this journey, neither were options.

"I have not. Ula will be my first and only wife. It is a strange thing to find life never really ends until it ends. Old is not dead you see. And old is me, Ashlon."

Ashlon remained uncomfortably, impatiently, silent.

"Your friend is wise to recommend us to you. Now, then, what may I be of service to you this morn?"

"My lord?"

"Your wish to speak in privacy, Ashlon. Let us be on with it." Niall's gaze remained on the window, his hand wafted in the air.

"The Grand Master of the Knights of Solomon, the Templar Knights bade me come to your doorstep in my hour of need. Specifically, he gave your name as a person who would offer aid and trustworthiness in completing a task he set me to before his tragic death. I petition that aid now."

"Ah, yes. I do know of tragedy, my good man. I do know of that." His stare lowered. "I confess your friend was not only wise but careful, as well. Terrible betrayal that business. You will not be the first of your brothers to seek solace within Ireland's long arms."

Ashlon's patience waned. He did not want to lose it with this kind man, but the chieftain was quashing both his hope and bearings in fast order. The first mention of Jacques' name had little effect and the full title and explanation seemed to have less. Had Jacques misspoke? Had Ashlon remembered inaccurately?

"It is unfortunate that both our tragedies will show

up in heaven together. I'd say the two will have a large, long laugh of it, too."

"My lord. I apologize, but I fail to comprehend your meaning. Might you explain?"

Niall frowned at him and Ashlon feared he had offended him. It was impossible not to ask though. A glimmer of clarity had come shining through and he needed make certain he'd drawn the correct conclusion.

"Some sixteen years past," Niall said. "It was spring as it is now, glorious and green. Imbolc festival was a resounding success, as it is nearly every season in St. Brigit's honor. And much the same way as you came to us, he did also."

"Who, my lord?"

"De Molay, of course. He brought his head to my advisor Heremon. He needed the priest to decipher his head, you see. I know not more of the meeting except from Heremon's own mouth, which is buried now, and bending another, better man's ear. You see, Heremon met a tragic fall this week past and has died."

Ashlon bent his head to show respect and hide the race of emotions circling his heart like vultures. He was sorry to have doubted his master, however briefly. His mysterious course depended on unquestioning trust and would likely end with it, as well.

"Please accept my deepest condolences, my lord. I had not heard and was not aware of the two men's friendship." Most of what the king had said suddenly made sense, miraculously. Ashlon regretted the surge of scorn he'd felt for Niall O'Donnell.

The events that had led him here had significance now. A jolt ran through him. Had his arrival in some way caused Heremon's demise? Jacques had sent him to Niall to get him to Heremon. Might Pope Clement have discovered his trail?

He needed more than ever to speak with Breanne O'Donnell.

Ashlon cleared his throat. "I thank you your majesty, for your time and insight. You have been most kind."

"My pleasure, as always. He lies in the Abbot's churchyard, if you would like to pay homage to his rested soul and honorable life." Niall gestured to the door. "If he were here, I'd be asking him to calm these blasted nerves of mine. The man always had a tonic or two, you'll come to know."

Ashlon smiled and bowed as he retreated from the room. A brawny, redheaded man with an ugly throat scar barely discernable with the heavy beard, eyeballed him and Ashlon met his stare evenly. "Can you point me in the direction of the priory?"

The man MacSweeney stabbed a finger through the air and followed with specific directions. His air was not haughty so much as severe and Ashlon pitied the man who faced him in battle.

Beards appeared to be the fashion of the area. Ashlon counted most men as having one, though none hid friendly smiles that greeted him on his walk to Heremon's gravesite. He doubted the man's mound of dirt or headstone would offer insight but felt compelled to pay respects. The man might have died because of Ashlon.

The sky was hazy, the weather mild and damp, the air clean and fresh in his lungs. Ashlon had meant it when he thanked the chieftain. The welcome these people gave went unsurpassed in all his experience. And Ashlon had many to compare it to. Hospitality to strangers ran cold or hot through his past, never warm, until now. He wasn't sure he could count the fact as stupidity or confidence but was leaning toward the latter. After all, would a man, beholden to such extent, bite the hand that fed him so well?

A large painted, carved cross acted as a beacon outside the simple stone priory. Approaching it, Ashlon studied the pictorial carvings. He'd never seen the like. Each rectangular portrayal seemed to tell a story in vivid color. He traced a finger along the base of the mammoth cross as though to make it real, less foreign. More Irish than ourselves, Niall had said and the idea nagged him.

"Beautiful, isn't it?"

Ashlon turned, pulled his hand back as though caught then felt silly for it upon seeing the man who spoke. "Unique, certainly," he said to the robust, bald man clearly of the cloth.

"Sir Ashlon Sinclair, I presume?" His wide grin got wider, his forehead wrinkling upward.

"My name precedes me," Ashlon said. He waited.

"My sister, Lady Ula has spoken well of you and as we see few welcome English in these parts, I knew the name to be yours." He spoke as though he'd solved a clever puzzle.

"I've come to pay respect to the recently departed, Father Connelly. Would you be so kind as to direct me to the site?" Ashlon didn't miss the glimmer of insult when he returned the play of names. But the man's smile held and he led Ashlon without further remark.

"Our door will be open, should you need solace, my son," the Abbot said.

Ashlon bowed and waited until the man left before giving his full attention to the headstone. Heremon was buried under a birch tree, still too young to offer shade but would someday. The thick square headstone lacked ornamentation aside from carved dates and Heremon's full given name.

He knelt and placed a hand on the dirt. What direction did he follow now? How would he locate the cargo Jacques had entrusted to him and would he endanger any other innocent lives in the process? At what price should he resign himself from Jacques' command?

No man could answer him but a single ugly vision came to mind. The full-lipped mouth he'd pressed his lips to as though in a dream, open to scream. Possessive fear shot through his heart and brought him to his feet.

He left the priory yard for the pension he'd taken temporary residence in, a strategy forming with every purposeful step. She could not hide forever. But, she could prolong his cornering her. Rather than chase the rabbit, he would draw the rabbit to him.

And he knew just the man to help him lure his prey.

Chapter Ten

"Just the man I was looking for," Quinlan said. He approached Ashlon outside of the pension house at the edge of Tir Conaill, as accurately shown in the map he still carried.

"Master Blake," Ashlon said, clasping the proffered hand. "I did not realize you required further time this morn. I would have waited."

"I hadn't, actually. Didn't intend to speak with you again—that is to say, I only now came, only just—," Quinlan said and paused to exhale loudly. He ran a hand through his hair. "I've come to strike a bargain, Sir Sinclair. Have you a moment?"

"Yes, of course."

"May we walk?" Quinlan glanced about.

Ashlon joined him in stride, waited for the man to broach whatever topic had him so disconcerted. A bargain. Convenient, to say the least, that Ashlon had the same endeavor.

"You have met the Lady Breanne, have you not?"

"Aye."

"Her mother, Lady Ula is set to marry Niall O'Donnell."

"I see." What was it he found so difficult to ask?

"Breanne will become his daughter." Quinlan paused, then resumed walking. "I have professed my intention for her hand to Niall."

"Congratulations. The marriage will bring you in line for the throne."

Quinlan's brow rose. "No. Niall has named his successor and to be clear, I have no desire of such a position."

Love then? "I see."

"Breanne is to choose her betrothed by Beltane feast. I have discovered I am among several—."

"She will choose, you say?"

"Aye, and there are s—."

"And she has no entitlement through her mother wedding the king?" Ashlon heeded Quinlan's flush at his interruptions. "He has a son?"

"No. She has title, lands, properties. But you miss my point, Sir Ashlon. Her inheritance, considerable as it is, is not my concern." He blew out his air. "My competition is."

His interruptions looked to have tried the man well. "What bargain do you propose?" Ashlon hid a smile.

Quinlan pulled the collar of his tunic. They neared the outer bailey of the O'Donnell keep. "I ask for your help in winning her hand."

Ashlon snorted. How could he not? The idea was preposterous. Him school Quinlan in the art of wooing?

"You are a knight, trained in courtly love, chivalry, the laws that rule society, well, most society. If you help me learn a measure of grace, composure, I will be eternally in your debt and I ask now that you seriously consider my plea."

"She is a woman. Treat her as you would any woman you wish to cherish. How I could conceivably aid—." They stopped.

"By instructing me in the very specifics of it. On the ritual of it." Quinlan lowered his voice, but it did little to mask his eagerness. "On the physical nature of courtship."

Ashlon's eyes popped wider. The physical nature? Christ's bones, was he sincere? Quinlan's sober nod said as much.

"I must say, Quinlan, that I am surprised. Have the ladies not flocked to you your entire life?"

"Nay! I do not mean to say, that is, I have not lacked for companionship since my fifteenth year. With offers long running. But the sensibilities of a high born lady are, Breanne is, different." Quinlan held his thumb to his forefinger. "What I ask is a polish of my roughly hewn stone so that I may seduce her mind and her heart."

"And in exchange…." Ashlon flexed his jaw.

"Name your price."

"Allow me time to consider?"

"Of course," Quinlan said.

They entered the main hall.

"Will you again join our table this eve?" Quinlan asked, making Ashlon realize the dinner hour approached.

"Yes, thank you." How had the day stolen away from him?

"Have you considered joining the galloglass guard, Sir Ashlon?" Quinlan separated from their stride. "Should you petition to join our clan, we would benefit from your knight's training."

He left Ashlon to ponder the notion. Join the clan? Was that possible? At present, he had a bargain to consider and a bath to see to. He'd learned that arriving unwashed to the king's table, or any man's, was an insult.

Though he had not found a moment alone to speak to Breanne, he might have thought of a faster means to her.

Walking to the main doors, Ashlon came up short

when the Grianan door creaked open. He saw her nose before her face, but knew it instantly. With few around, perchance he could ask her now for a private, secret meeting.

"My lady," Ashlon said low and discreetly.

* * * *

Unmindful of the ladies rapt in conversation, Breanne peeked out of the Grianan door. She saw him nowhere and sighed in relief. To think she'd actually heard and recognized the daft man's voice outside the door. And a good thing or she'd have run straight into him on her way—

"My lady."

The door shut like a shout announcing her exposure. Breanne straightened and faced him, ready to act on her first instinct and be damned of the stares she might earn. But just as she felt to run, Ashlon stepped forward like a barricade.

Breanne fought the urge to step back from him and forced a smile on her face. Her eyes fell to his mouth. Her chest warmed, her body remembering what his kiss had done to her.

"Aye, my lord?" Thankfully, her voice did not squeak.

She looked back to his eyes, aware of every other person in the hall. And even more aware of him. Within a moment, so many details filled her senses. He was taller this close, and broader and the image of his naked chest clouded her mind. If she tried, she might be able to smell his spicy….

"You have no need to fear me," he said quietly, drawing her attention back with a jolt.

"I do not fear you," she said, a bit too loud, confused as to why he would think so.

Ashlon glanced around. Breanne followed suit,

though not as surreptitiously, to be sure. She could not account for her sudden nerves. But it was no wonder he thought her afraid. She was nigh trembling.

"What I mean to say is you need not fear I will expose our previous acquaintance. Also, you have my gratitude." His gaze returned to hers; something indefinable shone in them.

Unbidden, the memory of his lips on hers struck her. Breanne lowered her gaze.

"That said, you no longer need avoid me, as well."

"I have not avoided you," she said, ready to explain fully her time spent within the Grianan, but footsteps approached from behind. So she curtsied deeply and readied to make for the stairs at his back.

At Ashlon's first glance at whomever approached, she hurriedly bid him farewell. He didn't object or follow and Breanne did not run, leastwise not until she'd passed the corridor wall.

She closed her bedchamber door and sighed against it.

"Who are you running from?" Finn asked from his perch in the narrow window.

"I have not run from anyone," she said, swallowing. "Not that you would know either way."

"Care you mean. Not that I would care."

"Then why do you ask?" She sat on her bed and began to undress. Her bath waited.

"You're right, Breanne. Why ask when one already knows the answer? To force an admission, I suppose."

"Somebody is feeling the nasty effects of over-imbibing." Her gown fell to the floor.

"As I thought. Avoiding the subject. Redirecting the conversation. You're quite transparent."

The hot water was delicious on her aching muscles and she closed her eyes while the knots in her shoulders untied. Finn's baiting was time and energy wasted. Naught could penetrate the haze of bliss this bath was giving her. Who knew spinning could be so wearing? She'd happily never pedal another strand of wool to life so long as she lived.

"Avoiding and redirecting will only delay your problems. And in the meantime, you'll create far more of them."

She wasn't listening. She wouldn't. He was looking to fight, but if she didn't respond, would he not give up? The heat was leaving the water. Two more minutes, then she'd wash and dress. It wasn't a lot to ask.

"Truly, Breanne, what would Heremon think?"

Her eyes flew open. She ground her teeth. "If you continue your games with me, Finn, I swear I will not only never practice a rite on your behalf again, but I may lay another curse upon you."

"Aha, she speaks."

Water sloshed over the tub's edge as Breanne sat upright. "Aye, she speaks. And may you hear my words. I warn you, Finn, play with me no more." She scrubbed her elbows.

"Fine. I will not. I will ask you, though, because I must. I have seen the stranger. I know he is among us. I need to know what you are doing about it."

"What am I doing about it? There is naught to be done. He has no consequence outside of being in Heremon's care at the time of his demise."

"Then why does he stay?"

"How should I know? He is no longer my concern." She stepped from the bath. "My concerns lie in choosing a husband, lifting your curse." Helping Rose. Avoiding that man. "Heremon's death has been decided as accidental. We must move on."

"I'll move on when he is gone from here. Or when I

136

am."

"That is your choice. But do not force your choice on me." She whipped four thick strands into a fishtail braid. "We need to attract goodness, purity, forgiveness or we'll never return you to where you belong."

"Don't forget basic skill and a good dose of talent."

"Why, you vile beast, I ought to toss you out on your ear, the ungrateful way you treat—."

"Breanne?" It was Rose. "Are you all right?"

Adjusting her dress, Breanne opened the door. "I'm sorry, I lost track of time soaking. Can you fasten this broach for me, Rose?"

"Talking to yourself is one thing, Bree. But yelling at yourself is another."

"I wasn't yelling at myself," Breanne said. "I was yelling at Finn."

"Ah, well, then. Nothing mad about yelling at an animal, is there?" Rose fixed the pin through the fabric.

Breanne glowered at Finn, daring him to speak up now, in front of Rose, but knew full well he wouldn't risk it. Perhaps she should take to sharing her chambers and garner further silence. He'd choke to death on his mean, unlived words.

"There." Rose smiled and brushed Breanne's shoulders. "I don't know how to bring up our earlier conversation smoothly, but I need to finish it with you."

"Not here," Breanne blurted. "On the way, if you please, Rose. I hate being late and not having seating to choose from." Safely down the corridor she said, "I know you haven't said it and I don't want you to have to. I wouldn't feel right, though, if I didn't try to dissuade you, and at least ask you try a tonic first."

Rose sighed and took her hand as they reached the hall. "Aye, Breanne. I'll try one. But, if I make my choice, I--."

Breanne put her hand up. "Say no more. I'll ready one and we'll go on from there."

Ignoring the center of most diners' attention proved harder every day. Three uneventful days later, he still drew eyes wherever he walked and not just Breanne's. Rose practically gawked at Ashlon Sinclair whenever present, making Breanne's disassociation of him all the more difficult.

"He's a man without a home, Bree." She clucked her tongue. "If Ryan doesn't return soon, I may entertain thoughts of making one for him."

"Rose, do you hear yourself? I thought you loved your husband." Her reprimand fell on deaf ears and Breanne's decision to keep her distance from the man was all the more reinforced.

"Ach, now, Bree, looking at a man with open eyes does not mean my love is less for Ryan. And my current peeve with him and his prick have cleared my vision a bit. Don't be such a prude."

Breanne saw no way to explain she was not being prudish, but prudent. If Rose knew the devastating effect that man's kiss had on Breanne's sensibilities, she might understand. And that would not happen. That kiss would remain a secret buried away with all her others.

She'd rather expose her studies than reveal that kiss. A shiver tickled her neck at the memory.

"When will Ryan return?" Breanne asked, trying to change her mind's course.

"Tomorrow mayhap."

"Can you tear your eyes off of him long enough to eat then, Rose, or shall I find better company?"

"Ah, don't be jealous, Bree. He'll not replace my affection for you." Rose poked her in the ribs, finally facing the food rather than Sinclair's direction.

A round of deep laughter echoed from the king's

table. She should have known. Sinclair looked to be telling some splendid joke, by his animated gestures. She shouldn't have looked.

He was something to behold. Tall, broad, masculine. She remembered the hard muscle under those ill-fitted clothes, likely lent him by Quinlan, as they'd become so disgustingly chummy of late. Everyone had taken to speaking in English, a sure sign he was in the vicinity, even Rose.

"He may stay, I've heard, to work and earn. I'd imagine he'd be able to meet Brehon law requirement sooner than most. Picture that blood joined with the clan's."

"Will you tell him?" Breanne told herself Rose's moan of approval was for the sweet bread she chewed, rather than the fantasy of Sinclair.

"Of Sir Sinclair," Rose said. "I don't doubt he'll already know. And of other things, not yet."

"But the tonic helped, did it not?"

"Aye," Rose said. "But two days is not enough to judge, Bree. Do not badger me of it. Rest you'll know first as my progress goes." She kept her voice low and warning.

Breanne knew better than to press the delicate affair further than the dangerous length she already had. A rumble of applause grabbed her attention back to Sinclair, saving her from finding a neutral topic.

"I wonder what he's told them," Rose said, audibly awestruck.

"I don't."

"Why do you dislike him so? I'd thought at first you've just been sour, and then that you wanted my attention, but now I wonder."

"I don't know what you mean. I do not even know the man to have chosen between like and dislike." She filled her mouth and shrugged.

"I think you have." Rose's gaze narrowed. "I believe you're quite decided and I mean to know every last detail, Breanne O'Donnell."

"Have you gone mad?"

"You're the only person in the room not reasonably taken with Ashlon Sinclair, the only one among four full tables that looks upon him with scorn. I'll know why? Or shall I ask Sir Sinclair?"

"No," Breanne said. "Don't look at me that way, Rose. All right, I admit it, I know the man. Now, if you please, remove that gloat from your face or I will not tell you a single detail." A fine sweat broke under Breanne's bodice. Another lie. More than a lie, a full fabrication. She'd better start writing these things down else forget what was what.

"I met him the day he arrived. He—."

"By night? Oh my," Rose said.

"No, not night. By day, he—."

"But he arrived well into the evening meal, remember, brought by Quin?"

"Aye. Well, I expect it was not *the* day he arrived then, but the following day." She rolled her eyes, but was glad for the time she'd just earned to think up her web to weave. "I bumped into him, literally ran straight into him, turning a corner on my way to the kitchens. I was hungry for eggs and though it was past breaking my morning fast, I couldn't give the idea up."

"Does he smell good?"

"How should I know?" Breanne shifted. Her mind filled not with memory of his scent, but of the way he'd tasted. Sweet. She remembered the surprise of the taste after rinsing his gullet with bitter broth, wine, meat, where had his sweetness come from?

"You ran into him. Did he smell badly, clean,

manly?"

"Clean," she said. Spicy. Earthy. Her thighs tingled.
"He smelled clean, and as I was saying, I had a taste for
eggs, scrambled with a bit of cheese. I turned and ran
straight into him."

"And what happened then? Did you fall?" She
leaned closer. "Did he catch you?"

"No, I did not fall. I am not clumsy, Rose. What
happened was Sir Sinclair looked at me stone-faced and
said not a word." She would burn in hell for certain,
telling such a giant fib. But Breanne could not exactly
speak the truth, that she'd felt as though she'd collided
with him. Or that it had *not* hurt. It had felt good,
familiar. Staggering.

"No."

"Oh, aye, not a peep. I apologized for not seeing him
there and curtsied and when I looked up, saw him
completely unmoved." Lies, lies.

"I can't believe it." Rose looked past Breanne to the
king's table. "Certainly, he's English, but so friendly that
I hardly held it as suspicious. Though I can see what you
mean by stone-faced. I have caught a hardness about his
expression. There is passion under that cool surface,
mark my words."

Breanne gave up. Even an insult Rose twisted into a
romantic notion. Her only prayer was that Ryan would
arrive early on the morrow and put his wife right with
plenty of romping affection.

When laughter filled the room once more, she gritted
her teeth. If he wouldn't soon be leaving on his own, she
might have to find a way to help him go.

Ashlon finished his most recent tale among the many
nightly requests Niall made. Not that Ashlon minded.
The shared stories and rapt audience reminded him of

days long past, days he didn't realize how much he'd missed in the last seven years. Only these men weren't the polished, low-voiced, winking sort. They were bawdy and blunt and refreshingly real. No subterfuge here.

He drew attention aplenty, even hers. Lady Breanne certainly seemed to try not to look, not to notice him. But she failed and every instance she did, he caught. He was careful not to meet her eye or even her face, but every turn of her head in his direction felt a victory.

In the last two days, it became his personal challenge. He counted the number of looks he earned and wagered with himself how many more he'd get by the week's end. Being so thoroughly hidden away in the Grianan as she'd been, and as she expeditiously retired each night, these looks were the closest contact he'd managed. Aside from one startling moment from which she'd fast escaped speaking to him.

But he had a plan. Quinlan began training with him in the morn and by day's end, Ashlon vowed to have roped the man into unknowingly gaining a secret meeting with the object of his affection.

Ashlon sat after his deep bow as the next man stood to share. Shane MacSweeney took the focus. A few moments into MacSweeney's hunting tale, as fellows in arms joined in during familiar parts, Ashlon watched her. She spoke with her friend, Quinlan's sister, waved her knife about, the speared meat flopping at her gestures. Whatever she said had her flustered and her cheeks were deliciously pink from it.

She shrugged, looked heavenward and in a breath, looked directly at him. Her eyes widened when they met his. Her pink cheeks flushed to red and color spread down her neck. A slow, knowing smile formed across Ashlon's face as he understood the true nature of her avoidance.

The kiss. His kiss.

Her stare went to his smile. Her mouth opened. Closed. Back to his eyes. Ashlon winked and when she visibly gasped and turned away, triumph surged through him.

His plan dictated patience. Gaining a meeting with her tomorrow might be too soon to hope for. But upon seeing the naked flash of heat in those eyes, tomorrow felt like an eon to wait.

Ashlon chuckled deeply and returned his attention to MacSweeney in time for his apparently hilarious conclusion. He laughed with the others and no one noticed the difference.

Once trenchers were cleared, most adjourned to the large hearth to hear the five bards play. Ashlon waited. When Breanne soon retired, without a hint of expression his way, he chuckled again. But the room was colder without her in it.

In her room, Breanne rushed to the long, narrow trunk at the foot of her bed. Finn opened his eyes and stretched from his usual spot. She pulled out two candles, one scarlet and one black, her book and four carefully selected jars. The first three items she dumped, the last four she set delicately aside until the lid closed and she laid her spread.

"Where's my wine?" Finn asked.

She dug the wineskin out of her cloak's inner pocket, sewn in for this purpose, and laid it on the floor. He drank from the mouth, a paw pressed to the bag and she didn't care if he spilt. Right now, she cared only about her altar.

She set each candle to an upper corner on the gray wool. In the first fifty pages, she found what she wanted. It was a simple enough incantation, given to her by

Heremon as a simple starting point. While she had never worked its magic, he hadn't reproached her. Surely he'd held faith that she could, and this time, she would make it work.

Breanne lined up the four short jars and reread the instructions. Simple really. Combine, chant, combine, circle, scry. She'd forgotten her athame and mirror.

"What mischief are we about, love?" Finn purred at her feet.

"We are making magick, Finn."

"Not tonight, love. I'm of no mood for it. Let us do something else." The wine had warmed him to her.

"It is not for you, Finn. I have other intentions for this conjuration. And I'm sure you'll find my practice as entertaining as ever since I am more determined than ever." She retrieved her athame and drew a circle in the air around them and the altar.

Finn kept quiet for once. Breanne began. She chanted the words, combined the herbs and liquid, Finn giggled. "Sshhhh," she said.

"What exactly are we attempting?" Finn whispered, his humor clinging to his words like honey.

"I am attempting to find a means to make Sinclair leave Tir Conaill."

"I say let him stay. He seems a good fellow."

Breanne stopped mixing to stare at the cat. "You canno' be serious, Finn."

"Pish-posh, Breanne. There's no reason 'tall to force the knight out. You did your part, now leave him be." He swayed a bit.

Pish-posh? The difference was night to day when Finn imbibed, though either version adored disagreeing. She wasn't sure she liked him better this way, the amicable protester. She refocused on the incantation.

"Why will you make him go?" Finn said. "And

how? He's done naught to you outside of needing a bit of tending and may I remind you that you are, in fact, a healer."

"He's done plenty to make me happier once gone. His remaining puts us at risk." She traced the page with her finger.

"I cannot imagine him putting his own neck on the block by telling anyone about Heremon." Finn squinted up at her. "What aren't you telling me? It's something important and I can nearly smell it on you, so you may as well tell me now and save a fit."

"Will you let me work, please?"

"Not until you explain that phrase to me. What plenty has the good knight done, Breanne?" Finn said, his tone teasing.

"He's put me at risk, is that not enough?"

"He did not put you at risk, you did. Aiding him, presaged or not, was your choice. And although you had to sneak about and heal him, you cannot convince me that is enough to rid yourself of his innocent presence in the clan."

He was right. Even besotted, the cat made keen deductions and astute observations. Well, he'd have to guess the truth because she refused to speak the words. That smile, that damned smile, gave her such a start, such panic, what could more cause? Another dizzying kiss, or worse, more? She couldn't risk it.

Breanne chanted the rhyme three times, cutting the air with her athame in the symbol of flight. She visualized Sinclair walking the road away from Tir Conaill, heading north and carrying a chest. She willed the image of him to walk onward, away, to journey elsewhere. She spoke the words and she wished him protection on his journey.

Back to the beginning, she replayed the sequence in

her head, chanting, cutting in chains of three, until suddenly, the image took on life. Ashlon walked, arms loaded, sword sheathed. He paused, he turned, and looking right at her, he smiled.

Breanne opened her eyes, coughing to catch the breath that knocked out of her like a fist to her chest. The mixture toppled, spilling. His smile lingered in her mind, changing from thrilling to cloying, and she realized she'd had her first experience of second sight.

She had chosen the spell entitled safe travel in hopes of encouraging the man's spirit to hunger for new adventures and doubly count him protected, in case her duty to him was not yet done.

Instead of completing a charmed concoction, she'd been hit with her first presage.

Until that moment, breath caught and sitting stunned with her hand to her beating heart, Breanne had denied the notion that her linkage to Ashlon might not have ended with his returned health.

A thrill of fear gripped her.

Chapter Eleven

"The man was beheaded by sword, the story went, for a minor crime such as theft, or something of the like," Ashlon said above their trotting horses. "And the raconteur swore on his mother's bones that upon the thief's head being severed, a young and beautiful woman emerged from the uproarious crowd, placed a chalice under the neck and gathered the dripping blood."

"Horrid," Quinlan said.

"Worse, the woman drank the blood, all the while staring into the witness's eyes."

"Ashlon," Quinlan scoffed. "You cannot have believed such a gruesome tale as all that."

"I hadn't reason *not* to believe its validity."

"But you are a learned man, trained and schooled in such an esteemed and unique way. For you to believe the story and then use it as example for all of Ireland to be compared with, I find surprising."

A spiky range of mountains broke through the rolling green landscape.

"It is a sad truth, I fear, that most of England and likely other areas, view your country and people as wild, and godless, capable of inhuman violence. Until you met me on the road that day, I considered the same idea. Had little reason not to."

"Ludicrous," Quinlan said. "A woman, or a man for

147

that matter, drinking blood from a beheaded corpse. Who would say such a thing and be believed?"

"A monk swearing to have just come from travels there at the behest of the crown." Ashlon's pride only slightly stung. Thinking back and now knowing these peoples, ludicrous described the notion precisely. "I am glad to have been proven so wrong, Quinlan, on my word."

"I'd say more than glad considering the state I came upon you in." Quinlan chuckled. "Clothes muddied and tattered, face gaunt and wanton."

"A sight, was I?"

"More. You looked like you'd tangled with the wrong giant."

Ashlon laughed.

"You must have guts of iron to have come to us with such sordid expectations," Quinlan said. "Obviously, it concerns me not, is business between Niall and you alone, but I must admit I am curious after your tale. What was it that sent you here, if I may be so bold as to inquire, worth facing blood drinking heathens?"

Quinlan slowed his horse to a walk. Ashlon followed suit. Their morning tour of the area could use a short rest.

He used their dismount near a sconce of birches as an opportunity to find his answer. Easily, he could offer none and Quinlan would leave the issue be. But Ashlon felt secrecy now could impinge on trust he might need later. He would need that trust intact if he were to gain contact with the Lady Breanne.

"You've likely heard some version of the truth by now," Ashlon said. "A community as closely united as yours must have drawn conclusions."

Quinlan shrugged.

"The truth of it is that I am formerly of the Knights of Solomon and before his death, my mentor, the Grand

Master bade me here. Any of us not directly captured, accused of heresy, and tortured to confess such, were given instruction on where to safely go. Mine brought me here." Ashlon's throat tightened and he swallowed.

"The Knights of Solomon. I knew it." Quinlan stared openly at him.

"Aye." Knights no more.

"But you are not surprised. No other has spoken of the supposition to me; in fact, I believe I am the only one to rightly suspect your origins. How are you not surprised?"

Ashlon tied his borrowed gelding to a low limb. "You betrayed your impression firstly, by asking for my help in courting the Lady O'Donnell and secondly, only now in reference to my unique schooling."

"Aye, I can see I did." Quinlan attached his lead near Ashlon's on the branch. "I arrived in France a year after the inquisition began. Horrific tales I heard, and unlike the gory one you just shared, I don't doubt the validity of these."

Ashlon's nightmares' flames rekindled in his mind. His skin sweated and he had to shake his head to keep composed.

"Yes, I'm sure they were. What business had you in France?"

"I studied at the University of Paris, a wide variety of subjects, none of which held my interest long and few that will aid me in my current needs."

Ashlon matched his polite smile with his own, grateful for the man's smooth transition away from hell's edge. "A matter we shall see to then," he said.

The agreed upon exchange for Ashlon relating his most relevant knowledge on women would be Quinlan's returned instruction on all subjects Irish. It wasn't that Ashlon any longer felt out of his element. It was a way for him to learn Gaelic and better know his environment should it become dangerous.

"First, Master Blake, we must consider the subject. If you please, relay all you know of Breanne O'Donnell." A surge went through his body when he spoke the words. Anticipation. Under the guise of servitude, he would gain insight to the mysterious woman who had saved, and now snubbed him.

Ashlon leaned against the tree trunk and chewed dried meat. Conceivably, if he knew of her better, he could not only win her confidence, but her interest in his cause. For the more he contemplated his next move, the more her name came to mind. It was as though events were leading him to her.

"Where to begin?" Quinlan raked a hand through his hair and plucked a strand of grass. "Breanne and I were childhood friends, well, moreover she followed me like the plague until I gave in and paid mind to her and my sister, Rose. She's quiet when she's wary of you, but warm and adoring once you've won her.

"Rose and I were orphaned during an English assault. The clan pressed them back, but my father died in battle and my mother in protecting her babes. We were fostered at the keep, under my uncle's care, then among Niall's elite warriors.

"When my uncle died raiding cattle to feed the clan three winters later, Niall kept us on. He is who I thank for my opportunities abroad, as well."

"He is a good man, a king better than any I've known." Not greedy and imperious as his experience showed most nobles to be.

"Aye, that he is and would even do well as Ard-Righ, Ulster's high king, but the O'Neill's legacy of fearsome rulers will not see him there and Edward Bruce has an eye for it." Quinlan shifted, tossed the shredded blade of grass. "Might we ride?"

Ashlon didn't question the abrupt turn of mood, attributing it to the unnerving topic. Women were strange draws and his years of exile were the only blame for becoming intimate in their ways. Perhaps returning to horseback would help ease Quinlan back to their subject.

A few galloping strides brought them around a low hill and in view of the township.

"Breanne, my sister and I," Quinlan said, "became constant playmates and confidantes and, I daresay, when my sister recently related Breanne's affection for me, I was shocked."

"You did not know she cared for you?"

"I knew she loved me well, aye. I did not know that she loved me in a way such as a woman does a man. What I took for sisterly affection, she held as wifely." Each word chucked forth with the hit of hooves to earth.

"Do you tell me, Quinlan, that the Lady Breanne is in love with you?"

"Aye," Quinlan said. "Rose blasted me with the admission one night after I had apparently rebuffed Breanne, and Rose reached her sisterly and friendly threshold. She hollered to the rafters about my dimwittedness and Breanne's closed mouthedness.

"And your sister made clear that the Lady Breanne is in love with you?" Ashlon couldn't have heard right, understood correctly. Not after the way she had looked at him last night, not when her lips had awakened such a hunger inside of him.

"Aye. Apparently, Breanne has held such affection for me for years and I had been blind to it. I never thought of her romantically. Until now. And my first attempts have been nothing short of dreadful. I blame my inexperience."

Dreadful. Ashlon shouldn't feel happy about that.

He had no claim to the lady or desire of her aside from the physical. Certainly, he could not offer any honorable intentions for her, being an outsider, the country-less knight, youngest landless son with naught to offer in marriage. Nothing yet, he amended. Once this business was concluded with the missing chest, he would rectify the other less significant affairs.

"Breanne is the only child of Ula and Jock O'Donnell," Quinlan continued, unaware of Ashlon's regard. "Her father died as mine did, but in protecting Niall's life instead a year previous. The English were a plague on us for some time back then. Jock was a good man, was named as Niall's successor nary a month before his death. The whole of the clan felt his loss. I remember my mother crying terribly upon hearing the news."

Their horses returned to an easy walk as Quinlan retraced other lineages and verity about Breanne, all of which bore little on who she truly was. Quinlan seemed to be circling the subject like a bird of prey, staying safely outside of what Ashlon had asked for. If he were to help the man, he needed to know her likes, dislikes, habits. Her dreams. When would the man come to the heart of it?

"She favors the lad Danny quite well. He is the only son of the Lady Isolde and Ferris Maguire, the clan's Brehon Law advisor." They approached the tuath from the north.

"What is a Brehon advisor's function?"

"Brehon Law," Quinlan said, "refers to our laws that govern man's punishment for crime, as well as other civil matters such as property rights, debt repayment, marriage contract. It would behoove you to familiarize yourself with the main points, which you may through Ferris Maguire, if you would like to petition joining the clan as a free man."

Somehow, the conversation seemed to be turning in his education's direction. Consciously or unconsciously, Quinlan had begun relating rather than revealing.

Three separate properties gained Ashlon's notice due to their impressive size. Two of the three were almost as large as the O'Donnell keep and combined with it, all lay in four points. A smart tactic, to surround the vulnerable with stronger keeps and spread the clan's power against attacks.

"Are all of these O'Donnell holdings?" he asked and brought his gelding up short at the top of the hill. Rolling green spread the valley below, craggy rock, heather laden mounds breaking up the smooth lay.

"Nay, that there is houses O'Neills, though not of Niall of the Seven Hostages as Niall himself boasts blood from. And that southern keep is MacSweeney. You may recall Shane MacSweeney among Niall's warriors, his family is the one and same MacSweeney, though he lives at the main."

"And the last?" Ashlon recognized the clan head and referred to the smallest.

"That as well is O'Donnell property, though only a handful of persons take residence there now. It is Breanne's and until she marries, it lays virtually empty."

"That doesn't seem a safe or clever course. It leaves the clan vulnerable, does it not?"

"Aye, I don't doubt it is among Niall's reasons in dictating Breanne marry by Beltane." Quinlan nodded absently.

While interesting, they'd tarried from the original issue. Breanne. Ashlon needed more detail about her, and more importantly, an opening for his own request: to get a missive to the lady using absolute discretion.

"It will be yours then, if you win her."

"Aye," Quinlan said and straightened a bit. "I hadn't considered the ramifications of that. Think you it too forward of me to inquire as to its security concerns?"

"That would depend on the lady herself. How would you describe her temperament?" Ashlon resisted smiling wide. He had done it. He had managed to redirect the young man's attention back to where they both needed it to be.

"Breanne would probably defend it herself before allowing me to see to it. And as resistant as she's been toward my affections, I warrant she'd like anyone else to handle the job." Quinlan inhaled loudly and smacked his thigh. "You've just given me a brilliant idea, Ashlon."

Ashlon's brow rose and gathered. He didn't like the look on his new friend's face as he chewed whatever notion popped into his young head. It looked best not to encourage him by speaking.

"There are considerable details to be worked out, but it is possible and might make all parties involved happy. You see, Breanne would be right to wish another to protect her holdings as I have little training or experience and will admit even less interest in it. It has been my favorite threat to tease her with for years, that I might join Niall's forces and—."

"Master Blake—Quinlan, forgive my interruption but what in Christ's name are you attempting to say?" he said.

"That you offer Breanne your services," Quinlan said, unperturbed by Ashlon's force. "Your knight's training and experience is perfect for the holding, vulnerable as you yourself noted. Acting as her sentinel would be a means for you to possess income and further a request to join the clan should you choose."

"Why do you not make the same offer and simply see to manning it yourself?" Eventual residence was an option to consider. Immediate actions in doing so were not.

"As I've said, she would not grant me that role. She loathes the trade her father died honorably for. She views a man's duty to protect his family should reach no further, that soldiers are a necessary evil of life."

"But you would not be that soldier." Ashlon pointed to the obvious and watched Quinlan squirm. "You would be seeing to her interests, relieving her of what is likely a dislikeable duty for which she has no skill."

"There, you are mistaken. Breanne can protect herself well and I'd prefer not to divulge the nature of my confidence that she will reject the idea were I to offer it. If my courtship had gone better thus far, I might say otherwise. I can see, though, that you are not convinced."

What had the young man done to so offend the woman and what could he mean in saying she could protect herself? He couldn't ask. Quinlan's clamped and sealed mouth looked more than determined and he would not meet Ashlon's eyes.

It wasn't that the idea was bad. He liked it, in fact, and that was what worried him. He couldn't afford to get attached to this place or people when he might be forced to forever abandon both in seeing the chest to its resting place. The danger therein might require that he leave, never to look back, not only in the chest's placement, but in insuring its secrecy also.

So, it was no use investing himself overly much into this community until he knew he was safe to do so. Safe for the chest, for the clan, for him. The loss of his entire belief system, of what had become his family—he would not endure the kind again.

Better to continue his strategy, get the missive to the lady, gain a secret meeting and then her help. All other themes, he would do better to keep at arm's length.

"The day has gained on us, I fear," Ashlon said, ending the cold silence, urging his steed forward. Quinlan nodded sharply and rode, as well.

"May we continue on the morrow, Sir Sinclair?" His voice was tight, shoulders squared.

"I look forward to it." Ashlon didn't smile, kept his gaze on the keep.

"You have my gratitude, Sir." Quinlan bowed his head tersely then heeled his horse into a full gallop.

Ashlon followed him, though not closely.

* * * *

The portent replayed in her head over again, intermittently, throughout the day. Breanne couldn't help it. The thrill of getting her first definite second sight contrasted sharply with what it had revealed. Neither Rose, nor any of the other ladies, noticed her deficient attention span, thankfully, and chatted about the day's work and Ula's upcoming nuptials.

"The O'Doherty clansmen arrive in three days time, O'Neills the day after. We will be bursting with bodies and I fear we haven't enough stock to cover the event, let alone the days before it." Ula didn't look nervous at all. She looked thrilled with her open smile and jubilant shrugs. "I cannot believe it, ladies, the Ard-Righ, coming for my wedding. I know he's family to Niall and that he favors us, but to actually show. It is a compliment and I do mark it shows approval."

They all nodded in varying degrees. "Of course, he approves Ula," Isolde said and patted her longtime friend's knee between needle threads. "You've mourned your Jock well long enough and what better man to marry than the one you lost's dearest friend. All approve the match. And don't forget the MacFearsons may come, as well"

"Don't be sure of that, Isolde," Rose said. "Danny's

heart could very well be broken. He may have to marry Breanne instead."

Isolde's hand went to her heart. Ula and she exchanged a warm look.

"I admit it, I am taken with your son, Issy," Ula said. "Can you forgive me for it?"

Chuckles rippled over the gather of women. Breanne smiled. The boy was a born flirt. She promised herself to seek him out soon. Cooping herself up in the Grianan had kept her from their daily visits. Her mother and Rose loved it here and though each day got easier, Breanne still longed for her old routine and would rather be keeping books than stitching.

She'd rather be attempting another presage. Again she went over the details. She'd chanted, she'd mixed, she'd scried the mirror. She'd envisioned him walking away, holding his belongings, no, a chest where his belongings resided. He'd walked up the north road on a clear bright day. The ground and hills looked lush with summer's overgrowth, the air buzzed with its hum around his figure. She'd wished him safety, wished him well and to continue his journey, seeing it to an end, on his way when he stopped, turned, smiled.

The smile shocked her. It was full and warm and his eyes looked at her as though in person, as though he knew her, saw her. The image rushed forth then, swirling and readjusting. His smile was the same, the chest he still held, but it was night and he was not smiling at her, but at it. A shot of fright ran through her and she looked up, around him. The full moon glowed yellow and rings of color hazed the azure sky. The fright turned to clenching panic.

Ashlon held his hand out. She knew she was there with him when she recognized the edge of her sapphire cloak pooling before her. Then he spoke—"Breanne, can you hear me?"

She opened her eyes. Rose and Ula's faces were above her, hands fanned her face. She'd fainted.

"Are you well, Breanne, can you hear me?" Rose looked angry with worry, her brow squished, lips pinched.

"Aye, I hear you. What happened?" Silly question she knew the answer to.

"You toppled over of a sudden like you'd seen a ghost. You said 'Don't go in' in a great shout in the middle of my very hilarious story and fell over flat on your back. Now, what's all this and are you well?"

She'd never seen Rose so forceful and serious. Her mother sighed and gasped in turns, nodding at Rose's words, petting Breanne's brow. Breanne sat up, swaying the slightest bit when her sight warbled. She forced a weak smile, hoping it would stop all the gawking and fussing. The terror of those last instants lingered in her belly.

She needed to see him. He must leave Tir Conaill and no doubt of it because she knew down to her bones that his life was in danger if he stayed.

"Rhiannon, fetch the nearest available man you find. She needs be carried to her room," Rose said. Ula nodded.

"No, I promise, I am well. I can't say what happened, but I assure you I am fine now."

"You've succumbed to stress, without question and I mean to see you rested."

Breanne didn't argue when Rose pierced her with her angry eyes. She'd scared her friend, who was with child and sensitive for it. Arguing would gain nothing but more scolds. Besides, she'd much rather be back in her room.

Rhiannon returned as Rose helped Breanne to her

feet, with Quinlan Blake in tow. Breanne's stomach sank like a stone in water. The only other advantage of hiding from Ashlon Sinclair was that it also kept her from Quinlan. The beaming smile on his handsome face practically screamed his feelings otherwise.

With easy grace, Quinlan scooped her into his arms. His breathing stayed easy and he might as well have carried a sack of flour for all the exertion he showed.

"My lady, I am sorry to hear you do not feel well. I offer my services to use, as you need. Make any requests to better your health." He exited the Grianan into the dinner hall and went to the corridor of stairs so efficiently Breanne didn't have time to protest his attentions.

"Thank you, but I assure you I am well. I need only rest and only do so at Rose and my mother's behest." Was he taking two gallant stairs at a time? Breanne forced herself not to roll her eyes. She would be laid into her bed and given privacy soon enough to stew and eye-roll over her misfortune.

Quinlan led a trail of ladies and only the last glanced back at Ashlon Sinclair in step behind her. A single wink had her giggling and running ahead, too shy to look back for him. Ashlon paused at the top stair, in shadow, and watched the entourage enter the last door to the right after the potential couple. The whole scene looked very much like any newly wedded couple on their way to consummate tender vows.

Ashlon didn't like the view one bit and worse, knew he should count it as a blessing. Quinlan had an opportunity to make a good impression on Breanne, whom he desired. Breanne got fussed over, which in his experience, ladies adored. And Ashlon got a chance to act on his plot.

But when he saw Breanne cradled in his new friend's arms, something angry pricked in his chest. Jealousy. He recalled her mouth parting, her eyes open with wonder as heat pulled her to him. The image caused a weight to slide into his gut. What fate had Jacques sent him to? What would wanting this woman cost him before it was finished?

The door closed heavily, sucking the gaggle of noise inside the room. Surreptitiously, Ashlon stepped forward. There were three doors on either side of the corridor and he didn't have much time to abscond into one and conceal there until the gentleman and ladies left her.

Ashlon skipped over the first set, favoring proximity to her. Were those brown eyes warming for Quinlan as they had for him? He shook the useless thought away. He had no right to think of her so. And he'd be the last to repeat his first offense in kissing her, or doing worse, again.

The laws and customs here might vary from the norm he knew, but he had no doubt that a lady compromised and ruined was a universal wrong he'd be held accountable for. He didn't want to contemplate just what punishment such a crime warranted in these parts and took care to tread softly.

He knocked only loud enough for an occupant to hear. He prayed one would not because an answer would end his venture. None answered. Ashlon tried the knob. Locked.

He continued on, his heartbeat thumped in his ears louder than his footsteps or the muffled voices past the door. At the second door he tried the knob first. Locked.

The last door, his final chance. Ashlon looked skyward and pleaded the heavens to grant him an additional boon. He put his sweating palm to the metal and turned. Locked.

In a whoosh, he exhaled as his anticipation fell to keen disappointment. What had looked to be a perfect opportunity to seek her out unnoticed proved false. The voices had softened and his gut told him they would soon leave her. He stepped to the window slit at the end of the corridor and chewed his thumb.

There must be another way. There must be another person he could enlist, trust to get her a note, unread and unspoken of. Quinlan looked to be less a candidate after their ride, leastwise not in a timely manner, which was exactly what Ashlon needed right now.

Each day that passed with the chest missing seemed to lessen its chances of being found. If it had been taken, whoever took it would be farther and farther away until finding their trail would take a miracle.

The book lay tucked under his mantle, no longer foreign, but a comfortable weight. Inside laid the note he wrote to her nights ago. His final hope was to linger where he stood and attempt to slide it under her door.

Ashlon dug inside his mantle and retrieved the volume. He opened it to the page he needed Breanne's help deciphering and plucked the folded and sealed parchment. He snapped the book closed as the door opened, three ladies scrambling out at once. He bowed to them as they left down the corridor. Quinlan and two others remained, his sister and the Lady Ula. All three could be heard giving turns at instructing Breanne to rest.

Holding the book behind him, Ashlon leaned forward and peered through the ajar door. He saw nothing other then three backs and a small table near the doorframe. If he stepped softly and slid the note in, he would only have to walk away and hope she found it. It was the safest and most effective option, certainly. Once Quinlan left, he had no excuse to remain without him.

"Is she all right then?"

Ashlon's breath caught. He straightened and faced the boy who'd asked him. "I believe so. I await Master Blake now." He covered the note with his hand held to his thigh.

"Seamus told me she passed out and hit her head. Is that what happened?" the boy asked, hushed. He peered through the door, then back at Ashlon.

"I cannot say. I was not present."

"Do you want me to call him for you?"

"Call who?"

"Quinlan. If you need him and you're concerned about disrupting, I can call him for you. They won't pay me any mind," the boy said, his voice rising.

"No." Ashlon waved his elbow. "Thank you, but I will happily wait. It is no urgent matter."

"What's that there?" His voice returned to a hush and his eyes lit on the edge of paper Ashlon's large hand didn't hide, eyes bright with interest.

"Personal business. A letter," Ashlon said.

"For Quinlan? Are you certain I cannot call him for you?"

"No, thank you, but the two are unrelated and as I said, I will wait."

"Why do you wait here and not below if it is not so urgent?" he asked and cocked his head at the simple puzzle.

Ashlon smiled at the rascal. "Curiosity, I suppose."

"You're not worried then? She looked well?"

"Aye, she did and no, I am not."

The boy went to the window, shifting his weight like an exaggerated trudge with each step. Ashlon promptly tucked the book under his shirt back, wondering what the boy was building the courage to ask when all of his other questions had come so easily.

"Are you Sir Sinclair, a real knight, from England?"

he said, fingering the drapery.

"I am. And who might you be?"

"Daniel Maquire." He stood straight and shoved his hand out to Ashlon.

"It is a pleasure to make your acquaintance, Master Maguire." He shook the proffered hand firmly. "You must be the son of Lady Isolde and Master Ferris, friend of Lady Breanne. Your good reputation precedes you."

Daniel beamed and nodded at Ashlon. "As does yours, Sir Sinclair. May I call you Ashlon?"

"I think you should and what name do you prefer Master Maguire?"

"Danny is what Bree calls me. And me mum. But the men call me Daniel. I like both." Daniel shrugged. "Is that your sword then, I mean, your knight's sword?"

Ashlon choked on a laugh. "Yes, it was given to me when I became a Knight of Solomon some fifteen years ago. My master and mentor, Jacques De Molay, bestowed it upon me in a secret knighting ceremony."

Daniel's eyes widened, but held locked on the sword's hilt and Ashlon saw opportunity materialize.

"Daniel, I wonder if I may ask an errand of you, important and I must admit clandestine business that I feel you may do well at?" Daniel looked at him. "In exchange, if you find it worthy, I offer my sword. Not to keep as your own, mind you, but that you may practice in arms, using it under my tutelage."

Daniel clapped a knee before he could finish and nodded vigorously. Ashlon glanced at the door to ensure the three backs had not turned to retreat. He showed the note. "I need this missive to reach the Lady Breanne. I cannot over emphasize its importance and its delivery would need to go unnoticed by any other eyes save yours or mine."

Daniel reached for the note, eyes narrowed, mouth

firm. "You can trust me, Ashlon. This will not be my first secret task and you have my word of honor that I will see it delivered."

"If anyone should come upon this note—."

"I shall die before they pull it from my clutches."

"Dear lord, no. Die not for my sake, good man. But if any should place hands or eyes on its contents, will you say not from where it came or if possible to whom you take it?"

Daniel had the folded square tucked inside his shirt, stuffed through the neckline, within seconds. He licked two fingers, slapped them to his arm and crossed his heart. A final curt nod apparently closed their negotiations.

Ashlon ruffled the boy's hair and nodded back. "Good day to you, Master Daniel," he said and bowed.

Daniel bowed, as well, then Ashlon returned to the main hall. Quinlan, Lady Rose and Lady Ula followed shortly and Ashlon forced himself not to await the boy. He didn't like having to behave so secretly. It struck him as dishonest and he longed for his life to return to honor and honesty rather than constant distrust and furtiveness.

Chapter Twelve

"Danny, is that you?" Breanne asked, sitting up in bed. When she got no reply outside of her closed door, she readied to go to it, but still found herself woozy.

She didn't know which she despised more, being carried to bed or being left there with strict instructions not to make an appearance for another day. Her mother had assigned her newest handmaid to tend to Breanne and if it wasn't Danny she heard, then mayhap the girl?

"Whoever is out there, please simply peer in as I canno' get up," she said. Where was that blasted cat when she needed help? Off on a binge in the woods, no doubt.

The door creaked open and Danny's tousled head poked through. "Hello there."

"Danny! You half killed me with fright. Get in here this minute and give me a hug."

Danny swung the door closed behind him and plopped onto the mattress next to her.

"Who were you speaking to in the corridor?" Breanne smoothed his hair and he smacked at her hand.

"Speaking to?" His eyes went from her face to his hands. "To myself, I suppose."

"Are you sure? No one else was about? No maid, perchance, that you might have thought funny to turn the other way and send to another room?"

"Nay, Breanne, I swear it, just myself outside your door. I wasn't sure I should be bothering you and was deciding with my mind if I should knock or come back another hour."

"Well, I am glad you chose to come in over leaving. Not ten minutes abed and I'm already thinking up ways to leave it."

"If you feel well, I see no reason for you to stay in it." He gave her a deep shrug. "And especially if you might have somewhere important to be and then what would you do? Stay abed and make others wait?"

"What are you about, Daniel Maguire?" She could read it all over his face that he was up to something. "Out with it."

Danny scrunched his face and handed Breanne a note. She took it from him, earning another deep shrug.

"What is this?" she asked, but didn't need an answer when the paper fell open, the seal broken. Quickly, she read the scribbled contents:

Lady Breanne, Though I have already received more than deserved, I must beg your assistance yet again. The issue I seek help with does not concern my health, which is good, and which I thank you for. I may not yet explain or give detail, but do assure you is a matter of life and death and that you alone may offer the aid I need. Please consider meeting me by cover of night in the location you last placed me. I additionally believe to have information useful to your purpose, as well. I dare not divulge more for both our sakes and will await you.

No signature was needed for Breanne to know who wrote it or its meaning. Recognition lit in her the moment her eyes landed on the script. She breathed out and looked at Danny.

"When did he leave it with you? When did you read it, Danny?"

"He gave it to me before the others left." His gaze returned to his hands, fumbling with a thread. "I don't know what got into me. I read it, telling myself I'd only take a peek. A poor conspirator I'm making." He stood and walked a circle, heel to toe around the floor rug's pattern. "But I dinna understand its meaning. And I won't tell another living soul, I promise you that." He stopped, sat, and plunked his face into his hands. "I am sorry, Breanne."

Breanne half smiled at his pitiful countenance. "I know you meant no harm. It is not so serious a matter, Danny. You have not wronged me." Her words sounded calm in her ears above the rush of thumping blood in her veins. "With the recent talk of marriage about, I suspect the man who spoke to you is only protecting my virtue by keeping it secret." She was more than thankful Danny didn't read English well yet. She didn't know what she would do to Ashlon Sinclair if he put the boy at risk.

Danny seemed appeased and lifted his head to smile at her. "Have you chosen yet, Breanne?"

"I wish I had. But I've not had much time to receive attentions or give them on the matter."

"Is it true that Quinlan favors you?"

"Aye. It seems he does. And the scribe Gannon O'Shannon, as well. But, I fear I have not yet spent enough time with either to know my best match." Her head began to hurt and she laid back into the mound of pillows forced on her by Rose and her mother. Quinlan had supervised, his gaze uncomfortably warm.

"I almost forgot," Danny said and suddenly stood. He reached deep into the belly of his shirt, crouched over, and pulled out a small wrapped bundle. With a flourish, Danny handed her the gift.

Refusing to give in to the pain in her head or the pound of her heart, Breanne smiled and pulled the tiny blue string. The misshapen corners of cloth fell away, exposing a necklace of leather attached through the center hole of a shining green cloc cosanca. Breanne gasped.

"I found it yesterday down in the grove. Do you like it? Does it not look like a fairy might have made it and left it for me to find and give to you?"

Breanne's eyes and nose stung. She swallowed down the knot of emotion. "It's beautiful, Danny. Prettier than any I've seen. Thank you."

"You're welcome." He sat at her feet.

She put the amulet around her neck and pressed it to her chest. "How does it look?"

"It looks nice." He stood. "Well, I best get downstairs or my mother will wonder if the elves stole me." He put a hand sidelong to his mouth. "That's what she always says."

"All right then, Danny. If you see a young handmaid, will you send her in the right direction? I'm getting right hungry doing all this laying about like a princess."

Danny laughed and agreed, but left like the wind.

Breanne read the note again, but felt no better. She couldn't meet him tonight. After the spell, her mother would have the maid underfoot and Rose promised to check in. She dismissed the idea of returning a note as soon as it entered her mind. Too risky. She loved the boy to the world's end, but he was right about being a poor conspirator.

She wouldn't enlist him again, shouldn't have when she asked him to lookout, but she hadn't had another choice. The guilt and worry simply wasn't worth it and now he'd proved himself a normal child with ample curiosity and little fear of life's follies. Breanne would have to impress upon Sinclair the same for all their better interest.

But how, when remembering the simple foresight had caused a collapse and left her more guarded than ever? A tonic would do, so long as she didn't make the poor girl sleep for days. And then to slip away, perhaps a cloaking incantation?

It was a lot to hope for, but worth a try if she could reach the cave and warn the daft knight to leave Tir Conaill and not look back. She saw his image again, walking away from her and shook it off like a chill. She couldn't yet replay the prophecy and didn't like the ache it weighed on her chest.

Her duty to him was not yet over, regardless of her resistance and denial. Were he here, she would demand an explanation from Heremon's own mouth. She would ask the sage why she should protect Sinclair and moreover, how? She could barely blend herbs for his fever, let alone arm him with magickal defenses.

And even with explicit warning to him, he had ignored her aid and come to sit in the lion's mouth. If a single man in the tuath knew of his presence that night, prone and unconscious or not, he'd change from honored guest to suspect prisoner within a blink.

Breanne punched a fist into the deep blankets. "Bloodthirsty. The whole lot of them."

A soft knock aggravated her worn nerves.

"Lady Ula sent me to tend you," a brisk voice said through the door. She didn't wait for Breanne to answer and kicked the door open to accommodate a large, steaming pot. Following her, two men brought in a small bed and crammed it into the far corner, shoving her trestle desk and chest of drawers out of the way.

The woman placed the large pot on the rug and helped Breanne sit up without explanation. "Steady there," she said and shot looks to the men assisting her.

When they soon left without so much as a nod, the woman plunked Breanne's feet into the water, the privacy of her exposed calves well kept.

Though the blissful hot water sent warm shivers to her bones, she didn't like being treated so abruptly. "I appreciate my mother's thoughtfulness, but please inform her that I need a minimum of care."

The woman put a hand up. "No, m'lady. I am here to tend to you. Food and wine will arrive shortly. In the meanwhile, rest and soak." As she spoke, she straightened the dishevel left by the men, then sat upright, hands in lap and silent until another knock came.

Along with a laden tray, she brought in a footstool, delivered by whom Breanne could not tell, unable to see past the large sturdy back of the woman. "What is your name, please?"

"Erlene, m'lady. Eat this," she said, then took a seat on the stool before the now cool pot of water. She pulled one foot out, dried it and rubbed the entire sole in vigorous circles.

Breanne gripped the mattress for fear of falling off and almost moaned at the painful pleasure in her feet. Erlene's arms flexed, but her brow was smooth and even. "Eat."

She did. And while Erlene's tending put her body at full ease, every passing hour rubbed tension back in. She should have sent Danny with a responding note, nosy or not. Now what would she do? Ask Erlene to turn her back while she cast and mixed, then offered her a nice bitter bedtime drink?

Feet done and thrust back into bed, Breanne finished the meal and wine under careful watch. Was it too much to hope Erlene would see the tray back down? Aye. Erlene sat on the cot just past dark, freed two wool socks from her bulky calves and lay down. It was.

"Don't fret, m'lady, I'm a light sleeper and will wake should you need anything at all," she said louder than necessary.

Did she think Breanne deaf in her fatigue? Breanne rolled her eyes and did not reply. She tossed and turned and stared at the slit of starry sky, not caring at all if her loud thumps and sighs bothered Erlene.

Would he be there now? How many hours would he wait until giving up, disappointed? She cursed herself for caring that he might be offended by her absence.

She told herself it was better this way, that he would finally heed her warning and leave, perhaps going this very night directly from the cave. Hard to believe he'd lain there prone and bare, her hand on his heart while her own pounded so hard she could first only feel its pulse, almost a fortnight ago.

Breanne rubbed her hand over the coverlet to rid the memory of his smooth heat from it. Would she ever touch a man and feel so moved again? She closed her eyes and let her mind relive what it would about him.

Erlene's snore came so strident, a low growl of her nose into the stillness, that Breanne almost shrieked. Her startled pulse soon became a trill when she saw chance's gift to her. Without delay, she swung her legs to the floor and tiptoed to her trunk. She set up her altar in the corner where Erlene's vision would be partially obstructed.

It was difficult to be quiet in her hurry to cast and run. She located the page she'd earlier planned, then she dressed. Shoes on, she went over the chant again, leaving off mixing the herbs the sleeping maid couldn't drink. For luck, she rubbed the amulet Danny gave her and chanted and cut with her athame in the dark.

Finished with her fourth whisper of the incantation, Breanne braved a look at the snoring Erlene. Her serious face was slack and peaceful. Breanne slipped out with a long look at the stuffed figure in her bed. It looked good enough in the dark and so long as no one approached it, would work.

She put the hood of her cloak low on her head and stole down the stairs. The air was quiet. The neat line of pallets on the far wall showed no movements. In a breath, she moved to the kitchen and out of the stone keep.

She gulped the cold night air in as she paused and peered about the bailey. The moon was descending and she guessed the hour around two in the morning. She prayed he was there, kissed the cloc cosanca around her neck and raced to the gate. The wind billowed her cloak, despite her pulling it close.

Outside of the gate, she ran, skirts lifted, elbows high, down the narrow path she'd worn so well. The copse of pine and oak trees grew tall in the night sky as she sped there. Her eyes felt wet in the cold air, her nostrils icy.

Once inside nature's sanctuary, Breanne slowed to a fast walk. She cut through brush, leapt the small stream relying on instinct to feel her way back to the cave, back to him. Instead of tiring, her body zinged with anticipation. A hundred phrases tossed about in her head, tests of what she'd say. But none of them seemed the right words and the single prayer returned. Let him be there.

She didn't think about Erlene. She forgot her wish for Heremon. All she remembered was him, waiting, the heartbeat, the danger. Breanne stepped past an oak and slowed, the entrance in her view. She paused a moment, concealed in shadow to listen to the trees.

Nothing. Not a twig's snap nor a leave's rustle sounded apart or amiss from the night's soothing song. With a deep breath, she stepped into the moonlight, telling her heart to steady before it made a fool of her.

She moved the foliage to allow room for her to pass and ducked inside. There he was, legs askance, sword ready to kill. Breanne stopped and met the shadow of his face, her heart tight and high.

Ashlon lowered and sheathed his sword. She had come. He couldn't believe it, had just given up to leave, and there she was glowing and panting and making his mind swim. He couldn't speak for it, and stepped forward, his hand out to take hers.

Breanne gasped, he stopped. He didn't want to frighten her. He should reassure her, but couldn't speak past the lump of emotion in his throat. She'd come.

In the hours dragging by in wait, he'd realized just how stupid a request he'd made of her. To ask a lady to come to him in the dark of night, alone, on matters of life and death. Preposterous to think she could or would.

Then he had damned himself for entrusting the note to the boy, eager and capable or not. He promised from that point forward to involve no other life in his quest, save his own. And that included hers. She was young and generous and on the verge of beginning a new, wedded life. He had no right to expect her help. He'd decided to find another way.

Then she had arrived and now she stood, her breath calming, but her eyes revealing equal emotion, unmasked. He forced himself not to stare at the high valley of cleavage rising and falling, pressing against her gown with each inhale and exhale. Even without looking directly at them, they shone in the slit of light.

"Thank you for coming, Lady Breanne."

"I had no choice." Her voice shook and he thought her angry with him.

"As did I. You are the only person I may turn to in a matter— ."

"Of life and death, yes, as I read. What you do not realize, however, Sir Sinclair, is your tactic to ensure I take your note as grave, will prove true. Your life is in danger."

"Aye."

"Aye?" She gasped, searched his face. "And yet you stay? You are more fool than I credited you for." She turned away.

"Please, don't leave." He reached for her, but she stopped and faced him on her own.

"I don't intend to. Leastwise, not until you've left Tir Conaill. Mark my words, Sir Sinclair, someone means you harm. Heremon's murder may not be your design, but I've no doubt now is related to your presence. Whoever poisoned him will come for you."

Ashlon saw now she was not angry, but impassioned, trying to convince him and shaken by it. This was not the reaction he'd anticipated. He'd thought to explain himself, calm her ire at his audacity in sending the note, then enlist her help with the text. Once deciphered, they could be on their separate ways. But she appeared genuinely afeared for his life.

"I cannot depart Ireland or here until I've discovered where Heremon hid an item I traveled with when he found me."

"And I urge you to replace whatever you've lost at the nearest port's market. If you stay, you will court your own demise."

"The item is irreplaceable and be not overmuch concerned with what I court. I am capable of protecting my own neck and have utmost experience in it."

She crossed her arms. "If you will not leave on your own, I will be forced to assist you. Do not doubt that I will report your connection to Heremon's death if it means ridding your welcome here."

"It won't. Lady Breanne, I asked you here to the same end you seek. I will leave, but cannot until my belonging is found. If you wish me gone, you can be key to my efficient departure. You can help me find what I require."

"I don't see how. Heremon left me with little to no information beyond seeing you well. I know of no hidden belongings." Her arms remained hugged to her and her words came more softly.

Ashlon pulled the book from under his tunic, slowly so she would not think the movement suspect. "In the room you bade me remain while I healed, I found this. Immediately I sensed its importance, if not to me, to the man who saved me."

Breanne's eyes landed on the book and widened. Her mouth fell open and her arms shot out to take it. He let her.

"Thief," she said, running a hand over the surface, turning it over. "You took this from him."

"Not from him, from his residence, yes. I felt compelled to keep it with me, with no ill intention. Were he alive, I swear to you, it would be returned with severe apology. But somewhere, somehow, when I found it, I...."

"You lie."

"I do not lie. I did not feel I'd stolen."

Her eyes darted from his eyes to his mouth and back to the book. "Did you know Heremon was already dead then? Did you see something? What have you kept from me?"

"Kept from you? I've hardly laid eyes on you to have kept anything from you. To all of your questions, I gave honest answers."

"Yet you take from a dead man, who died protecting you." Her eyes were narrowed on him.

Ashlon raked his hair and stepped forward. "I have no memory of his death, that I swear. I admit, though, that at no point did I feel wrong in taking this volume." As he spoke, he realized the strange truth of his words. How had he not considered this before? Why had taking the book seemed a natural thing to do? "The tonic you ministered, could it have dulled my senses enough to remove guilt?"

"No. It might create false happiness, a sense of the surreal, but does not prevent the opposite." Her eyes were back on the book, her voice more calm. "Are you certain you saw, heard nothing? I found you outside, lying in brush. Could you have come there on your own, followed Heremon or someone else?" She hugged the book where her arms had been before.

He wished he had a better answer, one that would diminish the desperate look in her eyes. He could not even go so far as to be able to place a sense of lapsed time to frame what memory he did have. Heremon's kind eyes, the cloth soothing his brow, the bitter broth similar to that which she'd given him at some point later. "If I did, I am unable to recall."

She nodded, turned to the entrance. The tip of her plaited braid swished at her hips, their curve outlined in shadow and draping cloak. "Thank you for giving it to me. In exchange I will try to help you find your missing belonging."

"I thank you, Lady Breanne, but I did not, in fact, intend to give you the book."

She spun back around. The sky seemed lighter.

"I meant to show you something in it, what I believe is a rendering of the item I lost." He reached out for the book.

Eyes tight on him, she released her hug of it and handed it over. Curiosity seemed to have won out over possessiveness. Ashlon smiled slightly. He paged to the one he sought and returned the book to her waiting hands.

Breanne stepped out of the dark cave and into the growing light. Ashlon followed, half fearing she might try to leave with the book. He hated how much weight he'd placed on her translating the book and leading him to the chest. It made him feel vulnerable and worse, he also liked her there with him, near him.

He refused to embroil her further, though. Once she had told him what information lay on those pages, he vowed to act independently heretofore. Ashlon rubbed the soreness from his eyes and blinked. Breanne read and slowly walked, knowing her way without looking. She headed toward the cottage.

Ashlon followed quietly. He tamped down the urge to ask her what she read. Once she'd finished, he would ask her. Not before. She had no reason to help him now, or ever. Pushing her couldn't behoove his situation or strengthen his position.

Mid-stride, she paused, turned a crisp page, then continued onward. They were close to the cottage. Did she intend to go inside? The ocean rushed and roared against the frogs and crickets. She paused again, flipped and watched a page fall in dips down to the grass.

She knelt to retrieve it, her cloak pooled around her, the hood falling from her hair. The moonlight bathed her in silvery light. Ashlon stopped next to her, ready to stoop down when she looked up. His gut tightened. The look of wonder shining in her gaze struck him and a small buzzing began in his veins.

"What have you found?"

She stood slowly, her eyes searching his. She placed the page to her heart. "He wrote this." She closed her eyes and when they opened, wetness shined in them.

"The day he died, he wrote this, to me."

Ashlon watched her struggle to remain composed, not sure what to say, knowing what he wanted to ask was not appropriately empathetic. He wanted to know about the drawing, about the chest that looked so similar to what he had lost. But that was self-serving and if she were to help him, he should focus on her.

"The two of you were very close, then."

"I did not know we were. He was always kind to me, but never so much that I would guess to be foremost in his mind when death came to his door."

Ashlon did not point out to her that timing likely had much to do with whom he wrote to in his last hours. If only a man could be so blessed as to know when death was imminent and have time to write letters, visit loved ones, speak last words of devotion. Though Jacques had.

The realization hit him. Ashlon breathed in to steady himself. Had Jacques known what lay ahead seven years ago? Did he know he'd be tortured, imprisoned, his reputation defiled only to be ultimately burned? Impossible. To have known, even suspected, and then follow destiny down that terrible road was the act of no sane man. And Jacques may have looked crazed that day, but he was by far the wisest man Ashlon had ever encountered before and since.

Breanne read the letter again, smiling, but also frowning. Slowly, she shook her head. "I do believe you've just gotten much more than you bargained for, Sir Sinclair."

Chapter Thirteen

Heremon's cottage door sat ajar. Breanne entered carefully with Ashlon behind her, sword drawn. She didn't feel it necessary, but didn't argue when the man unsheathed his silver blade and put his finger to his lips. When they found the dwelling empty and undisturbed, she almost gloated.

If she wasn't awake with anticipation, she certainly was with expectancy now. She couldn't believe it. She actually held Heremon's own Grimoire in her hands. The pages were soft and heavy, the binding smooth from years of oils. The work of decades, the secrets of nearly a millennia, all for her to behold and keep.

Even more, he'd written her a letter. Her. Not Niall, not Finn, not some other Druid from another territory. Her. And in all its wonder and instruction, her denial collapsed. Since the day she'd come upon him in the wood she'd resisted his words, his death, and the truth.

She could deny it no longer when it was literally spelled out for her. To think she'd almost not come to him first, by her own contempt and second, by her situation. She had no inkling the importance of the affair she'd done so much to shirk her role in. Now she did.

Erlene could wake and call the whole keep to come find Breanne and she would not care. Coming here tonight and receiving these two things were worth any punishment. Well, save death.

Breanne lit a candle, then a fire. Ashlon's intent stare followed her to and fro and made her belly dance all the more giddily. He didn't appreciate the depth of its seriousness. It was up to her to make him **see**.

She sat before the hearth and indicated a seat for Ashlon. He still gripped the sword hilt and sat at the edge of the chair.

"Does he write of the chest in the drawing, Lady Breanne?"

She turned back to the page in question. She ran a hand over its silken surface.

"Aye, he details the chest and its significance here." She pointed to the words scrolling a frame around the picture. "You've come a much longer distance than I originally thought. When I found you…."

"Does he offer a location?"

"In a manner of speaking, yes, he does. Here." She offered him the letter.

Ashlon took the parchment, but only returned it, shaking his head. "I do not understand the language."

"It matters not. You likely wouldn't understand even if you spoke Gaelic. You see, the script tells a riddle." She smiled at the paper.

"Forgive my candor, Lady Breanne, but I must impress upon you to relay the riddle to me. I have wasted much time and cannot afford to continue to let the chest in that depiction remain hidden."

Breanne frowned. "I appreciate the seriousness of this very much, Sir Ashlon. You do not need to explain."

"Again, forgive me, but I need only for you to translate. You will then be free of my dependence, as you have demonstrated is your wish. I implore you to translate these words now so we both may return undiscovered."

"I will translate them, but you are wrong to believe our affiliation ends there."

"I fear it must."

"I fear it is not your decision. Discovering the chest's location depends on us both."

Ashlon ran a hand through his black curls. "When I wrote to you stating this is a matter of life and death, I was not merely luring you forth. I dare not—will not—put you at risk."

"You do not put me at risk. Fate does."

He stood, sheathed his sword. Breanne's stomach flipped. He did not look pleased, to say the least.

"Will you read the letter aloud as well as the inscription surrounding the drawing?" He spoke through tight lips.

"I will, but I assure you it will make little difference. And I must say I am surprised. I thought you sought my help and would therefore continue to appreciate it."

He held a hand out as though to stop her. "I will appreciate more than you will ever know. Please, simply read both items to me so we may leave."

He didn't sound grateful. He sounded plain irritated. Almost as irritated as she'd been over these last few days with his constant presence in her home. But the grating feeling proved unwarranted. She should have known that ministering to his health was only part of her expected duties. Heremon must have intended more.

Finn would have said this was obvious, that she always missed the obvious. Now was her chance to keep her eyes open, as well as her mind, and live up to the calling Heremon had trusted her worthy of. She took a cleansing breath.

"My dearest Breanne, I pray this letter reaches you safely as I will not be here to ensure it does. I know not my killer or his weapon of choice, but be assured that I face both readily and without fear. Trust that he will expose his true self to you and prepare for it.

"My death is not the reason for this letter, however. Life is. The lives of Tir Conaill, the lives of all of Ireland, are tied to your destiny and fulfilling it. A stranger has come to us and he holds the key to the future I refer to. You will know him when you see him by trusting your inner voice. He is on a journey of his own, which you must help him carry out. Your lives are inextricably linked and have been foretold of.

"Protect him, Breanne. See his quest rewarded."

Breanne placed the letter back into the book and held it open in her lap. "These inscriptions are encoded to tell us where this chest lays."

"It is what I seek."

"Although you seem certain it is what you lost, I should point out that this page is quite old. Should you look again to ensure that we don't hunt the wrong object?"

"How old is quite old?" Ashlon reached for the book.

"Based on its placement within the pages in the center half, penned chronologically I would estimate a few decades. I will need to study the book further to ascertain a more exact timeframe."

"Impossible. I only arrived a fortnight ago, no more. You must be wrong."

"I'm not wrong," Breanne said. "If you look for yourself you can see the aging variation within the pages themselves. Heremon began at each end and worked inward as is customary for a text of this kind."

"I see no difference." Ashlon paged from the rear, to the front and reverse. He shook his head. "Perhaps he skipped about, or missed a page?"

"He did not, but it makes little difference of when he drew it, so long as you can distinguish that it is the chest you seek and not, definitely not another."

"Have I not stated this fact?"

"There is no need to get annoyed, Sir Sinclair—."

"Ashlon. Please, call me Ashlon. The knighthood you refer to leaves a bad taste and I prefer the informal whenever possible."

"As I said." Breanne lifted her chin. "Becoming annoyed with me will do little to aid your task. I am only attempting to help."

"You may help…." He took a breath, eyes closed. "You may help by translating the bordering script. I am certain the drawing matches. Please." His eyes locked to hers, his mouth set.

She didn't know why the look in his eyes burned her so badly, but she had the inclination to stand right up and leave him there. Ungrateful was the first of a few descriptors she could use for it. Breanne narrowed her eyes, but refused to break contact, despite how fast her heart trotted.

"I will need some time to translate the script."

Ashlon crossed his arms.

"It is the truth," she said. "And I have naught to gain by lying to you. In fact, I give you my word that you will only hear the truth from me, though you may not like it." The suspicion in his stare lessoned a bit, but Breanne's anger rose nonetheless.

"How much time?"

"I canno' say really. A day or so."

He clearly disliked her answer. "I must impress you to rush. I need to find this before another does. I don't know how your man Heremon knew so much to have drawn it before I arrived. I don't care. All I know is that I am responsible for it and the sooner I search, the sooner I locate it."

"I will work on it in every available hour. You have my word." She resisted placing a comforting hand on his knee. "It may not help to hear, but we will have little chance to search now, anyhow. In two days time, when guests begin to arrive for the wedding of my mother and Niall, we will be less noticed as missing."

Ashlon leaned back in the wooden armed chair. He suppressed a yawn. Circles showed beneath his eyes.

"We must return. If I am discovered gone, I will no doubt be bound to my room, mayhap even chained to my bed. And your health will suffer if you do not rest." She didn't wait for him to follow after extinguishing the fire and candles.

As she left the cottage, she sensed rather than heard Ashlon.

"Was it wise to light a fire? Will smoke not draw attention to our visit?"

"As Niall has completed his search and none others have reason to, I can't see the fire as a risk, no. And I put it out."

The light of dawn crept in as they strode their way back, he following her noisily. She stopped. Ashlon bumped into her back.

"You should go another way," Breanne said, facing him. "If someone came upon us...."

"You should not be alone." His hand went to his sword hilt.

"I will be fine. I know these woods well, have walked them a thousand times alone."

Ashlon shook his head.

"Sir Sinclair, I insist. It is far more dangerous to risk being seen with you than alone. One would immediately assume we'd been on a midnight tryst and your hand would be forced."

"I see it otherwise. I will go with you. If we hear someone, I will hide."

Breanne snorted. She couldn't help it. "You hide? Where? And I hardly think we'll hear anything with all the stamping about you're doing." She resumed walking, faster this time.

"I will not leave you."

"Then at least allow some distance between us." She heard silence and knew he'd stopped. She refused to thank him, or turn around. Or feel disappointed. Breanne shook her head. Why in all the stars would she feel disappointed in his maintaining a distance? It was the only compromise and he'd taken it. She should feel relieved.

If she were caught with him, she would not be choosing any husband at Beltane. She'd be standing next in line after her mother and Niall wed. And he was the last man she wanted standing there with her. He was a knight, distasteful or not, had belonged to the most esteemed and well-known company of knights.

He chose a life of potential war and battle, not out of necessity as a man did in Ireland. In Ireland, the men might be battle-ready and mayhap even battle-hungry, but that could be expected when their land and country was continually coveted by others.

The snap of twigs far behind told her just how far a lead he'd given her. She wanted to look back, but knew better. If she looked back, she looked weak. What she should do was let him know just how capable she was in caring for and defending herself.

Breanne smiled as she pictured the outraged look on his face upon seeing her weapon or worse, upon being overtaken by her. A trill of giddiness leapt in her belly. Without a glance back, she saw her opportunity approach with a bend in the path she'd led them to.

* * * *

"Stubborn wench," Ashlon said to himself, finding it hard to keep one eye on her and the other on the tangled path she traipsed down.

He should have let her go. His being out of the keep was just as risky, he could have let her know. Sneaking about in the dark alone, let alone with the chieftain's near stepdaughter, supposedly bedridden, in tow would get him gallows.

A branch scratched his cheek, stinging a path through his morning stubble. He growled, slapped it back and heard the satisfying snap. It made him grin. He'd like to break a few limbs over his thigh right now. Anything to get his roiling frustrations out before he gave in and screamed.

The dark green of her cloak blended too damn well and she moved too damn lithely. The reddish gold of her braid was the only thing he glimpsed while finding footing. Then the path widened and broke through foliage. Ashlon moved faster to catch up as she disappeared around a bend.

The woman had no sense of self-preservation, let alone decorum. Firstly, she had cared for him under secrecy. Secondly, she ignored his presence to the point of outright rudeness. And now, to insist he leave her to fend for herself in a dark wooded area when no one knew she was gone nor where to. At the very least, a wild boar should incite some degree of fear in a woman. He'd seen brave men quake over far less.

Where in blasted hell had she gone? He wouldn't be surprised at all if she'd left the new path and trudged through the trees and growth again just to spite him.

To hell with it. Ashlon slowed his pace. He chose the path before him, trusting it would lead him back in time to meet the morning sun breaching the sky. The forest was already awake. Birds sang, leaves shuddered and dew glistened on the ground.

Two days minimum. Ashlon hated the idea of waiting so long. His gut told him he didn't have so much luxury. But without a clue as to where to begin his search, he had no choice but to wait for her.

And to trust her.

For some reason, he did. He could see, not just in her eyes, but in her eagerness, how forthright she felt about the entire matter. She needn't know he would not involve her further once she'd done the translation. That might give her ideas about withholding information in order to gain interest in the task.

Heremon's note was vague, but he readily saw how she could mistake the meaning and latch herself to his cause, unknowing the substance or its imperiling nature. She was more than stubborn. Plainly.

An arm snaked around Ashlon's waist and the unmistakable feel of metal pressed his throat. Ashlon stilled, barely breathing lest he get cut ear to ear.

Alarm shot through his head. Where was Breanne? Ashlon scanned the foliage and path for a catch of gold. None.

He swallowed. The blade moved with his throat, leaving his skin unharmed. He opened his mouth to speak and the sharp edge pressed in and slowly slid upward to his cheek, scraping loudly in his ears.

"You need a shave," she said near his ear.

Breanne! What in Heaven's name was she thinking? The laughter in her throaty whisper tickled his lobe. She showed him her blade laden with his stubble. Clever girl. Ashlon allowed a slow smile to laze onto his mouth.

Impressive. Soundless and lithe.

In a single swift motion, Ashlon swept Breanne over his shoulder and under him, pinned to the soft ground.

"Yes, I do need a good shave." His smile was almost as wicked as he felt.

Breanne gritted her teeth and glared up at him. Ashlon laughed, enjoying the feel of her comeuppance underneath him. Suddenly, as she panted and writhed beneath him, another sort of wickedness drank his thoughts dry.

"Let me go," Breanne said, but she'd stopped moving and passion glazed her eyes.

Ashlon's groin ached and grew in want of her, nestled perfectly to fit between her thighs. The wrists he held above her head relaxed and she dropped her blade. Her lips were wet and plump with color. Need charged through his body. Need of her.

He bent his head, let go of her arms and touched her face.

Even as she shook her head, she closed her eyes. She leaned her cheek to his hand. His mind and body flooded with the memory of their kiss, the same fog of sensation with it.

He pressed his mouth to hers. She returned the pressure and opened her lips to his exploring tongue. Ashlon groaned, tasting her warm sweetness, feeling her body awaken under him, hips turning, thighs tightening.

He deepened his kiss and her legs inched open, hips arching. Her softness met his hardness, squirming against him.

Somewhere, he recognized that he should stop. But her arms held his head close, her fingers laced through his hair and her pelvis reached up to feel his rigid prick. Her full breasts teased against his chest, the nipples stiff and probing. His mind clouded with craving. Visions of her flesh exposed to his bare touch, to his tongue and lips, filled his mind. He would stop. He promised he would. Just one last exquisite taste of her to last him. One more touch. A little farther. A bit deeper.

He wanted to forge his prick closer to her, to rub the tip against her mound. Her legs opened further until mere fabric separated them. Layers of material that seemed to do little good in blocking such keen pleasure, he could spill his seed. He forced himself to rein his desire for her. She was an innocent and would certainly break the spell at any second. He needed to make this surreal moment last.

Breanne moaned into his mouth as he cupped a breast, teasing the hard nipple that pressed the soft fabric. Lord, but they felt better than he imagined, and he had far too often since their kiss. The vibration of her sound of pleasure satisfied a deep part of him. Ashlon sunk the weight of his hips downward, rocking gently onto her core. Christ, she felt good.

Was she wetting for him? Did her body throb as his did, begging her to chase the pleasure and fulfillment that beckoned? Certainly she felt as he did. She must, for her small moans sounded desperate yet awed in his ears. Her hands pulled at him, her body gyrated under his.

Her response to him was far from virtuous. Her response was untamed. It awoke the primal part of him. The part that wished to take her, make her his.

Her nails dug into his scalp, sending a flush of shivers down his neck. Ashlon nipped her lower lip. The kiss took on a frantic feel.

He should stop. Her hips squirmed, pressed. A small turn, a quick lift of her skirt and she could be his. Hot, wet heaven called to him. His prick pulsed, urging him.

He wanted more. He wanted to give her more, to fill the aching void that wanting her created deep inside of him. He wanted to watch bliss wash her features, to know he'd given that bliss.

Ashlon wanted to feel her naked skin against his. He

wanted to part her thighs and delve his tongue into the deepest part of her, to taste her honey as it poured in release onto his tongue. He drew a hand from her perfect breast, hating yet adoring her whimper, and grazed down her length. His fingers sought the hem of her dress as he told himself one mere touch of her silken skin and he would cease. He would stand and leave her. But when his hands met her ankle and her hips bucked beneath him, he nearly—.

His groan sounded like a growl. He pushed away from her before he was too far gone. Her lips were swollen and red. He imagined them on his body. Her eyes searched his face and emotion evolved through them. Disappointment and want, then confusion, and finally realization.

The next he expected would be anger and he readied for a hard slap. He squinted as she sat up and righted her gown. His body screamed with disappointment. But he did not reach for her.

"My," she said a bit breathlessly. "That was a lesson well taught. Here I thought I'd show you and low and behold, you've quite shown me instead."

"I did not mean it to be a lesson, Breanne." Ashlon frowned, but a grin tugged his mouth. He swallowed, his pulse at last slowing.

"I doubt that. Rather than allow me my triumph, you overturned me and proved my gender's vulnerability in a very obvious manner." She wiped her brow. "Though, were you truly raping me, I promise you'd be gutted before you finished."

She might be right on more than one count. "The lesson was not meant to be so—."

"Thorough?" She quirked a sardonic brow.

He laughed aloud. "I was going to say demonstrative, but thorough well covers it, I'd say."

"Or uncovers," she said and righted her bodice to cover her exposed skin. "Now, if you'll wait a moment here, I'll have gained enough space to ensure our discretion." Breanne tossed her braid over her shoulder and a red mark sat on her neck.

"Christ," he said. "I've marked your skin."

"What? Where?"

She was handling their encounter far too admirably, should be up in arms, outraged, at the very least still wanton. But she managed to keep her voice and gaze steady while his felt opposite.

Ashlon reached his hand out and touched her nape. Breanne flinched and for some inane reason, he found it reassuring. She was not so immune, then. She feared him touching her again and losing control.

He didn't waver and slowly brought his fingertip to the spot. He'd kissed her neck there, too passionately, and it couldn't easily be passed off as a bruise.

Her throat moved when she swallowed. Ashlon watched her lips part. Her eyelids pressed closed. He let his fingertip drag down the line of her neck, fascinated by the goose bumps he left behind.

God, but she was heavenly. And what she made him feel was worse than wicked. His heartbeat pumped his body like a drum. Ashlon lowered his mouth. Time stopped and hung like fog around them, alone on the soft mossy floor, in the early dawn twilight.

His tongue touched the spot of redness and traced a small circle around it. Breanne gasped and bent her head back.

"Why do you this to me?" she said in a voice nearly a whimper.

He didn't know. He shouldn't do this or anything like it. It took advantage of her aid, of her secrecy, placed both at risk. But the pull was so strong and again he thought one last taste would quench him.

He suckled her skin and held her close. Her panting breaths sang a sweet song to his soul. He kissed her as tenderly as he suddenly felt.

He heard a voice. Ashlon stopped. He pulled away. Breanne's eyes fluttered open and when they met his countenance, became as serious as his.

"Did you hear that?"

She shook her head. The voice came again. It was somebody singing.

"Danny," she said in a gasp. "Quickly, hide."

Ashlon looked around. "Where?"

Breanne looked about, as well, and had no answer. "Stay here." She leapt to her feet and sprinted up the path.

"Breanne," he whispered, but it was useless. She'd already gone.

Ashlon punched the ground, ignoring the smart in his fist. What was she thinking leaving to meet the boy? A boy of ten couldn't protect her and she shouldn't still believe herself able to when he had clearly demonstrated how easily one could overtake a woman, or a man.

Why she'd had to stand on a rock just to get to his jugular. How many good-sized rocks could be counted on to be ready for her when a true threat grabbed her?

Ashlon laid back his head and felt her dagger beneath it. He withdrew it from its grassy nest and, with a curse, threw it into a tree trunk across the path. It stuck, wobbled and sang a dull twang. Ashlon shook his head. She'd forgotten the single thing that gave her some degree of advantage over man or beast.

Yet, he stayed, as told. He couldn't have the boy seeing them alone together. She'd be able to use their bond to keep him quiet and, alone, would likely seem innocent to a child's mind. But even a child could guess something amiss when a man and woman came from the dark woods.

And her. She'd up and left as though they hadn't just been entangled and repeating the same mistake. Unless she didn't see it as one. He hadn't considered that she might actually want him to kiss her. She was looking to secure a husband, after all.

Ludicrous idea. She'd told him to leave at once. That was not the message of one wanting a courtship, now was it? Or did she think their encounter would make him leave, the threat of marriage clear?

Women. They were far too mysterious. No sooner did he think he understood one, they changed.

Chapter Fourteen

The only good thing about her mother ordering her to bed was that Breanne could sleep the missed hours from that night and morning after safely returning.

Danny had come just in time and she'd have thanked him if it were possible. He had not only saved Breanne from a full seduction right there on the forest ground, but from Erlene discovering her gone.

Thanks weren't possible when she could only act as though naught was amiss, the two of them happening upon each other as they had. She'd needed some air after being cooped up in her room all day and had to sneak past the chambermaid. Danny had nodded soberly at her excuse and offered his own. He couldn't sleep.

With a loud grumbling yawn, Erlene had woke the moment Breanne's head hit the pillow.

Breanne closed her eyes and pretended to wake soon after. Erlene didn't seem at all suspicious as Breanne worried at her lip, twisting the tip of her braid. More than once, she had to remind herself to hide the mark he said he'd left, although it might have been a ruse to kiss her again.

Moon and stars, his kiss was mesmerizing, dangerously so. All logic fell away to physical sensation when his lips touched hers only to slam back when they rudely stopped.

She liked those kisses far too much. If she were to be a success at helping his quest, as Heremon indicated was in fact her own quest, she would need to control her senses when he was near. No more kissing, to be sure.

Tossing about, she'd recalled every last detail, sending flushes through her. Erlene only raised an inquisitive eyebrow once, sending her into a full blush.

It amazed her how much a difference the book and note made within her. Yesterday, her only fervent wish was that Ashlon Sinclair leave Tir Conaill, whole and well, but certainly gone. She'd avoided seeing him to such lengths that her mother and Rose thought she'd joined the ranks of women, a long hoped for thing.

She couldn't even glance his way during dining a day ago without hating her lot and all that came with finding him. Even her belly had clenched and rolled with one smile.

Now she saw the truth. She'd just refused to see the obvious, which was that he needed her. Whatever this chest meant or held, and that must be important for Heremon to have gone to the effort of drawing it, she had to help Ashlon locate it.

And then he could leave.

Breanne winced. The wish she'd had didn't seem as good of one now. Not that she meant to keep him here. How could she? Why would she? A few hypnotic kisses weren't enough to want him to stay and become a clansman.

She was set to marry—someone--within four short weeks. Little sense she'd have to be dwelling on the fact that she was not to be his.

No more kissing.

She would treat the transgressions of lust as lessons, intentional or not, and use them as a guide for what she should feel when her husband did the kissing.

That way, she could still consider the memories without feeling badly. And he certainly set the standard high. Why, if Quinlan's kiss had been half as wonderful, Breanne had no doubt she'd still be fully and absolutely in love with her childhood friend.

And then Rose would be happy, her mother would be happy, Niall would be happy. And she could be....**u**nhappy.

It wasn't that she didn't still love Quinlan. She did. She just didn't want to kiss him, or feel his hands on her body, like Ashlon's hands.

Was she being too hard on Quinlan?

Perhaps she should give him another chance as he'd asked, but truly this time. She should kiss him. She should kiss Gannon, too. Mayhap. And why not Ashlon again while you're spreading your affections about, a tiny voice said?

She sighed again and rolled again.

Erlene tsked, folding her bedcovers. "If you like, I can ask your mother up to check on you, but I'll promise you she's never changed orders on me before and I don't liken will do so now."

"No, thank you, but I know you are right. I do need rest." More than Erlene would ever guess. "But my mind is busy as a bee in summer. I canno' seem to clear it."

"What you need is something tae read. I 'ave a small book of lyric and it puts me tae sleep before I even finish one page."

While the last didn't surprise Breanne, that Erlene owned any book did. There she went again, judging and misconstruing what was right in front of her face.

Reading was an excellent idea, though, and Breanne closed her eyes, remembering the book she'd tucked into her truck. Heremon's Grimoire. Wonder filled her just knowing she possessed it. The knowledge comforted her enough that she promptly fell asleep.

* * * *

Ashlon woke from his short rest to a visitor. Quinlan Blake. He'd forgotten the agreed upon lessons. He was supposed to be helping young Quinlan catch Breanne's heart and simultaneously learn the language and land. He rubbed his eyes and answered the knock, pushing away the guilt niggling his brain.

He'd been ravishing the very lady this man had set his heart on and Ashlon didn't need it pointed out how dishonorable that made him. Not only to have given in to base need by tasting her delicious lips again with no intention of marrying her, but he also must keep their association from Quinlan. And this bargain, from her.

A matchmaker would not do to be weaseling the territory he was asked to aid conquering for another. Not that he'd made any progress in the issue. Their single conversation could hardly be counted as a lesson. Still, the whole situation smacked indecent.

He felt to be a rogue.

He longed for the day that he could end subterfuge and secrecy from his life. Never before had he been a user of other persons to meet a desired end. The fact that Quinlan had come to him with the bargain and that Ashlon's intentions with Breanne had been platonic a day ago did little to help him feel better.

He must end the lessons and find another route to learn the language. Mayhap he should skip learning Gaelic altogether now that he had secured Breanne's help. But then if he needed it further….

Quinlan knocked again, called his name.

Ashlon answered the hostel room door ready to end their partnership with a grimace on his face. Quinlan entered the small room unfazed, beaming brighter than any man should at the early hour.

"Why have you not moved to the keep?" he asked while Ashlon put on his boots.

He didn't give the truth, that he was loathe to be so close to Breanne after their heated embrace only hours ago, or that it might make him so much more fond of the people here.

"I will be traveling on soon. It would only improve what I sleep on and I can't see a reason to overextend my welcome."

"Nonsense. Niall has already mentioned to me that you should consider a private chamber in his keep and to get you into one before the wedding guests arrive and all are one on top of the other."

The chieftain had only tried to persuade Ashlon once, but apparently had not given up, as he'd thought. A private chamber that might only be doors away from hers couldn't be a good idea, except that they could better communicate.

But they'd be doing no communicating aside from polite conversation in passing once she translated the script.

"When will the guests arrive?"

"Within this sennight, no later. As much time as we will spend in your tutelage and since you already dine with us in the great hall, I cannot see a reason to refuse." Quinlan followed Ashlon out the door. "Or is there something you're not telling me? Sir Ashlon, is there another reason you wish to stay away?" They stepped outside and Quinlan's eyes narrowed on Ashlon.

And what could he answer to that? Yes, Master Blake, I cannot seem to keep my thoughts or hands or mouth off of your intended bride?

"I'll consider it," Ashlon said. What he would consider was a more irrefutable excuse.

Quinlan clapped him on the shoulder, beaming once

again. He couldn't be more than twenty and three and still had an innocence about him that Ashlon found reminded him of his brother Christophe.

His chest panged at the realization. They had different coloring, heights, weights, but their practical way was identical. Also similar was how each handled uneasy topics through veiled avoidance, circling and dancing the matter to death, as Quinlan had done yesterday.

"Shall we ride again?" Quinlan suggested, gesturing to the already saddled steeds in wait for them.

Ashlon took a breath of the chilly morning air to clear his head as they rode north. The thunder of hooves and brisk air did little more than make him feel more alert and thus more aware of his missing Christophe.

The pain's freshness still surprised him, as well as how sudden it could come upon him after so long. The older brother he had lost by tragic accident contrasted with the man just ahead, riding carefree and unaware of his companion's thoughts.

Yet another reason to stop their meetings.

Quinlan reigned in his stallion so that it was nose to nose with Ashlon's.

"I've considered what we spoke of yesterday. I broached the subject with Niall and he took to the idea amiably."

"I thought I made it clear that I have no interest in Lady Breanne's keep," Ashlon said.

"You did and I have honored your decision. I asked Niall that I might see the holdings and that I would be asking your consult on its security."

Ashlon's anger cooled a bit.

"He saw it as a gesture of courtship and assumes I have made progress with Breanne. I probably should have dissuaded his assumption, but interest in seeing the keep outweighed my sense of obligation." Quinlan's horse nickered. "Since her father's death, I'm not sure of any aside from those handling upkeep have entered it."

Ah, so that is why he smiled like a boy today. The promise of small adventure.

"And what will you tell the Lady upon seeing her?"

"That will depend on what we discover, I suppose. Niall won't mention it as I asked it remain a surprise in the event that I do secure her hand. Not that I doubt I will. She has loved me for nigh ten years. And with your help, I can live up to expectation and be a befitting husband."

Ashlon suspected the ride to the keep was more for Quinlan's benefit than Breanne's. This way he could estimate how much he'd be biting off to chew by winning her.

It was an ideal time to bring up ending his help, but Ashlon found himself a bit curious, as well. To leave it unoccupied in such a prime target position, he wondered if Niall were either less than competent, his meandering ways notwithstanding, or had another motive.

He'd also be lying to deny that a small voice whispered to him that an abandoned keep could be an excellent hiding place. A small chest among a bevy of forgotten furniture could be left for all to see and none to suspect.

The voice grew louder, negotiating the notion with his rational brain that said it could never be so easy as accidentally coming across the chest. And Ashlon found his own anticipation grew with it. So much so that the pain of loss faded to the background and he was able to live in the present again.

Well, the near present, anyway. Approaching the home Breanne had grown up in, played in, made him think of their encounter last night. Before the kiss, before her attempt at bravado, he thought of her stubbornness.

Giving her the book had earned her cooperation far more easily than he had expected. Worse, she seemed to think that she was meant to help him, that Heremon had spoken from the grave and told her that Ashlon was her continued responsibility.

She'd gone from resistant and annoyed, to optimistically determined so fast it had made his head spin. He didn't look forward to the stubbornness she'd displayed rearing its head again when he ended her convoluted notion that she and he were a part of this together.

Hell, she hadn't even asked what the quest was that she supposedly was fated to help him with. She didn't even question it.

The outer bailey was surrounded in a tall and thick stone wall. The only entrance or exit was a narrow but heavily banded and barred gate. Quinlan managed it open and soon they entered the keep itself.

The couple and their small son, the family in charge of its upkeep these last years, stayed out of their way, going about their daily chores with no more than a few curious glances.

He wondered if they suspected the future master might have just walked in. The furniture gleamed, dusted and polished, and was unworn save for by time itself. They strolled through each room in silence akin to respect for the dead.

Dead is what the place was in its own way. Though the items within were still new and cared for, none of the manicured rooms were lived in. They reminded Ashlon of his childhood estate in England after Christophe's death. They were equally empty and silent then.

Ashlon shook off the past, cleared his throat. "Should we inspect the tower's parapets?"

Quinlan seemed startled from reverie, as well, nodded after a quick jerk close to a shudder.

Ashlon kept his eyes peeled for the chest and wouldn't allow himself to be disappointed if he didn't see or find it. Looking over the rooftop edge of the tower, the valley and community spread out before them. It was a beautiful view and he counted Lady Breanne auspicious in inheriting it. Did she recognize or know that none of her gender in other lands could hope for land entitlement alone?

Few men even received such a generous amount. He wouldn't upon the death of his father, being the youngest of four sons. He was fortunate to have been chosen to join the Templar Knights and still carried that first sense of pride when Jacques hand-selected him.

It was a strong and smartly built fortress, despite its age being centuries older than Niall's or the others. Niall's in fact was new by comparison, a decade old. This keep had a separate kitchen and, possibly, dungeon. Quinlan offered some history surrounding it.

Breanne's stronghold had once been the main of the community, before the Normans invaded. A female warrior had once defended it against invaders. The woman was conceivably one of Breanne's ancestors. But the Normans were determined conquerors and blended with the Gaelic residents, becoming more Irish than the Irish, and so the saying came to be.

Standing and gazing upon the beauty of the green valley was as good a moment as any to end their agreement. Ashlon cleared his throat and put lingering connections to his past to rest.

"Master Quinlan, I am sorry to say that I can no longer act as your instructor in matters of the heart."

Quinlan faced him, crestfallen. "No. I cannot ask another and, Sir Ashlon, I need the help. I have mucked things up so badly that you are my single hope."

"Surely, you exaggerate. The Lady Breanne does not seem so unapproachable as you imply."

"She is not. I easily approach her, it is what comes out of my mouth after the fact that gives me trouble. I implore you. Do not abandon me yet."

"I dare not stay here long enough to offer any suitable help and I fear to receive any returned education as we agreed. I feel it will waste both our time." Time he should spend searching.

"Not at all. Why you've already helped immeasurably."

Ashlon frowned. How was that possible? They'd discussed little yesterday that he applied to Quinlan's situation.

"Sir Ashlon, you made me realize something quite important during our last talk. I realized that before I was made aware of Breanne's feelings for me, I had no nervousness at all in her presence. Now that I know, I do. I feel if we work on relieving my nervousness, I will soon succeed."

It was hard not to smile at Quinlan's eager countenance, nodding his head, gesturing his hands for emphasis. He looked like he talked of a plan of attack not a design to woo a woman.

Ashlon suppressed a chuckle, imagining Breanne's reaction to being attacked into marriage, as it were. They seemed such an ill-fitted match, Quinlan and Breanne. While he was sober but innocent, she seemed intent and worldly. Perhaps that was what intimidated Quinlan.

"I also must admit something to you. Some time ago, the very night my sister related Breanne's true feelings toward me, I imbibed. A lot."

"We all have and will in the rough course of love, Quinlan. 'Tis naught to be ashamed of." The breeze brought the scent of rain.

"Please, allow me to finish. As I said, I imbibed. And as I've recently related, I am not experienced in the ways of ladies. Which is not to say, I am not experienced. But Lady Breanne is of good breeding and is a lady, despite having somewhat masculine tendencies."

"She seems not the least masculine to me."

Quinlan's face reddened a bit and he lowered his head. "I kissed her."

Ashlon went quiet.

"I kissed her that night and I fear that I destroyed her feelings for me in that single kiss."

Ashlon needed to the get the direction of the conversation back in hand, feeling more than curious. He felt annoyed, as well. Thinking of Quinlan in a heated embrace the likes of which he'd experienced only hours before was more than annoying. He didn't like it and that unsettled him.

"She slapped me." Quinlan looked at him.

Ashlon struggled to keep his features unreadable, to hide the sudden relief the last statement shouldn't have given him. Quinlan's was opposite. All of his discomfort showed openly on his young face.

"If you're asking me for help in the art of kissing, I will have to disappoint you," Ashlon said.

Quinlan guffawed and the stretch of uneasiness between them vanished.

"No. I thought not. And I've never had a similar reaction, if I may be so boastful."

"You may." They headed back in, the subject officially dropped. He'd failed to end their bargain, but since he had no honorable designs on Lady Breanne other than the translation, he might as well continue it. In a few days, he would have the chest back in his possession and be on his way, away from Tir Conaill.

* * * *

Of all the sordid ways Finn fancied waking Breanne, she cringed most over his licking between her toes. While it wasn't surprising that he welcomed her awake with the tactic, she was surprised to see him.

"Where were you off to this time?" she asked after scuffing away from his disgusting tongue. Though groggy, she was glad he woke her. "Where is Erlene?"

"Dismissed. I sent her to your mother posthaste for a new chore."

"I am not a chore and I know very well you did not speak to her. I'd have woken to bloody screaming, to be sure." She swung her feet to the floor, rubbing the sleep from her eyes.

"Your mother came for her shortly after I arrived this afternoon," Finn said, switching his tail.

"Is it evening already, then?"

"Nearly the dinner hour. I imagine a bath will arrive shortly since Lady Ula said to Erlene she'd never seen you rest so soundly since you were a babe and then dismissed her."

Breanne smiled. She'd hardly had time with her mother in the last few months, even during her time among the ladies, Ula was rarely present long enough to enjoy her company. Ula had a thousand and three arrangements to complete in less than enough time, as she liked to say these days.

"Oh, I almost forgot," she said and went to her trunk. "I've found Heremon's Grimoire."

Finn perked up and followed her. "Where did you find it? When did you get it? Is there something we can use for the curse?"

"I don't know yet, Finn. I just got it last night. But my hopes are high. Mayhap it will unlock my gifts, finally."

Finn nosed through her arms and into her lap as she opened the volume there. "Have you seen it before, Finn? Do you know how it works, backward, forward, scattered?"

"No. I haven't and I don't. While Heremon asked much of me in your training, do recall, I was never his. Only yours," Finn said. "If he held any tool in aiding me, he refused to offer it."

"There's no use in being angry with Heremon now, Finn. Unless the dead can hear, or care, which I doubt."

Finn kicked off of her lap and went to her bed. He scratched the bundled covers. "Yes, well I hope he hears and hates it. I hope he turns in the grave. And when you do release me, I hope I see him in the Otherworld and I will tell him further then, as well."

Breanne drew her eyebrows together. "I'll thank you to not take it out on my bedding. You've been gone stewing in your anger these last days, then, haven't you?"

Finn lay into the nest he created, silent.

"Fine. Don't tell me. I care not what you've been off to. I rather like the freedom of it and encourage you to go again whenever possible."

"And allow you more time with the knight? Or did you not notice he spends most time with your beloved Quinlan nowadays?"

"I don't know what you mean."

"Of course you don't. By the by, Breanne, how goes the husband hunt?" Finn closed his eyes, his mouth curled.

Her bath was delivered at that very moment and Breanne swore that had it not, Finn might have been tossed out the window.

The damned feline not only managed to ruin her excitement over the book, but also knew too damned much. Yes, she'd spent time with Ashlon and no, he had not been keeping company with Quinlan. She was sure of it. Finn could only be finding the right chords in her to play her well. She should know just how proficient he was at it by now.

Chapter Fifteen

He hadn't been at dinner that night or the next. Breanne tried to keep her mind off of the fact by translating Heremon's book but it made it all the worse. Finn's silence didn't help. In fact it made his statement actually seem potentially legitimate.

She didn't want to believe it. Certainly, she had seen the two men together and it wasn't untoward of Quinlan to continue to befriend Ashlon. After all, he had been the person who had come upon the knight on the road and brought him in.

But, why did Ashlon no longer join them at dinner? He had been a staple every other night since his arrival. She tried to tell herself that it was a good thing, that it allowed her time to work without added pressure. But, then why had the 'life and death matter' suddenly stopped being so vital as to lure her into a midnight meeting by moonlight?

Exasperated, Breanne tossed the book aside. Her head hurt, her eyes ached and her brain felt numb. She was making little progress and at this rate, Ashlon would be here through winter solstice, if he weren't dead by then. And she would have failed Heremon.

What could a wooden box hold that could be worth such trouble? Her first thought, that Ashlon was merely attached to the chest, evolved when he'd shown her the drawing. The chest must hold significance for the Druid to put it to paper. And, with the riddling script border, doubtlessly it was worth far more than she could guess.

Perhaps Heremon's death was linked to the chest. But who could know of it or of Ashlon's arrival? If she ever solved the puzzle she'd be using it to find out from Ashlon exactly what lay inside.

The first wedding guests arrived that morning and she had nothing to give Ashlon. She didn't doubt at any moment he would come knocking for answers she didn't have. What in the world could he be doing with himself in the meanwhile? Certainly, Quinlan and he had little in common, and to what end if he truly meant to leave soon? It felt too much to hope his absence from the keep was an attempt to become the unremarkable visitor as she'd advised.

The clang of metal on metal echoed up from the yard. The clang in and of itself wouldn't have called her attention but when a round of cheers followed it, Breanne shot to the window, mindless of disturbing Finn.

She peered down but couldn't see past the growing crowd in the yard. Without a second thought, Breanne left her room to look out the corridor's window. She gasped when her eyes landed on Ashlon, sword raised in arms against Quinlan.

"What in the world are they thinking?"

She returned to her room to grab her sapphire cloak and replace the book in her trunk. Finn gazed at her through sleepy eyes but didn't ask what she was hurrying about for.

Breanne almost tripped down the flight of stone stairs, she went so fast. Upon reaching the yard, she was shocked at how large the gathering had grown in the small space of time. Rose and Rhiannon stood at the edge. Rose waved her over.

"Can you see much from your chamber, Bree?"

She shook her head. "What are they about, then, Rose?"

"It's a test of skills," Rhiannon said with a faraway smile. "Sir Ashlon means to take on every last man among Niall's guard."

"We need a better view, girls," Rose said. "Come now, let us think a moment before its over and done and we miss the lot of it swooning here in the back of it."

"I don't understand," Breanne said. "He battled Quinlan just now, might be still. Are you certain they do not fight, Rose?"

"Of course not. My brother counts the knight as a friend. He is simply the first in line to take Sir Ashlon to test. Now, look there. Do you both see that window?"

Rhiannon nodded expressly while Breanne held her hand to block the sudden slant of sunlight. She couldn't see much at all and looked back to Rose. Her friend was walking away with Rhiannon, back into the keep. Breanne rushed to catch them.

"He can't mean to take on every man. That would be more than twenty."

Rose led them up the west stairwell. "He'll take on every man he can and whoever bests him will take on the next and so on until the winner is named. Whatever man succeeds the most, with the best skill demonstrated, to be judged by the O'Doherty's. They've men in, as well," Rose said as they climbed.

Rhiannon clapped and squealed. After her spinning lesson with the girl, Breanne counted her as a friend. Rhiannon had taken pity on her once it became obvious to them both how terrible a hand she had at the needle and wheel.

But, as she gushed and blushed over the games in the yard, Breanne found herself getting quite annoyed.

"How many do you imagine he'll sustain?" Rhiannon said to Breanne. "I'll wager he has more'n a bit of stamina, that one. Think you five, or six? More?" Her pretty blue eyes sparkled.

Breanne wanted to point out that Ashlon would not be up to so many after his recent illness and that he really had no business engaging in arms at all. But, neither Rose nor Rhiannon knew about the man delirious with fever, stripped bare and ministered to by her in absolute secrecy.

And the risk was worth this of all things? All her worry and sneaking about, suffering the mindlessness his kisses put on her, the very distraction of it when she should be focused on finding a husband or helping Niall find Heremon's murderer.

She almost hoped he got wounded. No not wounded, fatigued, really and suddenly fatigued. That would teach him making a spectacle out of himself for every man and lusting woman in the whole clan. By the time they reached the window Rose had spotted, Breanne was ready to go back to her room. But when she glimpsed the shillelagh coming down fast at Ashlon's head, she stood her ground.

Rhiannon squealed, her hands fluttering in the air, knocking into Rose and Breanne. Breanne suppressed the overpowering urge send her away.

Ashlon deftly blocked the heavy club and with a fast twirl of his silver blade, unarmed the man. He'd beaten Quinlan then, and was securing his second defeat. The tall man knelt in defeat before Ashlon and bowed. The crowd roared with cheer and applause.

The next opponent stepped into the circle, which widened its berth in anticipation of the coming spar. Ashlon and the burly man holding a mace were in their direct line of sight.

"Ah, but he's all man that one. Do you see the muscle on him?" Rose asked.

Breanne didn't need clarification on which man she referred to with all the fat on his opponent hiding any muscle tone. She flushed, remembering just how muscular he was. His smooth nearly hairless chest, hot to the touch, glistening in the moonlight, recalled far too freshly in her mind.

The flush raced from her cheeks to her belly, spreading lower. Her heart leapt as the huge opponent suddenly ran at Ashlon, swinging his mace in crisscross motions and sending him backward. The crowd swam with the men. If an onlooker got too close, they'd be surely injured, possible killed with that mean looking thing.

"I cannot watch," Rhiannon said.

The larger man wasn't as swift on his feet and Ashlon had him on his back with a move so fast Breanne couldn't have explained its process were she to retell what she had witnessed. She found herself leaning forward, gasping.

The crowd roared again.

"Blimey, that's more man than I knew existed," Rose said.

Breanne rolled her eyes. "He'll tire soon." She said the words but hoped he proved her wrong. He wasn't a peacock about his wins.

Rose shot her a curious look, one eyebrow raised. "What has the man done to you this time, Bree?"

Breanne frowned. The image of his mouth sucking her neck popped into her mind. "I don't know what you mean, he's done nothing at all to me." She cursed her cheeks for the heat climbing into them. Worse, for the warm ache far lower.

Rhiannon was blissfully unaware of Breanne's cold

gaze, so enraptured by the sight of Ashlon taking on yet another opponent, this one a mite smaller than the last. The loser had finally managed to get back to his feet and didn't seem the least bit offended by the expedient end to his turn. He accepted many a handshake, nodded at Ashlon with a look on his face that seriously smacked close to admiration.

"Pardon me for not being utterly smitten with the man as everyone else seems to be," Breanne said, and crossed her arms. But the scowl on her face was doing little to stop the heat in her belly. His bare biceps were so well defined. The strong set of his jaw, the ease with which he danced around his opponents....

"And, may I say, I'm glad to hear it," Quinlan said low, behind her. Breanne started and swung around, almost bumping into him. "Are you ladies enjoying our brutish sport, then?" He kept his eyes on Breanne.

"Oh my, yes," Rhiannon said breathlessly. "Thoroughly enjoying the fine display of prowess. I must say we've the best view thanks to your kind and clever sister." Her eyelashes fluttered, her gaze torn between the fight below and the man before her.

Breanne almost rolled her eyes again. Glad to hear it, he'd said in that husky tone. Of course he was glad to hear it and that meant he still had her hand in mind. He'd made no overtures in the time since their ride, discounting carrying her upstairs when she'd fainted. She'd not only begun to hope he'd given up the notion of marrying her, but had nearly forgotten his interest these last two days.

Ever since she'd returned that morning, she'd been too consumed with other things to recall his vow to try to do better. That husky tone spoken far too close at her back was more telling than the words themselves and had instantly chilled the heat in her.

"Was your turn over as quickly as the others?" Rose asked, a half smile curving her lips.

Quinlan gave his sister a mocking glare. "More," he said, rubbing his backside.

Rhainnon burst into laughter. Rose chuckled. Breanne smiled, as well. She did miss him. He'd always managed to make her laugh, even in the worst of moods.

Quinlan smiled warmly and equally at each of them and, for a moment, Breanne counted him as back to himself, not in the least bit awkward.

"Are you very much attached to watching Breanne? If not, I would ask a private word with you?"

Breanne swallowed, glancing at Rose, who had her gaze on the clash below, for help. Rhiannon eyed them suspiciously.

"Will you return after, Quinlan?" Rhiannon asked.

He nodded, taking his eyes off Breanne's for only a moment, long enough for her to close her eyes shut and re-open them determinedly. If he wished privacy, she saw no way around it. To help quell rising nerves, she reminded herself of his promise not to kiss her again without permission.

"As you please," she said and took his offered arm.

They walked to the end of the corridor and up another flight to the rooftop.

"Did he really best you that fast, Quinlan?" Breanne clung to the earlier topic, hoping to sustain its relief now.

"He is very skilled. It was over much faster than I anticipated it to be. I'll not be surprised if he lasts another ten men at this rate."

Too bad. He'd taken her question as serious interest when all she'd wanted was another jest. They came to a stop near the wall, the fighting behind them.

"Thank you for speaking with me. I know you are distressed in doing so."

Breanne winced. "It's not that I'm distressed Quinlan. It's more that I'm nervous, I expect. We used to be such friends and now…."

"I have gone and muddled it with a kiss."

She didn't know which she liked less, the memory his statement brought or the fact that he'd brought the subject up. She'd rather it stayed dead and buried on both counts.

"I have no good excuse for it, Bree, other than to say I'd had drink and was nervous myself." He clasped his hands behind him. "But I believe I have a solution that will help rid both of our nerves."

Breanne looked up. "Truly?"

"Yes, truly." He rocked on his toes. "What do you say to returning to being no more than friends?"

Breanne didn't know what to say. Relief flooded her but also guilt. "But, I thought you spoke with Niall, that you've asked for me?" Was he giving up then? Had she crushed his hope?

"I have and I do not rescind that request, no mistake. I simply feel that if we return to being friends, then mayhap we will both remember the ease with which we handled each other's company and the next kiss will not go so badly." He smiled broadly.

Breanne's relief ended but she did remember the resolution she'd thought of the morning before. She could try the kiss again, to see if he could create the wonder Ashlon had.

She toyed with her cloak hem. The wind billowed it. Quinlan's gaze pierced hers, hope shining there. She wouldn't deny it went badly, as it wouldn't comfort him and only prolong the memory of it.

"How do you propose we do such a thing? How can we act as friends and yet try again to test those waters?" She tried to keep an open mind.

215

Quinlan looked down. "I don't know, perhaps I can make you laugh a bit and then when you're ready, we might sit and proceed slowly and then give each other an honest opinion of it. Is it not what a friend would offer?" He peered at her through his lashes.

Breanne's stomach got a funny squirm in it. She gulped in some air and gripped her cloak. She didn't need him to spell out his intention of trying the kiss again here, now. She could tell in his shy manner and didn't doubt he'd been working up the courage to ask it of her for some time.

"It sounds friend-like, to be sure. And what will we do if the same happens as the last?"

"Well, I must say I'm hopeful that you'll not slap me," he said and rubbed his cheek.

Breanne smiled and tilted her head. He was jesting with her again. It helped lighten the heaviness that occupied her squirmy belly.

"Alright then. I expect now will do," she said.

Quinlan brought his head up. His Adam's apple moved down and up. He nodded and stepped closer.

As his head lowered, Breanne placed a hand on his chest. "Do you mind very much if we talk it through as we go? I think it will help my own nerves, that is if you don't mind."

Quinlan smiled.

"I know, its not terribly romantic this way, but I really believe it will help," she said.

"Fine then. What would you have me do?"

"You might put your hands, well, upon my shoulders?"

He did.

"And I could keep mind about your waist? There, how does that feel?"

"Fine. It feels nice, I suppose."

Breanne stopped from frowning. "All right then. I'm ready." She closed her eyes. Her heartbeat thumped in her throat so hard she could nearly feel its pulse in her tongue. Would he shove his tongue in like the last time? Would it weaken her knees like Ashlon's had?

Ashlon's face swam into her mind's eye. The hazy look his eyes got when they were on her face, on her mouth, the way her whole being seemed to buzz in awareness of him. The squirm in her belly changed to a flutter.

Quinlan's lips met hers. They were soft and gentle and kissed her tenderly several times. When he was pulling his away, she seemed to be bringing hers close, like their rhythms weren't in sync. Then his mouth lingered a moment. Breanne swallowed. She concentrated on breathing through her nose, though it didn't seem to be getting her enough air.

His lips parted first, his tongue warm and wet on her upper lip and Breanne found herself envisioning a serpent's tongue slithering in and out as his was now.

Breanne parted her lips and tentatively pressed her tongue to his. Quinlan's body flinched slightly, his tongue pulled back then he seemed to return to his earlier determination. Gently, he returned her kiss and they allowed their tongues to explore, their lips to press, part and reconnect. After several moments, Quinlan closed his mouth to her, pecked hers rather quickly and stepped back.

Both exhaled and Quinlan's gasp struck her as sounding quite relieved. She wondered on what count. Had it gone better than he hoped for or was he just as glad as her that it was over?

She didn't ask. The warm smile he bestowed on her was answer enough.

"I'd say that is significant progress, wouldn't you? I

must say I found it rather nice."

Breanne pinched her lips together, resisting the urge to wipe the wetness he'd left there for the wind to chill. She nodded. It was an improvement after all. It hadn't brought her to her knees with desire but mayhap that was better. With Quinlan she would never have to fear losing all thought and wits.

And it hadn't turned her stomach. If she allowed, there was a small warmth there now. She was right to have agreed to this trial and it must have been meant for if they each considered the test separately.

Quinlan stepped forward, his smile suddenly eager. He bent his head. Breanne closed her eyes and braced herself when a throat cleared behind them. They jumped apart and turned to see Ashlon and Rhiannon joining them.

Rhiannon had her arm linked through Ashlon's and her gaze was so consumed with watching him that she certainly didn't see Quinlan and Breanne about to kiss or how quickly they came apart. She also couldn't see the flush of red heating Breanne's cheeks.

Looking at Ashlon's half smile and cold stare, however, left Breanne with no question as to whether he'd witnessed it.

"Do you promise, Sir Ashlon?" Rhiannon said, fairly clinging to him. The wind fit her gown to every perfect curve and she seemed to know it by the way she arched her back before looking prettily at Quinlan.

"Promise what?" Quinlan asked and stepped away from Breanne.

The wind pushed her cloak and gown against her back, furrowing it in front of her so well that she had no doubt every line of her was obscured and padded. Gathering the material close was useless and only seemed to attract more of Ashlon's cold gaze onto her.

"He has promised to join us tonight for dining," Rhiannon said and stepped apart from him so that she was evenly spaced between the two men. "And for dance after."

What was he so upset about and nearly glaring at her for? She wouldn't for a second entertain the possibility of it stemming from jealousy. He couldn't have seen more than the two of them about to kiss, and what could be wrong with that?

"Wonderful. You will be able to witness how lovely a dancer Lady Breanne is. Oh, forgive my rudeness, Sir Ashlon. Have you two been formally introduced as of yet?"

"No, we have not."

Ashlon bowed deeply as Quinlan made introduction.

Breanne curtsied equally deeply and didn't miss the flash of emotion in his eyes as they peered at her. Did he need to speak with her then? Of course, he must have been searching her out to ask of her progress, having finished his round in the games.

Silly of her not to realize it sooner. Quickly, though, she remembered that she had nothing to tell him.

"You are masterful in the art of movement, Lady Breanne?" Ashlon asked. His eyes flashed again.

"I can be, given the proper setting and music," she said.

"And partner," Quinlan said, giving her shoulder a brotherly nudge. "Even as a girl, she could go through a dozen partners, wear each one out and be ready for the next, so much stamina she has."

Breanne smiled tightly and hoped the wind could be blamed later for the incontestable color blooming again in her cheeks.

Ashlon raised both eyebrows in an expression that looked both accusing and amused. Breanne bit down the jabbing barb that prodded her tongue.

Quinlan had not intended the double entendre and blast Ashlon Sinclair for making her feel wrong about kissing Quinlan. Who was he to be so amused when he was the one who couldn't keep his hands or lips to himself? Why he'd probably already given Rhiannon a taste of his wares in the short time they'd spent together. She knew firsthand how quickly he moved when the notion took him.

"Oh, I can hardly wait," Rhiannon said, clapping her hands. "Breanne, would you like to join Rose and me in my chamber to ready this evening? Rose promised to put my hair in a twisting braid coiled around like so and she has gold baubles that Ryan brought back for her. I imagine they would look ever so nice in your hair."

Quinlan cleared his throat. "Shall we return and view the remaining fighters, ladies?" He bent an arm for each of them to take.

Ashlon followed behind. Close behind. Breanne could smell him on the wind. And as they descended the stairs she fought to ignore the distinct tugging of her cloak. He wanted to ask her about the book and she had no good news and if she paused or turned, she'd be forced to confess that.

Breanne struggled to appear graceful as the three, linked, attempted the stairs together but Rhiannon kept losing her balance and falling into Quinlan who in turn almost knocked Breanne over.

After the third time, Quinlan shrugged Breanne's arm loose and offered an apologetic look. Breanne shrugged and waited for them to pass.

Ashlon waited, too, a step behind. Rhiannon and Quinlan passed the curve. She didn't know why she'd stayed there. She could easily have simply continued after. But, she didn't. And now they were alone and the corridor became warm around her. Her belly fluttered as Ashlon stepped down and faced her.

She couldn't look up at him and her breathing became difficult with the fluttering sensation growing. Would he ask her? Would he remain silent?

He reached his hand out and laced his fingers into her hair, his thumb soft on her throat. He grazed over the faint mark no one had commented on and she had forgotten about until he touched it.

Rhiannon's laughter floated up from the window she imagined they had returned to. Breanne's heart started, she looked up.

The ice in Ashlon's gaze had melted away and left a steaming heat in its wake. Breanne's breath caught in her throat. Before she could think or move, he kissed her.

And her body sighed with welcome. Ashlon backed her against the wall and slipped his hands inside her cloak. A thrill ran through her. His hands were cold through her gown, but hot to her skin beneath. They roved from her waist upward to her breasts, cupped both and thumbed over her nipples.

From somewhere deep inside, Breanne moaned into the mouth assaulting her senses. His touch was so sure, his lips so perfectly fitting for hers, his tongue magickal. She arched into his palms, grateful for the wall supporting her watery limbs.

Warm, wet wonderment spread between her thighs and she parted them to feel him there. He accommodated her body's wish, pressing her exactly where she craved. Her mound throbbed and the ache and warmth climbed. His very contour seemed a blessing against her, tall and erect, stunning her with accuracy.

Ashlon lifted the edge of her gown and hooked his arm under a bare thigh. His arm aided in opening her body to him, so close to her need. She arched toward it. His hand grazed her rear then gripped the flesh there, pulling her impossibly closer. Breanne might have gasped, "Aye, please. Aye," could she have spoken past his ravaging mouth. He lifted her up as though weightless. He pressed his prick to her sex making short, divine turns.

He broke his kiss and found her neck. Breanne leaned her head back as his exquisite mouth teased her throat. Her breaths were short flutters that matched the same strange beat as each time before. Like a heartbeat within her, but of need rather than blood. Each touch brought pleasure beyond the prior, escalating her sensibility into an abyss of bliss.

Deft fingers tugged aside her undergarment. Her mind begged him not to cease. His forefinger traced a line up her inner thigh, close, oh so close to her moist heat. *Please*. Breanne pressed her hips forth, driven to feel him touch higher. Yet he remained achingly slow in his assault. Her body wept and beat in want. Somehow, she knew his touch, his hand would fill the dizzying need.

Ashlon granted her body's wish, slowly slipping his finger into her slick sheath. Pleasure washed through her as his teeth dug into the flesh below her earlobe. His erratic breathing danced on her skin. He whispered her name and it sounded nigh painful to say. Breanne wiggled. Ashlon complied unbidden. He stroked his finger out of her, then back in, twisting and delving deeper. The sound of her wetness seemed to echo off the stones and much to her shock, deepened her pleasure. This is what her body wanted. His touch. And each delicious stroke brought her closer to something she could not name but might die without. All matters of where and who they were had long ago escaped relevance. Desire roared in her veins and, as suddenly as it started, Ashlon stopped and broke away. Her hem fell to the floor as quickly and silently as the spell he'd wrapped her in.

"Go now," he said. He sounded in keen pain.

Breanne could scream, she felt such a loss. Her body ached for more, but her mind penetrated the charm he had cast upon it. The risks they had just taken, the gamble, was not lost on her.

Go, now. His words reverberated through the haze.

Breanne balanced and stepped downward, feeling stunned as Rose peered about the curve and called up, "Think you they lost their way, Quin?"

Chapter Sixteen

It had been too close a call. Rose had immediately noticed Breanne's flushed color and imbalance. She'd used her only ready excuse, feeling suddenly ill, to explain their delay. While a deep part of her longed to, Breanne couldn't very well tell Rose that Ashlon had been ravishing her for the brief moments they went missing in the stairwell, could she?Leastwise not yet.

Rose had believed her without question. Thanking St. Bridget for such a boon, Breanne was happy to be sent straight back to her chamber to rest. With her mother's wedding in three days, and Ashlon needing to leave Tir Conaill before he either got killed or ruined her, rest sounded heavenly.

She couldn't count herself safe near him after the instant overwhelmed reaction he'd given her with a single kiss that lasted no more than a moment but suspended time.

Thank goodness he'd stopped. Rose would have kept

it secret had she come upon them, Breanne knew, but would then feel absolutely betrayed on her brother's behalf or become Ashlon's proponent and start a campaign for her to marry him.

Neither suited Breanne. And so she was grateful to Ashlon Sinclair for that single save, although she didn't forget he was the one she needed saving from and so it didn't very well elevate his character in her mind.

Finn was in the window, watching the scant view of the men in arms and gave her no more than a cursory glance when she walked in, kissed Rose goodbye and locked the door.

"Hiding out are we?" Finn said over his stripey shoulder.

"Aye, I've much work to do and those silly games should not have taken me from it."

"How did your knight fare?"

"He is not my knight and he did quite well if you must know. But, that is not why I left to watch as I'm sure you are about to imply. I simply wondered. I was curious. And he was fighting Quinlan, whom we both know is not highly skilled."

"Or was not when he was but sixteen, the last age you saw him practice in arms."

"Yes, well, even so. I got distracted and now I am back and ready to solve this damned code of Heremon's before the day ends."

"The knight has found a friend. Interesting." Finn leapt down.

"It is not surprising that the two are companionable. Quinlan found him--."

"Not Quinlan. Another knight, it looked to be from the similar swords and unusual greeting they just gave each other."

Breanne scowled at Finn and opened the book she'd

retrieved. What was that beast trying to bait her into saying now? Well, whatever his aim, she'd be sure he missed. She would not inquire his meaning regardless of how much she now wanted to know. She wouldn't even go to the window.

She would stay where she was at her trestle desk and focus on discovering the hidden meaning in the script. This was more important than any ally of Ashlon's down in the yard. Ashlon Sinclair needed to leave Tir Conaill before something terrible happened between them.

She might not have liked the idea of marriage but that did not mean she spit in the face of a union. She desired a happy marriage built on love and trust. Whatever uncontrollable magick existed between Ashlon and her, it threatened to consume her.

If she did not keep her bearings when near him long enough to see him safely gone, she risked not only shaming her family but ending the chance for a solid future with her husband, whoever she chose.

Quinlan was still an option. A safe option to boot. Their second kiss was a measurable improvement. Why, if they made as much progress with every one, she'd be soon melting in his arms rather than in Ashlon's.

Breanne sighed. Damn it but his mouth and hands could enchant her. She didn't like how much it changed her or how masterfully he could accomplish her total mindless consent.

Finn returned to the windowsill when she buried her attention in the book, or at least appeared to.

There was also Gannon to consider. He was charming and smart and were she to pay him a visit, she might find her heart a little more inclined his way. He might be lovely to kiss. Not a whirlwind like Ashlon, nor procedural like Quinlan. Perhaps his kiss would fall somewhere safely in the middle.

"Intriguing. Sir Ashlon and the other knight appear to be in deep and serious conversation. His face looks rather severe. I wonder from where in the past they are linked and what topic could cause such distress?"

Breanne closed the book and glared at Finn. "I don't care."

"If you need an easy excuse to see for yourself, I would not object to you procuring a skin of wine. I am right thirsty."

Breanne opened the book back up. The sketch stared back at her. She didn't need an excuse to go spy on Ashlon and though her mind itched with curiosity, she refused to scratch.

She focused on the words again. Then like a frog on a lily pad, an idea jumped into her head. Gannon. Of course. Why hadn't she considered his assistance earlier? Though she could not take the book itself to the priory, she could take the translation to him, pass it off as a riddle she couldn't break or something equally innocent sounding.

And if she happened to see Ashlon and whomever he spoke with on the way to the priory, well, what harm could come of it? As long as she avoided Rose and hoped that her mother did not yet know of her supposed dizzy spell, she'd be there and back before her evening bath for dinner.

Breanne smiled smugly to herself as she scribbled the lines onto the blank parchment. A couple blots of ink would not matter much, would it? She could find an explanation for it if Gannon were to note the wasteful appearance. Being a scribe, he would appreciate that a mistake here or there was natural for beginners such as she.

Finn looked lost in interest in the goings on below. Breanne rolled the parchment, tucked it into her cloak's inner pocket and left. "Don't forget the wine," Finn called as she closed the door.

Breanne rolled her eyes and hurried down the stairs. She took care to avoid the Grianan and came out the front rather than side of the keep. The crowd surrounding the games was dwindling and spreading into smaller groups.

She had no true reason to meander through them, as the gate was directly ahead, but she gave in and did so anyway. She only wanted a peek and what harm could come from passing by?

But as she weaved through, she did not find Ashlon.

"Who are you looking for, Bree?" Danny took stride next to her.

Breanne ruffled his hair and smiled. "No one in particular. Having a look at the masses, no more."

"You look to be well. The walk did you good then?"

She resisted frowning. Had she not known better, she would think he was digging for information. "It did wonders."

"Where are you off to now?"

"To see my uncle, Father Connelly, and pay visit to Gannon O'Shannon while I'm there."

Danny's eyebrows shot upward. "Really now? He'll be pleased to see you I'm certain."

"Oh, and why do you say that?"

"He asked after you when you were abed. Not long after we met that morning," Danny said, eyes glancing around when he referred to their secret. "I told him you were more than well."

"What else did you tell him?"

"Oh, no more'n that, Bree. I swear it. You can trust me not to speak to anyone of that morning. I'd be in more trouble than you, I think, if my father were to find out."

"Well, I won't be telling anyone either, Danny." She hugged an arm around him. "Off with you now before Father Connelly sees you and has your ear to bend the next two hours."

Danny kissed her cheek and left her. Whatever he'd been about, she hoped her promise was what he'd been trying to gain with all those questions and references. Strange behavior. But, then he was getting older, changing to a man.

She didn't knock and found Gannon on her way through the door. He looked distracted and walked toward her with his eyes on the floor and a fist tapping his chin.

He started when she spoke his name. "Breanne, what a lovely surprise." He took her hand and kissed it warmly, pressing it to his cheek after. "My but the walk looks fine on your features. Glad to see you're in good health."

"Thank you, Gannon. And I appreciate your patience, as well. I know it's been too long since I promised to pay visit to you here."

"None of that, now. You're here and just in time to witness the delight of my day's work. Follow me."

Gannon led her, holding her hand. His long legs reminded her of a colt's, eager and yet sure as he walked through a short maze of doors and corridors. Abruptly, he stopped. "Did you want to speak with your uncle first, Breanne?"

"No need. I'll catch a moment with him on my way back if it's all the same with you," Breanne said.

Gannon winked and continued, stopping again in front of a door. "Are you ready?"

Breanne smiled like a kid. "I expect I am. What are you about, Gannon?"

"It's a secret." He put his finger to his lips, flashed

his eyebrows up.

Breanne giggled, forgetting her own mission for a moment, caught up in his giddiness. He opened the door slowly, bringing a candle from the corridor in with them.

The bare windowless room held a slim straw pallet and a large rectangular chest propped open with a stick. Gannon waved her over and motioned for her to kneel with him. Breanne shook her head in wonder.

She opened her mouth to whisper but clamped it shut when a small sound echoed from the chest. Breanne inhaled sharply as Gannon opened the lid and exposed seven mewling little balls of fur and one large black cat. They laid in a nest of gray wool lining the oak chest carved on the inside but not out.

"Kittens," Breanne said and Gannon squeezed her hand then let it go.

"Three weeks old. And this is Minerva. She's a good mother. This is her first litter and though she lost one--."

"Oh, the poor thing. Did she know?" Breanne pressed her hand to her heart where it hurt.

"Oh, aye. She kept it with her, licked it clean for some time after the others got to feeding and then lay her head on it, closin' her eyes like she meant to say goodbye and then looked up to me. I knew she wanted me to take it then, that she was asking me to."

Breanne held both hands to her chest over the pain. Nothing could be worse than a mother losing a child. The idea of it terrified her and made her wonder if she could bring life to the world when it could so easily be snatched away.

She remembered the weeks after her mother lost her child more'n ten years ago, all Ula's sadness and putting on a brave face. Ula's best friend Isolde delivered within days of Ula and Breanne often caught a strange pain in her own chest when Danny was near.

Ula's had been a boy, as well, and she had struggled for two days and nights to give him life. Her father had been gone and Breanne's brother, Justin had already been buried when he returned. Then her father had died only eight months after and before he could fulfill the promise to his wife to try again.

Seeing Danny growing and thriving all these years must have been so hard for her mother and must be why Ula saved her affections for when Isolde was not around. Perhaps to save both of their feelings from hurt.

"What did you do with the poor baby?" Her voice choked.

"I buried him. I named him Alabaster. He was the single white kitten of the litter." Gannon's voice held emotion, as well.

"Can I touch one?"

"She doesn't seem to mind my handling them but if you don't mind overmuch, I'll ask you to wait. Just until they are a bit older and on their own more."

Breanne nodded and swiped a tear that slipped out. "Aye, a better idea to be sure."

"You get the pick of the litter, Breanne. I believe Finn is the sire and so you should have the first honors."

"Finn? That little beast. I can't believe it. I thought he must be too old for that sort of thing." In truth she thought his being an enchanted pooka, only taking the form of a cat, would make him not fully feline. After all, he drank like a person, ate like a person, spoke like one, too.

"I spied him here twice in the last month. I like to think he's been checking on her progress."

"Interesting. It would explain his absences. So long as he's not causing chaos in the kitchen for the Brehon to get fined for, I never wondered much about what he went about."

If he did sire the litter of all black cats, he'd left no sign of it in them. Unless some showed to inherit pale green eyes. Minerva's were yellow as a Beltane moon.

Beltane. Rather nice of her mind to remind her of that little holiday just as she forgot her woes for a time. She needed to focus on her original intent, to ask Gannon's assistance and doubly get to know him well enough to garner a kiss.

"Danny insists that Finn promised him first choice and already has it picked. If you won't mind my telling you which it is, and if you consider the others first, I can indulge the boy."

Breanne chuckled. "I can't see a reason why not. He gets attached right securely in your heart, that one. I have a hard time saying no to him myself."

A small kernel of suspicion lodged in her belly. It was the second time he'd said to another that Finn spoke. She wanted to dismiss it as a child's fancy and had she known better about Finn, she would. But then she couldn't see Finn risking the kind of exposure any other soul finding out his secret would cause. Without a doubt, were any to know he was a talking cat, he'd be burned as the devil's servant before she could remind any of the old ways, of fairy mounds and magick.

Her kernel of doubt dwarfed in comparison to her endearment for the boy, who was more like a brother, when she remembered the one she had lost. She hadn't understood the loss well then, when she worried more about losing her mother than anything else. But, now she appreciated the missing piece.

A brother. Family. With Niall having no children from his dead wife, Breanne would likely never know the feeling outside of that she had with Danny. Unless what she'd heard that day outside their door were true. Unless Niall meant to replace the baby Ula lost and begin a new family.

"May I ask your word not to tell a soul?"

"What, oh aye, of course you may Gannon." She shook off the uncomfortable idea of her mother bearing Niall's fruit. "But, why?"

"Father Connelly is a mite suspicious of animals, cats particularly. It took some convincing to allow Minerva to stay here with me." He pet the cat's head as he spoke.

"I promise. Although I should warn you that Danny is a poor keeper of secrets." Too late she realized she'd just implied having some secrets of her own. "That is to say, often he tells me a bit more than I believe he should be of other's personal matters." Though she stumbled over her tongue, Gannon didn't seem to notice.

"Aye, I know. But, as he's known for a sennight with no folly, I'm hoping he'll stay quiet. And I take pains to remind him every chance I see him."

"Speaking of personal matters, Gannon, I must confess, I have come with somewhat of an ulterior motive."

"Oh?" His eyes sparkled.

"I have come across a riddle of sorts that I find I canno' yet solve. I thought of you."

His smile widened, displaying a set of even and cleanly white teeth. "Let us have a look, then."

Breanne's discomfort instantly eased. She should have known he would take pleasure in such a commission. Without preamble, she retrieved the roll and handed it to him.

Without comment on its garish appearance, Gannon read the lines as he moved to sit upon the pallet. The kittens mewled in the vacancy. Breanne watched them, glancing occasionally Gannon's way and considering him well while he was occupied.

His face was narrow but not unhandsome. His hair was straight and a dun brown. His eyes were probably his best feature and those only because they held such humor and charm in them. Had he a different personality, he might seem quite dull to her.

She watched him mouth the words. His lips were thin and his beard was kept short, unless it didn't grow well yet. She tried to imagine those small lips pressed to hers in passion. She couldn't. She could envision them and even could see a warmth about them kissing her. It wasn't detestable but it didn't send her stomach aflutter either.

She could see a kiss from him to be loving, enthusiastic but not particularly ardent. Breanne sighed. To imagine was one thing, to know, another. She would not consider attempting to find out today though. Three men's kisses in a single day seemed too much to ask of one woman's lips.

Gannon tapped a finger to his mouth and lowered the page.

"Intriguing. It is not obvious, is it?"

She shook her head and smiled. He looked far from daunted by the lines. He looked indomitable.

"May I keep it and work on it?"

"Aye. But, only if I have your word as well not to share it with another," Breanne said. Gannon's eyebrows shot up and urged Breanne to find a quick explanation. "It was given to me in challenge and I wouldn't want the originator to gloat my defeat quite yet."

"Ah, I see. You have my word then, Breanne." Gannon reached down and kissed her hand to seal their trust. "I also need to tell you something and I'm not sure exactly how to go about it."

Breanne's belly tightened. She'd like nothing less than a proposal right now. Even a mild declaration of affection would send her running from the room if she didn't get her nerves under control fast. "What is it?" she asked, seeing no way out of it.

"You'll likely find this a bit funny, well, I'm hoping so. I asked Niall after you not so long ago. Not an official declaration of interest, mind you, but just was curious, I guess, as to why you've not married."

"Oh?" Breanne swallowed the growing lump in her throat.

"The funny part is that, well, methinks Niall took my question as a serious inquiry. He asked me yesterday how our courtship went." Gannon chuckled uneasily. "I told him well, not knowing what else to answer, and thought the man a bit daft or confused."

"You're not intending to ask for me then?" Breanne asked in a rapid spurt of confidence.

"Course not. I mean no insult, Breanne. I think you're lovely, right enjoy your company. But, I thought I better set the issue right in case I mislead Niall or you unintentionally." He met her gaze.

Breanne didn't know what to say. On the one hand she felt more relieved than she should or than she wanted to show him. On the other, Gannon had just shortened her suitor list in quick order and it did sting just a bit.

In the end, humor won out. "But, Gannon, I've already sewn my gown. My mother has spoken with yours."

Gannon's eyes bulged and Breanne couldn't contain her laughter any more. The joke was a bit cruel and petty but damned if it didn't make her feel better. Not to mention clearing the palpable tension from the room.

"Which is it, by the by?" Breanne said.

"Which is what?"

"Which cat has Danny selected?"

Gannon grinned, his gaze on the open chest. "The

runt. He's named her Legend."

"Aye, and good you warned me, Gannon, as I may have picked her myself. I've a soft spot for those beset with a challenge."

"When would you like this by?" He gestured the page in the air, returning to their common ground, learning.

"Well, as soon as you can so long as it's not a burden to your work. I'm a bit impatient to snub the nose that looked down in giving me the task." It was a slight truth.

"Can I ask if it was your uncle the abbot that challenged you so?"

"Aye, you can, but he's not the one." Breanne watched the little kittens clamor over each other for food, their mother heavy lidded and looking content. "Does he like a bit of mystery, my uncle?"

"That he does. I've told you of his expected arrival?" She nodded.

"If it does not arrive shortly, I fear he'll go mad in the wait of it and every day has a new supposition of what it might be. He believes the papal missive is coded well enough to conceal the identity of the relic." Gannon chuckled. "Not a dull day goes by in these halls, Breanne."

She smiled up at him, enjoying the dance in his eyes. Such a charmer, that one. And if she was not mistaken, Gannon was flirting with her own interest in intrigue.

"I should be getting back afore my mother sends the guard. I'm hoping I'll be allowed to dine tonight and join the dance after." She rose to leave. "Can we work on the puzzle together on the morrow, Gannon?"

He checked the hall for Father Connelly before they exited and hurried back to the entrance. "I'd like that." He kissed her hand and bid her farewell.

The sun was nearing the horizon and Breanne decided a visit with her uncle would have to wait. If she walked fast, she might be able to take Rhiannon up on her invitation. What harm could there be, after all, in looking her most tempting when every other lady there would be sure to shine?

Approaching the outer bailey, Breanne remembered the fact that Ashlon might be looking for answers regarding her progress. Her belly tightened at the thought of telling him the truth. While she trusted Gannon not to suspect anything untoward, Ashlon might dislike a stranger being involved.

She couldn't lie to him. She took her vow seriously for he needed to trust her. Otherwise, they would make little progress in finding the chest and securing his safe departure.

Ashlon would be gone as early as days from now if Gannon's help proved fruitful. She could simply avoid him tonight and hope he did her, as well. But, considering this afternoon's events, she found the possibility farfetched.

Well, she would simply have to be honest. No matter how difficult his reaction might be.

Chapter Seventeen

Though the dinner marked the beginning of the wedding festivities, few talked of the coming nuptials. Far more interesting to most men and women among the closely packed tables was discussion of the day's games.

Who won, who lost, who fell flat on his arse. And none seemed at all insulted that among the ten declared champions, an outlander was ranked in third. If Ashlon was welcomed before, now he felt embraced.

The many names he'd learned were difficult to match to the many bearded, ruddy faces who joined Niall's table of men that night to feast on soda bread, smoked venison and pulled pork. Ale and wine flowed freely and as well as the compliments, jibes, and wagers on the games scheduled for the morrow. A day of rest would do him good and he might even be able to search the coast line, today's goal gone awry with Niall's petition he join the games.

And glad he was that he had stayed. The day had been eventful to say the least. Not only had he attained third in line for the championship rounds, but, he'd been reunited with a fellow Templar, Sir Ramsey Johnston. Ashlon's elder by fifteen years, they had attained equal rank and shared in its ceremony.

Ashlon had not seen Ramsey in more than eight years, though. While Ashlon had spent his last year in France, Ramsey hadn't left his home in England and had served there until Pope Clement and King Philip began their campaign to destroy the brotherhood and gain its considerable wealth for their own.

While Ashlon went from place to place in hiding, Ramsey came straight to Ireland, joined the O'Doherty clan and also hired on with Robert Bruce as gallowglass in his crusade against English tyranny.

"Do you know, Ashlon, there is law on England's books forbidding an English noble to dress, speak, or participate in activity that is Irish?"

Ashlon shook his head, his mouth full, but wasn't surprised. Such a good-hearted, lively people grew on the soul, lifted it up unexpectedly. Even in the short time he'd been there, he found it difficult to suppress.

"They made me one of their own when the whole world seemed set to believe the lies and rot slurring a legacy of generosity and courage. Mark me you'll be hard pressed to leave. And why would you, I ask?" It was the seventh time Ramsey had asked.

Ashlon half-smiled and chewed. He wouldn't answer. What was the point in doing so when he meant to leave and could not tell the man why? Not that he did not trust Ramsey, he did. But Jacques had been clear. "Tell no one. Trust no one save those who do not, will not gain from aiding you. And that will be one and only one soul."

He'd thought the words too marked by fear at the time, but he held to them and trusted that his mentor would make sense one day. They had parallel lives, Breanne and he. She had had Heremon. He had had Jacques De Molay. He received a grave speech, she a cryptic letter, but both were asked by others to protect solely based on the trust and faith instilled by a teacher.

He wondered for the first time what it was that she belonged to. What was the nature between Heremon and her? He felt a bit badly for being so self-consumed with attaining the chest and ending his journey, the scent of home, and new beginning so fresh and clean in his mind that he'd not once considered it.

Ashlon leaned back far enough to see past Ramsey and glimpse her. Healer, angel, stubborn, proud. Who was Breanne O'Donnell? What was her life before he arrived and it turned upside down with death and secrecy and passion?

She smiled and spoke to Rose. It was dangerous to feel so drawn to her, to forget himself so well when she was near. He'd kissed her again, had allowed a bite of jealousy to rule his actions. It maddened him. And it pressured him.

Ramsey still spoke of all of Ireland and Northern Scotland's comely attributes and Ashlon nodded when appropriate. With each trait listed, the pressure grew, with each glance her way, the hole in him widened.

Breanne could feel his eyes on her. A tingle on her neck, at her shoulder told her he peered her way. She fought not to glance back, to keep her eyes and, more importantly and more difficult than it should be, her attention on the meal and table she sat at.

When the meal cleared and both bards and players began to set up. Breanne's belly fluttered as a familiar scent closed in. It was Ashlon and she didn't know what was worse, that she recognized the spicy clean scent of him or that he was so near.

"You look beautiful this eve," he said in low tones at her shoulder.

His words were a caress and she shivered despite the warmth inside her. "Thank you," she said but did not turn or look at him.

Guests and residents milled about in anxious wait for the floor to be cleared. Their bodies pressed around the pair, pushing her closer to him.

"Have you yet discovered the text's meaning?"

Quickly, she shook her head. Expecting him to ask, to approach her was one thing, the reality of it quite another. She suddenly felt hot and a bit dizzy. "Excuse me, please." Hurriedly, before the panic threatening her chest took hold, Breanne snaked through the crowd and out the main double doors.

The cool air washed her face and cooled her breaths as she fought to steady her mind. Inside the music began with the rhythmic beat of a bodhran. It slammed as loud as her heart and as the music joined and spread around it, Breanne found a sudden feeling of epiphany taking over the panic.

She saw the chest suddenly in her mind. Ashlon lifted it from its resting place, wiping it clean and dry, gathering it into his arms as one would a child. His face wore relief and amazement. He looked at her with gratitude shining in his eyes and another emotion that made her heart ache. One she couldn't define.

It was more than protection, fate required of her. And the certainty of knowledge went deeper than Heremon's presage, further than his letter, past her own prediction. She knew then that she must become like a rock in a storm as certainly as knowing her own name. The prediction was simple and irrefutable to her in that moment as the music swept about in waves of notes crashing and pulling hearts and minds.

Ashlon Sinclair was her fate, her destiny.

And that meant her destiny was in peril, not simply his life.

The doors opened behind her and she did not need his scent or deep voice to know it was him.

"Breanne."

Without turning to see the emotion that strangled his voice, Breanne said, "We must go tomorrow night."

She imagined he shook his head in the silence before replying.

"Where?"

"I know where the chest is."

"You solved the script. When? Why did you not say so? Where is it? Quickly, we must go now." He stepped close to her.

Breanne turned about. "We canno' go now. We would be missed."

"You would be missed. I will not. Tell me where it lies and I will retrieve it alone. 'Tis probably safer, as well."

"You canno' leave either. And you will not go without me."

"I beg to differ my lady. Clear of translating the script, I require no further assistance, would not have asked of it if another option were available. I will go now and without you."

Breanne didn't doubt he meant what he said. His eyes were fierce, his mouth set. He didn't seem to realize that they were intrinsically linked and not by the book or by the chest but by events set in motion by a generation past. And she didn't know how to explain this fact without sounding heretical or mad.

She searched for another, equally true, explanation while he searched her eyes.

Ashlon held her shoulders and stooped low. "Breanne, please, I know there is an invisible draw between us. I feel the pull of my soul and body to you, but I dare not risk losing that chest. There is more at stake in its loss than I am at liberty to share with you or even claim to know myself. Please, I need you to tell me where it is now. If I wait any longer, I fear the consequences will damage far more than my life but yours, all of Tir Conaill's even."

"Aye, I know. Heremon spoke as much in the time of your arrival and I realize now before it, as well. He has been long preparing me for this day and only now did I see it."

Ashlon ran his hands through his hair. The music inside took on a frenzied beat as the song reached the crescendo. The fast beats matched the tension between them.

"If you know, as you say you do, if what you say is true, then you will tell me now."

Breanne slowly shook her head and braced for his outrage. "Please believe me, Ashlon. I do not mean to impede you, in fact, the opposite. The chest is safe. I know where it lies, I must first discover how to get there."

Ashlon frowned. He shook his head. "You know its

location but not how to reach it?"

 She could see he did not ask her these questions, was venting more than naught. The music paused. Silence spread its wings around them.

 "When the moon reaches its zenith tomorrow night, we will go. Meet me outside of the rear bailey postern."

 "I will go. You will stay. I will not put you at risk." He sounded better if not a bit saddened.

 Breanne turned to go inside. He grasped her wrist.

 "Is there more riddle to solve? Is there some person to ask for direction?" He must feel rather powerless.

 "Aye. And I have."

 Ashlon nodded but his frustration was clear. He wanted to press her for detail but seemed to rein in the urge. The old ways were nigh extinct in England and elsewhere. So, she didn't think he fully comprehended the weight of her words, but trusted her all the same, or tried to.

 Something she had said must have rung true for him not to fight her further. She wondered what it was.

 "Strange that seven years can feel like a glimpse now and one more than eternity." A soft ballad penetrated through the doors and walls and cloaked the damp night air.

 Breanne hugged herself against the flutter inside of her. He was hers. To protect. Ashlon Sinclair was hers. He just did not know it yet. This was his home. He just had not discovered that yet. But, he would with her help.

 Breanne watched the play of frustration in his eyes and could see it was not from feelings of impotence alone. He was fighting something else, as well. When he turned and met her eyes, she no longer wondered what he fought. It read there clearly.

 He wanted her. She needed to distract him from any further wanton thought fast or he'd have her pinned and lost in heated bliss again with somebody certain to catch them.

"Gannon O'Shannon is the most clever man I know. I gave the script to him." She meant not just to distract him but to reassure him, as well. "He may have it solved now but, of course, we must wait nonetheless, for the full moon and last guests. It will be safest."

Ashlon's eyes narrowed on her. "You gave the book to another to translate? Is the book not so private and important as you led me to believe then?"

"Nay. It is both. I only gave Gannon the lines, rewritten and told him it was a riddle, a challenge. He will not understand the connection it has to you or even to me, let alone the chest." Though her words came well, they seemed to be worsening the look of things rather than improving them.

"You do not understand what it is you've shared, what it is you've put at risk. If any learn of this chest, if it is lost to me again, I will lay the blame at your feet."

Breanne gasped. "There is no need to become angry. I swear to you here before God and the universe that I do understand the gravity of your quest well. I might even understand it better than you yourself do." Outrage swelled inside of her. How dare he? From the start, she had done naught but aid him and without reward or gain.

"I can hardly see how that is possible. Life and custom may differ here than in the rest of Europe, but make no mistake that the knowledge I carry goes past the depth of an Irish lass."

Breanne's fists balled tight. She couldn't believe the gall of the man. "Absolutely unbelievable--."

"Exactly my feeling, my lady, unbelievable. If I were in a different position than at your mercy, I would demand to see this man and repair the damage you've inevitably done."

"You speak from the wrong end, sir," Breanne said, her arms crossed. "I am far more clever than you can comprehend due to the closed-minded mentality all English appear to favor."

"If I counted myself as one, I might take exception to such an insult, but since I do not, you have wasted your breath." Ashlon shrugged but his eyes shined with ire.

"Alas, I forgot, you are a man without a country, a noble knight without a cause, no more'n a bounder who I will be happy to see leave here."

Ashlon half-smiled. "Well, you have only to wait so long as you see fit. Go now, my lady, fetch your errand boy and let us be off to find the chest you claim to have found. Ah yes, I forgot, you only know the place and not the way."

Angry tears stung Breanne's eyes. She wouldn't let him do this to her. She would not let him see her cry. She had half a mind to show him exactly how clever and capable she was but couldn't think of a single trick at that moment. There weren't exactly a pile of unlit candles lying about the yard.

Behind Ashlon, the doors opened. A handful of flushed guests joined them to cool in the night air. Ashlon took a step back from her and though he still appeared angry, smiled for the benefit of the others.

Breanne did the same. A breath later, Quinlan appeared with Rhiannon on his arm. They looked handsome together, glowing from the dance they must've shared. Breanne turned to go inside before they saw her among the crowd.

Ashlon managed to bend close enough to whisper, "It appears yours is not the only hand, Quinlan is interested in, Breanne."

She inhaled sharply and looked at him. Ashlon knew

she meant to marry, then? Did he also know her impending choice was at Niall's behest? So be it. She should have realized that he would ask of her, being forced to depend on her as he was. Breanne strode toward the door then stopped and faced him. She would not let him get the best of her.

"You make it clear how little you know of an Irish woman's heart, Sir Ashlon. I have no need to compete with another. The man I set sights on will fall to my feet in love and make no mistake, will never take interest in another." She squared her shoulders and resumed her return.

At the doors, Breanne pressed her lips to her hand in a kiss. She let a small flame dance on her open palm then blew it out as if blowing him a kiss. She didn't linger to enjoy the astonishment that lifted his features but the mere glimpse made the rest of her night worth dancing away.

Chapter Eighteen

Ashlon woke at dawn with more than a headache from over imbibing. His chest ached as well. An uncomfortable weight had settled there during the course of last evening. But, he did not blame Breanne. He blamed himself.

He had gotten too close to her and to here. It must account for his dread and sadness rather than the elation and anticipation he should feel. They would leave tonight to retrieve the chest and within mere hours of its discovery, his seven years of surreptitious living would end. He would be free of the burden Jacques left him.

So, why wasn't he feeling well, light and hopeful? He raked his hands through his hair and gave up on getting any more sleep. His mind was too tense. What he needed was a distraction.

Last night, the dancing and drinking turned out to be a poor attempt to keep his mind off the bewitching creature, Breanne. Today, the effects only worsened the strange longing he felt for her. Even in heated argument, his body responded to her. Something about her lit his soul on fire, so much so that his mind played tricks on him.

She'd garnered assistance and he should trust her in the decision's wisdom. She'd done naught that would make him believe her otherwise capable and honest, yet he'd attacked her. Last night, he was sore to admit it, but in the growing gray light of another Irish spring day, the truth came more readily to him.

It was not the idea of her asking for help. It was that he felt enormously useless in his own quest. He hated his dependence on not only her but a stranger's charity, as well. His independent and self-sufficient nature found the ongoing dependence more than distasteful. He found it abhorrent. But, he had no choice.

Also, though he'd never say the words aloud, under torture even, he'd been jealous. It was the fact that she had asked a man. Women and men did not make good friends in his experience. Which meant that she had more than Quinlan in mind for her betrothal.

First, walking upon her and Quinlan ready to embrace. Then to find out another suitor wooed her, one she trusted enough to beg a favor. It went beyond the grain.

Ashlon stood and shoved his boots on. Aside from his mantle, he'd left all clothing on before passing out on his pallet. And though his head now ached, he was thankful for the oblivion the drink had given him.

If he lay another night torturing himself with images

of her mouth and body pressed wantonly into his, he might go mad. One single day, and he would be gone. Once the chest was laid in its rightful and permanent rest, he could go completely raving mad, could entertain ridiculous thoughts of love and family, of settling down. Until then, he must remain sane and busy. The thought should have offered comfort. Instead, it made his chest feel all the heavier.

After breaking his fast, curing his weak stomach, with a biscuit and dried meat, Ashlon headed toward the O'Donnell keep. The wedding was tomorrow. A shame he would not be here to witness the celebration. He didn't doubt it would well shadow those he'd already participated in. Damned but the Irish knew how to live.

Not a single soul went without a hearty dance, singing, and clapping, and laughing. The energy of the music and joy had pulled him in and lifted him up. So much so that he forgot his anger and thoroughly enjoyed the remaining evening.

Breanne had been mesmerizing. She only rested a moment here and there to wet her lips on wine and water then returned to dancing. She oftentimes was the center of the dance, being hailed and applauded as was well deserved.

She had an angel's grace and a devilish spark.

Ashlon shook his head. He needed her out of his mind, fogging it up with her draw.

Few men were about at the early hour, likely sleeping off their own night's worth of drink and cheer. Aside from a few servants, fuidir, Quinlan had called them, Danny was the only other person in the bailey yard. He sat leaned against the stone wall, a black and gray striped cat at his feet, and ate a pear. He was talking to himself.

Ashlon chuckled and approached as silent as

possible though he was in plain view. He hoped Danny was distracted enough in daydreams and pretend that Ashlon might give him a bit of a scare.

"Dead wrong you are there, Finn. Breanne cannot be in love. She hardly seems to like Sir--."

"Gotcha."

Danny nearly shot straight up into the air and did knock his head against the stone in a hard thump. Ashlon chuckled but felt badly when the lad rubbed his head and appeared more than perturbed with him. He looked a mite panicked.

"Sir Ashlon. I did not see you."

"Aye, I know it. Are you all right? I did not mean to scare you unconscious." He knelt before Danny, touched his head gently.

"I'm fine. You got me good, though. I did not hear or see you at all."

"I could tell. You were talking to yourself, arguing with yourself in fact." Ashlon took a seat on the ground and leaned his head back. It deservedly throbbed.

"To myself? Oh, aye, I sometimes do. When, no one else is about to hear it. What is it I was saying, that is, what did you hear?"

"Naught to blush about, Danny. It sounded like you were considering Lady Breanne's affections. And you referred to the name Finn."

"Finn is the cat, Breanne's cat. When I talk to myself, I use him to do it is all." Danny spoke fast.

Ashlon winced inwardly. He hadn't wanted to make the boy feel awkward. "I've done the same myself. But, I chose a horse to speak to myself with. A fine stallion I was forced to sell some years past."

Danny smiled wide. The cat named Finn, swished its tail in the dirt. It narrowed disturbingly light green eyes on him and seemed to look right into Ashlon. Feeling silly at the notion, Ashlon reached to scratch behind its ears. It ran, hissing a stream on its way.

Danny laughed. "He's not a friendly one, Finn."

"No, I'd say he's not." Ashlon pushed Breanne from his mind. "Seeing as we're both about with not much to do, is now a good time to see to your swordsmanship, Danny?"

Danny leapt to his feet. "Aye, Sir Ashlon, it is."

By the noon hour, Danny was worn out and Ashlon was warmed up. His head's pain dulled considerably and the exercise had done a fine job of preoccupying his mind. The continuance of Niall's games, kept it that way.

By the third round, five warriors remained: himself, two of the O'Doherty clan, two of the O'Donnell clan, one of which was Quinlan.

Ashlon had not heard Quinlan's name announced the previous eve, but was not surprised to see the man join the ten that began the day's battles. They'd had only time enough to exchange a nod of acknowledgement before Niall called the games to commence.

The crowd today seemed twice as big and ten times as loud. Ashlon took each man on with vigor. He did not mean to win, only to wear down the ache inside. Every time he felled a blow, blocked a stab, sidestepped a thrust, the heaviness dwindled. In its place a wonderful numbness took residence.

The hours swept by him. So, when Quinlan came to stand before him, and Niall announced theirs would end the day's competition round, Ashlon was surprised. Not because his newfound friend remained a contender, for Quinlan had done well yesterday against him, but because the day was gone.

He would meet her within hours, he realized. And for the first, he allowed Breanne back into his thoughts. The ache was gone. Only new anticipation filled him as he lifted his sword ready.

"You've done well, Ashlon. I should have asked your help in swords, rather than in love." There was a subtle edginess to Quinlan's statement.

"Would it be such an upset to have an outlander win out?" Ashlon half-smiled and brought his sword down onto Quinlan's.

"Ashlon, you should know by now, that you are counted as one of us. You have only to petition for your official status to call yourself an O'Donnell clansman." He blocked the blow well and swooped down one in return.

The clang of metal rang in the yard and the crowd was more than usually hushed. He could tell Quinlan then and there that he meant to be gone before morning light but saw no reason to. Better to sever clean and quick. If any knew aside from Breanne, many would try to stop him.

Ashlon grunted as Quinlan parried and turned. The day's work began to show. His movements were a degree slower, his arms heavier. Quinlan must be equally fatigued, but his blows came without sign of it. In fact, they, too, held an edginess to them.

With each block, a flash of something akin to anger lit in Quinlan's eyes. As they approached the call of time, Quinlan's eyes took on a frenzied glint and Ashlon became sure that the man was bent on winning. But, there was something more, as well. Ashlon couldn't fathom why Quinlan would suddenly harbor anger for him.

Unless he knew of Ashlon's encounters with Breanne and, thereby, the inevitable breach in trust. Impossible. The only two that could speak of it wouldn't. Breanne would not for the sake of her reputation. And Ashlon would never risk a lady's social virtue even if he were able to honor it with marriage.

Niall announced the round's end and applause roared around them. Quinlan and Ashlon grasped forearms in a sturdy shake, pleasing the crowd all the more. Quinlan's grip tightened and his eyes narrowed on Ashlon. "May the best man win," he said.

Ashlon merely nodded but when he followed the path of Quinlan's gaze to the open window, he understood the man's sudden ire. There, with her hands clasped to her heart, waving a square of sheer blue and beaming an ear-to-ear smile at Ashlon stood Lady Rhiannon.

Her flirtation was unmistakable and her eyes did not move from his face to Quinlan's. Ashlon's did. On it, he saw fleeting but clear dejection before Quinlan strode away. He looked back to the window and found Rhiannon gone. Only Rose remained and she appeared to be lost in thought.

The crowd dissipated, most leaving to ready for the evening meal. Ashlon needed a bath, too, and left for his small room, feeling more excited than before. He shouldn't have been so happy to see the source of Quinlan's ire, but he was regardless. It meant that Breanne's reputation remained intact and that their encounters, were they discovered, might not mean a betrayal of his new friendship with Quinlan.

It meant that Quinlan did not love her.

Ashlon bathed and dressed in quick order, telling himself he hurried because of the hunger gnawing his gut. When he shaved his face clean, he reminded himself that it was an issue of preference not of appeal. Just because the local custom was of wearing a full beard, didn't mean he had to.

His rush and care were not for her. The thought crossed his mind more than once that it was their last night, last time seeing each other. What could the harm be in leaving a good memory in her mind?

When he arrived at the main hall, diners were already seated and the meal begun. Niall's table was always the first to fill and looked to have some time before. In fact, only one table still had available seating. He credited mere chance that it was the same she sat at.

His stomach tightened as he approached. Fortunately, Quinlan sat there, as well, and Ashlon could count on his invitation to join them. Particularly since Rhiannon sat at the man's left and Breanne in front.

He took one steadying breath and approached slowly. A clap to his shoulder stopped him.

"Showing off for the beauties today, Ashlon?" Ramsey asked. His hair was still wet and slicked back.

"Every opportunity that I can," he said. "Did you not participate yesterday?"

"No. I'm a mite too old to be playing with the bucks. But, I watched and I do believe you've learned a trick or two since we last met."

Ashlon half-smiled and continued to the table. Ramsey followed. "I've had time and travels aplenty to see to it. New tricks, as you put it, helped pass the time and saved my hide."

"Oh, aye, I imagine. I must admit I envy you a bit there, Ashlon." Ramsey took a seat, nodding to the diners. Ashlon did, as well, next to Breanne. "You must have such adventures to tell your grandchildren."

"I suppose adventure is one way of considering my past years. But, don't trim your plight overly short, Ramsey. You've a family, a home, a nation."

"You forget that all these things can also be yours, should you only ask." Ramsey spoke a bit louder and nodded to Breanne, Quinlan, Rose and anyone else within earshot.

Ashlon gave him a hardened look in hopes of
quelling the fellow's urge to sell his point. Ashlon did
not need a rally of supporters just now. He needed a
different and safe topic.

"Do you know, that I myself have said the same to
Sir Ashlon," Quinlan said, then introduced himself to
Ramsey. The two men then became so engrossed in their
own perspectives on why Ashlon should remain in Tir
Conaill, or the very least, in Ireland, that they left him
out of it.

Breanne sat stiffly next to him and hardly touched
her food. He didn't need to look to know she was equally
engrossed in the conversation but, he suspected, for her
own reasons. She wanted him gone. He wouldn't be
surprised if she had her own contributions to the debate
outside of the life in danger angle, which she certainly
wouldn't use.

So that he would then not be able to further seduce
her would not be an easy argument to offer either. Not
that he'd been seducing her. If anything, she had been
seducing him with those bewitching eyes, luscious lips.

Ashlon drank from his cup, his throat suddenly tight.
His body was too aware of hers next to his. Sitting here,
being late, was turning out to be a bad idea. And they
were supposed to meet in only a few hours and be alone
in the night. Ashlon shook himself and tried to focus on
the conversation.

"Aye, I agree, why is that Ashlon?" Ramsey said.

"Pardon?" Ashlon had not a clue as to what the
fellow was asking him.

"Why is it that you never say you will and yet don't
say why you will not stay on?" Ramsey clarified with a
chuckle.

Breanne faced him suddenly, her eyes full of
concern. He had at least five others staring him down

along with her, each with a separate degree of interest, and he didn't want to consider how many more listened with equal intensity.

"Never one to beat around about the bushel, were you Ramsey?" he said evasively.

"You needn't actually answer him, Sir Ashlon," Breanne said. "In truth, your decisions should not concern us at all. Your choice to leave or remain is yours, not ours."

Was she trying to keep him quiet, trying to help? If so, the opposite effect took hold of him. Suddenly, he wished he could make clear to all exactly why he could not stay. He wanted to tell them all that the choice was not his, that it was made long ago by a man now dead. He wanted to tell her he wished circumstances were different.

As he opened his mouth to speak some fragment of these truths, Ramsey took pity and spoke up. "Or perhaps, his heart is torn, belongs someplace other than with us?"

Ashlon knew Ramsey referred to the brotherhood, that he had not recovered from the loss of it. Quinlan might guess as much, as well. The ladies, though, leastwise Rhiannon, must not have known overmuch about his past.

"Were you in love, Sir Ashlon? Does your heart long for love lost?" Rhiannon asked breathlessly.

Rose snorted. "Lust is more like it. It's all you men ever think about, isn't it?"

"What was that you said, Rose? I couldn't quite hear over Lady Breanne's enjoyment of the meal."

Breanne jabbed him in the ribs. A chorus of laughter relieved the tension and Breanne's shoulders dropped a notch. Ashlon wished he could feel relieved, as well, but that filthy ache from the morning was returning fast. He finished his meal quickly and made excuses for his early departure, blaming the days games and fatigue.

He didn't go back to his room. He walked. The night was cool and clear and the moon was low and yellowish. He had naught to do but wait for her.

Breanne watched him from her window as his shadowy outline transversed the inner bailey yard. As she estimated, Gannon had come through, an hour ago. Sitting next to Ashlon, she felt sure he would ask about the text. But he hadn't.

Gannon had found her after the meal and slipped her the small note. His expression brimmed with triumph. And while he didn't ask any questions, he made her promise to let him know every last detail regarding its success. And that if she ever saw fit, he would love to know who created the puzzle as they were masterful at it.

Near the stables, Ashlon walked heavily as though a great weight were on his shoulders. She wondered what the man would be like once the weight lifted. Would she see the boyish charm she'd glimpsed in his fever and with a former fellow knight?

Would he remain long enough for it to even become apparent or would he leave, the chest in his arms as she'd foreseen? Breanne wanted the time to swim past but stand still, as well. The unmistakable presence of change lingered near. She hoped she could weather its storm.

Another hour and she would know. Laughter and dance still carried through the keep from the night's festivities. Finn slept contentedly on her bed. The clear night air smelled dewy. She could go to him early, she supposed but sensed an unnamable reason to stay.

She began to gather what she would need, Heremon's book, her athame, three white beeswax candles. With one last glance at Finn and her room, Breanne snuck the door shut and tiptoed down to meet

Ashlon.

Her green cloak blended well with shadow and wall and though she got the feeling someone followed, saw no one along the way.

Ashlon sat where she had asked him to wait, pulling petals from a flower, sitting in the dirt and grass. He stood as she approached and Breanne was glad for the dark and her hood because she didn't want him to see what he did to her, or what his leaving would cause. He could not stay. She would force him away if she had to, but her heart didn't hear reason. It only wanted him near.

Well, it could have its way for a handful of hours more.

Ashlon gestured his hand that she should lead and so she did, unhurt by his silence. Down the valley slope, along the craggy rock path, she hurried and he followed.

His steps were noticeably softer tonight than the other morning. Breanne took it as a sign of support and compliance. Surely he finally believed in her. If so, that belief would certainly soon be shaken, for she didn't think her practice in magick would enforce it.

Ashlon could not call her a witch when his brethren Knights had suffered so much under the same accusation. But he might yet fear what she must do.

Soon he would know the old ways more intimately than she guessed he could comprehend.

Breanne weaved down the hill and to the stream. Without verifying he was near, she retrieved the chalice and bent to the stream. Ashlon remained quiet.

As they approached the Sacred Grove, she paused and performed the ritual blessing on the old oak's roots. She placed the empty chalice into her satchel and faced Ashlon.

"Before we enter, I must ask of you to clear your mind as fully as possible of all fear and prejudice. If you please, save any questions, or conclusions, for after your chest is retrieved."

Ashlon's frown deepened. "I will try. But, I warn you, the very telling me to do so has made me wary already."

"It canno' be helped. I know it is difficult to trust me so blindly, but I have given you my word and my actions show honesty thus far."

"They have." Ashlon cleared his throat. "Very well, I will try my best."

"I'm afraid mere effort will not be sufficient," she said softly. "I require your vow that you will work diligently to maintain a clear mind. If you do not, we may fail in retrieving the chest." Breanne kept her voice even and unassuming. "Unless you may stay among us another month."

"You have my word," Ashlon said, a bit too quickly for her heart.

But her heart was not important at that moment. Her head was. With a deep breath she cleansed it and feeling somber, entered the grove. From the first step Breanne became aware of the full moon's effect on the grove. Magick permeated the very air, sweetening it, creating a low vibration that her body responded to with a quickened pulse.

Nights like this were what she had lived for before Heremon's murder, what had kept her going through failure after failure over years of virtually lone study. On a night such as this one, she remembered why she had worked so hard and her commitment was inevitably renewed.

She wondered if Ashlon could feel it, too. Could he sense the tingle of it on his skin, smell its allure? She didn't look at him to see. She kept onward to the stone slab that her Druid master had used as his altar, to her destination.

The leaves and grass sparkled with dew and enchantment and the forest felt full of watching, curious eyes, all on her. She sensed they were there without having to see them in the flesh. Fairies, small, secretive little creatures were out to play and among them she wouldn't be surprised to know an elf or two came along.

They were said to be human sized, inquisitive creatures that sometimes lived recklessly and came through the Otherworld's veil to see how the human half lived. They weren't so easily hidden though, as a fairy might be and so Breanne never expected a sighting.

She pictured them green skinned with long pointy ears reaching past their head's top. In myths and legends they were hailed to be so beautiful so as to hurt the human eyes that could not break away, bringing tears and eventually blindness to witnesses of it.

Breanne was proud to share it with Ashlon, were he aware of it or not, because this was Ireland at its most magnificent and fascinating. If he opened his heart to it, he'd be smitten forever with its wonders.

Deep into the trees, the clearing came into view. The songs of toads and crickets softened as they stepped into the near perfect circle lit by the overhead moon.

Breanne turned to Ashlon, fighting down the panic in her belly. She didn't want to disappoint the trust Heremon had placed in her and she had promised his soul, wherever it might be in heaven or Otherworld, that she would find who had killed him and fulfill this task's completion.

Ashlon's face was upturned, staring at the moon above, his mouth open. A smile spread from her lips to her heart watching the awe touch him. What must it be like to have had his faith so shaken by past events and to see this splendor now? She hoped it nourished his soul and offered a bit of faith in her.

When he looked at her, questions showed in his eyes but he held them back and only nodded at her. Breanne didn't miss the swallow he took either.

She took his hand and led him to the stone altar. To him it likely appeared to be no more than a good and square-ish shaped boulder among others that were round. Breanne saw differently.

The stone slab glowed faintly and its energy vibrated through her. When she'd told Ashlon they could not come here, she had meant that they could not yet retrieve the chest. Gannon's deciphering did not spell the path she'd traveled countless times, it showed the words that would lay open the stone and reveal the chest inside.

But, revealing the chest depended on a level of magick Breanne had never experienced before let alone created. She took a trembling breath and knelt, as well. She withdrew the candles and placed them in a three points along the stone's tabled surface. Her hands shook.

From the corner of her eye she saw Ashlon press his eyes closed and mouth words she hoped were not heavenly prayers for escape or forgiveness. They needed the earthly Goddesses' ears tonight, not the heavenly father's.

Of Morrigan's trinity, she needed Macha for destruction. From Brigit, she would ask help in opening the well within the stone where the chest lay. And Sheela-na-gig for providence and help in birthing the chest forth.

Ashlon's mouth stopped moving but his eyes remained closed. No matter, so long as he did not intercede with the ritual.

Breanne opened Heremon's book to the image of the chest. She rotated the book so that the image became upside down. She read the words in reverse and then forward again. With Gannon's help, their meaning was now clear to her.

She lit the candles, thankful to have Ashlon's eyes shut, with a soft blow and whisper to each. She withdrew her athame and released a shaky breath.

"You're not going to try to kill me with that tiny thing, are you?" Ashlon whispered.

Breanne sagged and gave him a glowering look. "No," she whispered back. She returned her attention to the slab.

"It's much smaller than I recall. I can't believe you accosted me with such a puny blade."

Breanne glared at him. "I didn't. I accosted you with my boline. They are a set. But, I was a bit distracted that morning and fear I left it in the grass."

"Aye, you left it there. Then you walked away from me unprotected."

"Aye, now, please keep quiet, Ashlon," she said, exasperated, ignoring his scolding tone. "I need to concentrate and you should, as well."

"My apologies. Nerves, I suppose."

"Shhh."

Ashlon winced and closed his eyes again. But, she hadn't missed the bewildered look in them upon seeing the lit candles and her hand lifted ready to scry the air. She hoped he could handle whatever happened.

Breanne started over.

She took another breath and was relieved to notice it came out smoothly this time. The interruption had helped ease her tension, as well. She felt ready.

Scrying the air in a clockwise circle around them, Breanne spoke the words in Gaelic. She enclosed them in, feeling the energy compress and surround them. The magickal vibration was still subtle but present.

She began the chant in slow careful words, keeping

in counts of threes until the trance pulled her in and drew her up. The edge of trees surrounding the clearing blurred, becoming moonlit green, haze and mist. The stone shifted and the candles disappeared.

Breanne rose, the book with its glowing pages set aside. Ashlon remained as still as stone as she lifted her arms to the sky and reached into the depths of her being for her last draw of hope and love and need.

The night air roared in her ears, through her body as the vibration grew. With the words as arrows she shot them into the night air, willing them to find their target and splay open the stone well.

As her body drained, she fought to collect her composure and stay on her feet, terrified that she might fail. Like a bolt of lightening, something bright uncoiled from her. Breanne fought to harness the power and charged the altar with it, knocking her onto her back, unconscious.

Chapter Nineteen

Ashlon didn't believe his eyes. The silence brought them open in time to witness a blue-ish air of curling lights reach out and slice into the large rock she'd brought them to. He'd never seen anything of the like and it all occurred soundlessly before him.

When Breanne fell back in an apparent faint, Ashlon caught her, saving her head from cracking open on a sharp rock. He was torn between shaking her awake and demanding to know why in the world she had endangered herself so, and holding her close.

Holding her won out. His eyes flashed from the fallen chunks of stone to the extinguished candles, still smoking, and back to her pale face.

He bent his head close to hear she breathed. His heart galloped in his ears. He touched her neck to feel hers softly beat. Both her breathing and heartbeat felt far too shallow and he feared he might lose her.

Ashlon stroked her hair and whispered her name while he cradled her. The chest's lid crested the remaining square of rock, but he cared naught but for her. If she were hurt, he would never forgive himself or Jacques for bringing about such a disaster.

Her eyes did not move, nor her limbs. Her mouth's normally rosy hue looked whitish and dry. And worst of all, he had no inkling of a notion as to how to help her. The ache that had woke him that morn gripped him now, sharper than ever before.

He would rather lose the chest than her, would choose to lose his own life instead. He'd shout to the heavens, command them to open up and bless her, but he'd not risk letting her go. Instead he held her closer, kissing her cold brow.

He had never guessed the Bloodstone, resting inside the stronghold, would create this kind of harm. He'd have left it where she found it, might have sunk the rock into the depths of the sea rather than face this corollary.

"Breanne," he said, his voice choked. "Breanne, open your eyes. Breanne, please, don't yet leave this world. I beg of you, stay with me." He bent his head and pressed his forehead to hers. Her skin was dangerously cold, clammy. "Do not let him take you."

Ashlon lifted her closer, rocking her there in his arms, fighting off the sting in his eyes. He didn't know how or when she had become so important to him, but no longer denied it was true.

"Please, open your eyes. I need you here with me."

A rush of warm air passed through the wood, ruffling his hair. It washed over, between them. With it,

Breanne breathed in a deep, shaky breath and began to cough in his arms. Ashlon pulled back. Her eyes opened and adjusted, blinking several times.

"What happened?" Breanne asked like a child coming out of a dreaming sleep.

Laughter bubbled low inside of Ashlon and spilt from his chest, echoing in chortles through the shadows and moonlight. He couldn't resist hugging her tightly to him.

"You did it," he said after squeezing her close.

"I did what, exactly?" Breanne looked confused but returned the hug, somewhat.

Ashlon tilted her upward to sit in front of the exploded rock.

Breanne rubbed her head and got to her knees. She wobbled some and he supported her elbow until they both stood over the dusty chest and rubble.

"I did." She shook her head in amazement. Her hand covered her mouth, but it didn't tremble. "I always dreamed I would someday, knew somewhere deep down, that I could but, oh Ashlon—." She faced him, her smile reaching past her fingers' cover. "I charged the rock to break, and it broke."

"Aye." He nodded. "I don't believe you realize what you've just accomplished. And I cannot fathom how, but I will never question my faith in miracles again."

It was Breanne's turn to laugh deeply. The husky sound stirred his body. The color in her cheeks was rosy again; her lips plump and reddened. Relief could not fully define what surged through him as he watched her joy.

He laughed, as well, and swept her into his arms and spun her. She clung to him then dropped her head back, looking up to the stars and moon and sky.

"Do you know, it rather felt miraculous," she said.

"Like a life of its own that went beyond me, through me, like I was not me at all."

He set her to her feet but kept his arms about her waist. She did not seem to mind them there and he could not yet release her.

"I often considered what it would feel like. But, nothing prepared me for that. I don't wonder that Heremon warned me so frequently to take care of what I desired. The force of it was nigh powerful as, well, as love, I suppose."

Ashlon frowned, involuntarily tensing. The ache came back.

"As you feel when you love another so fiercely, so thoroughly, that your own existence seems secondary. Do you ken what I mean?"

The ache clutched his heart. Her eyes sparkled with delight and her words came out in pants of excitement. A hundred reasons why he should not kiss her sprang to mind. And not a single one managed to stop the beating need coursing through his entirety.

He knew the very instant recognition laced her features, her gaze falling upon his mouth, and took its invitation. He pressed his mouth to her and felt suddenly desperate to feel, to know, her every last living inch.

Her hands fisted into his mantle, she rose up on her toes to meet his ardor with her own, clamoring for the same closeness he sought.

Breanne's mind went blank save one thought. Tomorrow, he would be gone. She could not bid him stay or hope he would ever return. She appreciated the magnitude of his task's completion. Her portend, Heremon's letter. Tomorrow, he must be gone from there.

But, tonight he could be hers.

As though he reached her conclusion, as well,

Ashlon's hungry kiss suddenly slowed. Desperation left his touch and an exquisite tenderness took its place.

His hands stroked her in sure, loving caresses from her hair to her lobes to her collarbone and down the length of her arms. At her hands, he laced his fingers into hers as his mouth pressed and suckled hers. His fingers tickled her palms while his mouth inflamed her.

Shivers danced up her spine and over her scalp. A swirling warmth lit in her belly and roiled downward to burrow between her thighs. By now, her body knew this dream and opened to it like a dewy blossom at dawn. Her body knew this want for his as well, but now her mind and heart where in compliance. The difference it made was staggering.

What had felt like a clamoring storm, building and washing her in unpredictable turns changed to sweeping dawning.

With deft moves, Ashlon lifted her and laid her onto the bed of grass, never breaking contact with her lips. Without hesitation, she reached for him, parted her legs, already hungering for him.

Her mind grew fuzzy and images of the forest and trees and his hands upon her filled her mind. His hands roved from her neck to her breast to her ankle. Vivid anticipation emboldened her as well. She let her fingers entreat lower as well, down his broad chest, across his belly to the lip of his tunic. The magick that vibrated from without seemed to come from within her now. Reality spilled away.

Ashlon's hand slid her skirt upward, drawing a line up her inner thigh. Breanne gasped at the sheer delight of it and opened her legs further. The heat between her legs swirled and stoked. muscles there flexed and swelled at his approach. He paused, lifted and removed his tunic. Following suit, her eyes locked to his, Breanne unlaced her bodice. His gaze broke from hers and raked over her flesh. He helped her expose it, then freed his own, breeches and all.

Expertly, Ashlon undressed her and then himself. Her cloak became a blanket and the night, their cover. The cool air chilled as his body warmed.

His supple skin. His hard muscles. His soft touch.

Feeling his skin on hers satisfied and awakened a deeper part of her need than she knew possible. His hand lifted her thigh as he nestled his hips between hers. He was so close, so very close and she couldn't help but lift up to try to capture his touch. But his hand only paused and his hips drew away.

She whimpered, biting her lip.

Breanne opened her eyes and found his looking down into hers. In them, his question shone. He did not ask aloud, did not break the spell.

She didn't need to be asked. She wanted to experience him in the fullest realm.

To answer, she moved his head to hers, raking her hands into his hair. Ashlon groaned from someplace deep inside and it rumbled in the air and through her. She lifted her hips, need driving her closer, aching for more. She let her body lead her.

Ashlon cupped her breast and teased a nipple with his thumb. Her nipple tightened. Her need climbed. She moaned, closed her eyes. His hand returned to her thigh, higher, closer to her very core. Liquid desire pooled there.

He grazed her neck with his teeth. "Breanne." Her name felt like a prayer on his lips.

She wanted to answer it and moved her hips to his, hungering to take him in. But he was too far away. She reached her hand downward, desperate to find his hard prick, to feel its shape and size in her palm, to lead it closer.

Then she found his hardened flesh, grasped it, reveling when he physically jerked, groaned. Fascinated, she watched his face as she explored that which she could only imagine before. It occurred to her that while her body craved to feel this part of him plunging inward, he might not fit.

As though reading her thoughts, Ashlon half grinned and kissed her nose. Then he slid his hand upward and parted her swollen flesh for entry. She closed her eyes tightly, but opened them when his finger entered her, his thumb pressing above, sending charges of pleasure through her.

Breanne cried out and Ashlon went deeper, twisting and withdrawing, returning and pressing until a small fire kindled there, growing with every nuance. His name fell from her lips and she clutched at his shoulders. She widened her legs then narrowed them, itching for a relief she couldn't name. Then he replaced his long deft fingers with his prick's plump tip. Her entrance parted and clung to this new feeling and intrusion, inviting it forth.

Ashlon slowly entered her heat, cupping her face and showering her in kisses. A small sharp pain came and went as his length filled her fully and wholly, then stopped.

Ashlon did not move. Breanne's body felt completed by his.

But it was not enough.

Her need transcended the satisfaction and began to build anew. Breanne writhed her hips under his, eager for an unnamable prize. She bit into his shoulder, his neck, gasping his name.

She wriggled and pressed for more of what she could not define. More of him, of the wondrous pleasure swirling through her. Her mind begged him.

Ashlon withdrew and returned to her in slow, strong thrusts. Her body was so wet and the slippery sounds mingled with her own and her lover's labored breaths. Ashlon pulled away and pierced her with his gaze, heavy lidded and glassy. Breanne struggled to keep her eyes open but something was growing in her with each of his thrusts. In and out of her, deep and long, faster, then faster still until he buried himself so deeply her breath caught. Need tangled with pleasure to create a sugary sweetness that grew in turns, spread and tightened. Ashlon's mouth came to hers and she returned the deep kiss, moaning into his mouth as her pleasure reached a precipice.

He moved slowly and pressed his hips in perfect, sweet circles to hers. She rocked her hips up, driving him deeper, harder until she fell from the precipice into shuddering waves around him. Her body clenched and spasmed.

Ashlon called out her name and groaned deep against her neck. His prick throbbed inside of her, sending a wondrous new peak through her. The magick of feeling him swept her upward, coursed through every fiber of her body and carried her back to earth in a soft float.

Breanne opened her eyes. Ashlon's breathing came hard and trembling. Caught in her own sweep of pleasure, she just barely discerned him reaching his own. She kissed his glistening temple and wrapped her legs about him.

The forest around them became audible again as reality crept through the dark. Ashlon didn't speak, only kissed her brow or arm or shoulder, occasionally her palm, lying beside her.

He covered their entwined bodies in a cocoon of clothing and moved her head to nestle on his shoulder.

Breanne did not mean to fall asleep but without a single thought or worry, exhausted and replete, she fell away.

Listening to her breathe, Ashlon envied the luxurious slumber and yet thrilled in witnessing it. Her beauty and bravery stirred him. He'd never experienced such perfection before. Her skin had been creamier, her breasts fuller, her curves more tempting. Her returned passion shook him almost as much as how remarkable her body felt joined to his.

He would stay there, breathing in her breaths, trembling with wonderment for all his days. If he could. If he had a choice it would be her, here, for eternity.

But, he did not have a choice. His eyes rested on the chest, his fingers on her skin. Dawn would soon rear the ugly head of responsibility. Until the last of night, he would savor her. It would be all he had to take with him and he wanted it to last.

Chapter Twenty

Ashlon blamed the chill in the air for the water in his eyes when he carefully removed his body from the tangle of hers. Eyes closed, he pressed his lips to her brow.

"Dream of me, Breanne, as I will of you."

He retrieved the chest, still securely locked and otherwise undisturbed. Rock and rubble fell away but did not wake her. He bade her a farewell wish and made his way back to the keep.

He didn't have the courage to wake her and see her pain at his departure. And he couldn't risk her insisting she come with him, still under the insinuation of Heremon's letter, impressing her help.

Ashlon left feeling like a coward and a thief. The burden the chest bore was far heavier than its light weight. The walk back was hard.

As a measure to relieve the ache inside of him, he penned a missive to her and entrusted it under the seal of her door. He had only one other action to feel guilt over. He needed a horse and hoped Niall would forgive his taking one with him.

Mounted and armed, fed and heavy, Ashlon plodded down the road that led away from Tir Conaill and the Lady Breanne O'Donnell. With the wedding's ceremony and feast, he wouldn't be missed, nor the horse for some time. Only she would feel the absence.

He shouldn't have done it. He knew that now. But, he didn't rue it all the same. It had been the single most breathtakingly beautiful experience of his life. Were it never to recur, he would still count himself more blessed than any other man.

But, he left behind a broken heart and ruined woman. Breanne had the wherewithal and resilience to recover, he knew. He just wished she didn't have to. He wished he could finish this task, be freed, and return to her. But, Jacques had been clear all those years ago.

He might not survive after its completion. Securing the Bloodstone that lay inside the chest would the hardest part of all. For in doing so, Ashlon had been warned that he would face a choice that might end his own life.

Jacques had been vague but stern. At the time, Ashlon did not fear possible death. At the time, he hadn't anything to lose. He did now. He had a future to lose. But that future would never be possible with the past living and breathing into it.

Ashlon shook his mind from dwelling on what he could not yet change. The Blue Stack Mountains lay ahead. Ashlon slowed his horse and found the path Jacques had described. The thunder of hooves kicked his heart into a frenzied beat.

Someone had followed him.

The morning sun had nearly crested the horizon. Ashlon took to the nearest copse of trees, trying to hide the black steed in shadow while he still could.

He dismounted and listened, dismally hoping he was wrong.

The hoof beats slowed to a walk and a man's voice carried through the foliage.

"Sinclair," it said and seemed to echo in the deep, mountain walled valley. "Sinclair, answer if you can hear me. I've come to aid you, not ask your return."

Ramsey. He should have known the knight was up to something last night. A final effort?

Ashlon came forward reluctantly as Ramsey's steed came into view. "What makes you believe I am in need of any assistance?"

Ramsey chuckled. "Naught but your secretive air last eve and a refined instinct I have learned to trust in." He dismounted and joined Ashlon.

Ashlon couldn't help the wariness at Ramsey's following him. Jacques had been specific that he tell no one, no fellow knight, no friend. The only person who you may trust will not ask, Jacques had said.

"You'll miss the wedding celebrations, Ramsey. And although I appreciate your concern, I assure you I only mean to leave here."

"I don't believe you. Fair enough, Ashlon. I will not ask to know what you are about. I will however insist that you allow me to join you in it." Ramsey's gaze was intent. He did not even glance at the chest strapped to the black's back.

"Do I have a choice?"

"Well, we could take issue and come to blows, if you wish."

"Very well, but, I warn you, I mean to ride through

to eventide without rest." Ashlon's wariness subsided. What harm could come of Ramsey's help? At worst, he would try to open the chest or steal it and Ashlon would not let that happen.

If Ramsey had any idea of the valuable object within reach, he did not show sign of it.

Ramsey nodded, mounted his bay and followed Ashlon with only one question. "Where is it we are going, then?"

"The Giant's Causeway."

* * * *

Breanne stretched her sore limbs and yawned. The trees shaded her well and birds' songs melodiously awoke her. She had been having the most delicious dream about Ashlon Sinclair, and didn't realize anything was amiss until she finally opened her eyes.

A cloudy but warm day greeted her and upon mentally registering that the sky and trees were real, that this was neither her bedchamber nor a part of the dream, she bolted upright. Her gown fell from her chest and Breanne gasped as the cool air hugged her breasts and shivered her nipples.

She'd slept there all night long and it was well into the day. With panic panging her belly, Breanne scrambled to her feet, covering herself and dressing simultaneously.

Where was Ashlon? Gone. He'd left her there in the night and he'd taken the chest with him, she saw. Heremon's altar was no more than crumbles now. Its hollowed center did not even appear able to fit what had lain resting inside.

Breanne fastened her gown as best she could. Dread gripped her, sending nausea and prickles shooting through her guts in turns.

Her only hope was that the guests and residents still

slept despite it nearing the noon hour. It was a fragile attempt but kept her rational enough to gather all evidence of her presence, to thank the goddesses lest she displease them, and leave in a walk.

Should a guard of men have been sent after her, she did not want to appear disheveled and out of sorts. She needed to seem calm and leisurely. As she neared the edge of wood, and no guard could be seen, Breanne gave up the ruse and ran the remaining distance.

She focused on excuses for herself rather than ones for Ashlon's departure. He had not even said goodbye. Did he care so little for her then? Was the experience not a shared wonder?

Breanne shook her head to clear it, and blinked back tears. First, make a safe return. Regret could be saved for a private moment at some other juncture. Right now, she needed her wits, not her emotions.

The slender but heavy gate creaked when she pulled it ajar then came to a stop. Heavy iron chain linked through the top allowing no more than six inches gap. Someone had fastened the gate since the midnight last night. To prevent her passage?

She wouldn't entertain the thought. If it were true, it meant that someone had discovered more than her absence, they'd discovered the circumstance of it, as well. Chains do not go on gates when a person is missing, they go up when one has escaped and is not allowed to return the same way.

Breanne tried in vain to pull the base wide and squeeze through. She gained no more than a hand full of splinters and scraped skin.

She did not have another choice but to enter the bailey at the main. With a deep steadying breath, Breanne walked the wall's edge, resuming the ruse she'd earlier concocted. She had been unable to sleep and woke early to gather herbs. Using part truth would enhance her story's authenticity should Niall himself be doing the asking. And so she planned to say she'd fallen asleep looking at the sunrise dismiss the stars and moon.

What could be wrong in that? Surely, she would only be scolded for not taking an escort or guard, but no more. Her belly didn't seem to care how simple the matter should be. It roiled in dread.

She waved at the tower guard and smiled at all passersby. They greeted her equally politely and none seemed concerned over her arrival. She chose the kitchen side door to enter through as was her habit and was nearest to the stairwell leading to her bedchamber.

To calm herself, Breanne imagined herself walking up the stairs, after a cheery kitchen welcome, a stolen scone. Eating would settle her stomach and she would enter her chamber to find Finn fast asleep at the unused foot of her bed.

She would change, braid her mussed hair and return below as though naught in the world could be amiss, including the loss of her virtue or the missing love of her life.

Love? No, not love, passion. Desire, but let it not be love that tore inside of her. For if she loved him and he'd left, without likelihood of returning, that would devastate her. One night's magic was worth eternity and she would deal with her virtue loss later, when an impending wedding night became a reality rather than an idea.

The kitchen staff ignored her and she barely found a biscuit to take along. The small scrap helped little and she ran up the stairs only to come to a full halt at the top of them.

Looking quite grim, arms crossed and sitting on a stool directly in front of her door sat Niall O'Donnell. Breanne's belly fell to her toes and her hard breath knocked out of her.

Niall turned his head when she gasped. He stood and gestured that she might come to her room and enter it. With leaden steps, she did and found the room ransacked. Her bed was stripped, her bedding upturned. Her trunk lay on its side, the contents spilled and broken. Her book was not in sight.

Breanne inhaled sharply and walked through the door.

"What happened?" she said, her discovery forgotten. "Who did this?" What were they looking for?

"I know not, nor can I guess as you've seen fit to ensure, Breanne. I'll allow you a moment to locate your belongings and count the losses. Then, you and I have affairs to discuss."

Breanne met his eyes and saw the disappointment in them keen and fresh. It made her feel smaller than a field mouse. She nodded her head. It was clear he knew enough that any fabrication she'd managed would be seen through, particularly since her room appeared robbed.

"When was it found in this fashion?" she said and began righting the toppled furniture.

"Rose alerted your mother before dawn."

Her mother. She must be fretful to the point of madness after finding such a mess and no daughter to speak of. Breanne felt terrible, to be sure. What words could ever measure her level of regret? None came to mind and likely wouldn't. At best she could receive her penance and hope to one day repair the tatters their trust must be in for her.

"As I readied my guard, it came to light that you were not in the room when this violence occurred. I care not to know what you've done to incur this upon yourself. I only care that you do not have the chance to do so again."

Breanne nearly choked on the lump that rose in her throat. What punishment would fit this crime? Moreover, what exactly did Niall believe her crime to be?

"But you knew me to be safe," she said.

"Aye, we did. But, such matters will wait until we finish here. Are you missing anything of import? Do you recognize what the person was after?"

Breanne replaced the contents of her trunk, broken mirror, candles, cracked jars and bowls, her buried book. Naught was gone, only broken or torn. She hugged the satchel inside her cloak closer and shook her head. "I canno' know. I find nothing gone."

"Come along then, lass. Your mother and Quinlan await us." His voice was laden with emotion and sounded defeated.

"Before we go to them, my lord, I must speak of Heremon to you," she said, unsure what aim she had except a bargain for time.

Niall faced her outside of the doorway. "Ah yes, I should have spoken with you of it earlier. With all of the arrivals and preparations, it slipped my mind—."

"I believe I know why he was murdered. I believe I know the poison the killer used. Together, we may be able to ascertain who is to …."

"Heremon was not murdered, Breanne," he said, his voice a boom of thunder. "I found in his cottage a closet full of herbals and concoctions that he experimented with. I have established his death as an accidental, self-induced poisoning."

Breanne felt as though he'd hit her. It couldn't be. Heremon had been hiding Ashlon, the chest, it must be linked to his strange death. She shook her head in denial.

"I speak the truth. I found the mislabeled jar myself, quite by accident, and brought it here to compare its properties to that matching my own for the heart. By its pungent odor and consistency, I have concluded the facts just presented to you. I am sorry to have left you in the dark regarding the matter."

Breanne frowned, thoroughly confused. Heremon mislabel a concoction? She simply couldn't envision it. It went well past the Druid's habits of collecting, making clear inscription, and logging. The habit had been the bane of her study, her most hated role as an Ovate apprentice.

But, Niall did not look open to argument. He looked to be fast out of patience and time for her. Breanne snapped her open mouth shut. She could not very well tell him of Ashlon and the chest in any case, so she would have to find Heremon's killer on her own, once the current storm in her life passed.

Ula and Quinlan sat together in armed chairs on one side of the room, opposite the empty one intended for her. She'd last sat in this seat with demands of a husband laid upon her. She preferred the past to what loomed for her there now.

Breanne sat, adjusting the satchel under her cloak so that the book didn't jab her ribs, then rested her hands in her lap. Niall shut the door as softly as a serpent's hiss ready to strike.

She looked at Quinlan first in hopes of gauging what was about to happen. But, his features were schooled well and he did not meet her eyes. Niall had his back to them, his head tipped toward the sky outside the window.

"I marry today, Breanne," Ula said. Her eyes were on her lap.

"Aye." She did not know what else to say.

"It should be a happy occasion. And the lord knows, I deserve one."

"Aye."

"I've concluded your behavior must be an act of jealousy, a rebellion, and I will say this once so that my own conscience holds no regret." She looked at Breanne. "I love you. You are my first child and none can take your place."

"I love you, as well, Mother."

Ula closed her eyes a moment, smiled tightly. When she opened them, they were cold and sent a chill down Breanne's spine.

"I ask for truthfulness in your answers, Breanne, and please know that I will recognize a lie. Now then, who is he?"

Breanne swallowed. "Who is who?"

"The man Quinlan spied in your bedchamber window last night, the man you spent the night with."

"No man has been to my chamber save you, Quinlan, and that with your sister and my mother. You are mistaken in what you saw."

Quinlan met her eyes. He looked sympathetic but shook his head. "I fear I made no mistake, Breanne. He peered out your window, waved to me. Do you wish me to describe him? I am able to."

"Aye, I do wish, for I swear that no man has been in my chamber." She did not want to lie and so could not answer the second part of the question, not in front of Quinlan. "Mayhap you saw the man who ransacked my chamber."

Niall kept his back to them and seemed as though he were there only for support. She didn't realize until then that her mother was who she faced in reprimand.

"Do you deny you were with a man, alone last night?" Ula said.

Breanne's cheeks burned hot. Who could have been in her room? Why were they not interested in the same conclusion she easily drew? "Nay, I do not deny it. I deny that a man came to my room for the reason you imply. I insist that Quinlan witnessed a thief not a lover."

"I saw you leave with him, Breanne," Quinlan said. "And your chamber was in no disarray when I verified your departure, worried as you can imagine, by entering the chamber with Rose when you did not answer my knocks and yelling."

Breanne felt like a rabbit backed up against a wall of rock too high to jump, too wide to scurry around. She did not want to admit last night's deeds to any person, especially to the man who sought to marry her. Quinlan did not deserve to be so betrayed. It would crush him if he found out.

Not that she would continue to encourage, or rather not discourage, his attentions. She would beg off from his interest at the first opportunity. Though, Ashlon had left Tir Conaill and her, without a word, he could return within a few days.

She just needed more time get her bearings. So much had happened and now they asked her to reveal what she had thought no one would ever discover. Her intentions last night were to only have a single night with him, one moment to feel heaven. Time enough later to face the loss of his departure. "You say you saw me leave with the man. At what hour? How can you be certain it was me you saw?"

"I grant you, I did not see your face. I saw your blue cloak, the one and same my sister gifted to you, your favorite. And I saw the way he held you close, kissed your cheek, and rushed you out the main doors." Quinlan's voice was strained.

"You said you are able to describe the man?" She clung to hope. She'd worn her green cloak last night, still did now but what would it improve to point out that which she could not prove? Her mother looked well past impatient. Niall kept his gaze away from them.

Quinlan shifted and said, "As tall as me, lean, broad, black hair. One of the arrivals from O'Doherty no doubt," he said to Ula.

The description was too close to Ashlon's. He could have mistaken the cloak's color and spotted her joining Ashlon outside the gate. But, why would Quinlan lie about where he saw them, or their greeting?

"His hair was sparsed with nearly white streaks but I saw no other aging in his movements. He looked quite virile." His meaning was unmistakable when he frowned his mouth in disgust.

But, how could she tell them that she did not know who he spoke of, that she was with Ashlon who had no graying whatsoever? And who could that leave as the person's Quinlan truly saw? The fright from being cornered grew into confused anger.

"When did my room become in such disarray then?"

"Within an hour later when Rose returned to check on your return, telling me I must have been mistaken in what I had witnessed."

"You were mistaken."

Ula sighed in exasperation. "You are avoiding the matter at hand. I will play no more ruse. Give us the man's name so we may secure your betrothal."

She saw no way out of it. "I will not lie to you mother. I was not alone, nor in my room last eve. But, I promise you that Quinlan is mistaken in who he saw. It was not me. And the man he described is not one I recognize."

Niall was the only listener that did not gasp in outrage. Ula stood, her hands on her hips, looking more furious than Breanne ever recalled. Quinlan shook his head and looked as though he did not know her.

Breanne's chest welled with emotion. Why could

they not see that something far more important than her virtue's loss had occurred last eve? Because they knew not of Ashlon's circumstances. And she could not explain any part or the entirety.

"Do you require I ask Quinlan to find the man himself and bring him forward? Or will you make affairs simple for us all by finally being forthright?" Ula crossed her arms. Niall came to her side.

He gave Breanne a surprisingly understanding look. "Don't become distressed, Ula. Breanne will name the man. It is our wedding day. She has not meant harm, have you Breanne?"

"No. I wish no hurt to any and though you may find it difficult to believe, have strived to prevent hurting all of you." Breanne waited for Ula to be seated. "Quinlan, I would like to first apologize for misleading you. I in no way ever meant to deceive you."

Quinlan curtly nodded and if she didn't know better, looked supremely relieved. Well, seeing the issue over with must cause some relief. How long had he been forced to sit and wait with her mother and stepfather, all wondering what scandalousness she was about?

"I fear, mother, that my answer will greatly disappoint you for there will be no betrothal. The man I spent last eve with is gone."

"What do you mean he is gone?" Niall demanded.

"He left me last night at what hour I know not. He does not mean to return."

"He will have no choice," Niall said. "He will honor the promise made in bedding you, or were you not in fact bedded?"

"Niall, please," Ula said, blushing for Breanne's sake.

Strangely, the crude question did not embarrass her. She felt no shame in experiencing Ashlon to the fullest definition last night, ruinous or no.

"He is a man of honor, Niall but I fear, he may have no other choice."

Niall bent forward. "It will be his only choice. His name, Lady O'Donnell."

Breanne took a deep breath. Niall was wrong. Only one thing would bring him back. Love.

"Sir Ashlon Sinclair."

Chapter Twenty One

"I must admit I was surprised at your leaving. Now, don't look at me that way, Ashlon. I do not pry. I merely conjecture." Ramsey smiled up at the sun.

Ashlon didn't bite. He didn't know what irritated him more at this point, seven hours into their journey, the afternoon's heat wearing the horses even as they now walked, or Ramsey's incessantly cheerful disposition.

The man had discussed the passing beauty, his adopted clan, his love of hunting. And now, he had returned again to Ashlon as his favorite topic to dissect at length.

"I do not wonder so much as the reason as the fact that you left alone and at such a dreadful hour. Did you not comprehend the risks of doing these two things simultaneously?"

Ashlon clenched his jaw. "I saw no risk at all. In fact, I saw less risk." Of being detained, of being noticed gone.

Of course, Breanne would have noticed. Ashlon chest tightened uncomfortably. He tugged at his tunic collar. His sword banged at his thigh in beat with the steed's walk.

"None told you then, during your stay? Well, you

had not been there long, had you? A fortnight or so?"

Ashlon grunted his acknowledgement.

"And that explains it then. It's a good thing I saw you leave and was hard put to stay asleep this morn, then. I may have saved your life, Ashlon."

Ashlon chuckled derisively. "Oh, Ramsey, how's that?"

"Well, any good Irishman worth his weight in cattle would tell you that the whole land is enchanted and a full moon is an imp's playground for mischief and mayhem."

He guffawed aloud, the laugh erupting from deep within him. Ramsey looked better than pleased with himself, making him wonder if lightening Ashlon's heart was what he'd been about all day long.

"No, Ramsey, none shared that little tidbit with me."

"I can see you don't believe me. You'll soon enough know for yourself of the magick in this land."

Ashlon couldn't help thinking he already did and of Breanne. There were none like her. He found her to be bolder and braver than most men, yet honest and loving and utterly feminine. But, if she kept sneaking into his thoughts, he'd never make it to the Causeway.

"Not the kind we heard talk of in whispers and rumors among the Knights, mind you, Ashlon. What I speak of is the stuff of myth and legend. Fairy princes, Elvin kings," Ramsey said.

Ashlon only half heard his friend. He'd be galloping back to her with his heart in his hand and a seven-year vow in shambles at his feet.

"You're scared, aren't you?" Ramsey said.

Ashlon scowled at him in response. "I have long outgrown fear, my friend. The Pope himself, you can thank for that."

Ramsey snorted. "A grand lot of hog's shite, that one is."

"I assure you, years of evading assassins has a way about killing all fear in a man."

"Then you're not scared of what Ireland offers you? Home, kinship, a future, none of that shivers your skin, then?"

Ashlon shook his head. How could he fear what he might not have a chance at winning? "Overestimated, all of it, if you ask me," he said with a full grin.

Ramsey laughed. "The beautiful lasses, the welcoming homes and hearths, the ongoing revelry? None caught your eye?"

"Aye, who needs it?"

Ramsey took cue and said, "Right you are. Off with us then." He heeled his bay into a canter.

Ashlon followed suit, glad to be done, until Ramsey's next rising urge to prod him back the road they came.

Their horses' hooves were all he heard for some time, blessedly, until another distinct sound pricked his senses. Ashlon slowed his horse and motioned for Ramsey to do the same. They left the narrow road and came to a stop.

Ashlon listened to the sound of another rider approaching. Both men dismounted and crouched in the wood. Thankfully, Ramsey didn't question Ashlon and kept low and silent in the foliage cover. The sound drew nearer, grew louder, until Ashlon readied to watch the traveler pass them by.

But, without preamble, the sound stopped. It did not slow, or change or reverse. It vanished as though it had never occurred at all.

The hairs on Ashlon's neck stood up. Something was sorely amiss for a rider to thunder up the road and then disappear without a sound. No horse could come to a soundless stop, no rider could handle such a feat.

Ashlon stood. The two steeds nickered and pulled for their heads. The black reared up, spooked by what, Ashlon could not tell. Ramsey stood, as well, and gestured that one of them should go look while the other kept to the horses.

With a soothing pat below his black's withers, Ashlon carefully walked into the open to peer down the dirt lane.

No sign of another comer existed. No wafting dust, no trampled bush. He walked with his sword drawn and ready, should any hidden person spring upon him. But the farther he went, the more he worried he'd misheard.

Some paces away from Ramsey, he scanned the road and wood for signs of movement or trafficking. When he saw none, he lowered his sword and headed back to his waiting horse.

Ramsey still crouched and had rested his head against a tree trunk. He was making a poor guard with his eyes closed, looked ready to nap rather than keep watch over Ashlon's back.

Ashlon nudged the man's form with his boot, ready to rebuke his laziness for the duration of their trip. But, the nudge did not wake the man, only moved him enough to cause him to slowly slide sideways and on the ground. It was the limp appearance that provoked Ashlon's immediate alarm.

Ramsey was not resting, he was unconscious. His body hit the wood floor with a thump. No blood, nor sound signed the cause of his injury, but Ashlon held no doubt that Ramsey had been accosted in the short space of separation.

He spun about, sword ready to slice into any criminal in its path. Ashlon's mind raced with possibilities. A papal assassin was his first most likely drawn conclusion but he didn't discount the potential of a robber or other similar villain to come upon them.

The horses grazed unperturbed. The air was unusually silent. Not even an insect's buzz carried on the breeze. Something black flashed in the corner of Ashlon's vision. He swung toward it, his breathing coming in hard gasps as rage and fear warred his pulse.

He would not end this now, not in this fashion. He had come too far, had forgone too much to let another steal the chest now. If it fell into the Pope's hands it would be more heretical than any act the Knights were accused of, for he would possess the floating head that he so wanted, had tortured innumerable men to ascertain the location and validity of.

The Bloodstone inside of the chest was too valuable to allow the church to poison its meaning and use. He would die for it but death could only worsen its fate.

Another flash of black and gray streamed past him. He followed with his blade but did not move from his spot next to the chest strapped to his horse. In a spur, he mounted his steed.

He had no idea whether his friend lay breathing or dead and hated that he could not find out. But, he had to draw out the assailant and kill or be killed.

Ashlon rode to the path, his stallion leaping to life as though sensing his rider's urgency. Trained for war, the black bared his teeth and braced for battle unseen.

The blur of black and gray stripes came so fast, Ashlon and his horse were knocked to the ground before his mind could register the assailant's attack. The chest came upturned and loose, sliding down the black as it righted itself to stand.

Ashlon did not make it to his feet. Suddenly his attacker was kneeling on top of him and a small blade threatened Ashlon's throat. His eyes were an eerie shade of pale green. Something about the lanky form was familiar.

Wordlessly, he took Ashlon's sword from him. He turned the hilt over in one hand while pressing the knife against Ashlon's Adam's apple with the other.

Ashlon struggled to conspire a tactic to regain control of the situation. His only hope seemed to be that the attacker would take the emerald encrusted sword as enough goods and leave the horse and chest.

While his sword in the wrong hands was not good, without the chest its value was little. Ashlon pushed his abdomen against the weight of the man and breathed angrily, staring at him unwaveringly.

The man's eyes narrowed on him and his head tilted. He seemed to be measuring Ashlon up, unmindful of being out on the open road for incomers to witness.

Then he turned his attention back to the sword hilt, the emeralds. Dread overwhelmed Ashlon's senses. The man was eyeing the emeralds and then looked directly at the chest. Ashlon grasped for the sword, meaning to cut the attackers throat as his own might be, as well.

But, the man was off of him and on the chest so fast Ashlon had to blink to focus. He got to his feet and lunged at the man, ready to use a rock as a weapon if he couldn't retrieve either his sword or the small dagger.

Equally swift, the man moved again and was down the road, kneeling before the chest, using Ashlon's sword to open the chest. Ashlon screamed furiously, running for the man, knowing not what the man was or how he knew of the Bloodstone, seeing only his life's meaning being stolen, a legacy of secrets and power being lifted up and examined in the sunlight.

He reached the man, lifted the rock and, wailing like a bloodthirsty Viking of lore, brought down his crude weapon. It cracked into the chest, sending splinters to the dirt. The thief was gone.

Ashlon glanced about, terror striking through him like a bell. The man was gone, as though he'd never been there at all, and he'd taken the Bloodstone.

Ashlon fell to his knees and grabbed his sword. None knew of the key, Jacques had sworn to that, that it lay in the unusual encrusting of emeralds on the Toledo sword's hilt. And whoever stole the Bloodstone, found the sword and chest useless, as they were, once the contents were gone.

He had to get it back before the stone was used, or worse joined with any of its three brethren stones. The power and magic the stones held could easily be abused if the man could access them.

Returning to Ramsey, Ashlon found him not dead but still unconscious. He shook him, needing his help in identifying who the attacker was and where he might have gone to. The sense of familiarity was stronger now. Perhaps Ramsey could help piece together the clues.

After three hard shakes, Ramsey grunted and opened his eyes. "What happened?"

"It's what I would like to know. Did you see your attacker, Ramsey?" Ashlon asked in a rush. He helped his friend to his feet.

Ramsey shook his head as though to clear it. "I must have gotten my brain knocked a bit loose. I remember you creeping off to the road and then...."

"What?" Ashlon grabbed him by the shoulders both to steady and see him.

Ramsey rubbed his head. "Well, it was the damnedest thing. You left and out of thin air, it seemed, a cat approached me. A large tomcat of sorts, the like you'd find kept on to catch mice."

Ashlon's gut turned sour. But, he wouldn't let the disbelief overcome the clear instinctual certainty his mind just reached.

He'd seen enough in the last twenty-four hours to know his conclusion was at least possible. Which meant he needed to ride at double speed back the way he came. He must get back to Breanne.

"Can you ride?"

"Aye. I'll need to take it slow, but I can sit a few hours more."

"I'm sorry, Ramsey. I must leave you here. I forswear I cannot explain now but will you follow and bring this chest with you? It may be a matter of ...."

Ramsey held his hand up. "No explanation needed, Ashlon. Godspeed."

* * * *

"I knew it," Rose said. "I knew the very night he walked into the keep alongside my brother." It had taken her some time to get the truth out when her friend demanded to know what had happened to her.

Breanne wiped another tear away. "You did?" She'd sat crying at the foot of her bed for more'n an hour since Niall finally dismissed her, verdict in hand.

"Aye, you're a terrible liar, Bree, leastwise when it comes to me. I know you better than your own mother does, I'd wager." Rose had been waiting outside her door on the same stool Niall had left behind.

"And you're not angry with me?"

"Goodness no. Had a bit of fun with it, gushing over Ashlon Sinclair as I did, and figured you'd be telling me in your own time, as you always do."

Breanne almost didn't want her best friend to go so easy on her. Her heart ached and her conscience was bruised. She didn't deserve such understanding.

"Let's dry those tears now, Bree. There will be time aplenty to cry later, after the wedding. You don't want to be puffy eyed and make people wonder if you're against it."

Another round of sobs racked through her. "But, how can you not be furious with me? I've broken Quinlan's heart."

Rose sat next to her on her bed. "Because you haven't. Ashlon Sinclair has broken yours. Quinlan's pride is a mite bullied, but you'll be saving him from a worse fate."

She didn't see how. Quinlan not only knew of her maidenly ruin, but he had befriended the man who had ruined it. Well, not ruin, taken but not ruined. What Ashlon had given her shouldn't be treated as a soiled product of lust.

"He must hate me. I gave in to a baser need and never once thought it would impact another's fate aside from my own. In truth, I didn't think it would impact mine either."

"Things like this have a way of rippling through other lives, Bree. Do you remember when Ryan and I handfasted? How many people were hurt in the course of our happiness?"

Breanne sniffled. She tried to recall. "But, Rose, none were hurt by it."

Rose frowned and looked pensive. "Humph. Well, bad example. Well, look at it this way Breanne. It's better to have loved and lost than to never have loved at all. And you might be happier in the end."

"How so?" An inkling of hope shimmered inside of her. Her heart leapt at the image of Ashlon riding back to her, alive and ready to begin his life.

But that was not the angle Rose was taking. "I can speak for a marriage based on passion and primal urges. It is a rocky road to travel with ups and downs the like you've never known. It scares me to the bone sometimes, how much I need my Ryan. I've wished more'n once that I could love him a little less." Rose's eyes brimmed with emotion as they looked at her.

Perhaps she was right. She could not love Ashlon after all. He was perfectly wrong for her. He was a warrior and would live the kind of life her father had. Mayhap she would be better off with a man who she would not fret about each night, wondering if he'd lived the day.

"And," Rose said. "What better person to wed than your best friend?"

"Even if you betrayed that friendship?"

"He'll get over it, Bree." Rose gave her a reassuring hug.

"I can't see how. He's found a man he trusted has bedded the colleen he meant to handfast and now is forcibly held to his intention by his own chieftain." The tears came hot down her cheeks but the sobs stayed at bay.

"You'll be saving him from Rhiannon's lovely snare and in time, he'll thank you for it," Rose said with a firm nod and pat to Breanne's knee.

"I expect you're right." She wasn't all that surprised when Rose had told her of Rhiannon's intentions to steal Quinlan. If Ashlon had not left, Rhiannon might have won what with Breanne's attention so easily distracted in his direction. But, Quinlan wouldn't likely be happy for many years with such a conniver as Rose had discovered her to be.

"Of course I'm right. You yourself said, Ashlon Sinclair will never set foot in Tir Conaill again."

It wasn't that he wouldn't. It was that he couldn't. She'd made sure of that. By protecting him in getting the stone back to him, she'd prevented the mortal danger she'd seen in her foresight. And she didn't doubt that Ashlon needed little impressing to stay away when he'd so resisted the friendships and welcome of the clan.

The only one he seemed taken with, unguarded with, was Danny. She wondered if he told the boy goodbye.

And she understood. He'd grown used to a solitary life after the Knight's brotherhood's dismantle. She had sensed it in him still that night as he kissed her and touched her as though she were a treasure. He feared what returning meant more than what not returning might.

If she had months or years to wait, it might matter not. But, she did not. Niall had vowed that if Ashlon did not come back, or was drug back biting and hollering, Breanne would marry Quinlan.

At least he was safe. Somehow, knowing Ashlon would live and be well gave her comfort despite the disastrous turn of events.

The letter he wrote had been meant to comfort her, she could tell. Though it was a brief missive, the scroll of his writing was shaky and difficult to read. Breanne liked to think it showed how difficult it had been to write.

He made no declarations of love, no false promise of hope that she might wait. He'd only thanked her and wished her absolute happiness in a long well lived life.

The sweetness of it was what had caused the emotional downpour. It had been too much at the time, having just received notice that she was in fact betrothed to Quinlan, that the announcement would be made later that day and binding.

Breanne held the parchment in her lap, her breathing settling down from the hiccups and sobs finally. She glanced at Rose and gave her a weak smile.

She would make the best of it. She had to. Naught else could be realistically done about it. At worst she could leave in the night and go after the man her heart longed for, at best she could cast a spell and wish him back.

Breanne almost laughed at the idea. A spell. If only it were so easy as that. She'd been in study for so long and in it held on to a romanticized notion of magick offering solace and control over tragedy and pain.

She knew now that it complicated rather than bettered things. And what she thought magick was all those years had proved false. It was not a wish and a chant, it was a life-force and energy the like of which she still could not fully fathom.

"Come, let us get you dressed then," Rose said, squeezing her hand.

"I've been meaning to ask, Rose, how the tonics have been to you," Breanne said and wet a cloth for her face.

Rose patted her belly and warmed Breanne's heart with a beaming smile. "We've been right as rain, Bree, thanks to you."

Right as rain. Breanne rose, took the letter to her trunk and placed it inside the pages of her nearly empty Grimoire. Heremon's lay beneath it, its aged cover making hers appear juvenile in comparison. She would not need these things for some time as she would soon be busy minding a home, trying to forge a new bond with Quinlan.

Chapter Twenty Two

Breanne's eyes were puffy but nothing so severe that a brief compress would not remedy. She busied herself as Rose prattled on about the babe in her belly and what it would be like to have a son.

The wedding would begin within the hour and Breanne laid out the only gown she owned suitable for the occasion. It was a pale lavender silk, threaded through with silver and gray and white. The cape that attached at the shoulders was a deep shimmering gray, as well. Silver baubles in her hair and a plated silver and amethyst choker would complete the picture she hoped would make her mother proud, if that were possible after the morning's events.

She was nervous. Stomaching all the eyes that would be on her, all the whispers and conjecture that would buzz the hall throughout the ceremony, would be more difficult than any trial she'd yet faced.

The tightly knit clan warranted few secrets' survival among them. If most didn't already know the sordid details of her actions and repercussions, they certainly would find out while her uncle spoke lifelong binding words of love, honor, and fidelity.

Breanne's cheeks burned just thinking of it and she tried hard to focus on Rose instead.

"Ryan promised me to be home more with this one's arrival. Ah, but he said that with all my girls. I don't know why it scares them so badly, being fathers. You would think it'd make them feel more the man rather than like scared little boys." Rose pushed Breanne into the vanity stool and began weaving a coiffure, threading the tinkling baubles in as she spoke.

Babies. No one seemed to mind enough to ask or speak of the possibility of a baby. She could only hope Ashlon had not given her one. Forcing Quinlan to raise another man's child would be too much to ask her friend, honorable or not.

Breanne ignored the warm quiver in her belly at the image of holding Ashlon's baby. His dark curls, her brown eyes, a boy. A reminder of her one magickal night to last a lifetime. And Quinlan's, a voice reminded her.

Better to forget the possibility, to bury it along with all these feelings until the dust of so many changes settled.

"Ah, there, but you look gorgeous, Breanne. Rhiannon will be seething with her jealousy all the more when you walk into that room."

Breanne smiled up at her friend. The dull ache in her lifted a smidge under the breeze of Rose's effervescence.

"It will be nice, don't you think, to have an evening wedding," Rose said, plucking at tendrils just so.

"Aye, different and romantic, as well, though I'd have chosen a daylight hour were it up to me."

"I'm surprised it wasn't put off until daylight tomorrow what with the final rushing that had to take place. It's naught but chaos below. The ladies don't know their fingers from their toes getting it all finally together."

A knock sounded on Breanne's door. Danny poked his head through at their unison call to enter.

"It's time," Danny said in a low voice. He didn't look up to them and left as though the world were on his shoulders.

"What is the source of his long face, do you think?" Rose said.

"I couldn't guess," she said. But it was not true. She had a few estimations, one of which included Ashlon leaving Tir Conaill. Another might very well be hearing the sordid affair the clan's collective tongue likely wagged about all morning long.

Breanne suppressed the emotions threatening to gag her. She composed herself as well as she could and glanced at the mirror to verify she looked suitably aloof and reserved.

Rose took her hand, tucked at another scant curl in her coiffure and together they walked the long length of corridor leading to the main hall. Chatter bubbled up to them and turned Breanne's stomach. She didn't want to face them, but knew she had no other choice. She swallowed against the lump in her throat and took two steadying breaths.

Rose paused a moment with her, patted her hand. "It will be as easy or difficult as you make it, Bree. So, let us chin up and show them nothing but beauty."

Breanne nodded and watched as Rose walked down the stairs and away from her.

The first step was the hardest and when she reached the bottom, the half an hour that followed blurred past with the sheer effort of maintaining her serene smile.

* * * *

The black's hard breaths came out in puffs of steam in the dusk air. The moon was rising. The temperature was dropping and clouds menaced the horizon.

Ashlon hunched low over the stallion's withers and gave him his full head. What had taken him eight hours at least, he was fighting to make four. It wasn't going to happen.

The images of the Bloodstone's theft skipped and replayed in his head as his mind sifted for more clues. Breanne would know. Breanne would see what he could not. He had to return to her. And not simply to help him yet again, but because he knew down to his soul that her life was in jeopardy.

The black grunted and heaved up the low hill, whose crest Ashlon prayed would reveal the towers of O'Donnell keep. He didn't know how much more he could ask of the stallion if not.

As the grassy hill gave way to cloudy sky, a square-ish and undeniably stone formation reached their view. Ashlon cried out in triumph and patted the black's neck. "Not long now, my friend. We've nearly won the race."

He had no doubt his attacker had returned here long before, although he couldn't name why. He credited the

Knighthood's constant guarding ceremonies warding evil for the bill of trust he now paid. The Pope's forced confessions of a floating head worshipped by the Templar Knights were in part true. The bloodstone was no head, and had not been worshipped. It had been studied, revered, and protected from the earliest times of their brotherhood's formation.

The Bloodstone was not proof of heretical practice, of devil worship as the Pope and throne wished to prove. It was a resource that only a few could utilize due to its complex nature and giftedness.

The signs had been there and he'd chosen to ignore them. Breanne might be one of those few. And the fiend that was clearly not of this world, might be, as well.

His only hope was that nothing catastrophic had transpired in the time it took him to rejoin the fiend. If something had happened to Breanne due to his hardheadedness, he could not forgive himself.

If the spawn of demon life that took the Bloodstone lay…. Ashlon stopped himself from carrying down that road. He would get the stone back and see the villain's blood drawn in the process, that he swore before God himself.

A lather of sweat gathered on the black's coat and brought Ashlon back to reality. He slowed the steed to a canter and then a trot. No sense in blaring up to the doors and raising alarm or leaving the horse dead tired.

He needed to keep stealthy, find Breanne and not draw undue attention. In fact any attention would be undue since he had absconded with a horse and might very well be summoned to answer for it wedding feast or no.

The stable boy took the black's reins and gaped at the sight of both. "You've raced back for naught and missed both nuptials, Sir Sinclair."

Ashlon did his best to look disappointed. "Both, you say?" He tried to swallow against his hard breathing.

"Aye sir, the Lady Ula and the O'Donnell's with the last minute addition of the Lady--."

"Brian Patrick O'Toole," a booming voice called from the rear. "Get your lazing arse back here this minute afore I come up there and--."

"Coming," Brian called in return and scurried away, black in hand.

Ashlon was glad for the boy's distraction and his mild curiosity at what he'd spoken of gave way to immediate need to locate and find privacy with Breanne.

He did his best to appear unassuming while he walked through the kitchen entrance. The staff there looked busier than a honey hive and only one member caught sight of him. The wide mouthed look of recognition made him nervous and he flashed the girl his best charming smile, the one practiced for many a young welcoming widow over the years.

It worked well enough to raise a pretty blush to her cheeks and force her gaze back to her work. The priest's voice held melodiously and clear above the noisy kitchen and drew Ashlon out. He stood in shadow, his pulse pounding, his heart aware she was near.

* * * *

When Father O'Donnell announced the newly wed couple to the onlookers, Breanne realized with a start that it was over. Her mother had tears in her eyes and Niall's shone wet, too. She'd never seen either look so happy or so obviously in love as her new stepfather bent down and kissed his bride.

Breanne joined in the applause and riotous cheer that followed as Niall and Ula sprinted like kids back down the aisle, Niall nearly knocking over several guests. In an eager swarm, the lines of waiting spread and gathered into circles while the servants reassembled the banquet's tables.

Her mother was wedded. Shortly, she, too, would be and Niall had made clear that he would announce her betrothal this very eve to ensure neither she nor Quinlan lost spine or procrastinated it off.

Quinlan had stood at her side, silent but strong through the service. He had not yet met her eyes but then she'd equally avoided his. Her belly still rotted with guilt and loss, but her face showed no such torture.

Might she have been wrong in thinking her mother to be the only one to accomplish a peaceful visage? Perhaps she'd learned more'n she'd credited from her mother, similar or no.

It made her wonder what Ula kept hidden beneath. But, not today. Today her mother shined like a star in the sky. She looked vibrant and younger than her years.

A peal of laughter carried above the din and brought her head to the left. Quinlan's notably followed and stopped as well upon the vision of Rhiannon gushing at the side of Timothy O'Doherty. Their wedding had taken place as a quick opening for the main event of her parents' ceremony and now Rhiannon seemed desirous of a piece of the crowd's focus and well wishing.

Her mother would never say so, but Breanne thought the spontaneous request for Rhiannon and Timothy to marry as well today a bit contrived and without good taste. Ula had been gracious however and postponed her vows just long enough to allow Father Connelly to wed the youngsters.

Breanne hooked her arm through Quinlan's and laced her fingers through his. "She does not know what she's lost, Quin."

He looked down at her, pain and anger brightening the blue of his eyes. "And you do?"

She might have deserved that and so she only lifted her chin higher. "Aye. I always have." She bored her gaze into his, trying to stare her sentiment home.

Quinlan lowered his glance and smiled a little. "Might we should play a bit of her game, then?"

Breanne smiled back. "A fine idea." Anything, to erase the pain.

They sat together at the table of honor on either side of Niall and Ula. Quinlan took effort to kiss her hand and bestow a loving smile on her before sitting.

"You look absolutely beautiful, mother."

Ula beamed at her, love in her eyes and no trace of the earlier anger and disappointment. "As do you, Breanne."

Shame mixed with gratitude. Mayhap she had not ruined her mother's happiness with her scandalous behavior. Mayhap things would turn out for the best, just as Rose had declared.

For the first time that day, Breanne smiled a genuine smile and cared not whose eyes were on her or what they thought about it.

A flash of sapphire drew her attention across the room. She instantly thought of her own missing sapphire cloak, the single item unaccounted for once she'd righted the room. But, when she turned to find the color's source it was gone, the main doors closing out a strand of night.

Another movement caught her eye. In the shadows, not far from the entryway, she distinguished a set of perfectly broad shoulders. The silver shine of a sword glinted in the candlelight. None else in the room seemed to notice the unmoving figure and Breanne's heart tripped a beat.

It could not be him. It was too dangerous and too impossible a hope to entertain. The form retreated further into dark as a handsome couple passed by. Rhiannon and

Timothy, hands held were making another round of the room for congratulations.

"Are you quite prepared, then, Breanne? Are you certain you can manage it?" Quinlan said low near her ear.

She glanced at him, her mind racing to the man in the corner, pulling him into the light to verify that her eyes were lying to her heart, teasing it mercilessly. "I'm sorry?"

"They come this way now." Quinlan nodded slightly in Rhiannon's direction.

Breanne looked back, torn, and found Rhiannon's lovely figure blocking her view. She nearly rose and peered around her but a nudge from Quinlan recalled her earlier insinuation.

She owed him far more than the planned display would repay and could not worm out of it. Quinlan put an arm about her shoulders, possessively so. Breanne acted her best coyness, dipping her chin and batting her lashes. She leaned in and pretended he'd just told her an enormously funny jest, timed exactly at the couple's approach.

"Lady Ula, King O'Donnell," Timothy said, his eyes barely able to land on any face, so enamored of his bride's as he spoke. "Please accept our eternal gratitude in allowing us to join in you in happy day with our own."

"It is our pleasure, of course, my good man. Although I must say we will miss our little Rhiannon come the morrow when you must away back to O'Doherty tuath," Niall said and speared a sweet meat to offer Ula.

Rhiannon's eyes were hovering at Quinlan and Breanne's close embrace. Breanne could see the barely discernable shift of the lady's brow at seeing them. They'd struck their mark. The jealousy nearly steamed from her ears.

"Ah, Quin, I'm afeared my smile might make me wrinkled before my time, so much laughing as you're forcing on me." Breanne plucked an invisible thread from his chest and allowed her hand to rest there while she looked amorously up at him. While Rhiannon pretended not to be watching the pair, the man in shadows behind them consumed Breanne's hopes and fears.

She wanted to see his face, to know the trick her eyes must be playing and simultaneously feared the truth the light would reveal. If it were Ashlon and he now watched her, what would he be thinking? Would he see the ruse and know her real desire for him or would he believe her a weak willed woman, given easily to whim and want?

If it was not him, then he had not returned for her. If it was then his life's thread still hung at fate's sharp blade prime to be severed.

Rhiannon's gaze fell on her face and Breanne forced her best, joyous smile, praying that only she would believe its lie. Quinlan deserved more than this tart of a woman had proved to be and Breanne could not let Rhiannon believe she'd won and upped him.

Breanne held her breath, seeing the movement across the hall. She glanced there and back again to Rhiannon, wishing an end to the couple's visit.

"You must be so excited, Rhiannon, to leave Tir Conaill and away to a new home," she said. "No doubt your many skills will do you well among new friends and family."

The barb struck. She could see when Rhiannon's radiant smile faltered. It took a moment for her to reply. "Aye, I will begin anew. I imagine it will be quite freeing, not having a past known to all in clear detail."

The insult was obvious but did not hurt. She cared not what this woman judged her to be, as Rhiannon would never know a love like Breanne had experienced. The sheer thrill that ran through Breanne when Ashlon was near, the plunge of passion deep within her soul, Rhiannon was ignorant of love like that. She was a woman too wrapped in her own immediate wants to see and feel and touch what Breanne had.

Breanne only shrugged, and the cavalier response appeared to irritate more so than any insult. Rhiannon glared openly at Quinlan and Breanne, tugged at Timothy's arm and began to drag him away mid-sentence.

Niall only chuckled at the inappropriate leave, unoffended. "He'll have his hands full with that one, mark me. Quinlan, I dare say you've escaped the gallows thanks to me."

"I do see you are right on that count. It appears I am in debt then to Breanne and Sir Ashlon, in a round about way."

Breanne winced as though he'd punched her in the belly. She lowered her head to hide the color stinging her cheeks. He was still very angry, then.

She should have predicted as much. A small act of affectation for the lady bounder was not nearly enough to compensate for a forced hand in marriage. Breanne waited until her cheeks cooled before peering to the entrance again. When she did, her breath stuck at her throat and her belly tilted. The man was gone. Without thinking, Breanne stood up.

"Are you well, lass?" Niall said.

"Come Breanne, sit. I will not speak of him again," Quinlan said low next to her. "Breanne, you are causing a stir."

She became aware of how she must look, with her

mouth hung open, her brow gathered with concern and her hand trembling over her breast. Quickly, she feigned a loud dramatic sneeze and sat back down.

Several blessings and a scatter of applause followed. She'd become quite the player today and would need one more act's success. Breanne waited a few moments and rose with a delicate smile, patting her belly.

"Too much wine, I believe," she said demurely.

It worked. She walked toward the stairs and slipped into the kitchen at the last step. Peeking through, she saw no one that looked her way suspiciously and ignored the few that did from behind.

"I need some cool night air," she said, fanning her face, for the benefit of those few that remained interested in her sudden appearance.

Breanne stepped out the door and rushed down the wall to where she hoped the man would be. She lifted her skirts and cared naught for the noise she stirred. Her forced equanimity was forgotten. All her mind and heart could care for was around the stone corner of wall she raced toward.

Her pulse raced. A cheer echoed from within. Muffled thunder of tankers and goblets hitting the wooden tables carried, as well. She slowed enough to make the corner without a fall and found herself square on her arse, nose hurting and dazed.

She shook her head. Had she hit the wall? She looked up and took the proffered hand in front of her. Ashlon. He was back and before she gained a full standing position, her world tilted again. He caught each elbow in his hands and her weight into his body. Then, as she struggled to collect her wits, he swept her up and hid around the dark corner she'd barreled into.

Chapter Twenty Three

The ground jarred her back to reality when Ashlon soundly set her down onto it. Breanne didn't know what to say or how to feel. She wanted to kiss him fully on the mouth and yet to slap him just the same.

"Why are you here? Have you secured the stone to rest in such a short time, Ashlon?" His life was foremost on her mind, the scenes she'd foreseen recalled.

Ashlon snorted. "My apologies for the rude interruption of your festivities." But, he did not sound the least bit rueful.

"They are not my festivities, but my mother's, as well you know. You did not interrupt but are avoiding my questions."

He ran a frustrated hand through is hair. "Please, keep your voice down. I've come back for you, that is to say, I need your help yet again." He did not sound like he wanted it, though.

Breanne ignored the trill that ran through her when he'd said he came back for her as well as its quick death after he clarified his meaning.

"Please do not say you've lost the stone?"

"Aye, it was taken from me on the road and I have reason to believe you know the--what did you say?"

"I asked of the stone. And you have answered." What had he been about to say?

Ashlon took hold of her elbow. "We must away at once. Someone is coming and I must demand you remain with me."

Breanne didn't have time to answer or ask his meaning or intentions. Soon he'd found cover near the gate and motioned that they should slip away.

Distantly, she swore she heard her name called. She winced. She could not answer and could not leave. Her only hope at no alarm being called was the excuse she'd used to make escape.

They slipped past the guard as he bent to tend a boot. Ashlon held tightly to her despite her compliance and they rushed through shadow, down the well worn main and under a crofter's thatch. The home was dark.

"Ashlon, please, tell me what happened." Fright fluttered through her body and she was close to trembling with it. Something had gone completely awry and her presaged fate for him weighted her heart.

"I'm not sure you will believe me and yet I somehow trust you will. Ah, my head is scrambled since last night. You've bewitched me so I no longer think straight, particularly in your presence." His words came harsh and low and he suddenly released her arm as though his hand had been burned.

Ashlon paced in the shadow, clawing fingers through his hair.

She kept silent and still, sensing he needed no further anxiety. He'd lost the Bloodstone, his life's mission. And it had brought him here, which meant....

"Who took it? You were saying that I know. What do I know?" Breanne kept her voice level in spite of the knots of emotion tying her up inside.

"It will sound mad, but I feel its truth down my bones, Breanne." He stopped in front of her. The light of the moon displayed his handsome features, showed his gaze come to rest on her lips. "It was the cat. Finn."

Breanne almost laughed. Had he said Finn had robbed him of the Bloodstone? "How is that possible?"

"I do not know or care. But I do know it is true. I'd recognize those eyes anywhere. We need to find him before he manages to unlock the Bloodstone's secrets."

"But, he's just a cat. Did he pounce you somehow?" She didn't mean to sound overly incredulous.

"He stood as a man and moved faster than, well, a wild cat. How, I cannot explain any more than I can explain how you gained knowledge of the Bloodstone."

Breanne's mind turned like a key unlocking a door to reveal a myriad of recollections that fit neatly together. The picture it formed struck a new kind of fear through her. "Oh, nay, please, not Danny."

She turned back the way they'd come, ready to sprint back to the hall and verify the boy was safe and that she was wrong. But, Ashlon caught and held her to him.

"Aye, the cat has been using the boy, I think, to do his ill. We must find them, Breanne." His arms were like warm, tender vices and she struggled against him. "They have the Bloodstone."

"You do not understand. Finn is not simply a cat, he has been held under curse for more years than I can guess and if he has been speaking to Danny …."

"He is in danger. Aye, where would they be, Breanne?" His chest was warm on her back, strong but yielding.

Breanne stopped struggling. She pushed against the well of fear and anxiety to try to see more to the puzzle. The woods that morning, Danny had come. Speaking not to himself, but to Finn of the note. The sapphire cloak, the similar height, the sorrowful trapped look in his young eyes as he told her and Rose…. She cursed herself for not seeing it before, for ignoring her suspicions.

He was just a boy and still so easily head turned and eager to please. An enchanted talking cat would appeal to his adventurous and romantic nature. But, where would Finn take him and what possible use could he need of him now?

"You knew of Danny, then? You saw them together," she said, turning in his arms.

"Aye, in the yard, in the hall, near the priory, the stables."

Breanne added the locations to those already listed in her head: the keep, the grove.... Breanne pulled back from him, ignoring the protest of her limbs that craved his touch. "The priory. Gannon had said as well that Finn had been about there when I asked for his help with the translation. What have I done? It was there, under my nose the entire time."

Breanne could scream, her anguish flooded her so.

Ashlon took her hand. He squeezed it. "We'll get to him in time. I promise you. You must focus on that, Breanne. You must not consider any other option." His hand cupped her cheek. "It is the only way to get through it."

Breanne wanted to lean her face against his palm and shut out the storm inside of her. She wanted to return to the cover of his arms. She'd led Finn straight to the stone. She'd failed to protect Danny, so blinded by her own circumstance that naught else penetrated.

But, no more. She nodded at Ashlon and set her jaw.

They reached the priory yard within minutes.

"Where?" Ashlon asked breathlessly.

"I do not know," Breanne said. The building's windows held no light, the stone carvings stared back at them. Breanne tried the door but found it under lock and key.

"Let us search for a way in," Ashlon said, meeting her eyes steadily.

His words and resolve helped her keep the panic further at bay. His strength and honor lent her courage.

She took the western, he the eastern lay of the stone edifice. Breanne walked slowly and with purpose, listening and watching for signs of life.

As she searched the canvas of rock and grass and

dirt, her mind hunted for reasons Finn might take Danny. She wanted to doubt that he had but knew Danny's face was not among her mother's well-wishers. And the heaviness in her belly spoke a certainty she'd grown to trust these last weeks.

Finn had him. And once she found them, she would know why. The only estimation she gathered was tied to Finn's curse. What else could be of enough import to steal the stone and kidnap a child? She wondered as well how long the bastard cat had been able to shapeshift into human form. Of course he could as easily be in his original Elvin form when he had come upon Ashlon, she expected.

Breanne crept low along the wall. She wished she'd spent more time in the structure, visiting her uncle as he and her mother often nagged her of in recent years. She'd meant no disrespect in staying away, to him or to the lord. Her dreams and ambitions had distracted her away and strangely now brought her.

She wasn't even certain she would be able to retrace the steps Gannon led her down and paused to consider what they could do to gain entry. Gannon had taken her through a corridor, down stairs, his room had a high window that should be along this wall she stood at.

Breanne knelt and felt along the wall behind a small hedge and found naught but more wall. The stones were cold and slick. Her fingers followed the curve of one as it dipped downward and discovered another seam connecting the next rock. The pattern repeated over and again, upwards and down. She strayed farther and still, nothing appeared where it should. No windows, high or low and, of course, no door.

Listening for Danny offered even less reward. All that seemed audible was her own heart, her own breaths coming out in gasps and streams. She would not cry, no matter how dismal, no matter how horrific. She refused to break down.

The baubles in her hair tinkled softly. Down the hill, in the keep, laughter and music faintly carried. Breanne took a shaky breath, fighting to steady her spirit.

She would find them. If not her, certainly Ashlon. He was more than capable even against Finn in whatever form he now took. Intriguing that Ashlon had concluded the cat was the man that had accosted him solely by the look of its eyes. Or was there more?

Breanne's fingers touched glass and she went still. She bent to the ground and shadow to discern the discovery. She was loath to break the thick stuff but hoped it was a sign that a door would soon appear.

She rounded the corner and saw Ashlon in the shadows. He motioned her near. Breanne treaded carefully to him through the underbrush and bramble. The moon's light silhouetted his figure, his sword glinted when he shifted his weight. He looked thinner.

"I found a window," she said.

"No need," he answered, but it was not Ashlon's voice.

Breanne opened her mouth to scream. Finn stepped from the shadows and wrested his arms about her waist and head. A sharp pain stabbed through her temples before the world went black.

* * * *

Ashlon pulled his arms down again against the heavy irons around his wrists. He clenched his teeth and gritted past the pain, focusing on feeling a sensation of give in the stone or links. Nothing.

He gasped and let his arms sag. Breanne and he had not separated more than a moment before Finn had found and taken him prisoner so easily Ashlon felt as powerless as a child. It must be far worse for Danny. He'd woken there in the dank stone cell with a single torch for light and echoes of cries filling his ears.

Ashlon had called out and fought against the binds, sent insults and challenges at the demon responsible but all for naught. No one responded.

He'd fouled it all to hell. Breanne was likely captured, as well, Danny's and her lives might now be at the fiend's whim to dispose at will. And he could not break the binds, nor bend them. But he could not give up either.

He had to get to them.

Ashlon wiped his brow against his bicep. He tasted salt when he licked his lips. The cell was small and short and smelled of earth. The irons were old and heavy. Ashlon stood and tested the length and spread of his body in the cell again. He could reach the ceiling but not the floor. If he stretched to full length he could touch the far wall with a toe.

But what good would any of these abilities gain him? From deep within, Ashlon allowed the throaty roar to rise and cried out in anguish. He kicked the wall behind him until his foot throbbed through his boot.

Blood trickled down his wrist and he cared not if his blood were poisoned. The clang of iron and his grunts echoed against the walls and clamored for kingship above the distant cries for help that he could not stop or save.

He cursed Jacques de Molay for ever coming to his father's estate and offering him a position in the brotherhood. He cursed the throne and the papacy for their greed. He wished them all, it all, to hell for the pain he now suffered.

But in the recesses of his mind he knew he would not take a moment of it back. He would relive it all, even this terrible hour, to be with her again.

He fell back against the wall and lifted his head heavenward. It was the only and last thing he could think to do. A pitiful and hollow act as it might be, he spoke the words, ignoring the anger staggering his heart.

"*Christus vincit! Christus regnat! Christus imperat! Exaudi, Christe. Ecclesiae Sanctae Dei salus perpetua. Redemptor mundi, Tu illam adjuva*," Ashlon said, his hands rising up with each word. Strengthen, assist, he repeated the prayer over and over until a low hum filled him.

He closed his eyes and recalled Breanne standing before the stone slab in the forest. He returned to that place and time and smelled the trees and felt the stars in the vastness impressing down upon them.

The dew shimmered, the night hummed around them. He looked at her, unafraid and watched the light uncurl. He softly called out her name.

* * * *

Finn woke her with a drench of cold seawater that had her sputtering and choking awake. He sat on his haunches before her with a smile that was more catlike than any he'd given her in feline form. She met his eyes and knew Ashlon's conclusion as accurate.

Breanne heard Ashlon's call deep inside of her. She could not answer. The features from her portend, the man that held Ashlon's life in his hands, stared back at her. Finn. The eyes were unmistakably his. And the color was not the single indication. The pupils were elongated as a cat's and coldly assessed her.

The look made her skin crawl at the nape of her neck and her stomach turn. In human form, Finn was uncomfortably handsome. No greenish skin or hunched backs there. He was tall and muscular and pretty faced. The gray streaks even added to his appearance and gave a distinguished air to him. But, it also looked like cat fur.

She had not seen the obvious similarity when the presage had occurred. But it was clear now as well as her need to stop the prediction's fulfillment.

"Where is he?" she said. Her throat burned and her voice was hoarse. Water dripped down her nose, tickling the tip of it.

"Which one, Breanne? The boy or the man?" Finn leaned close and licked the drip from her nose. His tongue was prickly and warm.

"Danny. Where is Danny?" She trusted Ashlon to be alright and alive. More than sensing his call, he was a man capable and used to maneuvering in and out of tight spots.

Finn chuckled and traced a sharp nailed finger down her cheek. He considered her, his head tilted.

"I once thought you would be mine, that you were meant for me. I should have known I would need to rely on myself in the end. Leave it to a woman to ruin a perfectly good situation with sentimentality."

"I am yours, Finn. You've made sure of that by bringing me here. You don't need Danny any longer. Let him go."

He shook his head at her. His eyes fell to her breasts.

"Can you imagine what it was like for me, Breanne, all this time being foisted upon incompetent after incompetent? Can you guess the longing I felt, the frustration?"

She did not care. "Retribution for your sins, I have long presumed."

Finn's eyes left her breast line and returned to her face. "What do you know of my sins? What do you know of any sin, aside from that of the flesh?" His tongue curled on his lip.

"What has any of it to do with Danny now? Leave him be if you want my cooperation or help."

"What makes you believe I seek either?"

"You've brought me here. You have the stone."

His gaze went back to her breasts. With her arms pinned back, sitting, she could do little to hide them as they pressed against the fabric.

"Perhaps, I only seek a taste of the feast you've paraded before me for these last, long years. Did you consider that?"

She wanted to cringe but couldn't allow him to see her fear. Bathing, dressing. It had seemed innocent enough to do before a cat, enchanted as he might be. She never thought of him as a man. A sense of filth crept beneath her skin.

"Not at all," she retorted. "I merely assumed you preferred to violate a beast over a woman. Minerva seems more your taste."

Finn slapped her soundly, leaving a ringing thud in her ear. He stood and paced the room. Quickly, Breanne gauged it. Several torches, irons hanging from the ceiling, a large stone table.

He circled the table, his hand trailing the surface. "You deserve to die out of sheer ignorance, Breanne. Never with all my Ovates, have I counted myself so doomed as when Heremon gave me to you. You cannot even boil water, let alone make a map of time to travel and see."

Breanne felt for give in her binds, her fingers were growing numb. She needed to help Danny. The door was behind Finn, behind the table.

"Then why am I here? To rape, is that all, Finn?" Breanne laughed. If she could get him close again, she might be able to hurt him, kick him, something. But, the farther he walked, the longer he gazed upon the table, the higher her fear climbed.

A sick feeling formed in her belly. Finn had not

answered her regarding Danny, not even once. Surely, he was alive, hidden somewhere. Certainly, Finn only used the boy as a lure and a pawn.

The only other act Finn might need Danny for, Breanne would not entertain the thought of. Finn might be desperate but he could not be so soulless as to attempt a sacrifice. In a blur, Finn produced a knife from behind. In another flash, he produced the stone.

He lifted each in either hand and smirked at her. He set them down on the table. It was her boline. She last used it to demonstrate her cunning for Ashlon in the woods, then left it on the ground, befuddled by his effect on her.

She kept silent, her brow arched and her face placid.

The Bloodstone glowed amber as though a flame danced within it but not from the torches' reflection. It held its own light and the color worsened her sickness. Finn's intentions tainted the previously blue light. Or had she only imagined the color, changed it based on her own desires for protection?

Finn stroked the stone's topmost surface with a finger and the light within followed his path, swirling and expanding. Breanne felt she might vomit.

Her heart hummed a moment. Ashlon. He was growing desperate. He'd come back, sought her help, and now might die for it. And if he died she could not forgive herself.

She loved him. She might not be able to ask for his heart. She would keep him safe.

But, first, Danny.

While Finn stroked and continued his silence, she coiled the energy inside her heart and envisioned it spreading out in wavy fingers, touching the floor, feeling the walls for signs of Danny.

Finn's gaze narrowed on her. "That's enough." He

came to her.

Breanne readied for another slap, or worse, but he only jerked her to her feet and dragged her to the table. He produced her dagger and slit the bindings. Within a blink, he stood opposite her and within another Danny lay upon it between them with the stone at his feet.

She gasped and touched his face despite the prickling sensation in her hand. His skin was pale, his lips were blue tingeg and she saw no signs of breathing.

"He lives," Finn said when she pressed her head to Danny's heart. "He must for the rite to work."

Breanne listened for a beat. She took his cold hand in hers and jiggled it. The room felt small, sickeningly warm, yet the door seemed so far away.

She needed to get her blade back. She needed to get help.

Finn opened the laces of Danny's shirt. A glimpse of the man he would grow to showed in the outline of his muscles and collarbone. She had to ensure he lived.

Finn placed his hand there on pale skin she knew to be as cold as the hand she held, willing it to move. Finn dusted his fingers in a hover.

Breanne inhaled sharply as color flushed Danny's skin. Warmth spread through Danny's hand, warm enough to draw tears to her eyes and a calm to her mind. He was alive. But he wouldn't be for long if Finn had his way.

"Tell me Finn, how did you manage a shapeshift into your original Elvin form?" she said, her lip quivered. She bit it. Mayhap a sacrifice would not be necessary to lift the curse.

Only during black magic in ancient times did some Druid sects use human sacrifice to further their inclinations. The rare practice died off when the priests who used it got more than they bargained for and evil consumed them.

"Heremon's book. In turns at each month's full moon, I've been able to resume this form thanks to a spell I found in his Grimoire." Finn didn't look at her. "He refused to help me make it permanent."

Her eyes widened. She should have guessed when Ashlon told her Finn had taken the stone that he had killed Heremon, as well. Breanne jiggled Danny's hand again. She willed him to wake up.

Danny didn't move.

"What makes you believe I will be able to," she said. "What makes you think I will even try."

Finn smiled at her and it almost looked sympathetic. "You will make it work to save my need of using him. For, you also know that with a sacrifice, I will make it work myself." He brushed the hair from Danny's brow. "And because you love your half brother, though not by your father."

Breanne swallowed the gasp. She had not misheard him. The lifelong connection she had felt for Danny was of blood after all. She had no time to question why her mother had given her son to Isolde nor what became of Isolde's baby. And mayhap she already knew. A vision of her mother being held down, a rutting invader atop her, flashed into Breanne's mind. Nausea rose in her gut, but she quelled it, pushing the dark memory back whence it came.

She did not have time to call Finn a liar and knew he was not.

Finn was right. She would never risk Danny's life, brother or no, even if it meant sliding within his evil, allowing it into her heart and through her veins. But, not without Danny safely out of his grasp.

"I will do it. I will do whatever you ask. But, only if you release him. Now."

"I cannot release him now. He is my insurance that you will succeed and that if not, I will."

He couldn't want to kill the boy either. She could not let him hurt Danny.

Breanne saw only one possibility. "If I fail, you may use me."

Forgive me, Ashlon.

Chapter Twenty Four

The cries stopped. Ashlon strained to hear other signs of life. He was running out of hope. Water dripped from the stone ceiling in steady repetition. The chains clanged with every movement. The prayer had done little to aid him. He felt worse. But, he would not consider failure.

There had to be a way out of the irons and cell. He wished he could borrow from Breanne's giftedness. Somehow, she would see an escape possible. He told himself to remain calm, to think.

His tunic clung to his body, sweaty. His wrists stung from the scraping metal. The dripping tapped a rhythm into the dirt floor and irritated his already weathered mind.

He needed something to pick the lock. Nothing on his person was suitably slim and hard though. If only he still wore the chain and Knight's emblem. But, wishing had gotten no help yet.

The water dripped and his eyes gazed upon it as his mind went blank. It was close enough to touch. Ashlon reached out his hand and let a drop run into his fingers. It was warm and smooth and not water at all but oily.

Without questioning such happenstance or possibility, he hurriedly slicked his hands and the metal cuffs in the dripping lubrication. A thud outside the door warned him someone was coming.

Wincing and pulling, he finally squeezed one hand through. His thumb knuckle could be broken but he did not have time to care. He forced the other hand free and stood next to the door ready with his only weapon left, his fists.

Whoever came through that door was about to experience Ashlon's full fury. He did not know what he would do if Breanne or the boy were harmed or worse in the course of his failed mission.

A key turned in the lock, jangled, and the door came open inward. Ashlon hid behind it, his fists laced and raised. His fingers squished with oil as the tightened together. He tasted blood. Rage rose like a fire in him so well he could almost smell smoke.

A tall lean figure shadowed the cell and turned just in time to meet face to fist and crumple to the dirt. Ashlon stepped into the open and went still.

Father Connelly lay in the dirt, a ring holding three keys lay in his hand.

"Christ's blood, what is he doing here?" He peered at the bald man and shook his shoulder. "Father, are you well, can you hear me?"

The man's eyes came open. They landed on Ashlon and Father Connelly edged backwards, his hands defensive above his face. "Do not harm me, I beg you, Sir Sinclair. I mean you no harm. I swear it."

Ashlon narrowed his gaze on the man a moment. He'd lost trust in clergy a long time ago, before the Pope's betrayal even. Too few carried any real faith in their hearts, more lived in greed and lust. He could not trust one simply because he released him, in fact, might not for that very reason.

"To your feet, Father." Ashlon dragged him upward

by the arm. "Where are Breanne and the fiend."

Father Connelly shook his head. "I don't know. I only found you by chance. I've come from the feast, urged here by what I cannot name. But, something has gone terribly wrong Sir Sinclair."

"Explain yourself. Now. How came you by keys to a dungeon cell if you did not aid in my placement there?"

The man's eyes danced with fear. His body trembled with it. "As I said. I found the need to return, my gut telling me something had gone awry. I am right, but I did not put you in the cell. If I had, why would I then release you?"

True enough but still Ashlon felt unsettled. "Where has he taken her?"

"Not here." The man began to cry. He tried to jerk his arm back. "Please release me. We must leave at once. There is a fire above."

Ashlon only paused a moment to gauge the man's expression. He saw no lie and shoved him into the corridor to lead the way. "How can you know they are not here?"

"Master O'Shannon is getting help. I stayed. I have trusted the wrong man. I have only myself to blame."

"You have not answered me." And he was making little sense. They reached a stairwell. The smell grew stronger. Where was Breanne?

"I searched every room in the priory and here, below. They may have been here but are now gone."

They reached the main. Flames licked the walls and were spreading fast directly above where his cell had been. The oil. Someone had set the fire then, intended to kill him a coward's way.

Ashlon followed the priest out. He spat on the ground. The metallic taste was gone and a tinge of bile replaced it. In the night air, calls could be heard. Help came, buckets in hand. The flames would be out fast, not yet out of control.

He had to find her.

Ashlon faced Father Connelly. His mouth turned downward. "What did he offer you to gain your interest, Father? Wealth, power, is he on orders?"

The priest shook his head, tears streamed his face.

"Tell me what it took to sell your faith and put your niece in harm's way. Tell me what price a boy's life is worth to you."

"The boy Danny is safe. I found him. He is with his mother."

"You lie."

Father Connelly gasped. "I held no ill intent at any moment in the course of my aid. I myself am a victim of lies. Never would I put a life at risk to further my own gain. You must believe me."

"What did he promise you?" Ashlon asked, his voice menacing. He curled his hands into tight fists.

Oncomers paid little heed to them and hurried to the building's interior. A chain of men formed and buckets lined and passed to and from the priory. Father Connelly stood taller and looked Ashlon in the eye.

"He duped me into believing a relic was to come to Tir Conaill. A most holy piece, and that having it would give us the credibility I've long craved. I admit my folly. I have helped the man to decipher code and its mystery and promise sucked me in. But, do not think to so easily judge me."

"If Breanne or Danny have been harmed, mark me, priest, my judgment is the least you will feel." Ashlon turned on his heel, his name a mumble in the foreground noise. Somebody had recognized him.

No matter. He might look the knave for abandoning the call to assist the fire's extinguish, but he cared not.

He strode away, ignoring the call, to the only place his mind concluded the fiend would take her. It was the same place Ashlon now realized he'd first seen Finn.

The black that had carried him back there was his first choice, but he couldn't see wearing the steed any further. He took the bay in the next stall and didn't bother with more than a harness. The bay seemed pleased to be getting a midnight ride and his neighbors whinnied their jealousy.

Nobody came to check the disruption, likely helping with the fire, and Ashlon made an easy escape into the dark. Strangely, he knew the way into the dark valley, skirting the wood's edge, the moon watching through heavy clouds.

Let it rain on him, on the fire. Let the pregnant clouds pour down, winds whip, thunder bellow. It would match the hooves and hurry and heartache he tried hard to keep at bay.

Danny was safe. Breanne would be, too.

Ashlon abandoned the horse at a sturdy oak and stole into the dark toward Heremon's cottage. He smelled the salty waves that crashed below. The cliff area suddenly seemed taller, as though a jutting arm trying to reach the stars ready to fall short and collapse into the water.

He heard her before he saw her and realized he'd sensed her there the whole time. Ashlon flexed his hands, went to the place his sword should hang and fell on air.

It had helped him naught on the road that day so he had no remorse. Instead, he stalked closer. Peering about the cottage's edge, he glimpsed blue billowing fabric. His chest tightened.

Breanne.

He crouched low and peered farther until he saw her in full view. She stood holding the stone, eyes closed and entranced similarly to last night. She swayed slightly on her feet and the wind moved the fabric of her cape and gown. Her skin gleamed in the moonlight, bare under the cloak.

The wind rippled the cloak away, exposing a perfect thigh.

Ashlon exhaled and only then did he realize he'd been holding his breath. The stone glowed in her hands, raised chest level. Her mouth moved but he heard no words carry to him.

He leaned out more. There, before Breanne, knelt and bowed was Finn, in human form. The fiend's eyes were shut. He looked to be at worship, her a pagan goddess ready to receive. Ashlon nearly choked on the impressible fear the scene faced him with.

Dew glistened bright as the stars on the grass around them. The cliff's edge dropped behind her.

One small push from Finn and she'd be gone.

Ashlon pulled at the neck of his tunic and swallowed. He wanted to rush the fiend unawares but knew he would thereby endanger her. If not for the noise, he would find a weapon in the cottage. His heart screamed for him to take action while his mind bade him wait.

He must trust her. She had found a way to free Danny, Finn's lure. She would not put herself in undue jeopardy, stubborn or no. Ashlon caught movement in Finn's posture and pressed back against the stony wall. He looked to the sky, wind whipping his hair and burning his eyes.

The moon was low, as low as the night he'd come to Tir Conaill, desperate to find sanctuary. He had found much more than that. He had found love and hope. The family and faith he had lost, that seemed so long ago, had become tangible.

Losing Breanne was not worth any price. He'd throw the stone into the sea to be forever lost, sell it to the devil to do with as he may, so long as she was safely back in his arms.

A mournful wolf's howl echoed in the night air. The ocean roared below. The grass hissed as blades pushed together under the wind. A hum grew in the air. It was the same undeterminable sensation he'd felt when she'd freed the chest.

Ashlon wiped his brow and bit his lip. Another moment. He peered painstakingly slowly around the wall. The wind prickled with energy, tickling his ears. He watched her raise her arms up, stone held and glowing molten amber.

Finn looked ready to pounce. Ashlon's mind fell blank and a baser part of him took hold. He shot to his feet and ran to her as a light unfurled from the sky down toward Finn.

Eerie green eyes met his and time became like a long silvery thread before him. Breanne collapsed to her knees as the light struck Finn.

Ashlon reached out for her, willing his body not to encumber his intention, to become graceful and swift.

Breanne opened her eyes. She shook her head and screamed. "No."

But, Ashlon could not hear her and could not stop. With one last leap he wrapped his arms around her, brought her onto him as he hit the ground and rolled away from the cliff's lip.

He could not see Finn but heard his unearthly moan rise up from the ground. It chilled his soul.

Ashlon closed his eyes and braced for an immeasurable fury, covering Breanne's head with one hand, clutching her close with the other. All the while, he could only reason a prayer of pleading with God himself to find mercy for them, to protect them from whatever evil Finn was.

The pain in the mournful cry tore at Ashlon's heart, yet he did not look. And despite the peril Finn had put Breanne or Danny in, sympathy for the creature tore in his heart. Its pain sounded so familiar and haunting, how could he not?

Then the cry stopped. The dull noise that had swelled and hummed around them suddenly swept away. Quiet enveloped the air.

For a long moment, neither moved. Ashlon held her tightly, reveling in her warmth and softness, safe though trembling. Safe. He breathed in her scent of wet lavender and heather.

Breanne lifted her head and met his gaze. "Are you completely daft?"

Ashlon could not help but smile. "Aye. When I am with you, I lose all sense, Breanne."

She looked furious and bewildered yet smiled, as well.

"You could have killed us both," she said.

"Better to die with you than to let you die," Ashlon said and pulled her face close.

But Breanne pulled back. "Finn."

Ashlon followed her gaze to a circle of ash where grass and rock had been. "What happened to him?" He scolded himself for so easily forgetting its eminent danger.

Breanne stood. Ashlon was loath to release her but the way she moved begged no argument. Breanne knelt at the circle and touched the ashy residue.

"He passed through the veil," she said.

Ashlon frowned. "He's dead then?"

Breanne shook her head. "I do not know. Perchance I killed him, or he may be facing his fate in the

Otherworld. Either way, he will not return here."

He didn't know how to verbalize the questions her statement struck in him and chose to remain confused. There would be time enough for her to explain her ways to him. For now, he only needed to feel her close, alive and vibrant, again.

Ashlon knelt next to her. The light of dawn was creeping into the eastern sky in front of them. In the center of the circle, covered in residue, lay the Bloodstone. The faint blue hue had returned to it, the color of Ashlon's memories of rites and secret ceremonies in a world gone.

With his heart in his throat, Ashlon took Breanne's hand. She glanced at their fingers laced together then looked up at him. Birds began an orgy of chirping. He saw it there in the light glow of her honey eyes. Promise.

Breanne thought for a moment she might have gone mad. It was over. Finn was gone. Trouble and tragedy and terror, stopped.

Ashlon was back, the stone safe and years worth of study fulfilled. She had faced the worst mortal fear a woman or man could and now, looking at the emotion shining bright in Ashlon's eyes, all she wanted was to feel alive.

A jolt of need ran through her and, mad or not, she had to feel his mouth, his touch. She needed to taste him and touch him. Her eyes fell to his lips. She tried to speak the words and could not find any.

Her breathing became shaky. She tightened her fingers on his. He responded by pulling her closer, then letting go to cup her face. Both of his hands furrowed into her hair, pulling softly, massaging and caressing.

His brows drew together. She let her hands fall from his arms and touch his chest. She wanted to feel his skin, hot and smooth like the day she had in the cave. That same wonder returned now and combined with the need growing in bounds inside of her.

Ashlon shook. His frown deepened. And for a moment she thought he might be angry. But, when his next breath melded with hers as he kissed her so wholly that the world spun, all her worry disappeared.

Their lips met and she saw and felt and smelled and tasted him alone. The salt of his skin, the sweet of his mouth. Her hands found skin and glorious muscle, her nails raked, trying to get more. His hands left their tender hold to find her waist and breasts and derriere.

Pleasure tickled her flesh and satisfaction sang in her soul. He was more than she ever knew she wanted and better than anything she had. He was the sun and the wind and sent stars of heat and need coursing through her body.

She helped him shed his clothes and let her gaze wander over the Adonis look of him in the breaking dawn of day. And she gloried in the appreciation his eyes shone when he removed her cloak and gazed upon her naked form. He lay her down.

Ashlon bent his head to her hardened nipples, making Breanne moan in ecstasy. He suckled them rhythmically while teasing the tips, taking equal turns whilst pressing his body between her thighs.

When she could stand no more, he broke away from her breasts. But, then he went lower. His tongue traced a shivery path down along her belly and hip and lower still until Breanne thought to grab her hands into his hair and stop him.

"Ashlon," she said. "What are you doing to me?"

"Loving you to the absolute fullest possible extent," he said, not looking up, his tongue skimming the top of her apex. "Making you mine."

Breanne closed her eyes and swallowed. He didn't

move. Her heart beat faster as she slowly released her tight hold on his hair. Whatever he meant to do to her, she must trust him not to hurt her. He had not hurt her before.

He still waited. She exhaled a shaky breath and let her thighs fall open. The ache of need throbbed there and only worsened when he moved downward and touched his tongue to her mound.

Breanne bucked with surprise. Ashlon waited again and took his time. He began at her topmost peak and drew tantalizing dips downward. Her body moistened and swelled. He groaned against her, his mouth making lapping sounds as he suckled her flesh. Astonished at his skill, Breanne arched into his wet touch as his tongue dove into her core. He cupped her rear, lifting her so as to bury his face deeper. Within crazed moments he enflamed her desire with his licks and touches and strokes. He sent circles of pleasure spiraling through her, building into a tunnel of want.

As she approached the same crest he took her to before, Breanne gripped her hands into his hair, willing him closer, deeper, craving more. *More.* Yet he resisted. He suckled and licked, pulling gently back until she felt his hot kiss there no more. The chill of air did little to abate the heat he created.

Desperate, her eyes flew open and found his. She followed his gaze until she saw his arousal standing proudly before her. She joined his kneeling position and grasped his length. Ashlon's head tilted back but his gaze remained locked to hers, asking for some unnamable gift. Understanding washed through her. The wet heat he created throbbed, emboldening her to lower her mouth to his prick and gingerly press her lips and tongue to it.

Ashlon groaned and stilled her head. "Your touch is too sweet. You'll unman me," he whispered.

He brought her upward and took her lips in a penetrating kiss. There, she tasted her juices on him and it shook her. Suddenly, she thought she would surely perish without feeling him inside of her. Silken and strong. Proving to her how alive she was, how magickal he made her feel.

"Please," she whimpered, pulled at him.

Ashlon groaned. His arms held his weight steady and as he kissed her neck, he entered her. As he filled her body, he filled the void and in slow circles and thrusts, he rebuilt her need higher and wider than before. Breanne met each stroke, demanding more, raking her nails into his skin. He answered fiercely, nipping her neck. He bent and took a nipple into his mouth. She gasped at the new level of pleasure yet wanted more. Then, with a deft roll, Ashlon pivoted their bodies so that she rode him.

Breanne paused at the turn then saw the daring in his gaze. She took the challenge and was happy for it once she felt the change in her pleasure. What was deep and resounding became like a caress. Slowly at first and ultimately with abandon, she rocked up and down his hard length, inspired by the slick feel of her body in the position of power until she screamed out his name and sweetness took her under.

She heard her name on his lips, as well, as her body clenched and climax spread in waves through her. His prick slid blessedly in and out with each grip around his flesh. Then she felt him pour into her, his strokes falling still as his body reached her depths. Ashlon hugged her close, rolled her back over then dropped his weight onto her.

Breanne let her mind and body linger in that perfect moment while her breathing returned to normal. She didn't mind his weight despite it straining her chest.

When she opened her eyes, a bright day was

blooming above them. It was the first sunny day she could remember in a very long time.

Chapter Twenty Five

"Isn't it strangely true, Rose, take care in what you wish, for it may come true," Breanne said as she watched Rose twine flowers into her hair.

Rose sent Breanne's reflection in the mirror an all too knowing smile. "Are you going to be complaining of this for the rest of your days then, Bree? Am I going to be old and gray listening to you tell my grandchildren of how you one day long, long ago had gloriously curly hair and wished it away straight?"

Breanne laughed, causing a painful tug on her head. "Ouch. Be careful, Rose or you'll have me bloodied."

Rose clucked her tongue. Breanne hadn't meant her hair, smooth as a pond's surface on a warm summer day ever since she'd rid the earth of Finn and his curse. Breanne didn't miss the curls she'd often complained about in her life. But, she had been referring to her girlhood feelings for Quinlan, to how inaccurate they had turned out to be.

She and Rose had not yet managed to speak of the wrong Breanne did him, though clearly there was no grudge from his sister. Worse, she and Quinlan had not spoken at all since she had left his side during her mother's wedding feast. It was the single gray cloud on her otherwise happy day.

She was about to wed the one true love of her life. So, long as he returned this morn as planned, from his final leg of journey in hiding the stone.

"I did not mean my hair, Rose."

"Aye, I know it. But, I'm not the person to be

offering advise on that which you did mean. He is my brother and you are nearly my sister and I cannot choose between. All I can say to you is what I said to him, time will heal the wound well enough."

Breanne's chest panged. She hoped so. She missed him and knew Ashlon must, as well. In the short time since Ashlon had come to them, Quinlan had acted as a friend, a guide, a confidant. In many ways, he had represented the whole clan. It was a shame that Quinlan would not be there today to bless Ashlon's official join to it.

In a few hours, when Ashlon safely returned with Ramsey from the north, he would wed her. And of all things, he would do so by choice. Niall had declared Ashlon would have no choice once he was found, but when she and Ashlon had returned to the keep that morning hand in hand, he'd not taken him in chains as promised before.

Niall in fact had clasped Ashlon's arm in welcome and taken him straight away to speak privately. Breanne had chewed her nails in worry and fatigue, feeling certain something might go wrong after their close won victory.

The worry grew to anxiety when Shane MacSweeney brought Quinlan in to join the private discussion. Obviously, her future and recent scandalous behavior was the topic burning ears behind closed doors. But the few persons up and about were thankfully too worn from the evening's festivities and near disaster to raise a brow in her direction.

Shane didn't even glance her way when she time and again paused near the door, stared at it as though the wood's grain might hold answers, then stalked away. Not even a chuckle.

When the door opened and Niall's booming voice carried notes of humor to her ears, she breathed easy.

And Ashlon's face told her all she needed to know, so much so that she took the coward's road and didn't face Quinlan or look at his expression when he left the room and keep thereafter.

Ashlon did not disarm her with a smile or rush to her side in glee. He appeared neither puffed nor awkward, as she'd seen many a suitor over the years look after a similar conversation with Niall O'Donnell. In fact, he did not even speak to her, just nodded and walked away.

It was in the way he walked. There was an unmistakable lightness in his step, an easiness in his carriage. Relief surged through her as she watched his back and had any doubt remained, Niall soon quashed it when he called her in to tell her the decision.

"He has given me his word and, hard pressed as you might think me to take him at it when he left afore as he did, I will trust him to return," Niall had said once the door closed. "Quinlan has taken the news as well as can be expected considering the whole of it. He is young. He will recover."

Breanne did not know what to say to him. The reproach she half anticipated had not come. Niall seemed in truth rather unsurprised and if she did not know better, she might think him gloating. But, that would not make sense at all. Why would he force a betrothal with Quinlan if he knew it would not see fruition?

"Ashlon will return in no more than six days time and will marry you. By Beltane, you will be a wife and living in your own home, running your own household," Niall said.

For the first time, her belly didn't clutch at the idea in fear or panic. Her own home. Her own household. She hadn't the first inclination for either until now. Now, both seemed a boon.

She also held not a pinch of concern over whether he

would come back to her or not. With Finn's demise, the weight of her presage that had carried like an extra bone in her body, was gone.

Ashlon would see his quest's end, may have already, and would become her husband by the moonrise. Ula had seen to all the preparations, including the small keep that Breanne had not set foot in since her father's death.

Breanne had decided never to let slip nor verify the secret that Finn had exposed. She would not ask her mother and not tell Danny. She would not even allow herself to ponder. She loved Danny as a brother, always had, and knowing he might in truth be hers made little difference.

She held a new respect for her mother. Breanne realized that through the years of war and peace, of joy and death, Ula had been strength itself and managed serenity to boot. There was no better queen to Niall.

It would be propitious to return to it as a wife, her mother had promised her. And one day soon, as a mother herself. Ula had spent many happy years there as both and the stone walls missed the cheer that a family would bring.

"None of that now, Bree," Rose said. "You'll end up washing away the berry stain and I got it just the right color."

Breanne came back to the present and blinked back the tears Rose scolded her for.

"I'm sorry, Rose. I just canno' believe how happy I am to have been so very wrong about what I thought I wanted."

"I know it." Rose smiled and patted her shoulder. "I'm glad for it, as well."

* * * *

They'd offered him the black and the steed had proved worth his weight in gold. With only a handful of hours rest, the black had carried him, albeit at a more leisurely pace, back up the same road. Ramsey had arrived just in time to join him, his head well and not a sign of lingering effects from his injury.

Ashlon was happy to have the help and company. Strangely, the anxiety and pressure that he'd grown so accustomed to feeling regarding Jacques's petition had left him. In its place was hope, large and free and glorious.

They arrived at the Giant's causeway on the tail of a downpour and ceremoniously laid the chest into its intended tomb among the round stilts of rock. Ramsey spoke reverently of their act, making Ashlon finally understand why Jacques had chosen him to follow this journey.

"Life is bigger than you and I, my friend," Ramsey had said so softly that the wind almost hushed it. "It is bigger than the whole lot of us, wherever we roam or call a home, home."

Ashlon had been struck not just by the words but by the way they made Ramsey appear. The man's face was not lit with warmth, his eyes did not dance with joy. He looked almost sad.

"In a hundred generations, another man will find this treasure and try to harness its goodness and power. We are a part of the tapestry of those generations. What we choose today, colors the picture of that tomorrow." Ramsey stared at the sea, stretched out past the bridge rock myth determined a giant had once created to reach love.

Suddenly, his Grand Master's final words to him took on new meaning. "Be brave of heart and soft of soul and love will bring you home," Jacques had said, so fiercely that Ashlon had hid his derision. The words had seemed so trite at the time, and later simply sad mumblings of a man who saw death coming to his door.

Now, though, he saw their truth. Jacques chose him, not only that day, but long before then. Ashlon had been chosen and prepared for this journey from the first and only now could he see his life's events as part of a whole. It was as though he glimpsed destiny's face for a brief wonderful moment of clarity.

Ramsey half chuckled, his eyes looking faraway. "Well, then, Ashlon. This ones good and buried then." He kicked the rocky tomb with his boot. "What say you we leave before my arse falls off frozen?"

"Aye." Ashlon laughed. "Damned chilly for near summer, isn't it?"

"Ah, but that is another wonderful trait of Ireland, Ashlon. All year round, you'll enjoy springlike weather that is wonderfully mild." They mounted and heeled their horses to a trot. "Of course, the summers are lush and full of bloom, yet the winter won't freeze you bones either."

Ashlon half listened to the ongoing litany of benefits Ireland weather wrought as they rode faster, got closer to what he now thought of as home. His heart beat in rhythm with the black's hooves as the past's obligations and horrors melted away.

The sun broke through the clouds as he saw familiar hills and peaks rise in front of them. Even from the distance he was at, he could see activity in Breanne's keep's courtyard. What would soon be his yard. The realization sent a new trill of hope through him.

Ramsey had been visibly taken aback when Ashlon had sought reassurance that the clan would not see him as an interloper on Breanne's fortune and lands. His friend had soundly rebuked him for 'the ludicrous idea', but nevertheless, Ashlon meant to repay Breanne in the only way he knew how.

He vowed to God and man that he would protect her

and hers with his life. He promised to make her holdings a profitable endeavor of which any wife could be proud. Her father's legacy, her legacy, deserved no less.

As they rode to the O'Donnell keep's stables, they were greeted and welcomed by any who saw them. Groups walked to the keep, already merry at the day's coming celebration.

Ashlon handed over the reins of the black. In his distraction he didn't even hear Ramsey call for him to wait and didn't. He was home. And his body was reacting to that reality with the least appropriate response possible. He felt lusty.

The few days had seemed thrice as long and his body sensed that what it craved was nearing. But, it would have to wait a bit longer because as soon as he entered the keep, he was overwrought with well-wishers and his bride's mother.

Ula O'Donnell had three maids in tow and ushered Ashlon directly to a private chamber where a bath waited, for hot water and food sat ready for his consumption. Before he could properly thank her, she was gone.

He ate quickly, glad that things seemed rushed and cared not as to why. Buckets were brought, the tub filled and as he moved to undress, a soft knock sounded on the door. Ashlon hoped it was not yet another maid insisting he need help in his bath and dress. From the first day he'd arrived, he'd seen just how helpful some of the staff tried to be and he was loath to make another one cry over rejection.

But, it was not a young girl at the door. It was Danny. Ashlon had forgotten their arrangement, made during his quick departure, in all the bustle. He bade the boy enter and offered him a good strong handshake.

"Were you able to secure what we discussed, Master

336

Daniel?"

Danny beamed. His shoulders squared further. "Aye, Sir Ashlon. I have brought it to you."

Danny produced a small but roomy satchel and laid it on the narrow table near the door. Ashlon decided a lukewarm bath was as good as any. This procurement was not one to be rushed through. Though the boy looked well, Ashlon knew he might feel a good deal of guilt for his part in Finn's plan. If none or any had talked to him of it yet, it didn't show. There was a solemnity in Danny's manner that had not been there a week ago.

Gingerly, Danny reached into the bag and pulled out the gift Ashlon meant to give his wife that night. Danny had had a terrible time keeping the litter of kittens a secret and Ashlon was now grateful for it. The small black bundle blinked from her cower in Danny's hands. Her eyes were the color of daffodils and her petite mewl made him grin.

"You've done well, Master Daniel." Ashlon clapped his shoulder. "Now, I have another task, if you are willing and able."

Danny cupped the kitten with his hands and held it protectively close. "What's that, Sir Ashlon?"

"I'm hoping to surprise Breanne with this gift after we wed. But, I'm in a bit of a shortage on time. Might you be able to escort this gift to Breanne O'Donnell's keep? I have been assured by her mother that all is ready there. This kitten will be the final touch."

Ashlon wanted to tell Danny the fire was not his fault, that Finn's deception could have been successful on any. But, he did not have the words to broach the issue and so did the best he could conjure. He gave the boy responsibility, knowing firsthand the improvements it would make over the course of his growth into a man.

"I will see her there straight away, Ashlon." Danny

nodded and set his brow determinedly. "You can count on me."

"Aye, I knew I could."

Epilogue

"Think you all wedding days pass in such a blur?" Breanne asked. She adjusted her head on Ashlon's chest to better hear his heartbeat. Sweat from their second wedding night lovemaking still gleamed over his sculpted torso.

She seemed unable to get enough of him. She could drink him into her were she able and still thirst despite repletion.

Ashlon stroked her arm, not answering right away. "I believe so. Leastwise, every one of mine has been."

Breanne poked him. He flinched and chuckled. He'd been more'n a bit of a tease since they had spoken their vows in front of what seemed like the entire clan. She had even glimpsed Quinlan in the crowd and that gave her hope that she would one day again call him her friend.

"I feel as though it floated by me from the moment Erlene burst in to tell me you'd returned to the parade walking us over. I hardly recall telling you 'I will'."

Ashlon's arms squeezed her closer. He kissed the top of her head. A dozen candles' flames danced in the window's breeze. The male scent of him enveloped her mind as she breathed it in.

"I have a bit of a gift for you, Breanne," Ashlon said, his voice thick.

Breanne sat up so she might see his face. Her heart thrummed with love.

"You've no need to gift me, Ashlon. Returning to

me today is boon enough to last me all my days."

Ashlon smiled, stroked a tendril away from her face.

"It is a wedding gift to us. Niall visited me before the ceremony."

Breanne's brow gathered. She wasn't certain she liked the sound of this.

"He came to tell me news of Heremon's last wishes. In his final search, Niall found a letter." Ashlon paused, a smile quirking his mouth.

"He enjoyed such things, it appears."

Ashlon chuckled. "Aye. But, this one named me as his heir."

"What? Heir? I do not understand. He found you near death the very day Finn killed him."

"I offered the same point to Niall. It appears my destiny was decided much farther back than I realized. Heremon and Jacques saw their fate and, together, gambled yours and mine in hopes of saving the stone."

Breanne's brow gathered into a tight scowl. "I don't understand." Yet, somehow, she did. Ashlon was meant for her and she for him. They were meant to face this path. "If Niall knew you were named as Heremon's heir, if he knew of Jacques—."

"He knew only that Heremon left me a letter." Ashlon took her hand. "The letter explains the plotting our mentors made for our futures."

"But, he did not give it to you until today?" Breanne couldn't shake her suspicion. Her king, her stepfather, had handled Heremon's murder so strangely, as though it weren't one at all. "Why delay such a boon? Such secrecy is not like him."

"He's had a lot on his mind," Ashlon said softly.

"Aye," Breanne said repentantly. "He has." She returned to his outstretched arms, deciding she knew more than she liked already. Whatever more influenced

Niall's mind, she no longer cared to know.

Something soft tickled her lower back and Breanne shot back up with a small shriek. Ashlon guffawed and scooped his hands into the bed's sheeting. Then, with little flourish but a brilliant smile, he presented her with a little ball of mewling fur. The kitten she'd chosen from Minerva's litter.

"How did you know?" Breanne gasped and took the small thing from him. The shy little thing was softer than a duckling in her hands.

"With a bit of help from the feine."

Breanne raised her eyebrows at his use of the Gaelic term for kinship, clan, family. He truly had embraced it, then. It warmed her. For what felt like the hundredth time, Breanne thanked any higher powers that would hear for bringing her this warrior to love. In turns he surprised, impressed, and frustrated her beyond her girlhood or grown dreams.

"Do you love me, Breanne?" Ashlon asked, his gaze suddenly piercing hers, his fingers stroking hers.

Breanne tipped her head and smiled. "Can you not feel it, Ashlon?"

"Aye," he said, with an impish half-smile. "I do, and I feel my love for you, as well."

"Aye, I know you do." Breanne might've burst into a thousand stars, she was so happy. "I feel it, too."

The End.

###

Dear Reader,

Thank you for coming away with me in this magickal romance. Since I was a little girl, it has been my heart's dream to write and share timeless love stories, characters who surmount impossible obstacles. Quinlan's story will be coming soon in Enchanted Moon as well as an extra epilogue to Irish Moon.

I love to hear from readers and can be contacted at amberscottbooks@gmail.com or I can be found online. Subscription to my newsletter and visits to my website, http://AmberScottBooks.com , will give you access to freebies, contests and all my imaginary worlds.

I believe love transcends and transforms. Do you?

Sincerely,

Amber

Connect with Amber Online:
Twitter: http://twitter.com/AmberScottBooks
Facebook: http://facebook.com/authorAmberScott
Smashwords:
http://www.smashwords.com/profile/view/AmberScott
My Weblog: http://AmberScottBooks.com

Join the Amber Scott Books' HOT Club! Why?
Because you are HOT!
How? Get your HOT Club logo and more at
www.AmberScottBooks.com

In between naptimes and dishes, Amber Scott escapes into the fates, loves and complications of her characters lives. A native Nevadan, she makes her home in Arizona now with her husband and two young children. She often burns dinner, is addicted to chocolate and believes in happily ever after.

First rule of the HOT Club: tell everyone you're in the HOT Club!

Official Member of

60674297R00203

Made in the USA
Middletown, DE
02 January 2018